CASTLE ON THE RIVER VISTULA

McSweeney's and colophon are registered trademarks of McSweeney's, an independent publisher based in San Francisco. McSweeney's exists to champion ambitious and inspired new writing, and to challenge conventional expectations about where it's found, how it looks, and who participates. McSweeney's is a fiscally sponsored project of SOMArts, a nonprofit arts incubator in San Francisco.

Printed in the United States.

2   4   6   8   10   9   7   5   3   1

ISBN: 978-1-944211-28-8

www.mcsweeneys.net

CASTLE
ON THE
RIVER
VISTULA

Michelle Tea

For Jude Finch

Chapter 1

As the girl and the mermaid swam toward the mouth of the river Vistula, the landscape around them grew lush and green with underground gardens of weeds: forests of bladder wrack, their branches dotted with bean-like bulbs of air; wide leaves of sugar kelp, their edges frilled as clamshells. Bright, grassy sprigs of seaweed sprouted in between coral, like shoots breaking through cracks in a Chelsea sidewalk. Everywhere, long, flat ribbons of sea wrack undulated on the currents, over rolls of verdant algae that looked like spring meadows.

"All right," Syrena said, pulling her tail in front of her and coming to a halt. "We stop here for some business."

"What sort of business?" Sophie asked, eyes wide. In all their underwater travels they had never stumbled upon such a fertile-looking seascape. Poking in and out of the drifting fronds Sophie spotted the fat bellies of jellyfish and scrabbling, big-eyed crabs; a tiny, pokey fish darted behind a weed before Sophie could even tell what color it was.

Syrena removed the heavy backpack she'd been carrying for Sophie, setting it gently between a couple stands of coral. She tugged it open, and began stuffing it full of seaweed.

"Come, you help. Gather as much of the weeds as you can." She lifted from Sophie's tangles the octopus that had been her companion for much of their long journey through the sea. "You, too. You have many legs, you can help lots."

Sophie watched as the octopus pulsed through the waters, grabbing at leaves with his many curling tentacles. Then she shrugged and joined the harvest. She tugged up tough handfuls of seagrass that nearly cut her palms. She rolled leaves of sugar kelp into thick, wobbly tubes. She reached out and snatched sea wrack as it floated past, and uprooted so much bladder wrack she could hardly wrap her hands around it. The backpack bulged with vegetation, tendrils spilling out the top. Syrena used all her might to squash the plants down, loading more in on top until the flaps could not be buckled, and the octopus was employed to splay itself across the top, its many legs stretched long, holding the bounty in.

"Now you," Syrena motioned to the girl. "I'm tired of that thing bumping and banging over me."

Sophie gaped at the backpack. It had begun as an oversize, saggy sack drooping with the weight of the laptop she'd salvaged from the crashing submarine. Sophie got chills as she remembered locking

eyes with the desperate scientist, how he wordlessly
pleaded with her to take the
computer so that at least his
work would survive—even
if he wouldn't. A terrible
moment, but she had done as
he'd asked, and the mermaid
had done her the favor of lug-
ging it through the waters.
But now that she'd stuffed

the thing fat as a trashbag of raked New England leaves in autumn,
she wanted Sophie to be the one to haul it?

"You want *me* to carry *that?*" Sophie asked.

"Is not heavy," Syrena said. "It only, how you say, awkward."

"How am I supposed to swim with that thing weighing me down?"

Syrena scoffed. "You no swim. Water swim for you. Come now, don't
be baby. Look how hard little octopus is helping! You can at least work
as hard as baby octopus, ya?"

Sophie felt annoyed by the sparkle in Syrena's eyes as she bent
down and laced her arms through the shoulder straps. The mermaid
was right, it wasn't very heavy, but it was ridiculously cumbersome
and almost knocked Sophie backward before she caught her balance.

The mermaid giggled. "Now who look silly in backpack?"

"Why are we even doing this?" Sophie sulked. "Is there no food in

Poland? Aren't we going to be swimming a river? Won't there be tons of stuff to eat along the banks?"

Syrena's face grew still at Sophie's questioning; all teasing, all giggles, vanished. She was the stoic mermaid again, the one Sophie had first found in the creek—somber, serious, even gloomy.

"Sophie." Sometimes the mermaid's words seemed to spout from her mouth like her language was carried in her cheeks; other times they seemed dredged from the pit of her gut. The way the mermaid spoke her name gave Sophie the shivers.

"What is it? Why are you looking at me that way?"

"You know, I tell you before, your body been through very much. Your body, your mind, your heart. You been through so much, Sophie."

"Yeah," Sophie tried to shrug, but the backpack pressed down on her shoulders. "But I'm okay."

"The sea water help you. The salt nurture you, help to work against the bad effects of everything that happen. From back in Chelsea, when Kishka attack the creek, to even right now. When you change into shark, Sophie, when you change into mermaid, all these things take toll, ya? When you confront the Invisible. When you go inside the heart of Blooughadda."

"How did you know I did that?" Sophie gasped.

"Is not bad, is fine. Is fine to visit whatever heart you like, Sophie. It only take toll. The heart of a Billow Maiden a rough, wild place."

"Tell me about it," Sophie mumbled, remembering Bloo's heart, how raw and hot and vast it was.

"We will be leaving the ocean shortly," Syrena said. "Take a peek above the waters, if you like. Go ahead."

Sophie was surprised to find herself hesitant. She hadn't been above the waters in what felt like months, years, a lifetime. She had entered the creek in Chelsea one girl, and now, as they prepared to swim into the mouth of the river, she was another girl entirely. Slowly she kicked her legs against the water, rising upward, the light growing brighter as she ascended, illuminating everything around her. She could see herself more clearly—her kicking, scuffed-up legs; her bare toes; the once-lovely linen jumper the Ogresses had fashioned for her, now in tatters. Her head tilted back, Sophie saw blue, a new blue, sharp and wide. Sophie saw the sky. At the sight of it she gasped, inhaling a mouth full of salty seawater. She broke the surface of the Baltic sputtering, her eyes tearing, her lungs heaving. Sunlight—sunlight!—caught the droplets that shook from her as she coughed, like bits of molten gold.

It took Sophie a few minutes to adjust to the brightness of daytime on earth. Her eyes ached; she could feel them pulse as they struggled to shift from the ocean's ambient darkness to this violent glare. She stared back down at the water, away from the sky, while they calibrated to this new environment. Slowly, she looked up.

Trees, and beyond the trees, meadow. She hadn't seen such green, such verdant, living green, in a long time. Actually, considering she'd come from Chelsea—not the greenest place on the planet—maybe she'd never seen so much unbroken, unsullied green. There'd been the green of the seaweed forest they'd just harvested, but that was a dark and murky green. These trees, these leaves and grasses, were every shade of green, most of them such a sharp tone it practically made Sophie's mouth water. She realized she was *hungry*. Hungry for earth food. Hungry for—a salad? Yes! Sophie wanted to fill her mouth with living green things torn from their roots. Were she able to reach those trees, still very far away, she would have pulled handfuls of leaves from their branches and stuffed them into her mouth like popcorn.

The water beside Sophie rippled as Syrena's dark head broke the water. "Arghch!" the mermaid yelped as the bright sun assaulted her eyes. She closed them, rubbing them furiously with her translucent fists. She stared down at the rippling waters, then slowly raised her face to the sky, shading her eyes with her hand.

"*Polska*," Syrena said as she gazed at the green, and her voice held all the sheen of the sunlight on the water.

Chapter 2

I t's beautiful," Sophie marveled. "I've never seen a place so pretty. It's making me hungry for human food!"

"Oh, the food the people eat in Poland!" Syrena laughed. "Sausage and pierogi and sauerkraut and cakes with tiny poppy seeds and *bigos* and soups with mushrooms and soups with cucumbers, or beet soup, and kasha. Long ago they eat bear, ya? Bear paws with spicy roots, or tongue of the bear."

"I was more thinking I'd like a salad, actually," Sophie said, scrunching her face at the thought of eating paws or tongue.

"You might have to magic yourself some salad," Syrena laughed. "Much food in Polska, but not much salad. Look—" The mermaid grabbed Sophie by her bulging backpack and spun her around in the water. Off to the right, clustered around the water's edge, was a rust-colored town. If she squinted, Sophie could make out the spires of churches or castles or towers, the reddish color stained pale green by time.

"Is Gdansk," Syrena said proudly, as if she had built the town with her own hands.

"Are we going there?" Sophie asked.

"*Nie*. Is not along our way. But just to see. A beautiful city, ya?"

"Yeah," Sophie nodded. From where she bobbed in the water, it looked like a fairy-tale place, something seen only in the very oldest books. Syrena, her hand still gripping Sophie's pack, spun the girl back around so that her eyes were filled with green.

"You see there?" The mermaid pointed to the place where the ocean cut into the green land like a wide, blue road. "That is River Vistula. That is my home. More than *Polska*, or *Warszawa*, River Vistula my home. I cannot believe we here. And that you here too, Sophie." The mermaid paused and stared at the girl, and Sophie was unnerved by her stare. Above the water Sophie's pale blue eyes were nearly silver, and in the sun they all but vanished.

"What is it?" Sophie said. "You're creeping me out."

"Sophie, the Vistula not salt water. Is fresh water."

"Okay," Sophie said. "So?"

"Salt water will be with us for little while, but not long. Gone very soon. Then you have the sea plants, ya?" The mermaid hit the sack of vegetation strapped to Sophie's back. "They contain salt. Good for you to eat, to chew on, suck on, just keep in mouth maybe. Look." With considerable effort, the mermaid lifted her weight of hair from the waters. Sophie could see strips of sea plants woven in and out of the thick tangles. "I bring more, I bring much as I can, ya? But we must swim the river quickly. We must get you to salt castle, and to Tadeusz. You will begin to feel sick on this river, ya? But you will fight it, you will suck the salt from these plants, you will swim very fast, we both will, ya?"

Sophie ingested all that the mermaid was telling her. She knew she was being called to be strong, and she bolstered herself. She could swim fast, she could command the waters to move very quickly. She would eat this whole giant bag of seaweed if it gagged her. She wouldn't complain. The iciness of the mermaid signaled how serious this was, and Sophie made herself icy in reply.

"Of course," she said. "I can do it. Let's go."

"Wait," Syrena stilled her. "Another change. Sadly."

"What?" Sophie's heart thumped quickly inside her. She didn't want so many changes. Although she'd known all along that the purpose of this epic journey was to reach Poland, leave the mermaid, and train to destroy *Kishka*, the ancient source of evil in the world who decided to show up this lifetime as her *grandmother*, Sophie had become accustomed to the rhythms of the ocean, the company of Syrena. Why couldn't she just travel the deep forever, living a mermaid lifestyle, never mind Kishka, never mind whatever magic Sophie had inherited, whatever massive effort was expected of her just because she happened to be half-*Odmieńce*. Sophie never *asked* to be the saver of the world! She was just a kid! Really she should be back in Chelsea, wandering the halls of Chelsea High, a freshman, getting slammed into lockers by mean girls and dogged by awful boys, prepping her brain so that she could someday get out and go to college and live a normal life, whatever that was. If Sophie couldn't shrug off her massive duty in order to live as a mermaid then—suddenly—she wished she could return to the daily misery of her old life. Enduring the taunts and bullying of her town's roughnecks was surely preferable to taking on the ultimate evil of the universe. Right?

Syrena had moved behind her and unfastened the octopus from the backpack, causing ribbons of seaweed to unfurl into the water, floating away. She brought the creature to Sophie.

"Octopus not coming with, Sophia. Can't live in freshwater. Is saltwater creature, ocean creature. Ya? You understand?"

The octopus, it seemed, understood. It wrapped its tentacles around the mermaid's neck and gave her a long nuzzle, the dome of its head snug in her neck.

"Oh!" The mermaid laughed. "Such sweet creature! To think I expect you to eat it once, when was just a baby octopus! Friend, I pledge to never eat octopus again, ya? In your honor. You will be sacred friend of the mermaid, ya?" Syrena stroked the octopus lovingly with her long, pale fingers, and untangled its tentacles from around her neck, holding it out to Sophie. "Say your goodbye."

Sophie's eyes were full of tears at the sight of the octopus, hanging there before her in the mermaid's hands, his tentacles undulating around him. What a strange and silent comfort he'd been on this journey, helping revive them from Kishka's illusions and attacks with his wise head-rubbing, from his time as a baby until now. The octopus was full of love. Sophie took him from the mermaid and clutched him to her desperately, the tears in her eyes flowing into the sea around them.

"You are the best octopus friend I'll ever have," Sophie said, snot clogging her nose and her eyes all stinging and blurred. "Thank you for being with me. I wish I could come visit you someday but I don't know how I ever could. The ocean is so big. Where will you go? Where will you live?"

The octopus took a tentacle and placed it over the girl's jabbering mouth, causing the mermaid to sputter with laughter.

"Octopus be all right!" Syrena said. "Octopus be in the sea, is where they belong."

Sophie smiled at her friend and nodded her head. "Okay," she said. "I won't worry about you. But I'll miss you. I'll never, ever forget you."

The octopus took his tentacle and pointed it back at himself in agreement, causing more tears to leak from Sophie's face. She felt like Dorothy in the stupid *Wizard of Oz* or something. As she went to release the octopus from her grasp the creature swam closer, and with deliberation placed all its tentacles on Sophie's head. *A last massage?* she thought, but as the cephalopod brought its beak into view, Sophie had a flash of the deep-sea Vulcan, the octopus that had healed both her and Syrena and given her visions, shown her everything that was going on back home in Chelsea while she was on the other side of the world, at the bottom of the sea. Was her sweet little octopus friend about to do the same? Were *all* octopuses magic, exhaling their very own crystal balls into the sea?

Apparently so. From the octopus's hidden black beak emerged a small bubble of air that grew in size as it floated toward Sophie. She braced herself—braced her heart—for a glimpse of her mother, or her best friend, Ella, or Aunt Hennie or Angel or her odd sister, her twin, like looking in a mirror and seeing a stranger. But the girl in the bubble was someone Sophie had never seen before. Her hair was long and glossy-dark, spanning out around her head in a way Sophie recognized. The girl was underwater, just like Sophie: no tank of oxygen, no breathing tube. She was smiling, happy, perhaps playing. When Sophie saw who her playmate was she inhaled sharply, and shouted for Syrena.

Chapter 3

Look!" She pointed at the fragile bubble wobbling in the water. There was another mermaid. So much like Syrena, and so different. The same tail, though this mermaid's scales climbed much higher up her torso. Same wild mane of hair, though this mermaid had grown what looked like tiny horns, or antennae, that cast a bioluminescent halo around her. Her eyes were thin, with an upward cast, and her cheekbones sharp as a fishbone. Unlike Syrena, there were the tiniest gossamer fins floating off the tip of this mermaid's cheekbones. But like Syrena her face was stern, as if she were trying to discourage the girl from being so playful—at a glance, it was a dynamic Sophie recognized. And then, the bubble burst.

"Oh!" Syrena cried. "I have not seen one of my kind in—oh! I cannot know! I cannot know how long it has been!"

When the octopus's clawed beak cracked open again, the two froze, watching the next bubble form and float toward them. Another girl, again Sophie's age, her face round, her hair in a sloppy ponytail sliding off the side of her head. She looked not playful but focused, radiating an intensity Sophie feared could pop the bubble. Her companion? A mermaid. Same ratty, wild dark hair as Syrena—wilder and rattier, if such a thing were possible, which Sophie would not have previously believed. The mermaid's face was marked with dark lines—not wrinkles but ink, tattoo marks that arced down her forehead, meeting in a point between her eyebrows. More marks, circles and dots, decorated her cheekbones, and curving stripes ran down her chin.

"Her hands," Syrena said, tearing Sophie away from the creature's face. The mermaid's hands were blunt, fingerless. "Arna," Syrena breathed, her voice holding a wonder Sophie had never heard.

"You *know* her?" The girl spun away from the bubble to face her friend.

"Know *of* her," Syrena said. "If is her. Arnakuagsak. Famous and powerful. Man chopped off her fingers, she use mermaid magic to turn fingers to seals. To seals, and fish and many other animals. Octopus, maybe." Syrena gave a smile and pet the octopus. The bubble came apart, vanished.

"Oh, Sophia," Syrena smiled. It was hard to tell beneath the salty waters, but it seemed the mermaid might be crying. "I have not seen mermaid in so long. I imagined I could be only one. Only one in all the waters of earth!"

"Syrena." Sophie clasped the mermaid's arm and directed her toward the octopus, where yet another iridescent bubble floated out from his ebony beak.

Like a diorama, like a snow globe, the orb held another girl and another mermaid. This girl's eyes had a sparkle that could be seen even at the bottom of the sea. Her hair, tightly braided at the crown, exploded behind her in a great, round afro. Beside her, lounging in the sea, a great mermaid, her hair a bundle of long cords that slunk into the water behind her, each one slightly resembling the slinky, striped snake that hung around her neck, sliding down her body toward her tail. From the mermaid's temples sprung spiny fins, and her eyes flashed blue-white against her dark skin. Syrena stared deeply at the bubble, her long, elegant fingers clamped over her mouth. Her head shook back and forth, slowly.

"I cannot," she breathed into her fingers. "I cannot believe this."

"Do you know her, too?" Sophie asked, and Syrena shrugged.

"Know of her. Mami Watu. The very first mermaid, perhaps a *ningyo.*"

"What is that?"

"Is mermaid, basically. Just from other sea. Oh, octopus!" The mermaid pulled the creature to her, pulling his tentacles away from Sophie's crown. The girl gasped and gingerly touched her head where the rubbery suction cups had stuck themselves to her.

"Syrena! Maybe he wasn't finished!"

"You finished?" Syrena asked the creature, and he blew the tiniest bubble from his beak, a bubble that floated over to the mermaid and popped in her face. Syrena laughed and hugged him. "I think that was all for Sophia, how you touch her head and all, but I cannot tell you. Thank you. You give biggest gift. Biggest gift to know one is not alone, ya? Biggest gift ever."

Sophie had never seen such a wide smile stretch across the mermaid's face. Her baleen was fully exposed, bristly beneath her upper lip that was pulled taut in happiness.

"That was for me?" Sophie asked, taking in the mermaid's words.

Of course it was—it was her head the octopus had attached himself to. And as shockingly delightful as it was for Syrena to see her kind, Sophie understood that the larger point was for her to see *her* kind. Girls. Three girls, all her age. Three girls, happy and serious. Three girls living and breathing beneath the ocean, with their mermaid companions. Three girls maybe learning to harness their magic, just like Sophie? Who *were* these girls? Did they all have evil grandmothers, too? Were there even more out there? And, she couldn't help thinking, did it mean that Sophie wasn't quite so special after all?

Sophie felt the kindly brush of the octopus's tentacle on her brow, soothing the furrow she'd made with her worries. Syrena looked at her, a slight smirk teasing the corners of her mouth.

"Oh, are you jealous?" Syrena asked in a teasing tone. "You think you only girl with mermaid friend and now you feel not so special?"

"No," Sophie scowled quickly, though that was exactly what was happening.

"Sophia," Syrena said in a stern tone velvety with care. "Is always better to not be alone. Is good to have people. Imagine if you alone under the sea all this time, without me, ya? What would happen to you?"

"I wouldn't have made it!" Sophie cried. "I wouldn't have found my way, I wouldn't have survived!"

"Maybe these girls and their mermaids help you find your way, ya? Maybe they help you survive, somehow. And maybe you help them, too: maybe you need each other."

"I know I'm being a baby," Sophie confessed, making the mermaid laugh.

"You just being human," Syrena asked. "All humans are babies. Is okay. You think about it. Think about these girls. I think you find you want to know them, ya? Perhaps your task so big that you can't do it all by yourself. Maybe you even want friend. Human-girl friend, who are magic also, like you."

"Maybe," Sophie said, uncertain. Uncertain, but hooked on the faces of the three girls she'd seen in the bubble. She could bring them into her memory easily: the girl with the fan of dark hair, a streak of yellow-blonde floating in the water, her smiling face; the stern, round-cheeked girl with the sloppy ponytail; the girl with the sparkly eyes and round puff of hair. And their mermaids, each one different from one another, and different from Syrena. The more Sophie thought about all of them, the more curious she became, and her upset at not being the *only* human girl in the whole world hanging out with a mermaid faded away and began to seem as ridiculous as it was; it was replaced by a wash of relief. Maybe she wouldn't have to face Kishka alone after all.

"Anyway." Syrena brushed aside Sophie's feelings like the human silliness she thought it to be. "Now is time we say goodbye to this friend." Syrena gathered the octopus' many tentacles in her cool hands and kissed them all. "A prince," she declared, "a king. A king among octopus, a king of the sea. May you grow large and mighty and live forever, may you swim deeper than any human dares to go." The octopus caressed the mermaid's cheek with the tip of a leg, and turned to Sophie, his tentacle held up as if to say, *One more thing.*

The mysterious beak in the center of the creature's face cracked open, and another bubble emerged. Sophie held her breath, hoping, hoping. The bubble grew, fat and shimmering, an image stretched across the fragile surface like a projection. Black and white, staticky as an old TV, Sophie squinted and puzzled over it until a small, humanoid figure became clear. Part human, part alien, its bones luminescent, giant eyes staring out at Sophie. When it finally popped a thumb into its mouth, with a laugh Sophie understood what she was seeing. "It's Ella's baby!"

The scene inside the gossamer globe shifted, and Sophie was looking at the baby's bulbous home, the swollen belly of her best friend, hooked up to a machine and smiling at the image Sophie'd just seen. Joy bubbled up inside Sophie; if she were back in Chelsea she had no doubt she'd be accompanying Ella to her many doctor appointments. It was almost like she was there with her, sharing the special moment. And just when Sophie's happiness began to level out the vision panned out and she could see, crouching and squinting for a better look, Angel, the smile plastered across her face a mirror of Sophie's own. She cheered; Angel *had* understood! She was helping Ella through what Sophie imaged was the craziest time in her friend's whole life. She watched as Angel straightened herself and clapped Ella proudly on the shoulder. The bubble popped.

Angel! Quicker than her conscious mind could register, Sophie's inner flares shot out, searching the ether for her friend so many miles away. Sophie's consciousness zoomed through ocean and air, through the fabric of time, hurling itself into her old mentor. Sophie gave a long, deep sigh. Visiting Angel like this felt like the closest thing to home she'd had in a long time.

Hey! she felt Angel exclaim in surprised delight. *I wasn't expecting this. Where are you?*

Poland, Sophie explained. *Finally. Still in the water, but so, so close. We're about to swim into the river.*

Everyone dreams of getting out of Chelsea, Angel teased. *But you picked the craziest way!*

The light vibe inside Angel's heart grew suddenly cool, as if a cloud had cut off the sun's warmth. *How's...* Angel faltered, not daring to think Sophie's grandmother's name lest the woman somehow appear.

So far so good, Sophie mused, uneasily. *Have you seen her?*

Nope. No one has. After your last visit, when you asked me to check on Ella, I figured I should check on your moms, too. Can you see where I am?

Sophie shifted her angle and was able to view the world as Angel saw it. Chelsea, Heard Street, her little house with the mismatched lions flanking the crumbly staircase.

Oh my god! Sophie gushed, full of emotion. *Is she—is everything okay? I mean, it's not. I know it's not. But—*

It is, Angel said, understanding everything. *It's totally okay, within the realm of everything being totally* not *okay. I've been visiting your mom, bringing her stuff.*

With a twitch Sophie could see what Angel was carrying. A tincture made from lobelia flowers, a bag of dark licorice, tea made of catnip and red clover.

Me and my mom have been making her things to help her resist smoking. We cook it up together and my mom blesses it, hard. I'm able to shove it into your house real quick. I don't know how we're getting it past… but we are. Your mom goes through it fast, though. Me and my mom are like a factory.

Sophie's heart ached as she recalled the glimpse into her mother's life the Vulcan oracle had allowed her so many waters ago. Andrea trapped inside her house, a kind of electrical force field keeping her there, hurting her when she tried to escape. Piled on the kitchen table were Kishka's gifts to help her pass the time: cartons and cartons of cigarettes. Sophie had watched her mother try to say no to the addictive things, and watched her fall helplessly into their clutches. She hated to think she was still engaged in such a struggle.

Without saying goodbye, her spirit full of alarm, Sophie rose up and out of Angel. Employing some new skill, she willed herself into her old home.

At first she thought it was under construction. So much white, and debris all over the floors. But as her eyes focused she saw what it was. Then she didn't believe it. Then she saw it again and knew it was true. Her mother was living inside a house built entirely of cigarettes.

They lined the walls and ceilings; were the raw material, it seemed, of everything she could see. Cigarette refrigerator and cigarette shelves. Cigarette couch and cigarette table. A mattress and headboard, pillows and sheets, all of cigarettes. Tobacco scattered the floors like lint or dirt, and among the mess of it were boxes and boxes of anti-smoking gum, of empty boxes once containing nicotine patches, and hundreds of empty jars once containing the various herbs and potions Angel and her mother were churning out.

Sophie was about to flee this awful scene when a slight movement caught her eye. Behind the bed, a tuft of something brown and frizzy. Sophie brought her mind's eye closer. It was the tip of Andrea's head, bobbing as she chomped a wad of anti-smoking gum almost too big for her mouth. She was polka-dotted with round patches. A final jar of herbal tea sat beside her. Sophie was chilled; the image wounded her. It was taking everything inside her mother to resist the insane temptations Kishka had encased her in. It was taking everything inside her, plus new mettle that nobody, not Andrea or Sophie or Kishka, had known she had. Sophie felt a battered pride, looking at her mom. In her own way she was fighting Kishka, too. Her eyes filled with tears as she tried to somehow kiss her. And suddenly, like a bubble disintegrating, that world was gone. Sophie came to on a bed of seaweed, Syrena gazing at her with a mixture of concern and annoyance. The tender pressure at her temples was the octopus, kneading her throbbing brow.

"You back now?" Syrena asked, impatiently tapping her luminous nails against her scales. "You ready to be here or what? You want to be back in Chelsea hanging out with friends or you want to conquer evil?"

Sophie was taken aback by the mermaid's harshness, still tender from all she'd seen and felt.

"I saw my mother," Sophie said. "And it's horrible, the things my grandmother's doing are—"

"Oh, ya, surprise surprise, Kishka's being a monster. Kishka *is* a monster. What did you think you would see? Do you understand that it weakens you to zoom into people like that? That when you go flying around your hometown like a ghost it is draining your reserves? And what did I just tell you, about the salt, and the water? You have no energy to spare right now. No dilly-dallying, no visiting, no becoming mermaid or sharks or whatever. You stay girl, you stay here with me, you relax and you do what I say. You understand me good?"

"I do," Sophie said. She felt humbled and a little ashamed. It *was* impulsive of her to jump into Angel. Impulsive and greedy. The octopus had been doing her a favor, but she wanted more. More contact, more information. More home.

Sophie lifted the creature from her head and looked into the octopus's large, watery eyes. "Thank you," she said, choking up again. "Thank you for everything. I wish I could do something wonderful for you—"

"You did!" laughed Syrena sharply. "You didn't eat him!"

"Oh, hush!" Sophie cried. What a thought! "Thank you, Octopus. I love you." She too kissed the octopus's tentacles, and then placed a kiss on the dome of his head. He tapped her face with the tips of his many legs, poking and pecking, and Sophie imagined a bazillion little kisses all over her face. She laughed out loud, and the octopus took a single tentacle and on her cheek traced the shape of a heart. And then he slunk away, behind them, back to the kelp gardens, back to the beluga whales, back, back, back and out to the endless sea.

"Now, we go," Syrena said brusquely. "Back to business. No time for crying over new friends or lost friends or any friends. Ya?"

"Ya," Sophie nodded, pulling herself together. They sunk deeper beneath the water, moving forward through the sea until the sea slowly, then quickly, became the river.

Chapter 4

Iwill tell you of how I met my love, Basil," Syrena said to Sophie. "Basil was fighter, like me, and like you. Basil fight for good, too. You must know of others in your lineage, other magical creatures fighting for good. You will meet more, ya? Be prepared. Be inspired. Though," Syrena paused and took a breath, "is hard to talk and also keep up with your quickness!"

"Well, you told me to go fast so I'm going fast," Sophie said, annoyed. A branch of bladder wrack hung out of her mouth. So far she felt fine, but the mermaid's warnings had spooked her, and she figured why not start loading her body with whatever salt she could find right away. The bladder wrack was surprisingly pleasant, and the little pockets of air that dotted its branches were fun to pop with her teeth.

"Yes, is good," Syrena nodded. "I want to get through here quickly too, you know. Very homesick for Warsaw. And also, my river there be *big* mess. I just know it. Much work for me to do. Besides," the mermaid glanced around her at the dark channel they sped through. "Mostly only bad stories around here."

"Why bad stories?" Sophie asked. "It's so pretty here. It feels magical."

"Is magic, ya," Syrena agreed. "But bad magic, mostly. Here, a little further up, is where I come onto land for first time."

"Like, out of the water?" Sophie asked. "With Basil?"

"I looking for Basil, it true," Syrena nodded. "I alone in the oceans so long, I miss my sister Griet, I miss my kind. Basil not my kind, but not human either. Basil was griffin, we meet briefly on my lonely travels. I kept his kindness with me. His eagle eyes, and fur and feathers, they look so soft. He understand what it is to not be human but to live in their world, with their cruelties. I find I longing to see him, to talk to him, learn more about what it is to be griffin. I know he go up and down the river peddling gold, so I go up the river to look for him. But I not find him. I find human men, or they find me. On their way to city, they follow me in boat. I swim near boats all the time, I not worried. I fast, I stay low, ya? But river not ocean. Sometime not deep, sometime suddenly earth right in the middle of river! Sometime river blocked by, what you call them, *bobr*—beavers. They make giant house smack in middle of river, how I get by? I having a fight with beavers when the men find me. The beavers, they all move quickly, they see boat. I so hot-headed in my fighting, I not even understand what happen until boat upon me. They think I girl skinny-dipping in river. When they see my tail, they waste no time. They toss fishing nets all over me, til I as tangled as a fish in my own hair." Syrena took a deep breath, which made Sophie realize she herself wasn't breathing at all.

"They kidnapped you?" Sophie whispered, as if the men, long dead, would hear and take her friend away all over again.

"Oh, ya. They take me from the water, lift me onto their boat. I try to cut myself out with my narwhal horn, but it only get tangled, too. I stab a man in the leg with it, though, I get him very good, very deep in thigh. He rips horn from my hand and he takes it to my head—" Syrena touched her temple gently, as if the wound were still fresh—"and that all I remember until I wake up in cramped little tank in *Warszawa*."

Chapter 5

What happened to her head?" The little girl, a wreath of flowers in her hair, poked the tank where Syrena's head lolled against the glass, smearing a bit of bluish-greenish mermaid blood along the pane.

"We rescued her." Syrena heard the loud, hammy voice of one of her captors, a booming voice full of bravado and cheer. He was addressing not just the little girl who would not stop tapping the glass, but the larger crowd that had assembled itself on the dusty grounds. "Out in the sea, this fair maiden was being menaced by seals—big, gruff seals, a whole pod of them! Why, one of them even got my leg!"

The crowd's laughter prompted Syrena to crack open her eyes and take in the façade. Her wild hair swirled around her in the tank, masking her, so she opened her eyes wider. On a slight raised platform beside her cramped and dirty tank, the ruddy-faced man, his cheeks scattered with stubbly whiskers, gestured to his bandaged thigh, which Syrena had pierced with her horn. Where was the horn now? No longer with her, though she was sure that at least some of her other weapons would have made it past their scrutiny, buried as they were in the thick tangles of her hair.

As the crowd's sympathetic murmurs died down, the mermaid's captor's voice rose again. "You all have parted with a bit of your change to behold this wonder—"

"Abomination!" a voice keened from the crowd. "It's an abomination of our Lord! It's the handiwork of the devil, what you've got there! A demon, don't care if it dwells on the land or in the sea, it's a demon all the same!" The voice was old, and it trembled as it delivered its proclamation.

"Ah, you might be right, my lady." The red-cheeked captor tilted the brim of his busted top hat toward the righteous woman in the crowd. "A wonder of our Lord, or a sea demon? Well, there's but one way to know, and that's to find out for yourself! For another coin you can climb right up here on the stage, like this little lady." He reached out and ruffled the flowers ringing the little girl's hair. For yet more coins you can stick your hands in the tank and have a poke—she won't mind! She's docile as a baby goat, this one! Some more coins and you can talk to the sea-lass, ask her yourself what she knows about the Dark Lord!" The audience chuckled, and the old woman scuttled away. "And gentlemen, if any of you would like to spend some private time with this sea vixen, come talk to me and we'll settle a price." His bloodshot eye winked at a pack of men idling at the rear of the gathering.

With a rush the crowd clustered around the mermaid's glass tub, blocking the light, stomping the wooden stage with their dusty shoes, rattling the glass with their fingertips. Syrena slunk down lower in her prison, just as a wandering hand entered her enclosure and pulled rudely on her hair. Quickly, a stick came down on the offender, cracking against the glass as it swatted the grabby fingers. Syrena's eyes darted upward from under her veil of hair—*her narwhal horn!* Her carnival captor was using it as a cane and a pointer, and a tool to keep the unruly crowds in line. Through the dirty glass Syrena saw the sharp tip of her sword poke cruelly into the chest of the little flower-headed girl who'd been transfixed to the tank.

"Make room, *dziewczynka,* you've seen enough."

Backing away from the horn's keen tip, the girl's eyes briefly met with the mermaid's before she tumbled backwards off the stage, the space she'd occupied quickly swallowed

up by the bustling bodies of those who'd paid their *zloty* to gape at the sea creature.

"Hey, hey, hey," they yelled, a clamor, banging on the glass with flat palms, trying to rouse the mermaid.

"She's dead!" accused one young fairgoer. "It's just a wig and a fish!" shouted another. More hands plunged into the tank, hoping to reveal the showman's hoax, but they were punished by swift, sharp raps and jabs of the horn.

"Ya little bastards!" the showman shouted, aiming the horn at their heads now, not caring if the fierce tip left a cut on a temple or cheek. "You cough up more *zloty* and the bitch will sing you a song of the sea and let you stroke her hair, but for the scant coins you paid you're lucky to catch a glimpse of such a creature at all! Now clear out!" With a *whack* the narwhal horn came down across the scrawny bodies of the row of children closest to the tank, sending them tumbling from the stage.

"Now who wants to *really* meet with the sea-lass? Gentlemen? A once-in-a-lifetime win for any of you, I'd say. Can't hardly put a price upon it, though I'll help you do just that."

Scrunched as low in her tank as she could go, Syrena wondered if she would die here, soon. A low-lidded peek through her hair, through the scummy glass that caged her, showed only peril. Her terrible glass tub and the dirty water that had been dumped into it to keep her wet—it was like being ensconced in a cloud of soot and ash. There was little in such a water to keep a mermaid alive, and Syrena doubted her captors cared enough to take proper care of their moneymaker. From the sound of the showman's complaints, she wasn't quite bringing in the *zlotys* they'd hoped. The mermaid found herself in the strange state of hoping she was profitable enough for them to give her some clean water and a bit of food, while fearing that she would in fact be profitable, for what exactly were they selling of her?

Outside her grim confines, there was the menace of her captors, sour-smelling, sweaty men with little care for her or anyone; Syrena's insides filled with dread at the nasty way the one had whapped and struck children with the stolen horn, while the others dragged them from where they'd fallen in the dirt. Not that the children themselves gave her any hope; no, they too would only poke and prod were they given a chance, peel her scales from her tail like the wings from a fly. Human cruelty was all around her, and in her bones Syrena could feel how far she was from the sea. There was no busting free from this shabby tank and making some sort of foolish crawl to the shore; her arms were weak from hunger and confinement, and her tail, that muscle, was no use to her on land. Syrena could imagine her rotten captors laughing as she flailed across the dirt, letting her have a go of it for their own sick entertainment before scooping her up and flinging her back into whatever dank puddle they'd prepared for her.

"*Szlachta!*" the top-hatted captor crowed, and through her slitted eyes Syrena watched him clutch his ratty headpiece to his oily scalp as he bent at the waist in deference to a new mark. The showman hopped from the stage, and Syrena lost sight of him, though his voice still echoed through her tank.

"Oh well, you must understand that will take much *zloty*, but a fine sir as yourself surely has pocketsful!" There was a pause as the mark responded in a voice too soft for the mermaid to hear. She shifted the slightest bit and affixed her ear to the glass, but still all she could discern was the booming, perpetually half-drunken voice of her captor.

"Yes, yes, privacy, of course, but you understand, we must stay close by, my associates and me, for the sea witch is our most worthy bit of property, ya? We are, after all, not *szlachta* as yourself, just humble working men, doing our best to scrape out a living, ya?"

The rage that Syrena felt inside her bones felt hot enough to boil the water that kept her. Oh, had it only been a fair fight—if a fight between a human and mermaid could ever be fair. If only she'd had her wits about her, if only she could have had a shot at them on *her* turf, the sea, how she'd have taken them all down—the drunken showmen, their feeble boat, the moneyed *szlachta* bartering with her captors about her very worth.

With a series of subtle movements, Syrena brought the thick batting of her hair down alongside the glass, like a curtain. Thus hidden, she slowly, carefully, ransacked her locks for the bits of this and that she often stashed there. A shark's tooth, sharp as a needle and fat as her palm. She could clutch it by its root and perhaps slice a man's jugular. Fish bones, slender and strong, any of them could do damage to an eyeball. A round shell, its edges filed down to near-transparency. All of these weapons were lodged in the mermaid's massive tangle of hair; all of them could be snatched by her quick fingers and used to hurt her captors and their marks, wounding, maybe even killing them.

But then what? Like a snarling animal, she'd still be trapped in her cage. Syrena was pondering her predicament, searching for a solution, when her tank began to move.

It was on wheels, apparently; rusty, busted wheels that locked and twisted, causing the mermaid to bump unpleasantly against the glass, causing the stagnant water to slosh over the sides, leaving a trail of mud on the dusty ground. Syrena watched with alarm as the level in her tank sank; she didn't realize how necessary the water was—even this repulsive, foul water—until she started to lose it. Dirty water was certainly better than no water at all.

Syrena peered through the glass, watching the dirt roll by beneath her, watching the trunks of trees grow more plentiful until they closed in around them. They were taking her into the forest. Syrena's heart wailed. Into the forest was farther from the sea, and all hope of her survival rocked there in its waters. She listened for the soothing rush of a river, but heard nothing, only the passing of rusty wheels over a carpet of pine needles, soft and crunchy.

"How's this for privacy, there, sir? What more could you ask for, I say?"

The *szlachta* murmured something that made the captor laugh.

"A curtain! I say! We're not in your fancy-house, here, are we? You'll have to let nature be your curtain, then. And you've only bought so much time with the lass, you're not going to be here all day, remember."

More murmurs, and Syrena was suddenly lifted into the air, still in her glass cage, the grunting, red faces of her captors all around her as they heaved her tank from the wagon and set it onto the forest floor. The low voice of the nobleman wove through the trees, like the hardly noticeable chatter of forest animals. The captors scoffed and spat in response.

"Ya hardly paid enough for all this, I say," the showman griped. "Ya better be considering a tip for all this special service, hear me?" And with that, the brawny, dirt-stained hands of the captors plunged into the water and dredged the mermaid from her tank.

Syrena did not know what to do. Instinctively her body tightened, ready to thrash against their touch, but she kept her stillness. *Play dead.* The thought echoed in her head, though it wasn't dead she was playing so much as docile, or sleeping; too unconscious to grasp what was happening, the better to strike when the moment arose. If she were to die there in the forest, bleeding her blue-green sea blood into

the pine floor, she would take these men with her. If that was the most she could hope for, so be it.

The men dropped her roughly onto the wagon, and the mermaid managed to land with her hands twisted in her hair, her fingers close to the sharp things tucked away there. She felt the blunt fingers of one of the men push her hair from her face. The smell of the sea, still sunk in her hair, was replaced by the fresh scent of pine, a deep green smell. How strange to die in such a lovely place. She kept her face slack, and heard a small gasp from the nobleman as he looked upon her.

"Ah—so you like what you see, then?" brayed the showman, still selling his showpiece even though the deal had been made. "Better act quick, then! The longer they're out of the sea, the uglier they become, I hear."

"So what do you intend?" asked the *szlachta,* close enough now for Syrena to hear his voice.

"Well, there's a lid for every pot, they say. Strange tastes, some men have. We'll see what she brings in, maybe sell her off for good down the line. You hear about the *ksiaze* in Copenhagen who took a sea-wench bride, ya? If he hadn't cut her all up, it might've worked out for him. He got a taste for the sea, maybe we'll set sail to pay a visit?"

Griet, Syrena thought, an electrical panic shooting through her. *They're talking about my poor Griet.*

"Then again, you traffic in gold, do you not? Perhaps after your time with the lass you'll make us an offer, ya?"

"Could be, could be," the nobleman said affably. "You'd best leave me to her, then. Gentlemen."

Syrena could hear the lumbering scuff of the pack of them on the forest floor. "We won't be far, now," one warned.

"Yes, I'll try not to make off with her," the *szlachta* said in a funny voice, and the men all laughed along with him.

Syrena tried to sense where the nobleman was in relation to where she lay, prone on the wooden wagon. Her tail, too long for it, flopped onto the ground, her fluke in the dirt. Her hair likewise slid from the back, trailing on the floor, pine needles getting caught up in the tangles of sea wrack and fish bone. She could feel the man circling her, a stirring in the air, a slight, shifting warmth. Her fingers dug into her tangles, finding the shark tooth. She pressed its root with the tips of her fingers, slowly easing it down toward her palm, all while continuing to track the man. The mermaid wished to open her eyes, but it wasn't yet time. She must play dead for as long as possible; her limpness, her deceit, was her strongest weapon.

The warmth came closer, closer, near her face. In the stillness of the forest she could hear the man's breath, and soon she could feel it on her face, a faint puff, and then she felt softness. Long hair. A long-haired nobleman, young and arrogant. The hair brushed against her cheek again—only it wasn't, Syrena realized. It wasn't hair at all. It was feathers.

Chapter 6

Snapping open her eyes, Syrena stared into the face of a griffin.
Basil the Griffin, to be precise. The creature she had ventured
out into the waters to find had now found her, in this terrible place.

"Shhhhh." The griffin brought a curved claw to his beak.

"I have this," Syrena mouthed softly, sliding the shark tooth from
her hair and showing it to Basil. The griffin seemed to think little of
the makeshift weapon, and Syrena felt briefly ridiculous. A mermaid
out of water, perched on a rattletrap wagon, about to slay a pack of
men with a single shark tooth?

"If you were in the sea, perhaps," Basil said kindly. "If this were a
fairer fight."

"They have my tusk," Syrena said. "My narwhal tusk. I could damage
them with that, even on land."

"Okay," the griffin nodded. Standing tall and strong on his

lion-furred haunches, his paws soft in the leafy dirt, Basil headed in the direction of the men. He did look like a nobleman, Syrena realized, understanding why the men addressed him as *szlachta*. He looked like a prince of his kind, his head high, his long, tapered ears regal, rising up from his stern eagle-face. Only the sly twitching of his long, golden tail hinted at what lay beneath Basil's show of gentlemanly pleasantries.

"Kind sirs," Basil called out to the men as he came upon them, hunched in a circle on the dirt, a tattered pack of playing cards tossed around them. "The strangest thing—I happen to *know* that sea-lass you're keeping." His voice was filled with delight, as if this funny coincidence was something the men, too, would find humorous. But they only looked at the griffin blankly.

"*Know?*" repeated the main showman, puzzled. He did not understand a mermaid to be something—some*one*—that one could know. They were *things*, weren't they? Things of the sea, like jellyfish and bladder wrack, like seals and shipwrecks.

"Yes, yes, her name is Syrena, and we made one another's acquaintance a fortnight ago, under the full moon. A very witty mermaid, very sharp indeed. You must know this yourself, you've been spending much time with her, eh?"

The showman scoffed, while his peers looked about, confused. "We don't *talk* to the wench, *Szlachta*. She's part of our zoo."

"Your *zoo*," the griffin nodded. "Tell me, did she come with you willingly, the mermaid?"

"I think not!" guffawed the showman.

"Gave him a scab on the head, she did," another joined with a laugh.

"Ah," Basil nodded. "So, she fought you on it. Even after you explained all the *zloty* she'd make?"

At this the men's laughter bulged and roiled. "Oh, sure," the showman said. "We told her we'd have piles of gold for her, certainly. She'd be the richest sea-wench in Pomerania. After we reimburse ourselves, of course. For our time and our efforts, and the cost of housing her, and feeding her whatever fish food the thing eats."

"Yes, rent on that tank of hers must be pricy," Basil jested. "But, quite seriously, gentlemen. This has been a mistake. You've captured a free creature, you've kidnapped her from her home, and you're displaying her like a two-headed sheep. Or worse. Yes, worse, actually. So, I'll be leaving with her. Bringing her back home. No need to say goodbye. Best you all be off."

The showman stood from his hunch on the ground slowly, as the griffin's words fell on him and took effect. Watcheing and mimicking, the other rose slowly, too. They formed a triangle around the griffin. His tail swayed and snapped.

"You're not taking our golden doll with you, *szlachta*." The showman spit the word to the ground on a splatter of tobacco. "You'd like to *purchase* the lass, then we can talk. You look like you've got quite the bit of gold, there, am I right?"

"Most right, yes," the griffin nodded. "I'm quite rich. Gold is my business. But I am not *purchasing* Syrena. She is my friend. We are simply leaving the forest together, and you will have to dredge up a new money-making scheme, the lot of you."

The showman cracked his fingers, and like a troop of monkeys, the others followed suit. The forest echoed with tiny snaps.

Back a ways, Syrena heard it all. Something quite foreign to her—perspiration—beaded up on her skin and rolled down her sides. She felt quite anxious, not only for herself but for Basil, playing it cool while surrounded by thugs. If only they were in *her* world, the pleasure she'd get from bringing them underwater! If only she had wings, like the ones folded neatly into Basil's feathered back. Syrena was used to feeling powerful. The only time she'd felt like this was when her sister was taken from the sea. Now she was close, very close, to suffering Griet's own fate.

"You're not leaving with the fish," the showman said. "Should I escort you from the woods or will you find your way out?" He spit again, blackness on the forest's green carpet, and his hand moved to the leather belt on his hips, where Syrena's narwhal horn was threaded, dangling against his leg like a sword.

"Am I to take it that you intend to stop me?" Basil queried.

"Do I intend to stop ya?" The showman ripped his top hat from his skull and flung it into a pile of pine needles. "You're freaking mad, bird-man! You betcha I'll stop ya. We all will. Now, get the feck out from here!"

The screech that curled out from Basil's beak was a sound the forest had never before heard. Snoozing bats woke, startled from where they hung by their toes, and flocked into the air, away, away, away from that noise. Long-legged storks rose in the distance and stretched their white wings to carry them far from the scream. A bristly pack of hogs, their blunt noses squealing, scrambled, as did a herd of bison so dense the trees shook from their roots at their passing. Eagles tucked their pristine tails and soared for cover, a gang of lynx leapt deeper into the woods, a flock of corncrakes headed for the clouds. Miles away, in the river, beavers heard the sound and dove deep into the mud, hiding beneath their woody homes. Wolves and elk, woodpeckers and bears, all that called the forest home bolted at the fury that the griffin let loose, a wild *zawolanie*, pure griffin magic. There was a lion's roar in the center of that eagle-screech, and while it drove the sensible animals of the woods from their homes, it had quite the opposite effect upon the men, freezing their scuffed, tattered boots to the forest floor.

Syrena bolted upright on her rickety wagon. Her mouth hung open as she watched Basil attack the men. She'd seen shark fights, she'd watched giant squid devour their prey, she'd even seen the wars of men enacted in her waters, but never had she seen such fury and violence, such *elegance* in battle. Basil sprung from his lion-pawed haunches and spread his wings, so long their edges beat against the trees and shook whole branches from the trunks. The men cowered and screamed, ducking the falling mess while shrinking back from the monster before them. The sun shone on Basil's wings, and to Syrena it appeared to be every shade of gold, and who had known that gold had quite so many tones? It mesmerized, the way the feathered muscle lifted him into the air. With his claws curved before him Basil descended on the showman, sinking his iron-gray talons into the man's shoulders. How like nothing a human body was when confronted with this beast. It was like tossing a bag of leaves, a soft pile of bread dough, a scoop of earth. The showman screamed as the claws pierced his body, and then he was in the sky, dragged through the air, blood raining down from his wounds. Basil hurled him into a tree, the impact smashing the branches, all of it coming down in a terrible jumble, man and tree, flesh and wood, blood and leaves. As the mass settled, nothing stirred. The showman was dead. Paws on the ground, Basil faced the others, the cowards, his claws extended before him, bits of the showman's flesh still caught on the tips, bloodied and rageful. His great beak cracked open and again the ungodly noise shook the forest, and the men scrambled backward, tumbling over themselves in the dirt only to rise and tumble again, finally crawling away from the griffin, crying like children.

"You're too useless to kill," the griffin said, shaking the mess from his claws. "But if our paths should ever cross again, the memory of this day might just move me to murder you. I'd head to Germany. What do you say?"

Hiccupping promises and gratitude, the men scrambled like hogs along the forest floor. Basil turned his back on them and approached the pile of branches that shrouded the fallen showman. Kicking away the debris with his paw, he finally bent to the man, looking for Syrena's horn. He found the tip protruding from the showman's soft belly. As if the wound the griffin's claws had made, the impact of the tree, or his subsequent fall—as if any one of those were not enough to do him in, he had fallen on the mermaid's stolen sword. Basil wrapped his claws around the hilt and with a powerful tug brought the tusk from the man's limp body. And so he came to the mermaid, bloodied and tousled, and returned her horn, its spiraled grooves sticky and crimson.

"Well," Syrena said simply, looking into the griffin's sharp eyes. "That was magnificent. Never have I seen such a thing."

"We griffins do not fight often," Basil explained, almost sheepishly. "But when we do, there are generally no survivors."

Syrena busily unwound a length of seaweed from her tangles and tied it around her hips, looping the narwhal horn through the weave. Her great, shiny tail was already dull; a bit longer in the air and the scales would become dry enough to cut her as they sloughed away.

"We must get you to the river," Basil said, taking in the sight of her.

"I'm no good on this land," Syrena agreed. "Please, take me."

Basil investigated the small glass box, still half-full with cloudy water. "This," he gestured uselessly. "You do not want to be carried in such a horrible thing, no?"

Syrena slid her tusk from the belt at her hips and with a sweeping blow shattered the glass box. The shards shone scummy on the forest floor, and the dirty water seeped into the earth. Syrena brought the horn to her face and inspected it happily. Not a nick, not a scratch. She felt good to have it again; it lessened the terror of being outside the waters considerably. She kept it in her grip as the griffin lifted her in his great, scaly arms.

"Your glory," he addressed the mermaid. "Onward, to the river."

Syrena felt the opening of his wings as a gust of air that blew over her, fluttering her fluke and shifting the dense weave of tangles that was her hair. And then the mermaid, who had just only touched land for the first time, was taken into the sky, the province of seabirds and bumblebees. Her mermaid heart lurched as she gazed down at the town, the stone smokestacks and crumbly walkways, the wagon heaped with fruit or meat, the still-grazing cows, the dots of children in colorful clothes scampering across the land. The green of the forest, the sun, that golden ball, lowering itself like a curtain after a successful performance.

And cutting through it all, the river.

The wind from Basil's powerful wings blew Syrena's wild hair one way, and the wind in her face blew it another. Her strong fluke fluttered like a mere kite. How wonderful it was to fly! Very much like swimming, actually; the gliding, the speed, the sensation of effortlessness. Syrena felt a pulse of actual pity for the humans she spied on the earth below. How they lumbered! So heavy were their bodies! Did they ever experience such a thing as Basil's soaring flight, or the mermaid's amniotic glide beneath the waves? Was there a human equivalent? Running, perhaps, but the pumping, sweaty effort of that was nothing like the easy bliss of flying for a griffin, or swimming for a mermaid. Poor humans! Perhaps that was why they were so cranky and hateful! Syrena's sense of kinship with Basil grew as she pondered all of this. Both, in their own ways, knew the ecstasy of flight. She flew below the world, and he above it, and both knew to be wary of the humans that toiled on that middle plain.

Basil stopped pumping his wings, angling them in special ways to allow them to gently glide while slowly descending to the ground below. The smell of his wings was sweet to Syrena, slightly smoky, like a nub of incense tossed into a fire. As the earth came closer, Syrena spotted a boat docked at the riverbank, wooden, glorious with color. Crimson red, lapis blue, mustard-seed yellow. It was shaped a bit like a gondola, but much larger, with a wooden cabin in the center. The wood was decoratively notched, and the boat's bow and stem curved grandly. Flags fluttered from banners—Italy, Pomerania, Russia, Greece. A pirate's flag, and the sorts of flags believed to contain prayers that only the wind can loosen and deliver to the gods. It was a beautiful boat, and it was Basil's boat. He came down gently onto it, and the craft dipped and swayed as it received him. At the edge of it he bent low and returned Syrena to the river, his feathers dipping into the waters.

"You freed me," Syrena nodded, quite serious. "You killed a man for me. I will be forever in your debt."

"No debt, your glory," the griffin shook his head, his own yellow-beaked face quite serious as well. "It was what any decent creature would have done. And did this trouble not find you here in the Vistula, and, if I may be so bold, were you not swimming the river in search of me?"

Syrena nodded her head. "It is true. You were much in my mind. The ocean so large, can make a mermaid feel like a fry." She looked around the river and smiled. "I like the river, actually. For its closeness. It like a hug, while the ocean, the ocean like a howl."

"Do you think you'll stay?" Basil asked, his eyes looking this way and that, at the fluttering flags, at the last bolt of orange in the sky, at the fiery torches beginning to blaze along the shore. "Or is it too close to humans for you? Perhaps it feels cozy now, but maybe it will begin to seem small, and you will long for the open waters."

Syrena looked intently at the griffin's face, his beak and feathers and evasive eyes. "I do not like the humans, it is true," she nodded. "But now I have my tusk again, and I will be on guard. And if I long for the sea, I will go to the sea. The sea will always be there. But you, Basil. Where will you be?"

The griffin finally looked at her, and Syrena was struck by the bald hope in his eyes. "Upriver," he said. "Warszawa. I will stay there, now. No more up and down the water. I've asked the moon god to secure me an inland post, and I've been heard. A little home by the Vistula, a little boat for my travels. Perhaps too provincial for someone who has swum the seas." His eyes slunk away again.

"Basil," Syrena said sternly, calling them back to her. "Are you asking me to come with you?"

"Yes, your glory," he said.

"Well, ask me, then." Her fluke tapped the water's surface, impatient.

"Your glory—"

"Syrena," the mermaid corrected. "Enough with this 'your glory' nonsense, I am not a queen."

"But you are," Basil insisted. "You are queen of the sea, queen of all that falls between the glow of the moon and the ocean's depths."

"Is lovely," Syrena nodded at the griffin's poetry. "Not mean to be rude. Just not queen. Syrena."

"*Rusalka*," Basil said, with what seemed to be a smile. How interesting, thought Syrena, that she could tell when he smiled, this yellow-beaked creature.

"What is *rusalka*?" she asked.

"River mermaid," he told her.

"Okay, yes, fine, I am river mermaid then. I am *rusalka*. Now, were you to ask me something or were you not?"

"I was to ask you to come with me," the griffin said humbly. "Down the River Vistula and into the city of Warszawa. To stay with me at the water's edge. For only as long as it suits you, and no longer."

"That seems to me a very nice invitation," Syrena said, smiling so wide her baleen poked from her lip. "I will come with you, Griffin Basil. I will swim beside your handsome boat. I will dig a cave into the wall of the river and I will live there, in the water beneath your home. And I will stay for as long as it suits me."

Chapter 7

And how long was that?" Sophie asked the mermaid. She reached out and skimmed the muddy edges of the river bank as she glided by on her current of water. She was still adjusting to the parameters of the Vistula. How small it felt after the vastness of the sea! She understood now why the mermaid had been driven to madness while waiting in shallow Chelsea Creek. It would be like folding yourself into a box! Sophie tore a wet chunk of mud from the bank and slid it into her mouth, searching for a bit of salt. There was none. She spat the out the dirt and looked to Syrena. The mermaid was lost in her memories.

"Oh..." she said, catching the girl's expectant eye. "Many, many years. More years than a human girl live on earth, was I with Basil. I get beavers to help me carve a home into the river's wall, right under his house. I threaten always to dig my way up and come through his floorboards, but I only joke. I like my cave in the river. Nice to curl my tail there and dream. Nice to know Basil was so close. Even when I sleep, I feel him nearby. I think I smell the fire he makes, the smoke from his chimney. The ashes blow into my river, I don't mind. Hundreds of years, we live like that. Hundreds."

"Did you miss the sea?" Sophie asked.

"Never," Syrena said. Once I come to the Vistula, I become *rusalka*. I still live in same cave, same home in *Warszawa*. Only Basil not there anymore. Basil's house gone, gone for many years now. For more years than it was there has it been gone."

"Is Basil…" Sophie wanted to know, but she didn't want to ask.

"Is Basil dead? Yes, child. Basil be dead long as Basil's home be gone. A war come to Warszawa. Not the first war, not the last war, not even the worst war, but the war that take Basil. He fought the men who come. I fight, too: I drown many men, I sink ships. My tusk very bloody. I use it on the man who kill Basil. I see it happen, there at the shore. A shock." The mermaid looked at Sophie, her eyes the color of water, fathomless.

"I think I not believe griffin can die. Such marvelous creature, so much magic. But all things living can die, Sophie. Even mermaid like me, even special girl like you. Even Basil."

Sophie was silent, letting the heart and bones of Syrena's story sink into her body. Everyone there on planet Earth, on its grass and dirt and beneath its many waters, fighting an evil meant to outlast them. The girl felt heavy.

"And so Basil died there, on the river bank," Syrena continued, "And so I send my tusk into the heart of the man who slayed him. It lodge there so hard, it never come out! Many men try to pry from dead body, but no. He taken like that through the streets, by the townspeople. He brought to their camp, he thrown into their camp like so. They take him back across the waters, when they retreat. They did retreat. We won: Warszawa, Poland, won. That man buried with my tusk in his heart so no one ever forget. We won. But I lost Basil."

"How could you stay?" Sophie asked, feeling emotional at the mermaid's story. "Didn't it make you sad to live there, after he was gone?"

"I be sad anywhere I go with no Basil," Syrena shrugged. *Warszawa* my home. Vistula my home. The people, they accept me, because of Basil. After war, after I slay that soldier, people love me. They know I mourn Basil, they bring me things—human food, cakes and such, too sweet for mermaid but very pretty. Some bring me fish as well. Bring me flowers and kindness. Say I help save the city. That when I become so famous. People start putting my picture everywhere, ya? Say I protect Warsaw. And I do. Not only Warsaw! I protect river. I protect all of Poland."

"And me," Sophie said. "You protect me."

"Ah," the mermaid laughed. "You protect me too, ya? Your Kishka, she not kill you but she can kill me! I need you more than you need me! How feel to be protector of mermaid?"

Truthfully, it didn't feel so great. Maybe if she felt ready to flip into a great white, maybe if she could *zawolanie* herself into a killer whale or, better, a sea monster with the sharp beak of a squid, the poison tentacles of a jellyfish, the endless teeth of a shark and the terrible spines of an urchin, maybe then Sophie would feel capable of defending a mermaid. But Sophie knew that any *zawolanie* she tried would come out pathetic as a hiccup. She felt weak. Weak like she had a cold, the kind of cold you know with intuitive dread is swiftly morphing into something worse, the flu, pneumonia, mononucleosis. Sophie wished they could bed down with some beavers, that she could take a long, long nap and wake up refreshed. But she knew she would not. It was the salt that was getting to her, the lack of salt, just as the mermaid had warned. A nap would only prolong her time in fresh water, she'd wake up sicker than when she went down for the slumber. The only thing to do was keep going, force the water to carry her as fast as the narrow channel allowed, and continue to snack on the rubbery sea plants stuffed into her backpack. Sometimes the texture repulsed her a little, but the taste of salt, as small as it was, was welcome. She kept a hunk of it tucked in her cheek, sucking and chewing the salt from it slowly.

Sharply attuned to the girl's condition, the mermaid noted her limpness. Sophie's normal bravado was filed down; her gusto was wobbly. She lay weakly upon the current that carried her, softly chewing on bladder wrack.

"You not okay," the mermaid observed. "It hitting you now. Your body very weak. Eat more seaweed, ya?"

Sophie opened her mouth grotesquely, showing the mermaid the wadded-up blob of green on her tongue. "Check it out," she said. The mermaid snorted a string of air bubbles from her nose.

"I see you not so sick to stop being rude," she said, truly relieved. "Is good news."

"Tell me more stories," Sophie demanded. "It helps take my mind off how I feel."

"And how you feel?" the mermaid inquired.

"Achy," Sophie said. "Like my bones are made of glass. Like I'm chipped and cracked. Like my blood is made of dirty, melting snow."

"You will be poet yet, ya?" Syrena smiled. "You should tell me story. Why not, eh? You bored with mermaid show already?"

"My life is boring," Sophie grumbled. "This is the most exciting thing that's ever happened to me, and you've been here for all of it. I don't have a story."

Syrena laughed, sending a stream of bubbles from her lips. "Your story bigger than this moment," the mermaid spoke wisely. "Your story begin the moment you born, and you can't even see how magic it is. But you will see. Others will help you. Your story is your magic. It will come to you in time."

When the mermaid talked in such a riddly way, Sophie's already overwhelmed brain got fritzier. "Please," she said, "Just one more awesome mermaid story?"

Syrena gazed around at the mudded river walls, the dark waters. "No good stories here," she shook her head. "More sad stories. Too many sad stories, too many wars. Near here is where big, terrible place built by humans. Like a prison, only the guards are the criminals and the prisoners just sad people, sad people being worked to death. No reason but human insanity. In the winter, that winter, so cold the Vistula froze. I stay low, at the bottom, under all the ice. But I hear the prisoners made to cut the ice, ya? Into blocks. They have bad, broken tools, they hack and hack and hack at the ice. They no do good job, they killed, just like that, right there on the bank of my river. So I begin to help. I have my tools, ya, my own tools, not so great either but they work, and from underneath I dig and dig to the surface, and I help the people chop the ice. We work together making ice bricks, the people pile them on the dirt, then drag them back to prison. We make many ice bricks. I think less people die, once I help. No matter, though. They all die anyway. Die sooner, die later."

"That happened here?" Sophie whispered. Syrena's tale made the dark, earthen walls of the river feel sinister, full of bad mystery. Syrena's tale made the walls feel closer, claustrophobic, closing in.

"Ya. You see? You no want my story. What your story. Tell me—that person, at the creek the day we go. Acted like they in love with me, who that person, eh?"

Sophia stretched her mind back to her last moments in Chelsea, wading into the creek, the pigeons and people who had gathered there to send her off on her great journey. Angel, who had gazed at the mermaid with a swirl of disbelief and devotion.

"That was Angel," Sophie said, smiling at the memory of her. "She was my teacher. She taught me how to hide myself from Kishka, or from anyone. And how to dig into someone's heart, even if they don't want you there."

"Well, she did very good job, ya?" Syrena snorted, recalling when the girl trespassed upon her own psyche. "She handsome, that one. She like part boy and girl both, ya?"

"I guess," Sophie shrugged.

"I never have great love with human. But, with most all other creatures gone now, who knows? Who knows, hmmmm?" Syrena smiled at the girl with a rare lightness, and Sophie caught a glimpse of what the mermaid might have been like had she not been placed in this world full of slain griffins and kidnapped sisters and ice-chopping prisoners.

"Tell more," the mermaid demanded. "Tell me, you have mother and father, ya? Why they not at creek?"

"Well my mom," Sophie began. "She was raised by Kishka, right? So she's—she's pretty damaged. She was an okay mom," she said thoughtfully, "considering. And my dad, I only found out about him like right before we left!"

"Mermaids no have 'dads'," Syrena shrugged. "We don't even know who is our mother. Whole village is our mother."

"That sounds cool," Sophie said, dreaming briefly about a whole village of mermaid-moms. "My dad, he's an alcoholic. He just sort of drinks all day and is really stupid. I mean, he might be smart underneath it, but the alcohol just makes him so dumb, he's not even human."

Sophie felt a pang of guilty sorrow. That broken man was what brought her to life.

"He sounds pretty human to me," Syrena scoffed. "Know many such men in *Warszawa*."

"And Kishka just *gives* him alcohol, to keep him like that. He works at her garbage dump, but he doesn't even work because he can't *do* anything. I didn't even know he was my dad. I just thought he was some creepy drunk. Nobody told me."

In her weakened state, Sophie couldn't fend off her tears. They drifted from her eyes into the water before her, giving the fresh river a tang that she slurped at as she spoke. "And I have a sister, a *twin* sister, if you can believe it, but she lives in this magic poison jungle inside Kishka's trailer."

"Trailer?" Syrena asked.

"It's like the opposite of a castle," Sophie said. "A really small little place to live. You can hook it to the back of a car and move it around. My sister, Belinda, lives there. It was supposed to be *me*. But my Aunt Hennie made a switch, she outsmarted Kishka because she's Odmieńce, too, so she has some powers. She owns this crappy grocery store that nobody even shops at, but it's like a cover for her witch studio. It's a glamour. Now I think she's helping this really messed up girl Laurie raise her baby. Laurie got possessed by the *Dola* after I was a jerk to Hennie, that's how they met. Laurie was hooked on drugs and had a baby even though she's a teenager, but I think she's doing better. And there's Ella, who was my best-best-best-best-best-best-*best* friend, but then she got weird over boys. Well, she was weird anyway, like, she gets really, really, *really* freaked out about germs. Even when she's totally okay she thinks there is something on her that could hurt her or make her sick."

"I hear of this human problem," Syrena nodded.

"What's so dumb is that the things that really *could* hurt her were these jerky boys she always got crushes on, and now she's actually pregnant from one of them."

"Good thing mermaids don't need to have jerks to have baby," Syrena mused. "Just have baby on your own, ya?"

"Lots of women have babies on their own in Chelsea," Sophie said. "But there aren't villages of mermaids to help them out, so it's really hard."

"Humans," Syrena shook her head. "All their life is such a mess."

It was true, Sophie thought, so true. And yet. When she thought about Chelsea, something stirred inside her. The smell of burning leaves in the winter, or the electric smell after a summer rain. The way the street got almost gooey with the heat, the way it would shimmer in the distance, like the world was turning magic just a little ways before you, and if you could just *reach it*... but you never could. The magic of Chelsea was always just out of reach, like the disembodied voices from the police scanners old women would tug out onto their front porches, spooky and crackling as the sound moved though the air. Sophie thought of the icy, sugary slush served from wooden barrels at the old corner store, of the pilgrims buried in the ancient graveyard in the center of town.

Kids rode their bikes down the rocky hills there, and even Sophie had disobeyed her mother and hopped the fence to climb the trees—trees that had been there so long, they'd seen Native Americans and witches, pilgrims and other immigrants. Sophie remembered sticking out a powerful summertime rainstorm from the bough of such a tree, and the way the gutters swelled and ran with branches and leaves, candy wrappers and pigeon feathers. Her heart swelled with longing.

"I really prefer the pigeons," Sophie said. "They live in this coop on the roof of Dr. Chen's house in Chelsea. The pigeons are really smart, and funny, and sweet. They've been through a lot. They don't like humans either but they're trying to help because I guess if the humans get better then they'll maybe stop trying to hurt the pigeons, and everything else. So it's good to help them. Even if they don't deserve it."

"Oh, Sophia," Syrena smiled softly. "Everyone deserves help, ya? Is true, what the pigeons know. Only sick people make so much trouble. If the humans become less sick, better world for everyone, ya? This your great job."

My great job, Sophie thought grimly. What in the world was *she* going to do about it? She could barely lift her arms to feed herself a fresh ribbon of seaweed; could barely move her tongue to spit out the salt-sucked wad of green tucked into her cheek. Syrena looked at her, a rare nervous expression on her strange and beautiful face. Syrena hardly ever looked nervous. Annoyed, exasperated, furious, yes. Not nervous.

"Am I that bad?" Sophie asked. "Can you tell?"

"I may have to drag you to castle by my hair, like how I bring you across the Atlantic Ocean," Syrena said. "Only now I have to drag dumb backpack with jewelry and computer, too. Agh. Try to stay strong, young girl. You stop talking about life now, yes? I sorry I make you. Maybe no war or camps in your life, but is not so good either, eh? We both be quiet. We be quiet and swim to my home in the Vistula."

And that was what they did.

Chapter 8

re we there yet?"

"Whaaat?" Syrena hollered back. The speed at which they traveled made communication hard. The water they zoomed through snatched the words from their mouths as they barreled forward.

Some miles back Syrena had seen fit to take not just the girl but her weighty backpack as well and rope them to her back with her strong length of mermaid hair. Though the mermaid had gotten her impossible hair sorted out by the Jottnar, after so much travel it was indeed insane once more. She had braided it with wide, flat strips of seaweed, more for Sophie to chew from once they hit fresh water. Sophie had located a matted chunk that looked somewhat like a hammock—tough, wiry locks alternating with the rubbery swaths of greenery. She'd pulled it around her, taking care to yank it back across her stupid backpack, and then grabbed a bunch of floating tendrils and tied them in knots all around her. The end result was like a patchwork sea net. And so Syrena began the unhappy task of swimming her charge up the river.

"Never mind!" Sophie yelled. "It was a joke!"

"You make joke?" Syrena yelled. "No make joke! No time for funny! Save your breath! You not well, Sophia!"

Sophie knew it was true. She was lashed snugly to the mermaid in her cocoon of hair and seaweed, but when she did move she could feel the creaky ache in every joint, the long pains that shot down her muscle. Her skull throbbed. It was like the flu, she thought. Like the flu, but worse. She found a stem of seaweed woven into Syrena's hair and, too weak to tug it free, angled her head to suck on it. Sophie fell asleep dreaming of that taste in her mouth.

SOPHIE DIDN'T KNOW if she had been asleep for a long time or a little, or if she had been asleep at all. Perhaps she had passed out—like sleep, but bad, a problem. A little wiggle brought a stiff pain up the back of her neck, so thick she groaned. Her fevered skin heated the water that surged around her face.

When she opened her eyes, what she saw made her gasp so deeply she choked on a lungful of water. Sputtering, her mind reeled. *How?* Sophie marveled. *How can she smoke a cigarette underwater?*

Kishka was perched daintily atop Sophie's chest, her legs crossed inside her flowered housecoat, her feet in kitten-heeled sandals which bounced lightly as they moved. She rode Sophie, still lashed to the mermaid, as if seated sidesaddle atop a horse. One hand elegantly fingered her cigarette, while the other held, as if it were a purse, something Sophie intuitively knew was no good. Round with a little handle, made of a heavy metal.

"It's a mine," Kishka explained, easily reading her granddaughter's thoughts. From the great war here, in the '40s. The Germans laid them everywhere, and the explosions were marvelous. They killed many people."

"The Nazis," Sophie said. She felt sick, and when she noted how weak, how salt-deprived she was, she felt sicker still.

"So many left behind," Kishka mused. "I know you can't see the riverbed, with how that crazy mermaid has you tied up, but if you could you would see that the muddy floor is strewn with them." Kishka tipped the mine flat in the palm of her hand and ashed her cigarette into it. "Of course," she said, "It would take but one to blast you both to smithereens." She drummed her fingernails on the metal; Sophie could hear the bing and clatter faintly, over the rush of the water around her.

"Please," Sophie whispered, her throat dry with fear. "Please stop doing that."

"Oh fine," Kishka said, flipping the mine around so that it dangled from her fist like a handbag. "I mean, since you said *please*." She gave a little laugh which morphed into a sigh. "My darling. I'm surprised you haven't figured this out by now, but I actually *can't* kill you. That's the thing. Odmieńce can't kill other Odmieńce."

Right, Sophie remembered. But it was so hard to feel invincible in the presence of such menace. Her open mouth filled with water. "I— know that."

"What tipped you off, the fact that you're still alive?" Kishka snorted. "You didn't think it was my grandmotherly love that's kept me from murdering you, did you? Or that your own 'magnificent powers' were saving you?" Kishka said, in a tone suggesting Sophie's powers were nothing but a ridiculous joke.

"Well, you're still alive, too," Sophie snapped. "Don't think I wouldn't have offed you if I could!"

"Oh, touché. Listen. Sophia. We need to talk. To sort this out. I can't kill you, you can't kill me, that means we're going to have to come to some sort of a truce, am

I right? And I have the means to make a very sweet deal with you. To coexist with me in splendor. I can give you everything you want."

"I can give myself anything I want," Sophie shot, remembering the gold bar she'd left for her mother; her shining, undulating mermaid tail.

"Please," Kishka scoffed, her face sour. "And I can't believe you would *degrade* yourself by becoming one of those trashy fish-women. It's frankly disgusting. And I'm sick of that one's influence on you. I'm about done with it."

As if swimming out from a portal in her chest, a bed of eels poured from Kishka and darted straight for Syrena, their hideous jaws unhinged, their teeth tiny but so sharp, and so many.

Syrena opened her mouth to roar at the swarm, baring her fangs all the way up to her baleen, stretching her body long, making herself as huge and monstrous as possible. A carved shell dagger was gripped in her hand and she swam to and fro, her eyes darting and fierce, ready to make her first hit. But the eels—there were so many of them, and they swam like ribbons in a wind, swift and elusive. The mermaid was weighed down by Sophie's leaden weight. Sophie felt Syrena calling out to her for help, quietly, without showing Kishka her weakness, without taking her eyes off the fry of eels that had swum from her grandmother's heart.

Even if Sophie could free herself from the intricacy of tangle Syrena had woven about her, she knew she could not fight off the eels. There were far too many of them. And what of the bombs lying in the muck below? Were they there or was her grandmother bluffing, were they simply illusions? Sophie thought fast. These weren't *real* eels, they were a part of her grandmother. Yet they could do real damage—Sophie noticed with alarm that Syrena was already bleeding from a bite on her tail. The blood bloomed in the clear water like a terrible rose; she had to act fast. She had to enter the eels.

With a push Sophie was not just inside one of the creatures, she was in them all. Of course—whatever hive mind the beasts naturally shared was amplified by the fact that they were all emanations of Kishka. They all shared a consciousness: a narrow, obsessive consciousness bent on devouring the mermaid. Through the animals' beady blue eyes she watched Syrena lash out with her dagger, making contact. More blood colored the water.

Sophie felt the eels' hearts beating inside their wily bodies and she seized on them, all at once. Sophie entered the fry and with a feeling like a clench, a bearing down, she squeezed the eels' hearts. Her own heart stilled at the effort, the audacity of stopping a beating heart. What a terrible way to kill! It was too diabolical; it seemed like something Kishka would do. But, as Sophie watched the eels seize, their slender bodies twitching, her own heart kicked back in relief and excitement. It wasn't a bed of eels she was besting, not really. It was her grandmother. Sophie and Syrena watched as the eels began drifting down toward the flat, metal circles at the bottom of the river, both dangers vanishing. With a glance at the astonished mermaid, to make sure she was safe, Sophie returned to her body and her grandmother.

"Syrena is the closest thing to a *family* that I've ever had, okay?" she spat. "She's my mother and my grandmother and my sister. Anything you do to her you do to me. If you're trying to get me to fight you, you're doing the right thing." Sophie felt flushed and wild, and realized it was true: if she had any family, any true family, the way people in books and on TV had families, people who loved them and taught them and protected them, then Syrena was her family. And Angel, and the pigeons back in Chelsea, and Arthur, and Livia. Livia, who Kishka had killed. Livia was her ancestor.

"Your ingratitude is outrageous," Kishka spat. "You've got a mother waiting heartbroken for you at home. You've got a sister, you've got a *twin sister,* she is part of you and you are part of her. And you've got me. A magic grandmother. What girl wouldn't *kill* for a magic grandmother? A person who has helped shape the very world we're standing in. You could have that power. The power to shape the world."

"I do have it," Sophie said.

"You do not," Kishka laughed. "You've got something, but it's parlor tricks, dearie. You do not have what I have. I can carve mountains and split seas. You, you give yourself a pretty tail and banish some imaginary sea worms, big deal. You are making a mistake. You are signing up for a life of misery. A life of insanity, of madness. And that's if you live."

"You can't kill me," Sophie declared uneasily. "You said so yourself."

"Just because *I* can't kill you doesn't mean you can't be killed, dearie. There are other ways to dispose of you. Others you will anger by working against me. But, living or dead, it's all the same to me. You won't be in my way. My plan is large, larger than this obscure little world you care so much about. It's big as the universe—and getting bigger all the time. You think you're going to find something in that computer you've got strapped to your back? It's *me* they're looking for, idiot. It's *me* they can't understand. Humans never will. They'll never see me and they'll never stop me. And neither will you."

As one long, spindly cigarette came to its end, another magically appeared in Kishka's fingers, sending its plume through the waters. "Keep your path, then. See where it takes you. Wherever you land, I'll be there. At the end of it all, you reckon with me, sweetie."

And with that, her grandmother was gone.

Chapter 9

Argh! Ugh. Ack! Go fast, ya?"

Sophie could hear the mermaid's familiar demanding sputter, too loud and too clear, as if it were being shouted into her ear. She grimaced and attempted to complain, but found that she could not speak. The effort of forming the words, moving her tongue, pushing it out from her mouth on a gust of air—all of it was beyond her.

"I'm trying, I'm really trying," spoke an unfamiliar voice from somewhere above Sophie's head. She willed herself to open her eyes, but even the simple mechanics of that were too tough. The muscles that operated that system had pooped out; they felt made of lead, of something heavier than lead, maybe the material Sophie pulled up to keep her heart safe, whatever that was. Sophie hoped, in her haze, that Kishka was not watching this, because there was no way the girl would be able to drive her grandmother out from her now. If she couldn't lift an eyelid, there was no way she could raise that iron gate up around her heart.

"Girl very vulnerable," the mermaid said with a bit of urgency, as if she were reading Sophie's mind, and perhaps she was. Sophie felt splayed open, a crab without a shell, an oyster without its pearly cave.

"Kishka come to her in the river, bringing eels. Sophia make them go away. I don't know how, but it took everything from her. I knew she would be hurting by the time we arrive, but I not think this bad."

Sophie felt pulling and tugging, heard grunting and understood there was an effort at play to untie her from the mermaid's body. The swift ride up the river had pulled on the knots until they were impenetrable. The reason, she realized, that the mermaid sounded so close was that Sophie was lying on top of her, squishing her with her cumbersome backpack.

"Tadeusz, find knife, ya?" Syrena pleaded. "Anything sharp. Cut hair away, you think I care? Look what hair I have! Cut it all off for all I care, just help her!"

"Backpack," Sophie managed to kick the word out from her mouth, slurred but audible.

"Backpack," Syrena scoffed. "She come back to life, what she care about? Stupid backpack full of human things."

Sophie geared up for the next word, taking some deep, slow breaths.

"Heavy," she breathed. "Empty?"

Sophie felt a weight lifted from her own back as hands plunged into the pack and carried away its contents.

"Jeez," said the voice, and Sophie heard a pile of seaweed slither to the floor.

"Don't ask," Syrena murmured. "Just keep working."

"Huh," said the voice, as another weight was removed. "Whoa."

The clatter of jewels as they fell to the floor had an echo, and for the first time Sophie wondered where they were. As she mustered the strength to unpeel her eyes, she felt herself being handled roughly.

"Sorry," said the voice, and Sophie could feel the heavy straps of her pack being sawed through and lifted from her shoulders.

"Aaaaaah," Syrena breathed. "More. Keep going."

Thanks to the diligent efforts of whoever worked the knife, Sophie and the mermaid were finally unbound. Sophie heard a splash behind her as the mermaid dropped off into the water, while she, the girl, was hauled further onto what her numbed face took to be stone. Stone, its odor faint and familiar. With tremendous effort Sophie cranked open her mouth, and willed her tongue to drop onto the floor. *Scrape, scrape.* It was as if her head had been placed on a hard pillow of salt! *Scrape, scrape.* She did not care how disgusting it was—and yes, she knew it was disgusting, quite disgusting, to be licking the *floor* of any place, in particular a place she still could not open her eyes to see. But the urge, her body's need, took precedence over propriety or grossness, and she continued to dig at the floor with her mouth.

"She's coming around," said the voice.

"I hoped it would not take long," Syrena said from behind her, "Once we got her here."

"What should I do?"

"Just let her be. She will show you."

With every lick of the salt floor Sophie felt revived. She longed to roll onto her back, to crack open her eyes and finally see what had happened to her, but she could not bear to pull her mouth away from what soothed her. So she stayed there, face planted, for what felt like hours, until finally her eyes snapped open of their own accord, and her arms, still weak, could move without much pain, and she pulled herself upward, her head ringing with the effort.

"Here, please."

Before her was a hand, proffering a good-sized chunk of opaque, gray salt. She popped it in her mouth as her eyes adjusted to the darkness and light in the room that held her. Darker than the world above the water, brighter than the world below it, she appeared to be in a cave of sorts. The walls rose above her in sheets of gray, doming above her head and dropping back down into a kind of pool where Syrena splashed about. It looked like an ice castle, but Sophie was not cold, and she knew that it must be a cavern of salt, like where the Ogresses lived, so far beneath the water, only this one was on land, made by humans. Just lying upon it, beneath it, inhaling its essence, was helping Sophie get better.

"Where am I?" the girl croaked. "Is this the castle?"

"It is." Syrena's hard, accented voice echoed around the little chamber. "Very vast, the castle. And built upon an old salt mine. Lucky for you."

"I am Tadeusz." The hand that had held the salt offering was attached to a long, gangly arm growing out of a shirt that was slightly too small, the cuff riding high on the wrist. And the arm was attached to a shoulder, attached to a collarbone, attached to a long, gangly neck that led up to the face of a boy not so much older than Sophie. As his shirt seemed too small, the glasses that sat on his face seemed too big, a rattling black contraption sliding heavily down his nose. He pushed them up, only to have them slowly slip back down. It was something, Sophie would learn, that the boy did all day long.

He's a nerd, Sophie thought meanly. That's what Ella would say, and then some. He was the opposite of the boys of Revere Beach, sunning in greasy suntan oil, the gold crosses around their necks sparking in the sun. He was the opposite of the boys of Chelsea, spitting as they popped wheelies on their stolen dirt bikes, quick with an insult, multitaskers of cruelty. Tadeusz was long and pale as a stalagmite, and he appeared to live in a cave. Sophie looked around for where the boy slept, ate, existed.

"How do you live down here?" she asked.

"Oh, I stay in some quarters upstairs," he assured her. "Inside the castle."

"Oh," Sophie said. "Will I live down here? In the cave?"

"Of course not!" Tadeusz cried, and Sophie could hear Syrena laugh.

"Fetch her more salt, Tad," she said. "Her mind has not woken up yet. Sophie, the Castle Vistula vast place, ya? Above is part open to tourists, they come to see where old kings and queens live. Very beautiful,

I hear. I never see, and you never see either. Other part of castle sealed off, falling down, abandoned. Tadeusz live there and you live there, too. Down here, beneath—salt. Salt and salt and salt and salt. Good place for you to recuperate. Good place for you to get some strength back. But you will not live down here, like dog! There is a room for you above. Ya, Tadeusz? You fix nice for girl?"

Tadeusz blushed and shrugged. He was awkwardness personified. He would get eaten alive in Chelsea, Sophie marveled. Every street corner would provide him with a fresh group of boys and a fresh beating. He would be bounced across the city like the spinning ball in a terrible pinball machine. Sophie had truly never seen such a boy before, and she regarded him much as she had the bioluminescent creatures at the very bottom of the sea.

"I don't know what you're accustomed to," the boy said nervously.

"Not much," Syrena said. "Her town, Chelsea, what you call, craphole?"

"It's not *that* bad," Sophie snapped defensively. "But, I don't need a lot. Just a bed, I guess?"

"Of course. There's that. There's a lot, actually. It's quite nice—well, maybe not nice, but, special. It is a castle after all. Just a decrepit one."

"Sounds great," Sophie said. "When can I see it? When can we start whatever it is I came all the way here to do?"

"You rest first, Sophie," the mermaid said sternly. "And once you well enough to go upstairs, you still come down to the mine every day, ya? Long time ago, even humans come down here to become well.

Salt heals everything. You will need much healing. Is perfect place for you to be."

"I feel pretty good now," Sophie said, despite the slight throbbing that lingered in her head, the edge of dizziness when she turned to look around her. How winded she felt from the simple effort of sitting up.

"You stay," the mermaid said. "You know when you ready. Don't rush yourself. Evil is eternal. It will wait for you to battle it, ya? Waited this long already."

Evil. Kishka. Sophie turned to look at Tadeusz.

"Do you know my grandmother?"

Tadeusz looked puzzled for a moment, then nodded. "Right. Syrena explained, you see the evil as your *Babcia*. No, I don't know her, not exactly. Not as you do."

"What do you mean, I see the evil as my—what?"

"*Babcia*. Grandmother."

"Kishka *is* my grandmother."

"Right," Tadeusz nodded, his glasses sledding down the bridge of his nose. He pushed them back up, and Sophie watched his eyes grow magnified behind the lenses. "But, you know, she's just, she's just *evil*. Like, evil the noun, not evil the adjective. So in that way she's not your grandmother, not a person at all. She's just this shape-shifting force."

"Yeah. And one of the shapes she regularly assumes is that of my chain-smoking, housecoat-wearing grandmother."

Tadeusz looked uncomfortable, but Sophie had a feeling the boy always looked uncomfortable. "I guess I would just encourage you to stop looking at her as if she's your *Babcia*—your grandmother. Because you will have to fight her. And that might be hard, to fight your own grandmother, yes?"

Sophie snorted. "It's not like she was ever that nice, even before I found out she was pure evil. Plus, I've already fought her."

The boy perked up in surprise. "You have?"

"Yeah. Just now in the river. I even became a shark once, in the ocean." Sophie's tongue flicked up to her teeth, the dull row of human molars lining her gums. She remembered how the shark teeth had exploded through them, row after row of lethal sharpness filling her mouth, a mountain range of tiny knives. She shuddered. "It was awesome."

"Huh," Tadeusz looked nervously between the girl and the mermaid. "Okay, then."

"Tad, I meet Sophie, I think, 'Oh, this girl is half-Odmieńce, half-human, ya? As if such things are neat and equal, 50-50. I now not think so. Sophie not so much part-Odmieńce, she part-human. She mostly Odmieńce, with a little bit of human thrown in to make her brat." Syrena smiled wide at the girl, so wide the bristles of her baleen poked out from her upper lip.

"Really?" Sophie asked, amazed. "You think I'm maybe mostly Odmieńce?"

"I do," Syrena nodded. "Don't get such big head about it. Human part still important. Is crucial ingredient. Make you feel with that human heart, ya? Make you understand human pain. You here for the humans, after all."

"Not entirely," Tadeusz interrupted. "I mean, yes, but there are other creatures you are meant to help, I believe. Some are here to see you. Are you well enough for visitors?"

"I guess," Sophie shrugged, and watched as Tadeusz walked away toward a large salt door that took every muscle in his body to pull open. She wished, as she watched the boy's long frame tremble like a platter of Jell-O, that she had the strength to get up and help, but she could only sit there weakly and wonder what new creature lay on the other side of the dense gray door. A gnome, a troll, a talking frog? Some conglomeration of creature she'd never before imagined? A unicorn? That would be nice. Tadeusz gave the door a final yank that nearly disconnected his arm from its shoulder and the door swung open and the cave filled with pigeons.

Pigeons! Their fat gray bodies swarmed the domed cavern like a pack of bats, the beating of wings a great, echoing rumble. Sophie caught flashes of iridescence where the faint light caught their throats, sparks of orange when the brightness hit their eyes. Their flutter was a cacophony, as if someone had tossed the flock of them at the ceiling, and it took them all a moment to gather themselves and drift back down to the salt floor. Sophie's breath caught in her throat as she beheld the lot of them, bobbing and cooing, so uniform in their gray and white, but each one different—a different shape and different tilt of the neck, different patterns of stripes and different quality of feather. Some had long legs and some were squat, and of course some of them had sustained injuries—a ruined foot tucked high up in the feathers, or placed bluntly on the floor. A busted feather, a busted wing. One blind eye, or two. Sophie watched quietly, respectfully, as they shifted and settled. Within the mass of them a pathway opened up, and out of the flock limped Arthur, wobblier than ever. He had lost weight, and his feathers were darkened with grime and mussed into tangles and spikes. His one injured foot was stretched before him. He looked totally different, but Sophie would have known him anywhere. Tears sprung to her eyes.

"Arthur!"

She reached for the bird, scooping him up, and the bird both resisted and loved the embrace.

"Careful, there," he spoke, and Sophie's heart swelled at the sound of his gruff, cranky voice. "I just flew all the way here from Chelsea. And boy, are my arms tired!" He waited for a reaction, and scowled when he got none. "That was a joke, right? A people joke?"

"I told you it wasn't as funny as you thought it was," scolded another pigeon gently. Like Arthur, the bird looked severely windblown and battered, and too thin. But Sophie only had to look into her tender, orange eyes to know that it was Giddy.

"It's *not* funny!" Sophie cried, the tears that had pooled in her eyes spilling down her face. "You guys flew here from *Chelsea?* All the way to *Poland?* That's insane! That's so dangerous! You all could have died! How did you do it!"

"It was rough, all right," Arthur nodded. "There were spans where there was nothing to land on—nothing! Not a boat, not a piece of driftwood, not even a mat of trash to give the wings a break. Those were the hardest parts."

"And the seagulls," offered another pigeon, pushing through the crowd, rumpled and battle-scarred, feathers missing from his wings. Roy. Sophie smiled hugely through the waterfall of crying on her face, and reached out to gently touch the wounded bird.

"Oh the seagulls, those jerks, don't get me started about the seagulls!" Arthur griped. "Do they know how to share? No, they don't. They're monsters!"

"But we're here now, and Tadeusz has taken great care of us," Roy said gratefully. Tadeusz shrugged.

"I've done my best," said the boy. "I don't really know about pigeons."

"Well, they could use a bath," Sophie suggested. Giddy blushed. "No offense," Sophie said. "But, you all have been on a really long trip!"

"*Somewhere I have never traveled,*" quipped a new voice, affected and familiar. Wings and feathers parted and Bix slid through the crowd and presented himself to Sophie with a tiny, pigeon-sized curtsy. "'*Gladly beyond / any experience.*' e.e. cummings, 1894 to 1962. Wonderful poet, terrible man—a supporter of Joseph McCarthy, that fascist. What sort of a poet supports a fascist?"

"Bix!" Sophie gleefully cried, clapping her hands together. "It's you!"

"*Grief of my heart, joy of my eye,*" spoke the bird. "Sir George Etherege, 1636 to 1692, poet and gambler. No, Sophie, not 'it is me,' but—it is *you.*"

"It's really great to see you, Bix."

"*Permit me voyage, love, into your hands,*" spoke the bird, and Sophie lifted him with her one free hand, as Arthur vacated her other with a grumble. "Hart Crane, 1899 to 1932. Lost at sea, sadly. Much as I feared we were, for a bit there. But it all turned out for the best, for here we are. And, I have this."

Bix lifted his ringed, pink leg to Sophie, showing her the tight curl of paper bound to his ankle.

"For me?" Sophie asked, confused.

"Ah, yes. Please remove it. It is little short of a miracle that it survived the journey—the winds and the rains, the sea and the seagulls."

"Seagulls," Arthur spat. "Don't get me started about the seagulls."

Sophie undid the bit of paper from the bird's foot. It had the stiff consistency of something that had been soaked and dried, soaked and dried. It was smooth and brittle and Sophie feared, as she gently unrolled it, that it would crumble in her fingers, but it did not. The paper, once white, was a wash of pale blue from where the ink had bled, but the message was still visible.

I'm sorry.

Sophie looked curiously at the bird. "It's from that girl, your friend," Bix explained. "Ella."

Sophie clutched the scrap of paper to her heart. "It's from Ella?" she gasped. "You saw Ella? She—she talked to you?"

"Well, we had to stay a few feet back from that one," Arthur grumbled. "She didn't want to 'catch anything.'"

"How rude!" snipped a pigeon in the crowd.

"Well, she's stricken, that one," Bix said kindly. "She's not well."

"It's true," Sophie nodded. "She's, like, a germaphobe. But a real serious one."

"I'm just saying," Arthur griped. "We hadn't even gone anywhere yet. We didn't look like this. We looked nice, like we normally do."

"I'm sure you all looked great," Sophie nodded.

"She did seek us out," Giddy said. "I think that was a big step for her."

"She found you?" Sophie asked.

"In our coop, at Dr. Chen's. She'd heard from Angel that we were coming to be with you."

"Ella is... with child," Bix pronounced grandly.

"I know," Sophie said. "An octopus showed me, in an air bubble. At the bottom of the sea."

"That's the craziest thing I've ever heard," Arthur said. "Octopuses don't talk!"

"It's true," Sophie nodded. "They don't. But they can do this psychic thing with tentacles, where they put them on your head and blow air bubbles from their beaks, and inside the air bubbles are visions."

"Please," Arthur said, waving his wing at Sophie. "I can't have my mind blown any more right now. I'm still recovering from the trip."

"Angel has a new occupation," Bix continued, "assisting the downtrodden in our shared native city. And Ella is now one of her clients."

"She's interning at a social service agency for youth," Roy translated.

"Aahhh," Sophie said. "How nicely everything came together. Almost as if it were meant to be!"

"Precisely," Bix nodded, quite pleased. "Angel arranged for us to meet with her, and I agreed to bring you this communication."

"Well, thank you," Sophie said. "It means a lot."

"And these are our Polish comrades," Bix said nervously, gesturing to the large flock behind them. "They've been wonderful."

"Hi, everyone," Sophie waved at the birds. After that, the group of them fell into an awkward silence. There was one more pigeon whom Sophie longed to see, one who had not pulled up from the crowd to greet her. The one whose feather was lodged in a tangle of her hair, a tangle so dense it would never come loose. Livia.

Sophie stroked the smooth, gray feather that hung in her tangles. "You guys," she said to the pigeons she knew best. "Livia." The tears began again. "I'm so sorry."

"We're managing," Arthur said toughly. "It hasn't been easy. Not a day passes that I don't feel for her. It's a thing with us pigeons—we mate for life, you know. And when we get that mate, they become part of us. You can always feel where they are. Every day I catch myself feeling for her. I feel for her, and can't find her, and then I remember." His body gave a little shudder, trembling his feathers. "Such a big thing, right? The most important thing ever. Livia's gone, and I *forget*. How can I forget such a thing? But I do. I forget every single day."

"How she would have loved to be here," Bix said, nuzzling his soft, feathered head under Sophie's chin. "How she would have loved to see you."

"She would have been a real help with the seagulls," Roy nodded solemnly. "She was gentle—the gentlest—but she could fight when she needed."

"Enough with the seagulls," Arthur said.

"Where are you staying, all of you?"

"They have a room, upstairs in the castle," Tadeusz offered, which made Sophie laugh.

"You're staying in the *castle*?"

"What, you think a pigeon isn't good enough for a castle?" Arthur demanded. "I'll have you know, there are a *lot* of pigeons in residence at this particular castle!"

"It's true," Tadeusz nodded. "Like I said, the wing that we stay in is pretty worn down. There are some broken windows, holes in some of the walls."

"Sounds great," Sophie said sarcastically.

"It ain't bad," Arthur nodded.

"'tis but a shadow of its former glory," Bix commented, "but ruin has its own splendor, does it not?"

"I'll let you know," said Sophie.

"Birds, birds!" Syrena shouted from the pool, smacking her tail on the water for emphasis and startling some pigeons who were bathing and sipping at the waters. "This girl is not well, ya? She needs rest. You all be together soon. Now, she sleep."

"But I'm not tired!" Sophie protested. She wasn't a child, and didn't appreciate the mermaid giving her a bedtime.

"Tadeusz, you have bedding, ya?" The mermaid ignored the girl's complaint, and watched as Tadeusz stepped into a darkened corner and emerged dragging some heavy, lumpy blankets.

"Ugh," Arthur noted. "Stuffed with feathers, I see. How barbaric."

"Sorry," Sophie and the boy spoke in unison. Tadeusz fluffed the blankets into a soft and dusty nest, and motioned for Sophie to roll into it.

"Do you need my help?" he asked uneasily. Physical labors were clearly not his strong suit, though if he had managed to heave open the salt door, it figured he could lift the girl into the bedding.

"I can do it," Sophie grumbled, still resenting this enforced resting. The salt cave *had* helped her. She felt sharp and renewed and didn't want to bed down in a puff of ancient feathers. She wanted to be with the pigeons, exploring the castle, peeking out the broken windows at Warsaw, at Poland. She'd never been anywhere! And now she was in Europe—*the* Europe. A famous place! She crawled into the bedding, and Tadeusz crouched down and arranged the edges around her, so that she was stuffed inside it like the filling of a pie. She was surprised at how cozy it felt. The bedding was old and dusty but soft and not smelly. Her body relaxed into the fluff of it, relieved to no longer be lounging on the hard salt floor. Giddy waddled up to her, and began to brush her forehead with the tips of her wings. It felt lovely.

"Go to sleep, little one," she cooed, which was funny, because Giddy was the little one, she was a pigeon, and birds are small, smaller than all humans, even babies. But Sophie felt small beneath the bird's caress, and it was a sweet feeling, unbearably sweet. "We've come so far to see you, and we will all be here when you wake up. Rest, rest." Sophie's eyes grew heavy under the pigeon's gentle command.

"Tadeusz," she mumbled before a great, healing sleep overtook her. "Please. Give these birds a bath."

Chapter 10

Time—the days and hours that had been so important to
Sophie while in Chelsea, useful for getting her to school on
time and in front of the television for the start of her favorite shows—
had ceased to mean much once the girl climbed into the creek with
the mermaid. Those initial lost days, when her body was broken from
Kishka's fist-shaped rogue wave and she was forced to ride on the mermaid's back, bound there with her miles of tangled hair. How long
had she traveled like that? How long had it taken them to arrive at the
underwater mountains that spit fire and healed her? How long had they
rested at the mountain, how long until they reached the Ogresses' deep,
deep home, how long did Sophie swirl in the swilkie gateway to their
realm? Sophie's mind boggled a bit when as she attempted to add it
all up. Her time with the Jottnar, in their golden cave; her time inside
Bloo's hot and fathomless heart. It could have been days, all of it, or

weeks, or, she supposed, *years*. So Sophie wasn't too alarmed when she awoke in her puff of bedding on the floor of the old salt mine having no idea how long she'd been asleep. What mattered, she supposed, was that she felt deeply, wonderfully *rested*—a sensation she realized she'd missed dearly. Her eyes adjusted to the dimly lit cavern, and as she smacked her sleepy mouth together, she tasted salt. Tiny, cracked granules of it lingered inside her mouth, crunchy on her teeth. She pulled herself up in her makeshift bed, the covers falling off her in a cloud of dust. She started to find a pigeon standing stiffly beside her.

"Hello," Sophie said, more of a snap than a greeting. She didn't appreciate being spied upon while she was sleeping. "What are you doing down here, staring at me?"

"I am Loosha, *moja pani*, and I am doing my duty watching over you and feeding you salt as you sleep. Forgive the intrusion." He gave a slight, pigeony bow. "I have long lived at the castle, and have heard of your coming since I was a squeaker. It is a great honor to serve you."

"Okay," Sophie relented. She supposed it was nice to have been given the salt by the bird. Perhaps she was not lying in old blankets on the floor of a cave, looked after by pigeons, but being kept in a sort of hospital, watched over by this medicine-dispensing night nurse. Her round-the-clock care only seemed to have helped. Inspired by how fresh she felt, Sophie pushed aside the last of her blankets and rose to her feet—only to grow quickly dizzy and fall back down into the mound of bedding.

"Oh no, no, no, no!" Loosha fluttered, flustered. "I was told you must not stand up on your own! You have been asleep for too long! And before that—the mermaid said—only being in water for so long, make it hard to stand on the earth as a girl again! Mermaid said!"

"'Mermaid said,'" Sophie grumbled. "Even when Syrena is gone she is still bossing me around!" She sat still in the pile of soft blankets until the buzzing in her head had stopped, and the hot feeling in her ears had cooled, and the little black spots that blotted out her vision had faded away. "And—where is she? The mermaid?"

Loosha shrugged his feathers. "She swam back out into the Vistula," he said. Sophie nodded. Syrena was home. And Sophie knew she had work to do, having been gone so long from the river she guarded and its many people. It occurred to Sophie that she would be returning to her own mess someday, if she were lucky—her pregnant friend, her cigarette-sick mother and alcohol-sick father. Still, Sophie felt an emptiness at being without her mermaid.

"Loosha," she started, "how long have I been sleeping?"

"Oh, I'm not certain, *moja pani*. Pigeons don't really concern ourselves with, what do you call it, *time*. But this is my second shift watching over you, and the entire Warsaw kit has had at least one shift."

"Okay," Sophie nodded, remembering the size of the flock of Polish birds. "And how long are each of your shifts?"

Loosha shrugged once more, and repeated, "Pigeons don't really concern ourselves with time."

It had occurred to Sophie, as she struggled to understand how long not just her slumber but her journey had been, that she didn't exactly know how old she was anymore, and this troubled her greatly. Had she had a birthday while swimming the oceans? Had she had a birthday while conked out beneath her pigeon sentinels? Was today perhaps her birthday, or would it come and go tomorrow, without her knowledge? It seemed a terrible thing to miss a birthday, and strange and awful not to know one's age!

"Well." She turned to the pigeon, conscious of her overall annoyance with her situation, not wanting to take it out on this one noble bird but finding her feelings quite beyond her control. "How am I supposed to get up? Are you going to help me?"

Her sarcasm was lost on the earnest Loosha. "I'm afraid I wouldn't be much help to you, *moja pani*. I can fly upstairs and fetch the boy."

The boy. He'd crumble like a pile of sticks! Sophie didn't need that eggheaded weakling to help her stand on her own two feet. She could do it herself. Carefully. She scrambled onto all fours and slowly—slowly—began to raise herself into a shaky squat.

"Oooh," Loosha cooed nervously. "You really must let me get the boy."

"Don't," Sophie ordered in a tone the bird could only obey. When she caught her breath she attempted to rise, but the trembling of her legs won out. "Okay," she muttered to herself. "Okay."

"Okay, I shall fetch the boy?" Loosha inquired.

"No!" Sophie snapped. "Let me do this. Okay?"

Back on all fours she crawled out of the bedding and moved toward the cave wall. Again she pulled herself into a squat, this time with her back propped against the smooth salt. Slowly—slowly—she pushed herself up against the wall until she was fully upright, leaning against it. She stayed there, her weight heavy upon the salt slab, until her body stopped trembling, her blood no longer rushing through her veins. She closed her eyes and her tongue instinctively sought the crumbs of salt stuck in her molars. She sucked at them. Then Loosha was before her, wings aflutter, a pebble of gray mineral in his beak. Sophie plucked it out gently and gratefully.

"Thank you," she said, and popped the salt in her mouth. Much more dignified than turning and licking the wall she leaned upon, something she was on the verge of doing.

"When you are ready, I will lead you upstairs, to where the others are," Loosha offered.

"That will be wonderful," Sophie said. It took her some time to feel confident that she could walk on her own feet, without a wall to prop her up, but eventually she took a step, and then another. Loosha fluttered around her, nervously.

"You're sure, *moja pani?* You're sure you don't need assistance?"

"I'm fine, Loosha."

"It's just that, were you to fall on my watch, I never would forgive myself." His orange eye looked into her brown ones with urgency.

"I promise I won't fall," Sophie said, wondering if she could actually promise such a thing on her noodly legs. "If I need help I will have you fetch Tadeusz."

With the slow, stiff lurch of a zombie, Sophie made her way to the large salt door, propped open to allow for the coming and going of the pigeons. She didn't have the strength to push it any wider, but managed to squeeze through. When she looked up at the stairs, her breath caught in her throat and she had to lean once again upon the wall.

The stairs, carved from salt, went up and up and up and up, as far as her eyes could see.

A curse word popular in her hometown of Chelsea escaped her lips.

Loosha was unfamiliar with the word, but understood the tone, and the sigh of desperation it came out on.

"Exactly, *moja pani*," the bird babbled. "This is why it was insisted that you have help."

"I want to do it myself," Sophie said stubbornly. "I don't care if I have to crawl to the top."

"As you wish."

"I'm just going to take it slow. Really slow."

"We are not quite a mile beneath the castle."

Not quite a mile. To be honest, Sophie wasn't sure how long or short a mile was. Not to mention the difference in climbing a mile's worth of stairs versus walking a mile on flat land. When she lifted her head to the top she could not see the end of the stairs, but she did see sunlight. She liked that. The brightness of it made her eyes ache in their sockets, but she liked it anyway, and like a flower felt her whole self turn toward it longingly. She would climb to the sun. An iron bar jutted out from the salt wall, running upwards. Sophie clutched it, and began pulling herself up the salt steps.

After only a few moves upward Sophie came upon a carving in a wall. *Carving* seemed too crude a word, actually; it wasn't like someone gouging their initials into the trunk of a tree, it was a whole tableau, artfully etched into the soft salt walls. A beast like a centaur, half-woman, half... duck? Duck-bat? The thing had a long tail and wings coming of her hips, and she carried a sword in one hand and a shield in the other.

"What is this?" Sophie asked, delicately running her fingers around the edges.

"Syrena. Our mermaid. Your mermaid."

The breath Sophie had been holding as she tenderly inspected the engraving now burst from her face with a cackle and snort. "*Syrena?*" Sophie gasped. "This thing? This is *not* Syrena. I don't know *what* this is, but Syrena, Syrena is... well, she's beautiful, to begin with. And she doesn't have any feet at all, let alone these duck feet! And she does have those little fins at her hips, but they're not bat wings!"

"*Moja pani,* I am not the artist," Loosha said simply. "Artist made this carving many, many years ago. Hundreds upon hundreds. When Syrena first come to the Vistula. She was very shy with humans and did not show herself often, not like her griffin. So this is what the people thought she looked like."

Sophie snorted derisively, taking one last dig at the work.

"More better up higher. But this, this carving is very, very old. Please respect."

All that scorn had taken the wind out of Sophie. She leaned against the iron banister, scraping a fine bit of salt from the wall with her raggedy fingernail and sucking it off. "Okay," she said, as the mineral soothed her. "Let's go."

Further up the stairs the pair came upon another carving, this time what looked like a queen, a woman with a heavy crown on her head and robes falling from her shoulders. She held her hands out toward a man who knelt before her, offering her a ring.

"Who's this?" Sophie asked.

"That's Kinga," Loosha said. "She was a queen and a saint. Came from Hungary and married a Polish prince. Her father wanted to make a great big gift of gold and silver to Poland, but Kinga thought they needed salt more than they needed gold. So she took her engagement ring and she threw it in a salt mine back in Hungary. Then, when she came to Poland to marry the prince, she had some miners start digging for salt and they hit upon a block of it, with her ring inside!"

"Come on," Sophie said. "Really?"

"Really," Loosha nodded his solemn pigeon nod. "And the miners continued to dig and they found this salt mine right here."

"Well," Sophie said thoughtfully, "maybe Kinga was an Odmieńce."

"Maybe," Loosha nodded. "She did love salt. And she did very nice things for the people. And when the king died she became a nun so she could spend all day praying."

Sophie shuddered, remembering the nuns that had taught her and Ella what felt like a million years ago. "Well, that's not what I'm going to do when this is all over, I'll tell you that. Maybe the nuns were different during Kinga's time, but the ones back in Chelsea are just mean."

Anticipating the next carving in the stairwell made the movements up the stairs bearable; in fact, Sophie hardly noticed the strain on her legs and in her lungs as she pulled herself up the steep climb. The next engraving was also of a woman, though this one looked much plainer, no crown or robes. Her hair was pulled back and parted in the middle. Her shirt collar poked out above her sweater, and she smiled a slight smile.

"And who is this?"

"Krystyna Krahelska," said Loosha. "Great-grandmother of Tadeusz. She's a big hero here. A poet. Come, see." The bird swooped up to a landing, and perched upon the banister, waiting for Sophie. The wall there, from ceiling to floor, was etched with Polish words.

"What does it say?" Sophie asked.

"You cannot read Polish?" Loosha demanded, aghast. "I thought you were magic girl!"

"Uh, I am!" Sophie floundered. "I am a magic girl. Probably I can read Polish?" She looked quizzically at the pigeon, as if he could know. The pigeon shrugged—a little haughtily, Sophie thought.

"I heard you turned into a shark and bit the great Kishka," said Loosha. "I wouldn't have imagined reading a humble Polish poem would be such a struggle."

"It's not," Sophie asserted, bluffing. She turned toward the wall and regarded the poem, her mind tripping and tumbling over the words, so many *z*s and *y*s, so many *p*s and *w*s! She didn't understand how such words could be sounded in her mouth; her tongue, curving around them, would tie itself in a thick knot. Never mind understand what the words even meant. Never mind that.

But the pigeon's challenge—and his bare disappointment—hung in the stairwell. Sophie could feel it, and it didn't feel good. She *was* magic. She had done incredible things. She had made herself a mermaid, for cripe's sake! Now she would know Polish.

It was like a muscle, a dormant muscle, was buried deep in Sophie's brain, hidden beneath layers of gray matter and weak from disuse. It was hard to flex—it took as much effort as it had taken her poor legs to stand upon the solid salt floor—but Sophie worked at it, and worked at it. She ignored Loosha's clucking and cooing; to even tell the bird to shut up would take too much precious energy away from her task, and so she tuned the pigeon out and focused all of her might on this one tucked-away muscle. So strange it felt, like hoisting a whale up from the deep, grabbing onto something alive and submerged. As

Sophie lifted it she felt a brightness in her brain. The words on the wall made *sense!*

"*Hey, boys, bayonet on the gun!*" Sophie read the words chinked into the tall salt wall. Her eyes scanned down, taking in the poem that had only just appeared as a jumble of jabberwocky but now made seamless, perfect sense before her eyes. "*A long way away, in front of us toil and drudgery!*" So true, Sophie thought. She herself had swum all the way from Chelsea, and for what? To arrive sickened at a dilapidated castle and learn from a nerd how to fight off her all-powerful grandmother. She returned to the verse.

"*After the victory, we are young, we're going to be afraid.*" Well, she thought, at least there was victory in the poet's future.

"This is poetry?" Sophie asked the bird, a little surprised. "She's just, like, saying what she's thinking. Right?"

"That's all poetry is," Loosha said simply. "The poet says what is on her mind, but says it a little bit better than most."

Sophie briefly wondered why pigeons seemed to know so much about poetry, then turned her attention back to the wall. It felt *good* to read Polish, to flex this muscle. The words, as they revealed themselves, felt smooth upon her brain. "*Because who knows, maybe tomorrow, or the day after today / come an order that now we need to go now.*"

"Not bad," Loosha nodded. "Not perfect, but not a terrible translation."

"Where was she going?" Sophie asked the bird. "What victory? What was she fighting?"

"The Nazis," Loosha said, and lifted off from the banister, flying higher. "Come," he cooed. "There is more."

Up along the stairwell, more dioramas were cut into the wall. Three women, huddled together on the bank of a river. The one in the center was immediately recognizable, what with her long fish tail and epic scramble of hair. "Syrena," Sophie breathed, running her fingers along the image, noting the detail of the scales notched into the salt. "This is more like it." Sophie turned to the pigeon. "This is what she *really* looks like, not that weird duck-bat back there."

"As Syrena allowed herself to be seen by the townspeople, so she became more beloved, and over the years many artists were inspired to paint her, or make a sculpture. She was put on the seal of the city after fighting off the invaders millennia ago. That woman to the right is an artist. Louise Nitschowa. Good friend of the mermaid, she made a statue of her that still sits on the riverbank. Very famous statue."

"Of Syrena?"

"Yes. Though Syrena didn't model for it. She couldn't be out of the water for so long, and the artist couldn't create her work in the river, so she had a human girl model for it. Krystyna, there on the left."

Sophie peered at the image. It wasn't like looking at a photograph, but the etchings were surprisingly vivid. "Krystyna, the poet? That's her?"

"Yes. Louise sat by the banks and did many sketches of Syrena, of her tail and form, but then the long work in the studio was with Krystyna. Come." Loosha fluttered up the stairs and Sophie followed, no longer even feeling her body, its weakness or its strength. She came to rest before the next tableau, a strong image of a mermaid, not Syrena but not *not* Syrena; not the poet but not *not* the poet. The poet's humanity had tamed the mermaid somewhat; her hair was shorn and neat and her tail, while powerful, was smaller. And the poet, who looked almost matronly on land, was transformed into a bare-breasted warrior as she merged with the mermaid. One arm held high a sword, as if to bring it down onto her enemy's head; the other held a shield to her side.

"This is here, in Warsaw?" Sophie asked. "I can see it?"

"Oh, sure," Loosha nodded. "Right at the Vistula. One of the only monuments in all of *Warszawa* without pigeon droppings." Loosha looked down at the stairs with what might have been embarrassment. "Out of respect. Deep respect. Come." The bird lifted himself into the air and led Sophie up to the next relief. It was simple; if she hadn't been in the midst of this art tour with her pigeon docent, she might have overlooked it: the letter *p*, with a bottom that split into twin curls, like a double-tailed mermaid.

"*Kotwica*," Loosha said, with a solemn pride that Sophie noted was rather common to pigeons. "Means 'anchor' in Polish." Sophie nodded, for the mark did look like an anchor. "But it is also a *p* atop a *w*, and has stood for many things through time, all of them good, all of them related. *Powstanie Warszawskie.* Warsaw Uprising. This was Krystyna's fight. When the Germans take Poland and come to Warsaw, a secret army fought them. Men and women and young people, even children. And pigeons, of course." Loosha shook his feathers proudly. "We fought with the *Armia Krajowa*, the secret army, to free Poland. When the uprising occurred in 1944, it was the biggest act of resistance against the Nazis in all of Europe!" Sophie trailed the bird up the stairs, the *Kotwica* seared into her mind like a tattoo.

"Here is the girl who create the *Kotwica*." Loosha brushed a wing softly against a carving of a round-cheeked girl, her face resisting a small smile, her hair pushed to the side like a boy's. A patterned tie—houndstooth or stripes, Sophie's fingers felt along the ridges—was knotted around her neck, and a tiny official badge was pinned to her collared shirt.

"Anna Smolenska," Loosha spoke the girl's name. "A member of *Szare Szeregi*, the Gray Ranks. She ran with the youth group *Wawer*, making sabotage and propaganda. And she helped the families of people who'd been arrested by the Nazis. There was a contest to design an emblem for the resistance, and she won it. She made the *Kotwica*. At first, the *p* and *w* meant *Pomścimy Wawer*—'We shall avenge Wawer.' The Wawer massacre, the first big killing of the Polish by the Germans. But then, later, *Kotwica* meant everything. It meant the resistance itself. It still does." Loosha took a breath and looked sadly at the portrait. "Anna was an art student. Twenty-three years old. The Gestapo took her. She was involved in an underground newsletter. The Germans wanted the editor, the publisher, but they found Anna instead. They took her and her family to Auschwitz." Loosha looked at Sophie with a tender eye. "I suppose you know what that is."

"I do," Sophie nodded, touched by the picture and the story, this young art student with the boyish style, whose emblem helped carry her fight even after she was murdered.

"Much sadness in this stairwell," Loosha sighed. "Come. There is more."

The next relief showed Krystyna Krahelska again, a younger image, perhaps Sophie's own age. A long braid hung down over each shoulder. *Danuta*, the word arched above her head, and beneath, *1914—1944*. And then that mark again, the anchor, the *Kotwica*.

"Those who loved her called her Danuta," Loosha explained. "She died on the very first day of the uprising. In a park, a lovely place. They were going to take back a newspaper that had been captured by the Germans, they were moving toward the press. Danuta—Krystyna—was a nurse, and a fighter. And she was tall. Taller than the sunflowers in the park. Brighter, too. An easy target for the Germans. They shot her in the neck and in the lung, and she lay among the sunflowers, she lay there until the sun went down because she didn't want anyone to risk their lives helping her. Once it was dark the resistance came for her, but it was too late."

Sunflowers. Sophie remembered an image, powerful and haunting, from when she dug inside Syrena's heart and tried to take her pain away. Bright yellow sunflowers, like happiness itself, streaked with dark blood. She turned to the pigeon. "Syrena—Syrena loved Krystyna."

"Oh yes," Loosha bobbed his head. "After Louisa selected her to model for the statue they grew very close. Krystyna visited Syrena often. And Syrena fought in the uprising too, of course."

"She did?"

"Oh, yes," Loosha nodded. "Syrena has fought in every battle that has come to Warsaw. She is our hero."

"So, did you win, then?" she asked hopefully, and the bird gazed at her with raw disappointment.

"Do they teach you nothing in your school, back in the United States?"

"Nothing," Sophie nodded. "Nothing worth very much."

"They fought for one month," Loosha said. "They believed the Soviets would come and help them, and together they would drive the Nazis from the town. But the Soviets stayed on the other side of the river. They never crossed the water to help, and so the Nazis took Warsaw. They destroyed it. Almost all of it. They left just the tiniest piece intact."

"The Soviets," Sophie said, feeling frustrated, as if she could figure out the puzzle and somehow change the long-ago outcome. "Why didn't they help?"

Loosha shrugged his feathers. "Perhaps they didn't want the Germans to win, but they didn't want us to win, either. *They* wanted to win. And in the end, they took our city. After the Germans left, the Soviets stayed for a long time."

Sophie's head was buzzing. "I never really paid much attention to history," she said apologetically. "Maybe we *did* learn this stuff in school, and I was just scribbling notes to Ella the whole time."

"History is different when it is right in front of you." Loosha motioned to the portrait of Krystyna Krahelska. "Different, also, when you are a part of it. Come."

Sophie could not believe it, but she had made it to the top of the staircase. The sun that had looked so far away was now shining on her face, and she felt herself turn her head toward the warm, familiar rays, like a sunflower.

"You see." Loosha snapped her from her reverie with a soft brush of feather against her cheek. "You are part of this story."

Chapter 11

O n the wall, at the top of the stairs, an image of Sophie had been carved into the stone. Her hair was a bit wild; the artist had carved the twisting strands deep and far into the salt wall. Dangling beneath her ear was a feather—Livia's feather. Sophie's hand rose to touch the real one where it lay snug in a tangle. She was shocked to see her likeness, so unexpected, so accurate with the inclusion of the feather. But she was truly struck by her face. It both was and was not her; familiar, but older, her expression fierce, yet calm. She reached out and traced the faintest mark of a scar upon the cheek, then felt her own face. Yes, it was there, a thin trace of the wound Kishka the sea monster had given her. She spun around to the bird.

"Loosha," she began, "Do I look like that? Does that look like me?"

"Hmmmm," the bird considered thoughtfully. "Stop making such a crazed face."

Sophie, unaware that her expression was crazed, tried to make her face look more neutral. She looked blankly at the bird.

"Uncanny," he nodded. "It is you, all right."

Sophia Swankowski. Her name was etched into the space above her head. And below, a string of words in Polish. Sophie pushed on the part of her mind that knew all language, and read aloud.

"*Heart pounding in the chest like a bird awakened,*" she began, noticing that her own heart was in fact beating its wings against her ribs. "*The sun rises over red silver rainbow / Hey, buddy, open your eyes and see! / It's not a dream you dreamed, or some sign.*" She looked toward the bird, who nodded.

"Pretty good," he said. Sophie continued.

"*Open your eyes! Listen: it grows singing / It's not the birds. The land is singing, the earth trembles / Silver dew falling apart as the purest tears / In red. A red gushing upwards as blood.*" Sophie shuddered at the imagery, the earth itself gone gory and red. "Gross," she said.

"Not gross," spoke a voice, a human voice, not a bird. Sophie spun around to find Tadeusz standing in the mouth of the stairwell. The sun lit up his glasses so that Sophie could not see his face; the glare bounced off the lenses and struck her own eyes, which she shielded with her hand. "It's a poem," Tadeusz explained.

"Well it's sort of a gross, bloody poem. I thought poems were supposed to be about like, nature."

"Well, there is a lot of nature in this poem," Loosha pointed out delicately.

"Nature isn't always gentle," Tadeusz said. "There are earthquakes and lightning and terrible storms, there are animals that destroy other animals."

"Well, I'm from Chelsea," Sophie said with a sulky defensiveness. "We don't have much nature there. And the nature we do have, it's true, it isn't pretty, but that's mostly because people have made it that way." Sophie thought of the creek, with its bed of rusted shopping carts, broken bottles, and stubbed-out cigarettes.

"This poem was by my great-grandmother, Krystyna Krahelska," Tadeusz said with quiet pride. "She fought for the resistance. She fought the Nazis. She knew what it was to see the earth turned bloody." He touched the wall softly. "It was in my mind as I made your portrait. So I put it there."

"You did this?" Sophie asked. "All of this?" She waved her hand down the dark staircase. As once she couldn't see the top, now she could not see the bottom, so far below her.

"Not all of them. Some of them are quite ancient. All of them are old. I did this one, the one of you."

"How did you know what I look like?" Sophie asked suspiciously. "It's not even from a photo or anything. You showed my feather. And my scar."

"I can see things," Tadeusz told her. "If it is important enough, and if I try very hard. And so I tried, and an image of you came to me."

"Are you Odmieńce?" Sophie asked. "Syrena told me you were just human, not magic."

"I am just human," Tadeusz nodded. The sunlight on his glasses flashed like a strobe as he moved his head, blinding Sophie with the glare.

"Could you take those things off for a minute?" she asked.

"Oh, sure." Tadeusz fumbled with his frames, then stood before Sophie bald-eyed and blinking.

"Can you see?" Sophie asked. "Are you blind without those things?"

"Almost," the boy admitted.

"Well, you look way less nerdy without them," she offered. "No offense."

"What is 'nerdy'?" Tadeusz asked.

"I don't know, like... super smart, into computers and math, shy, not very strong..."

"These are bad things to be?" Tadeusz asked this with such genuine curiosity it panged Sophie in the heart a bit. What a jerk she was.

"Just where I come from," she said quickly. "Probably not in the rest of the world. Probably not here in Warsaw."

"You are kind of a nerd too, ya?" he asked. "You are very smart also?"

"She better be," Loosha butted in when Sophie took too long to answer. "She's here to save the world for humans, pigeons, and everything else. She better be smart."

"I am!" Sophie nearly shouted. "I am smart."

But—was she? She didn't know anything about the Warsaw uprising, or about any historical event of any importance. She didn't understand poetry. But she could read it, at least. She could read it in Polish, which meant she could read it in any language.

"I speak every language," she proclaimed boldly. If pigeons had eyebrows, Loosha would have raised his.

"Every language?" Tadeusz asked.

"Yes," Sophie nodded. "I mean, I think I can. I just figured out Polish on my way up the stairs, and I think it's probably the same for the rest of them."

"Okay," Tadeusz nodded. "Well, that's what I mean. You're so magic, it's like being the smartest person in the world, because you can just figure out how to magic whatever it is you need to figure out. Isn't that how it works?"

Sophie thought about it. "I think so," she said a tad sheepishly. "But isn't that cheating?"

"Who cares?" Loosha interrupted. "You think Kishka fights fair? You think the Nazis fought fair against the people of Warsaw? You take your strengths, all of them, whatever they may be, and you use them, and you make them stronger."

Tadeusz looked expectantly at Sophie, his eyes squinting and widening, squinting and widening, as he tried to bring her into focus. "He's right," the boy said.

"The pigeons are always right," Sophie nodded.

Suddenly, the narrow stairwell felt very cramped, almost claustrophobic. A sweat broke out on her upper lip and the back of her neck felt sticky and clammy. She fell a bit against the wall, beside her portrait.

"Are you okay?" asked Tadeusz, shoving his glasses back onto his face with alarm. "You weren't supposed to come all the way up here alone. I was just on my way down to check on you—here, let me—" The boy reached out to help ease Sophie out of the stairwell, but it was too late. She slid down the wall as if her legs had turned to water, her arms twisting around her in a violent spasm, her head shaking furiously, as if saying a tremendous *no* to some unseen force.

"Uh-oh," Loosha cooed.

"Kishka?" Tadeusz asked the bird. "Already?"

IT HAD BEEN too long since Sophie had felt the interior tickling of someone working their way into her. There at the top of the stairs, still a bit weakened and reeling from all the pigeon had shared with her, she hadn't felt her grandmother slip inside her until it was too late.

"No!" she roared, and thrashed herself against the wall. And her grandmother answered with a voice so clear and close it was as if she were standing right in front of her.

"Why, yes!" Kishka exclaimed, her cheerful voice hitting Sophie in the guts like a sucker punch. "Yes indeed, my little chickadee! So you made it through the waters! You've come back to your homeland! I just wanted to welcome you, sweetie. This is my homeland, too, of course. In many ways, I never left it. I might have been stuck in the dump in Chelsea, raising some raggedy family, but I was here, too. I was always here!" The voice paused, and Sophie felt a sickening smoke blow through her. Kishka's cigarette. She sputtered and coughed.

"I was the bullet that passed through your poet's neck," Kishka crowed, full of pride. "I was the sun that took its time to come down while she lay dying in the flowers. I was each officer who dragged the little art student to the chambers. And I was the chambers, of course I was. And you are, too. Because you are of me."

"No!" Sophie raged again, twisting and twisting, as if she could fling Kishka from within her through the force of her spasms. "I am none of that!"

"This is much too big for you, dearie," Kishka began her familiar coaxing. "But if you join me, I will lend to you my largeness, and together we will be *huge*. Are you ready for that? Or should I just sit here inside you until you go mad? It certainly worked on your sister."

Sophie flinched at the word, *sister*. "Leave her alone," Sophie said, a blind loyalty springing up inside her. "Why would you bother her? She's never done anything."

"I had to make sure she was *mine*, and that she would always be mine. Not like you and your mother. Belinda is my little pet, my little dearie. I camped out inside her heart until it was as ruined as mine, ruined and wild. Of course, she's just a little girl, and mostly human, so she doesn't understand how to work with it. She's a bit like an animal. But *you*, you're the magic one. You could handle my power. I could infect your heart with it and you would be my heir, my *miłość*."

Though she could feel Kishka inside her, Sophie tried pulling up her wall. With a deep internal tug she felt it rise from some dark place, heavier than iron, yet pliable. The quake of it rising inside her toppled Sophie flat to the floor and set her trembling, but she held tight to the psychic reigns and felt the barrier seal around her heart, evicting all that did not belong. It made Sophie feel strong, to have this shield within her. Though Kishka was still there, Sophie knew now that her grandmother had not been inside her heart. Her mind perhaps, some other part of her, but not her heart.

With the fury of a bull in full stampede, Kishka took her wrath and slammed it up against Sophie's guarded heart. The ringing of the impact took away Sophie's breath, deafened her. She gasped hoarsely, each breath a dry choke. In the stairwell both the boy and the bird looked on with horror, powerless in the face of their friend's mysterious struggle.

"See you soon, dearie," Kishka spat. "Eat a pierogi for me, why don't you?"

It was the last thing Sophie heard before her consciousness evaporated, and she was gone.

Chapter 12

In her depleted state, half awake and half asleep, with no real understanding of where she lay, Sophie heard a knock-knock-knocking at her heart's heavy shield. Her first feeling was a cascade of relief; even in her unconscious state something in her knew to keep her wall high, her heart fortified. She felt grateful that this effort had become as involuntary as the filling of her lungs with air, her heart's steady thumps. The relief passed, and the sensation returned, a knock-knock-knocking at her heart. *Who is it?* Sophie said silently, feeling a bit silly. But soon enough, an answer.

My name is Isabelle Naoko, said a timid but friendly voice. *May I come in?*

Do I know you? Sophie said, utterly confused. Was Kishka tricking her into dropping her shield? She remembered her grandmother's last strike, brutal enough to hurl her into this state between waking and sleep.

A mermaid came for me, spoke the voice. *In Hawaii. She brought me to Japan, where my family is from. My grandmother is, like, completely evil. Michi is her human name. I think you call her Kishka.*

Sophie could feel, if she tried, the spirit of this girl. It was a beaming turquoise sensation of goodness. Love tufted around her, light and billowy as clouds. And though she was just a girl like her, there was something ancient about her. Ancient and joyful. Sophie lifted her shield and felt her heart become swarmed by this spirit, times ten. She burst out into laughter. It was all she could do.

I cannot stay long, Isabelle said. *Like you, I am training, too. And Michi came to me and hurt me, so like you, I am healing. But I brought you something. A piece of my magic. It will help you get strong faster, and it will stay with you throughout our big fight.*

A sensation of sweetness and bitterness ran the length of Sophie's body, inside and out. Cool, bracing, she *did* feel stronger. Rejuvenated. *Purified,* Isabelle offered, reading her thoughts. *Like salt, but different. It is guava leaves, soaked in magic water. Big, healing love magic.*

How do you know it?

It was practiced in my neighborhood, in Hawaii. And, here, to top it off!

Something sweet and fluffy engulfed Sophie. The taste of love itself, fruity and bright, pink and crimson and incredibly delicate. *Cake!* shrieked Sophie, and Isabelle giggled.

Isn't it the best? My favorite guava cake. Magic-style. It fills you with love.

Sophie felt awesome. Not quite awesome enough to snap out of her dream state, but she was no longer in the gray fog Kishka had knocked her into. *Thank you,* she said to the girl. *It is so great to meet you, and it is so nice of you to help me like this!*

Duh! Isabelle laughed. *We have to help each other, all of us. In fact, if you don't mind, I could use some of your Chelsea magic.*

At this, Sophie snorted. Chelsea magic? *Uh, Chelsea doesn't have any magic,* she broke it to her new friend. *That's sort of the point of Chelsea.*

Oh. Isabelle made an urgent sound. *But that isn't at all true! All the places have magic, and the place you're born, it is extra powerful. For you to share some with me would help me very much when I'm fighting Michi.*

A sad emptiness caught Sophie unawares. *I really want to help you. I can give you anything. I can teach you how to burst into someone's heart-space, so you don't have to knock.*

I know how to do that, Isabelle said, annoyed. *I was just being polite. Listen, you have Chelsea magic. I'm certain you do. Just bring me some before the big fight. Okay?*

As Sophie lay, reeling from her unexpected visit, she felt movement again near her heart.

Hello? A voice cried out inside her. *Hey? Uh—Sophie?*

Yes? Sophie responded. It was not Isabella this time, not her singsong lilt. This voice was heavier, weightier, more serious.

This is Pipaluk, the girl said. *I figured—I mean, I know we all know about each other, and things are about to get real, I thought we should meet. Plus, I know you got knocked down. My grandmother, Naja, just got me pretty good, too.*

Sophie lifted her heart shield and in came Pipaluk. Her energy was low but strong, a deep, glowing purple. An orange music came with her, the sound of a guitar, perhaps, but shot through with something otherworldly and silver. And around it all something twinkling and strong, something cold, as if her energy were trudging through a gorgeous blizzard.

Thanks, Pipaluk said as she entered. Then: *It's cozy in here. Nice. Like sitting in front of a fire.*

It is? Sophie asked. She knew the sensation of entering another's sphere, but had she ever stopped and wondered what her own felt like to another. A cozy fire sounded very nice.

Have you met any of us?

Isabelle was just here. She brought me guava water. And cake.

Well, I don't have cake for you, but I have some magic. Do you want it?

Yes, Sophie said. *We all need everything. Don't we?*

For sure.

The magic Sophie felt enchanting her was organic; it was hard like wood but it was not wood; like her shield, somewhat, but not nearly as leaden. And within it was something softer, something tender, something that possessed a steadiness that instantly comforted Sophie. She felt a slowness within her, something abiding and eternal. Maybe Kishka was ancient and forever, more element than person, but in her own way Sophie was too. She touched that place inside her that had been waiting, patiently, for this showdown for hundreds of thousands of forevers.

Whoa, Sophie marveled. *What is that?*

Turtle magic, Pipaluk said simply. *We always had turtles at my house, growing up. As pets. My mom is super allergic so we could never get dogs or cats. But we had a lot of turtles.*

You have brothers and sisters? Sophie asked.

A bunch, answered Pipaluk. *Five. But I'm the only magic one. Lucky me, right?*

Seriously, Sophie commiserated. How great it felt to bond over the strange hardship of being charged with destroying one's grandmother and saving humanity! She longed to spend more time, in real life, with Pipaluk and Isabelle. *When this is all done we should all, like, hang out or something.*

Definitely, Pipaluk agreed. *I wish I could stay longer but I'm not working with salt, I'm working with Cryolite, so I have to get back.*

What's Cryolite?

A toxic crystal. A bit trickier than salt but it's cool because it's a weapon more than a purifier. And I like to fight.

Sophie smiled at the girl's rowdy honesty. She hoped some of her eagerness for battle had come into her with the turtle magic. *I don't have any Chelsea magic for you,* she told Pipaluk. *Yet. But I will find some. Somehow.*

Well, better heal up and get it done, Pipaluk advised. *Grandmother could strike at any moment.*

With Pipaluk gone, Sophie knew it wouldn't be long until the final girl came bearing magic, the one with the sparkly eyes and puffy hair. Sophie felt her approach, and opened her heart to her.

Hello, she said.

Hello, said Sophie.

I know I'm last, said the girl, *But my magic is strongest. I'm Lesia.*

Sophie, said Sophie.

We all have our strengths, you know? Lesia said, a philosophical tone to her voice.

But Sophie didn't know.

I'm only now just meeting everyone, she explained. *And my grandmother came at me not long ago.*

Tell me about it, said Lesia. *Gennadiya is my grandmother, the evil one. I got a lot of grannies, human grannies but they are powerful, too. Witches. That's why I got such strong human magic. My specialty is repulsion. It's harder for Gennadiya to come at me. She still does it, but truthfully, I make her a little sick.* Lesia beamed with pride.

That's amazing, Sophie said.

Well, you got that crazy heart shield. None of us can keep her out like you can.

Really? Sophie asked. She felt ashamed of her pride. She wanted all the girls to have strong shields. They all depended on one another.

Yeah. And Isabelle, she's able to bounce back from her grandmother extra quick. Pipaluk's strength is harder to see, but it's there. She endures. She might be the strongest of us all, all things considered.

You know so much about us, Sophie said.

My family has known about it all for so long. Most places, the stories get broken up, turned into jumbled fairy tales. But my family held the story, untouched, for generations. I knew all about us before I knew I was one of us!

Sophie felt Lesia's energy as she listened to her words. It was long and limber and slid around, quick and flexible. Her color shifted between greens and oranges, warming and cooling. Her power was as massive as the most formidable sand dune, with such movement, the movement of millions upon millions of tiny pieces, sneaking and sliding in concert.

I brought you magic, she said. *Something from home, on the island. Now that my mermaid brought me to Africa it's all about the salt, but this is from the Caribbean, okay?*

Sophia felt the overpowering essence of sandalwood and gave herself over to the glorious smell. More essences followed, herbs that she couldn't distinguish, something like a gem gone liquid—wine! Oil. The sweet, warm advance of honey. She felt a light move across her, as if searing it all into her heart, and then nothing. But stronger. Sophie definitely felt stronger.

I know you haven't figured out your own home magic yet, Lesia said lightly. *But you will. We're all really smart, or else we wouldn't be in this situation.*

That's true. Sophie felt emboldened by Lesia, by all the girls' belief in her. And by their magics, of course. She had to repay them. She knew she would come up with something special, a gift from her soul and her city. Her dirty, tough, complicated city.

Gotta get back to my mermaid, Lesia said. *She gets mad* real *quick.*

Mine does, too! Sophie cried.

She could feel the roll of Lesia's twinkling eyes. *Mermaids,* she said, and she didn't need to say anything more. Sophie understood.

Chapter 13

The bed that Sophie lay upon was lovely. This was her third thought upon waking, the first one being a deep, primordial *Salt*, followed by a similarly profound *Ouch*. Sophie's chest felt like a giant fist had punched through it, crumbling her ribs like a stack of twigs. Her mouth sang out for the salt she knew would make it better. The tang of it on her tongue suggested someone had been tending to her. She let loose with a weak howl to summon her nurse, then sunk heavily into her pillows. A threadbare canopy swagged above her resting place, a heavy pink taffeta, soiled and torn but not without its charm. The same could be said of the chipped marble staircase that rose up from the room, deteriorating but still in possession of its former glory. With a soft pitter-pat upon the stone the boy Tadeusz appeared, tripping in his haste, reaching out to steady himself on a banister that tumbled from the wall as he touched it.

"Careful," Sophie choke-laughed as the boy scuttled to her side.

"Here," he said, and pulled a sizeable hunk of salt from his shirt pocket. Sophie ate it greedily, a blissful smile stretching across her chomping mouth.

"Where's my around-the-clock care?" Sophie demanded, teasing Tadeusz. He seemed like the sort of person who tended to not get a joke, but Sophie couldn't resist. Tadeusz's eyes furrowed, and his face took on a downcast expression of guilt and contrition.

"We were all with you until your breathing stabilized," Tadeusz insisted. "And many of the pigeons were with you around the clock, I promise."

"I'm just messing with you," Sophie said, wondering if she should explain the concept of 'messing with' to the boy. By his timid smile he seemed to understand. "The others came to me while I was out. They brought me magic. I think they helped me."

"You have seemed much better than I feared you'd be," Tadeusz nodded. "I've checked on you, but mostly I've been in my study. With the computer."

"My computer?" Sophie was surprised at her feelings of protectiveness, but she *had* lugged its weight in that cumbersome backpack through the ocean waters. Not to mention stolen it from a sinking submarine in the first place, a submarine she wasn't able to save. The memory of the workers inside the vessel gave her a chill. It all felt so very far away.

"Yeah, your computer. From the submarine. I'm sorry, I just—"

"Forget it, it's not mine," Sophie flopped her hand at the boy. "It's ours. I donate it to the cause. Right? Is it going to help us somehow? Is that what you were studying?"

"Ah, yeah," Tadeusz nodded. "There is much on there. Some I knew, and then some I didn't know. I know enough to begin to know more. Does that make sense?"

"Tadeusz," Sophie said weakly, "I know I'm magic-smart, or whatever, but you're smart-smart. *Really* smart-smart. So, no, you don't make sense."

"Oh," said Tadeusz.

Sophie let the last of the salt dissolve and slide down the back of her throat. *Yum.* "You got any more?" she asked.

"Got a whole mine of it downstairs," Tadeusz smiled, and Sophie smacked him happily in the arm.

"Tadeusz!" she hooted. "You made a joke!"

"Not really," said the boy, confused and rubbing his arm. "There really *is* a mine downstairs. It's not a joke."

"Forget it," Sophie grumbled. "Can I have another?"

The boy dug a handful of various rocks and crumbles from his shirt pocket and placed them in Sophie's giddy hands. She tossed the bunch of it into her mouth and slurped happily. The salt was like the best, purest energy radiating through her body, making whole what was broken, smoothing what was shabby. She pulled herself up in her bed, and caught a movement in the wall across from her. She froze, and the movement froze, too. The silvery, webbed wall was a tarnished mirror, and in the middle of the rusty splotches sat Sophie, staring at herself.

"No way," she whispered, and the girl in the mirror whispered the same.

"What is it?" Tadeusz asked nervously. Sophie ignored him, stumbling out of the bed, kicking off the blankets where they tangled around her ankles. The cloud of dust made her cough, and she quickly swallowed her mouthful of salt, too distracted now to savor its goodness. She walked over to the mirror, and beheld herself.

It was *her* alright, of course it was her, but how she had changed! Her hair would never be as wild as the mermaid's, but it was in her style, a magnificent tangle holding treasures and secrets—Livia's feather, of course, but bits of shell and fishbone, too, and pieces of seaweed that had dried to leather. The dense knots at the nape of her neck were still damp from all her time underwater, and when Sophie squeezed it she could smell a bit of the sea, and the river. Her hair—she couldn't tell if she loved its power or hated its mess. But it was her face that really took her breath away.

Sophie had gotten older. The question of time that had haunted her, it returned with new urgency, both answered and unanswerable. Yes, Sophie had been gone a long time. Her face had lengthened, and her scant diet of crab legs and bladder wrack had sharpened her cheekbones. Her eyes blazed with a new intensity. She looked down at herself, still clad in the ragged outfit the Ogresses had presented her with so long ago. It wasn't just the force of the sea that had corroded the linen and spoiled the leather; her own growing body was pushing at the seams, creating rips and tears and worn-away patches.

"Jeez, Tad," Sophie said, turning to the boy. "I need some *clothes*. This thing is a mess!"

"Sure, sure," he nodded. "We can do that. I can get you something. Maybe we can go shopping? Do you have money?" He smacked his head. "Oh right, you don't need money. Or you can just magic some." He paused. "Or, you can probably just magic yourself some new clothes. So I guess you don't have to go shopping. Never mind."

What *really* tripped Sophie out was how her baby pudge had melted away in the sea, how she'd grown taller and leaner, how she'd grown *breasts*. They weren't ginormous or anything, thank god, but they were there, right where they once weren't. Sophie wanted to share this weird marvel with someone and suddenly missed Ella with the sharpness of salt.

A lonely homesickness flooded her heart, tempered by the note Bix had flown to her: *I'm sorry*. Ella was sorry, she and Ella were friends again! Even though they were a million miles apart Sophie felt a surge of joy that they would come together again, maybe even soon; how Ella would marvel and joke and appreciate this strange, new version of Sophie, much as Sophie's mind would be blown at the sight of her own friend, a *mom*. Sophie realized her own transformation paled in comparison to her friend's, and pulled herself away from the mirror.

"I haven't seen myself for a while," Sophie explained. "I got older. I don't even know how much. I don't know how old I am. Isn't that strange? How old are you?"

"Thirteen," Tadeusz said.

"I used to be thirteen," Sophie nodded. "Last time I checked. I'm going to go make myself something to wear. Is there, like, a room—"

Tadeusz hopped to his feet. "This is your room," he said. "I'll be upstairs in my study, just come find me when you're done making magic clothes."

"Okay." Sophie watched the boy shuffle up the stairs, occasionally reaching for the handrail, only to have one of its rotting posts tumble to the floor below.

"Watch out for that," he said, turning back to Sophie.

"Got it."

When the boy was shut back into his study, Sophie peeled the ruined jumper from her body. It had been so nice once! She supposed she could magic herself a replica of it, but as correct as it felt to wear the garment while frolicking with dolphins in the sea, it just didn't seem right for Poland. What *was* right for Poland? What did girls wear around here?

Sophie realized all she'd seen were elderly witches, a mermaid, pigeons, and a nerd. She really had nothing to go on. She figured she'd just whip up what she normally wore back in Chelsea, and, flipping some secret switches in her mind, conjured a pair of cut-offs, a T-shirt, a hoodie, and a pair of slip-on skate shoes. She pulled on the outfit and checked herself out in the ruined mirror. She looked like a girl, like anyone, except for her hair. *A real rat's nest*, Sophie's mom Andrea would call her tangles, working them out with a comb and a bottle of conditioner. But this—this was something altogether different. A rat's nest? More like a rat's castle. Sophie couldn't imagine the effort it would take to fix it, how many bottles of conditioner spent, how many hours beneath her mother's stubbornly digging comb, how many tears cried at the pulling and the yanking.

You're magic, Sophie reminded herself, and the look of despair on her face brightened. *Fix yourself.* Sophie closed her eyes for maximum concentration, imagining the hair she *wished* she had on her head. Her mind scanned through hairstyles—the short, boyish cut of Anna Smolenska; the long, heavy braids of young Krystyna Krahelska. Ella's impossibly smooth and shiny locks, so sleek they never fell into disgusting tangles. Her mom's frizzy curls, like Sophie's but worse. It was probably why her mom kept her own hair short, a halo of twirls around her head.

Sophie settled on the braid, but instead of pigtail-style, like a little girl, she had hers woven into one long one that hung down the side of her head. When she opened her eyes, there it was. No flotsam and jetsam, no periwinkle shells and bladder wrack. Just a thick hunk of hair, neatly twisted down her shoulder. She hardly recognized herself. Too weird. She pulled the hood of her sweatshirt up over her head and stomped up the grimy marble staircase, in search of Tadeusz.

Chapter 14

The long, dim hallway was hung with the antlers of animals whose time on this earth had been very long ago indeed. Sophie stopped and marveled at them, reaching up to touch them. They felt like wood, or plastic; how wild that animals grew such things straight out of their heads! *When you think about it, everything is kind of magic*, Sophie thought, passing beneath them as if through a forest of bare-branched trees.

The hallway was lit by a hole in the ceiling where sunlight spilled in. At least it was sunlight spilling in now, Sophie observed; the stiff and moldy carpet beneath bore the impact of cloudier days in Warsaw. A pile of chalky plaster was matted into the carpet as well, and the hall was strewn with splintered furniture, furniture that once must have been very grand. A long, long time ago, when those antlered animals had roamed the woods.

Sophie could detect a soft but frantic clicking sound and deduced it was Tadeusz, hunkered above the computer. She shuffled around the debris-strewn hallway, the ticks and tacks getting louder. A splintery wooden door hung loose from its jamb, and a peek through the crack revealed the boy, sunken into a tufted pink chair, bits of feathers and other stuffing fluffing out from holes when he wiggled in his seat. The computer sat on a heavy wooden table, illuminating Tadeusz's face so that he looked whiter than ever, so white he glowed, a subterranean creature who lived in the salt mines below.

"Tad!" Sophie rapped her knuckles on the wood door. "Can I come in?"

"It's Tad-*deusz*," he corrected her. "And yes, please."

Sophie pushed the rickety door open, letting some of the light from the hall fall into the dim study along with her. While Sophie took in the room, Tadeusz took in Sophie. She looked a tad less magical without her strange attire, thought the boy, in spite of knowing it was magic that had brought the girl her unremarkable outfit.

Tadeusz's study was heaped with piles of plaster from the crumbling walls; a purplish color, the walls, though hard to say, mottled as they were with time and mold, spilling white crumbles from punches and tears. Another pair of antlers hung on the wall above the table. Sophie tilted her head and regarded them.

"When I first met Syrena," Sophie said, "She tried to explain to me that mermaids aren't magic, they're just creatures, and it's only because we don't know about them that we think they're magic. I didn't get it, but I think I get it now. Like, if you didn't know any better, wouldn't you think the animals that grow these out of their heads were magic? Wouldn't that seem like a magical thing to do?"

Tadeusz looked up at the horns, and nodded. "Absolutely. I think all magic is natural. Natural forces and abilities that are rare, or have become lost, or maybe were always hidden from us." He turned back to the shockingly ordinary-looking girl before him, her hair tamed, no longer hung with bits of the sea. "I think that is what I am finding here, in this computer. Here." The boy leapt up to offer Sophie his tufted chair, loosening a cloud of dust into the room. Sophie waved it away from her face and demurred.

"I'll stand," she said. "It's good for me. Build my strength."

Tadeusz angled the computer so that Sophie could see the screen, then opened document after document on the machine. At the sight of so many graphs and charts, spreadsheets and maps, Sophie felt her mind peacefully buzz away, as it often had in school when something bored her. She gave her head a shake and forced herself to pay attention.

"You're going to explain all this stuff to me, right?" Sophie demanded.

"Uh—yeah," Tadeusz nodded. "I mean, unless you can just look at it and figure it out magic-style, like you did to learn Polish?"

The thought exhausted Sophie. "I've sort of been through a lot the past couple days, okay?" she snapped. "Syrena brought me all the way out here so you could teach me something. So—teach me something." She plopped herself down on the desk beside the computer.

"Okay," Tadeusz said, and rubbed his face, knocking his glasses around. His eyes without the spectacles weren't giant-sized at all. In fact, they were very normal-sized, with a little tilt. Sophie wished he'd take them off; sometimes she felt like she was talking to his glasses and not his face.

"I don't know where to begin," he said.

"Begin at the beginning."

"Okay, well, in the beginning was the big bang."

"Are you kidding me?"

"No, no," Tadeusz shook his head. "It is how the universe began. All matter and—"

"Yeah, I know the big bang, Tadeusz. Even *I* know the big bang. Is that really where this begins?"

"Well, okay, so the universe. We still don't know a lot about it, right? Nearly 30 percent of it is 'dark matter,' and about 70 percent of it is made up of this 'dark energy.' No one knows what it is, but they know that it's out there, and that it's getting bigger, and bigger, and bigger— it's nearly everything that's actually in our universe, and the stuff we know, the planets, and the stars, and gravity, and all of that, is only a tiny part. And eventually, scientists think it's possible that this dark energy is going to destroy the universe."

"Destroy it how?"

"They're not totally sure. Maybe just like tear it to shreds? Or, maybe it gets *so* big that the whole universe snaps back on itself, like an elastic? It would be like the big bang all over again—but in reverse. Some scientists thinks that's what happens, actually—that the universe just expands and contracts over and over and over, forever."

Sophie felt a strange dizziness at the thought of the universe stretching and imploding, like some strange machine, or like a living thing, breathing. Just the fact of the universe—so unfathomably large, so final—made her feel off-kilter.

"These scientists, the ones who had this computer, they were exploring dark energy," Tadeusz said. "But rather than looking in outer space, they were looking for it here on earth. At the bottom of the ocean. They were headed to some sort of site that they thought would have information about dark energy."

"The Invisible," Sophie said. "I've been there. I've seen it."

"Please," Tadeusz said, shoving his glasses anxiously up his nose. "Tell me."

Sophie hesitated. She wasn't sure how to talk to this person, a human boy, about all she had experienced. *So, there are these twin Ogresses and they live at the bottom of this massive whirlpool, milling salt...* But Tadeusz wasn't a normal human boy. A mermaid was practically his aunt. He was already spending time with flocks of talking pigeons. A couple of undersea Ogresses wouldn't faze him much.

"It's far beneath the water, somewhere near Scotland, I think? Near some islands off the coast. To get to it—well, how I got to it—you have to swim down this massive whirlpool, the swilkie. It's really crazy! I couldn't get out of it, Syrena had to save me. And on the way out I had to turn myself into a mermaid to really hop out of it."

"Wow," Tadeusz raised his eyebrows, causing his glasses to sled down his nose.

"Anyway, the swilkie leads to where the Ogresses live in these giant underwater caves—like, *so giant*, because they're giants, right? *Literally* giants. And out back, in the ocean behind their home, is this... *thing*. Syrena brought me to it, but we couldn't get too close because it has this weird effect on you. *Bad* weird. Even though we stayed away it still made me feel so sad. Like, I can't tell you how sad. It was awful. It was like everything you knew to be good was wrong, it was bad and had always been bad and you were just realizing it, and it was *true*. Like the truth, underneath everything, is misery."

Tadeusz gave a little shudder. "That sounds awful," he said. "What did it look like?"

"Like nothing," Sophie said. "Like a ghost. You could hardly see it, it was just this shimmer coming off the sea floor in the distance. It didn't help that it's *so* dark down there. It's so dark that the fish and the animals grow lights and glow, and that's all you have to see by, and it's very faint. But still, it was like—do you know when it's very hot out, and it makes the air in the distance seem wavy? Like, shimmery?"

"Yes," Tadeusz nodded.

"It was like that," Sophie said. "And it seemed to be somehow coming out of the sand, out of the ground." Sophie tried to remember what else she had learned about the Invisible, but that night was a chaotic blast. She remembered climbing into Syrena and taking away her precious sadness; she remembered the Vulcan returning the mermaid's feelings and memories to her. It all felt so long ago, like the craziest dream, or a movie she'd once seen.

"Other scientists had come there and dropped equipment," Sophie nodded. "But it was always destroyed by something. The submarines aren't able to stay there long either, because it's so deep. But they keep trying."

"What happened to this one?" Tadeusz asked, pointing at the computer, and Sophie was filled with shame. How was anyone, even a boy who hung out with supernatural creatures, going to understand the sinking of the submarine, the deaths of the scientists inside? It was in everyone's power to save them—the Billow Maidens, Sophie—and yet, beholden to some cryptic command, the creatures brought the vessel down, crashing it on the ocean floor, and even Sophie, horrified Sophie, participated, helping the scholars to a peaceful death. And then she stole their computer.

What was I supposed to do? she railed against herself. *Fight the Billow Maidens and single-handedly save a submarine?* Here, today, in a castle in Poland, firmly on the earth with a fellow human, it seemed the answer was yes. Sophie *should* have fought the Billow Maidens. She should have magicked herself into the largest whale shark the ocean had ever seen, swallowed up the submarine, and swum it to the surface, spitting it out to safety. Here, today, in a castle in Poland, there seemed to be no logical reason why Sophie could not have done that. But down there, at the bottom of the sea, with an ancient family of sea goddesses, it was their rules that mattered, their baffling rules that made no human sense. And Sophie had trusted them, trusted the terrible wisdom of destiny, a force she could have no sooner gone up against than she could have the Maidens, with their formidable strengths and convictions.

"I'm sorry," Tadeusz said, nervously shoving at his glasses. "We don't have to talk about it."

Sophie was surprised to find herself crying; surprised also at how easy it was to cry in front of Tadeusz. *I guess that's the good part of having a nerd for a friend,* she thought. Ella, alarmed by her vulnerability, would have made some mean jokes to try to get her laughing again, and any of the boys of Chelsea would have seized on such a moment of weakness like a pack of wild dogs, mocking and berating her sensitivity. But Tadeusz just watched her with his magnified owl-eyes.

"We *do* have to talk about it," Sophie said, wrapping her fist in the cuff of her hoodie and mopping up her wet face. "It's important. I just don't know that you'll understand." And she began to tell the story of the Jottnar, and how the Billow Maidens rushed into the sea with all the joy and purpose of a hunting party, to take down this submarine. How Sophie had helped, in her sad way. How hearing the one scientist's thoughts—thoughts of dark energy, thoughts that she and Tadeusz were sharing now—she was urged to take the computer. And so she did.

Tadeusz's dinner-plate eyes were unblinking; Sophie wasn't sure he was breathing.

"Hey," she reached out and shoved him in the shoulder. "What? Say it."

"You've been through *a lot*." Tadeusz shook his head slowly. "No wonder you were asleep down there for so long. It's a wonder you aren't crazy!"

"It is!" Sophie said joyfully, feeling wonderfully understood. "It *is* a wonder I'm not crazy!"

"Well." Tadeusz turned back to the computer. "That place you went to, it's one area on the planet where they believe dark energy is entering the universe. There are more."

"Where?" Sophie asked.

"Well... according to their maps, there is one off the coast of Japan, and one near Greenland, and one in Western Africa, near Ghana."

"Huh," Sophie nodded. These were the places other mermaids had taken the other magic girls to. "How do you know them?"

"A vision, I guess. Like the one I had of you. I saw you, and I saw them. The other girls being called to fight Kishka. Or whatever the other girls call her. She's not really anyone's grandmother. She's a force, an energy. Sophie—" Tadeusz took a deep gulp of air and barreled on. "I think Kishka *is* dark energy. Or she, like, feeds off of it, or something."

"She feeds off pain," Sophie said. "Suffering. Human suffering. And—well, pigeon suffering, I suppose. Maybe all suffering."

Tadeusz nodded. "And you said that when you stood near the Invisible, it made you feel awful—"

"Worse than I've ever felt, pretty much," Sophie nodded. "But wait—the girls?"

"Sorry," Tadeusz nodded, and grabbed a pile of paper sitting in a disheveled heap on the table. "There's so much, so much to keep organized in my head, and more happens every day, it just comes more and more together." Shuffling through the papers, Tadeusz pulled out one sketched with the image of a girl. "Isabelle Naoko," he said.

Sophie took the page from Tadeusz and gazed at the girl rendered there in pencil. The girl from her vision, the happy girl. Her long, dark hair had a blond streak where it fell into her face, and unlike Sophie's own portrait, this girl was smiling.

"This is Pipaluk." Tadeusz quickly pulled another drawing from the stack. The serious girl, with long, messy hair pulled into a lopsided ponytail. "She lived in Alaska, until a mermaid from Greenland came for her. And the last one, Lesia, originally from St. Martin, in the Caribbean."

"Let me guess," Sophie said, taking in the sketch of the girl with the sparkly eyes and the braids and the afro.

"Yup," Sophie nodded dramatically. "Kidnapped by mermaids!"

"Yes," Tadeusz nodded. "One single mermaid."

"The one with the snake," Sophie nodded. "And those cool fins, right here." She touched her temples, where she'd seen the decorative fins flaring up from the mermaid's cheekbones.

"Tadeusz, you're a really great artist," Sophie said. "If this computer genius thing doesn't work out for you, you could probably do pretty well drawing and carving and stuff."

Tadeusz blushed, his white cheeks flaring scarlet as if suddenly fevered. "I'm not a genius, Sophie. You just think that because you don't know computers. If someone taught you, you'd get it."

"Or I'll just magic it," she relented. Sophie placed the pages back on the pile.

"So these places—Japan, and Greenland, and Ghana, they're where the other Invisibles are. Sophie," Tadeusz pushed his glasses back up the bridge of his nose, "I really think it's where Kishka gets her power!"

If Kishka is their grandmother, too," Sophie wondered, "are they, like, my cousins?"

"In a funny way," Tadeusz said. "I mean, no, not at all, but in a funny way you all are related. In a funny way, you're almost like sisters."

Sophie spread the images out in a line across the table. Isabelle, Pipaluk, Lesia. "What else do you know about them? Do you see them a lot?"

"No," Tadeusz shook his head. "I just know they're out there. My role is to work with you, Sophie. To figure this all out."

"Well, it seems as if you're doing it," Sophie nodded. "You've figured out a lot."

"Yeah," he said uneasily. "There's more to explain."

"Okay."

"The Invisible, the dark energy. It's sadness. Pure negative energy. The essence of sadness, or despair. It's what you felt when you looked at it."

"Yeah, I know."

"So, what you're meant to do, as far as I can tell, is remove the sadness from the world. From all the people in all the world. *That's* what will destroy Kishka. Well, not destroy, not exactly. She's a property of the universe. She can't be killed. It would be like trying to destroy gravity."

Sophie was very quiet, her mind reeling as Tad's information synced up with her own knowledge, what she'd learned and what she'd lived through. Her brain felt like a computer uploading a new operating system. She remembered her recent trip into the complicated heart of the Jottnar Bloo; she recalled her voyage into Syrena's strong heart, and the damage she had unwittingly done there. Tad didn't understand, and how could he? How could any human, so weighed down with suffering, really understand that some of it—a glittering shard, an eternal throb—was meant to be there?

"I won't remove all the sadness," Sophie said, heavily. "I will shrink it. I'll right-size it. It has gotten out of control, the balance has tipped. I'll tip it back, but some sadness—a lot, actually—will stay."

Tad looked hurt by the news. "But why?" he pleaded. "If you have this magic, if you can remove *all* the sadness, all the pain, why wouldn't you?"

"You don't understand," Sophie said, frustrated. "I wish that I could! Do you know how *impossible* it's going to be, entering the hearts of millions and millions of people and only removing the 'right' sadness?" It would be simpler, she knew, to just explode the Invisible to bits. But that would only bring about another problematic balance on earth.

"Well, great!" Tad persisted, even after Sophie had done all she could to explain. "Let's try living with *that* imbalance for a while! The imbalance of *no pain!* Maybe two great imbalances make a balance?"

"Tad." Sophie couldn't help but smile. "You are being *such* a human right now!"

"Well, it's what I am!"

"I know," Sophie nodded. Is this why Syrena was always so exasperated with her, for the ways her own illogical humanness came into play? Probably, but she knew it was also why the mermaid loved her. And Sophie caught a rare glimpse of herself then, the way she straddled these two worlds, magic and human, and she was glad she was the way she was.

"You're just going to have to trust me, Tadeusz," Sophie said in a soft voice. "It's really confusing. I mean, I'm half-Odmieńce and I'm still figuring it all out!"

"Well, whatever you do, it has to make *some* difference, right?"

Sophie nodded. "Yes. Whatever *we* do will make a big difference. It has to." Sophie reached for the boy's drawings, spreading them out along the table. Smiling Isabella, scowling Pipaluk, sparkling Lesia. "I think the four of you are probably splitting it up. Splitting the earth up into quarters. You get the West, Isabella the East, Pipaluk the North, and the South goes to Lesia."

The West. Would Sophie have to *go* there? Or would she just beam there in the magical way she was able? *Don't freak out, don't freak out,* she coached herself as a feeling of overwhelm rose in her body. She dipped her head between her knees. *Breathe.* Tadeusz shoved a chunk of gray salt at her.

"Here."

"Thanks."

"You should just carry a bunch of salt with you, like all the time," Tadeusz suggested. "My mom makes me carry nuts and fruit with me, because I get low blood sugar. If I get too hungry I'm sort of hard to be around."

"You have a mom?" Sophie asked, which made Tadeusz laugh.

"Of course I have a mom!" he said. "Everyone has a mom, somewhere."

"She lets you live here in this castle?" she asked. "She doesn't care?"

"She understands it's where I'm supposed to be. Sophie, we've all been waiting for you, for so long. You have been part of the myths passed down through generations. Syrena has known about you for a very long time, and she told my great-great-grandmother, and my great-grandmother, and my grandmother, my mother, all of us have awaited you. And now that you are here, I am the one to help you."

"How are you going to help me?" Sophie asked.

"I'm going to help you," Tadeusz said, "By bringing you to someone who can really help you. I am going to bring you to Jezda."

Chapter 15

Leaving the castle was quite a production. The ruined wing that Tadeusz and Sophie and the pigeons inhabited was so vast, Sophie didn't understand how there could be *another* wing, this one polished and restored and teeming with tourists. Then there was the underground salt mine, with its caves and ponds and tunnels to the Vistula. It seemed that the castle should take up all of Warsaw! The girl followed Tadeusz through a warren of rooms. In one, a giant, dark chandelier hung treacherously from the rotting ceiling, half-melted candles stuck in their slots. Paper cones hung beneath them were stiff with cold wax. The floor beneath their feet was sometimes splintered boards, the jabbings of wood catching the soles of their shoes; sometimes checkerboard marble, so smooth their feet slid over the tiles. When they passed through the room that the pigeons occupied—a dark room ornamented with the Polish eagle, its white plaster body crumbling, its gilded crown dulled—the pigeons themselves flew out from the holes in the walls where they'd made their nests. They shook dust from their feathers as they joined Sophie and Tadeusz, swooping beneath low-hanging chandeliers, funneling down windowless hallways that narrowed to passageways, that sloped down and then up and finally released them into a small brick building on the edge of the property. It was a tight square filled with pigeons, the beating of their hearts and wings filling the cramped room.

"Let us out of here already!" griped a bird that could only have been Arthur, and Tadeusz rushed to the metal bolt that secured the heavy wood door and flung it open. The birds were released into the sky and Sophie was blinded by the onslaught of sunlight.

Ack!" she cried, and with a thought—a powerful thought, but still, just a thought—a pair of sunglasses appeared on her face.

"Whoa," she breathed, reverential. Reverent toward her own power, able to conjure something as ridiculous as sunglasses onto her face with nothing but the fleetingest idea of them.

"Tadeusz, look!" She pointed at them sitting on her face, and Tadeusz nodded.

"Ya, you're magic, right?" The boy shrugged.

"Yes, of course, but I didn't even hardly *do* anything! I just *thought* about them and they appeared on my face!"

"Well, I guess you are feeling better, then. The salt and the rest have healed you good."

The two of them leaned back against the stone building and took in the majesty of the castle in the distance. It was made of brick and stone, red patterned with white and sand, rising into turrets here and there, flags streaming from their tops in the breeze. Sophie could tell that they were looking at their own busted wing of the estate—the windows that were covered with boards, the windows that lacked glass, dark as the space a knocked-out tooth leaves in a mouth.

"You can't see at this distance," Tadeusz said, "But there are many little holes in the walls, from gunshot, from the war. Not so many buildings in town show that. Most were knocked down completely. It's good that we have the ones we do. To show our battle scars, to show that we fought. Ya?"

"Yeah," Sophie nodded.

"The alternative is to forget," Tadeusz said, "which we must never, ever."

Sophie looked at the boy with a real affection. He was so lanky and frail-seeming to be charged with such a heavy task, carrying the memory of long-ago wars. But as Sophie adjusted to being outside the castle, feeling the energy of the city around her, she understood that Tadeusz was not alone in his burden. The city itself carried the memory of the war. For the city and its people, the war was not so very long-ago.

The pair trudged off the castle property and onto the street. Far behind them a line of tourists waited to enter through the castle's grand front doors. Sophie smiled at the ingenious sneakiness of it, that they would live and plot and plan right under the nose of such official opulence, like mice or rats or pigeons. The smile split her face in half, and she grinned at the people they passed, feeling a surge of goodwill ring through her body. Tadeusz observed her nervously.

"You mustn't," the boy instructed.

"Mustn't what?" Sophie asked.

"Smile like that at everyone. People will think you're up to no good."

Sophie burst out in laughter, her smile growing wider. "Because I'm *smiling* people will think I'm up to no good?"

"I'm quite serious," Tadeusz said, shoving his glasses up his nose in order to give the girl a good, serious stare through the magnified lenses. "Polish people don't walk around smiling like Americans. If you smile at a stranger they will think you are trying to trick them. Only criminals smile here."

"Tadeusz, that's nuts!" Sophie cried.

"It is the truth. If you should blend in here you must stop smiling."

Sophie experimented with the boy's pronouncement, offering a cheery grin to those who caught her eye—old women with scarves tied beneath their chins; new mothers pushing strollers full of baby; young men smoking as they strode down the street. Every time, her smile was met with a scowl. Some looked practically offended, as if Sophie had insulted them with her toothy grin. She turned to Tadeusz, amazed.

"You're right!" she exclaimed. "Nobody is smiling back at me! It's like my smiling makes them *angry!*"

Tadeusz shrugged, and gave his glasses a poke. "It's how I said. I know my home. You have to believe me."

"But why?" Sophie cried. "Why is it so?"

"Poland is a hard place, Warsaw especially. All of these people— especially the older people—they have had hard lives, many of them. Some remember the war. The years after the war, when the Soviets controlled everything. Communism, standing in line for food. All these things have a big effect on everyone's hearts, ya? They get heavier and heavier. You see some person smiling, it's like they're laughing at you."

"Okay," Sophie nodded. She wasn't trying to make anyone feel bad. She'd keep her smile to herself.

The usually serious Tadeusz allowed himself a brief, sympathetic smile at the girl.

"When you are done with your task, perhaps the people of Warsaw will smile at one another again," he suggested.

My task, Sophie thought with a different sort of smile, a grimace. He said it like she was to run an errand, pick up milk at the corner store, perhaps write a book report. Her task was to remove the heaviness from the hearts of all these people who frowned at her cheer. *All* of them, and then some more, and then some more, and then some more.

Tadeusz grabbed Sophie by the cuff of her hoodie and pulled her down a smaller street where vendors sold fruits and vegetables and baked goods. "Magic some money," the boy told her, and Sophie did, in her pockets. She pulled out a handful of paper and coin and passed it to the boy, who stopped at a bread kiosk manned by an old woman, an old woman Sophie dared not smile at. She regarded the woman blankly, with a neutral expression on her face, fighting the feeling that she was being terribly rude. Tadeusz purchased rolls spreckled with tiny poppy seeds and bagels strung on a rope like a big bagel necklace. He handed the paper bag to Sophie and they crossed over to another cart that sold the big, floppy heads of sunflowers cut from their stalks, the yellow petals withered. Tadeusz paid the man and lifted one of the heaviest, floppiest heads into his arms.

"What will we do with that?" Sophie laughed. Tadeusz looked at her blankly.

"We will eat it."

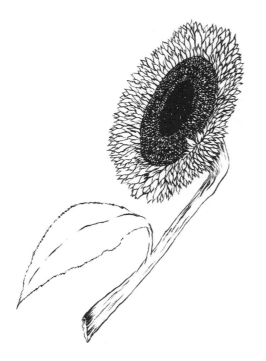

"How?" Sophie asked. Tadeusz appeared puzzled.

"Do they not have sunflower seeds in America?"

"Of course," scoffed Sophie. "In a bag, in the supermarket."

"Huh. Well, here is where the seeds live before they go into their bags." He flashed the flower head at Sophie, and Sophie saw that it was studded with seeds.

"You just pick the seeds off it? And eat them?"

"Ya," Tadeusz said, ever more confused. "Are you making fun of me right now?"

"No," Sophie said quickly, embarrassed. "I just haven't seen this before. A sunflower full of seeds."

"Okay," Tadeusz said. "For a person who is supposed to know so much important things, it is strange that you know so little simple things."

"Well, if you were in Chelsea I bet there'd be a bunch of things you wouldn't know either."

"Certainly," Tadeusz agreed. He pulled a seed from the wide, dry face of the flower, and cracked it between his teeth, offering the head to Sophie, who rejected it with a scowl.

After buying some fruit at a fruit stand that also sold the most lovely bouquets, flowers mixed with leaves mixed with small apples and berries, the pair headed away from the market and toward the river.

"Would you like to see the statue of my great-grandmother?" Tadeusz asked. "To most everyone else it is a statue of Syrena. But to me, it is my family."

"Of course," Sophie said, and they walked along the banks of the Vistula, gnawing on pieces of bread and fruit. Sophie eventually plucked a sunflower seed from the big, floppy flower and split it open with her two front teeth. All around them people passed on bicycles, or jogged, or strolled. Families with barely-walking toddlers moved slowly, gazing at the freshly stepping baby with wonder. Ahead, they could see the iron-colored statue sitting strongly on the bank. On one side, a woman in white—a bride—got her photo taken in front of it. On the other side, a thin, young woman in big, clunky shoes did model poses before a different camera.

"It is a very popular place," Tadeusz explained with a shrug, a movement that had become as characteristic as the nudge of his spectacles up his nose. The two hung back, noshing, until the photo shoots ended, and then made their way to the statue.

The mermaid—verdigris but not without her gleam—rode upon bronze patina waves, kneeling upon the ocean's surface. Sophie noted the vague outline of the Polish eagle upon the round shield the statue held at her side. She gazed at the monument, searching for the mermaid and not finding her. A loneliness for her friend awoke inside her heart.

"It doesn't look like her at all," Sophie said, a tad scornfully. It was a truncated, blunt version of the mermaid. Her tail stopped short of its wild, sinewy glory, and her mane of hair, wilder and longer than her tail, was short and combed and neatly collected at the nape of her neck. Where would Syrena keep all her snacks and tiny weapons? The statue was more human than mermaid—the simple, smiling face held none of Syrena's ancient mystery, and a clear outline of two human legs grew from beneath her belly before merging into a tail. Her blunt sword, raised in an arm poised to strike, was surely not as vicious a weapon as her narwhal horn.

"Of course not," Tadeusz said, smiling. "It looks like my great-grand-mother, Krystyna. Look at her smile. It is my grandmother's smile, and my mother's smile. Is it also mine?"

A hesitant smile graced the boy's face, tender but slight. A humble Polish smile the same smile the mermaid smiled onto the Vistula running calm and smooth before them.

"Yes," Sophie nodded. "You do have that smile." Hearing this, the boy's smile briefly grew, and then vanished.

"If this was a true statue of Syrena," Sophie continued, "she wouldn't be smiling at all, not even that tiny smile. She'd have a big scowl on her face, and you would see her fangs."

"Such a statue would scare children!" Tadeusz cried, laughing.

"Besides, Syrena will live forever, and anyone who wants to see what she really looks like only needs to sit by the river for a while and she will come to them. But my great-grandmother is gone, and she went too soon, and lucky for me and my family we can come here and have this vision of her. Ya?"

"Ya," Sophie nodded. She could see in the boy's longing for his ancestor her own longing for the mermaid. "So..." she started, "if we just sit here a while will Syrena come and say hello?"

"Usually, ya," Tadeusz said. "That is how she helps the people of Warsaw. One of the many ways. But sometimes she makes you wait for a very long time. And if she thinks your trouble is foolish, she will not be very helpful."

Sophie laughed out loud, knowing firsthand how Syrena handled those she thought were fools. Sophie had been that fool, again and again. "What if you don't have a problem, and you only want to see her? Will she come to you?"

"I don't think so," Tadeusz said. "I mean, she's pretty busy. She's the city mermaid."

"Well, what if *I* want to see her?"

"Syrena will come to us at the castle, don't worry," Tadeusz assured the girl. "You will see her again. But she has been away for a while. I imagine she has much business to attend to."

"The girls," Sophie nodded, shivering a bit at the memory. "The water-fairies? Binkies?"

"*Boginkis*," Tadeusz nodded. "Baby stealers. They are always a problem. In the olden days they were somewhat useful, because whenever they stole a baby they would replace it with an Odmieńce. It was an easy way to get them into the world of humans. It was how your family happened, ya? Not just Kishka, but her sister, too. Kishka has a sister?"

"Hennie," Sophie nodded. "She's a witch who runs this fake grocery store that's kind of old and gross, but it's just a front for all her witching. So I guess it's better that people don't really shop there very much."

"Does she have much power, like Kishka?"

Sophie shook her head. "Not as much as Kishka. Maybe not even as much as me."

Sophie wasn't bragging when she said this; in fact, the truth of it made her sad. How she wished Hennie were as vast and powerful as her grandmother! Sophie hoped that the three girls would at least match her own fledgling abilities, if not surpass them. Four girls. Would they be any match for Kishka? Would four hundred girls be a match? Four thousand?

Deep in thought, the two of them ate their lunch from the brown paper sacks, leaning against the statue's stone base, looking out onto the river, or to the bridge that spanned it, its steel cables like the string of a child's toy. A small pile of sunflower shells gathered at their feet. Then, passing over the bridge came an unusually large flock of pigeons. They zoomed low over the river, coming to a landing around Sophia and Tadeusz, busying themselves with a refreshing dip in the small water fountains that ringed the statue. Sophie scanned the motley kit for a friendly face, and spotted the familiar waddle of Arthur, who hobbled toward her with Loosha at his side.

"Hello, hello," the bird crowed.

"*Dzien dobry,*" said Loosha.

"Hey you guys," Sophie grinned, caught herself, then grinned some more.

"Hey Arthur, did you know that you can't smile at people in Poland? They think it means you're a criminal. Loosha, did you tell him?"

"Well, it is not really relevant for pigeon," Loosha said. "Pigeons don't smile either way."

"Sounds like a great custom to me," Arthur bobbed his head. "What's there to be so happy about, anyway, eh? Keep your smiles to yourself."

Arthur's crabbiness just made Sophie smile wider. "Do you like Warsaw, Arthur? It seems like your sort of place."

"Well, I am liking it, as a matter of fact. The pigeons here are real stand-up birds. Tough guys, even the girls. Loosha just took us by the Old Town Square—it's the top pigeon hangout in the city. I met a lot of great birds. They have a mermaid statue there, too," Arthur tossed his head toward the mermaid statue behind them. "This town's nuts about mermaids."

"That statue's okay," Tadeusz shrugged. "I'm not related to it so I don't really care about it. Every few minutes a fountain comes on and it kind of sounds like a toilet flushing."

"Well, this statue sure is something," Arthur nodded. "It has more dignity, I'd say. Though it doesn't really look like your mermaid."

Sophie took the floppy head of the sunflower and offered it to the birds, immediately wishing she had not. The pigeons swarmed the dried flower, harvesting the seeds with their hungry beaks. "Yikes!" Sophie squealed, dropping it.

"Why'd ya go and do that?" Tadeusz sulked. "That was our lunch!"

"I just didn't expect them to swarm like that!"

"They're pigeons," Tadeusz said, shoving his glasses up his nose so he could better glare at her.

"Well, sorry."

"We need all the sustenance we can get for this trip into the woods."

"Well, if we get hungry I promise I'll magic us something, okay?"

Tadeusz grumbled, and Sophie looked back to Arthur and Loosha, who had waddled away from the feeding frenzy. "Are you guys coming with us? Wherever it is we're going?"

Loosha responded to the question with a shiver that fluffed his feathers so greatly it looked like the bird had tripled in size. Arthur looked on, his orange eyes widening.

"I guess that's a no."

"You are going into the woods, to Jezda's house?"

"Ya," Tadeusz nodded.

"No way. No way we're going with you on *that* little journey." Another feather-fattening shiver.

"How come?" Sophie asked, looking from the bird to the boy and back again. "What's up with Jezda?"

"Did you not tell her?" Loosha asked. "Have you not prepared her?"

"I plan to once we're in the woods," Tadeusz said, sounding annoyed. "Away from the city and all the ruckus."

"You plan on *preparing* the girl to meet Jezda once you are in Jezda's *woods*?" Loosha sounded appalled.

"Syrena said she did not need much preparation. She is ready to meet Jezda. I only have to inform her."

"You know, I *hate it* when people talk about me like I'm not here," Sophie said. "And when I say people, I mean pigeons also."

"I know what *that* tone of voice means," Arthur said, backing away with a slight curtsy. "Good luck, you guys, with whatever it is you're doing. I'm sure we'll hear all about it back at the castle."

"If they return," Loosha said gloomily. "If they *return* to the castle."

"Loosha—" Tadeusz began, exasperated.

"What is *that* supposed to mean?" Sophie demanded.

"One does not simply *drop in on* Jezda as one might a friend. One *prepares* to meet her. One *trains*." The bird swiveled his head to stare down the boy. "Aren't you at least afraid for yourself, if not for the girl? Are *you* prepared to meet Jezda?"

"I've been preparing. Training, as you say. And Sophie is ready."

"I am?" Sophie scoffed. "I don't even know what you are talking about."

"*Odes!*" Tadeusz shouted, with a sudden force—a temper—that Sophie hadn't before glimpsed, and wouldn't have thought was in him. "This is none of your business. You have eaten all of my sunflower seeds and you are ruining my plan! All of you, begone!" The boy waved his long, lanky arms, startling some nearby birds into the sky, a contagious movement among the pigeons. They flew off as one, the strong *crack* of so many wings sounding like a whip snapping in the sky.

"See ya, kiddo," Arthur said, before joining the flock.

"I've said my piece," Loosha said ominously, and took to the sky as well. The boy and girl were left in a chaos of scattered sunflower seeds, the desiccated flower abandoned on the ground. With the lightest *zawolanie* escaping her lips, Sophie disposed of the mess with a bit of magic. She turned to Tadeusz.

"You better tell me," she said, "what all *that* was about."

"I will," the boy pouted. "And always I had planned to! But I wanted to do it in a special way."

"Too bad," Sophie said. "As they say in Chelsea, what the *frig* is going on?"

"Let's walk into the woods, ya?" Tadeusz said weakly. "And I will tell you all you need to know."

Chapter 16

So," Sophie began, her mind reeling but comforted by the peace of the forest. The trees had a soothing scent and blotted out the strong summer sun, dappling the soft forest floor with a flickering, golden light that made her think of butterflies. She stopped before a particularly majestic tree and leaned her back against it. They had been walking for some time, and before them stretched out more and more forest, as far as Sophie could see. "Jezda is a witch," she began.

Tadeusz nodded. Great, no biggie there. Sophie had witches in her family. Sophie perhaps *was* a witch, by certain people's definition, anyway. Sophie was down with witches.

"And, she lives in a spinning house, way deep in the forest here," she continued, repeating back to the boy all he had told her. "A house that spins on a pair of chicken legs."

"Three pairs, actually," Tadeusz specified. "They're sort of dancing."

"Dancing chicken legs. Okay. And the fence around her house is made of skulls and bones."

"Yes."

"And you have the key to the gate…"

"Uh… I do."

"But the keyhole is made of teeth and might bite you."

"Might bite *you*," Tadeusz corrected. "You are the one who must open the gate."

"That's convenient," Sophie snapped.

"It is your quest," the boy nearly whined.

"Don't say 'quest,'" Sophie complained. "It sounds like we're playing Dungeons and Dragons."

"Jezda *does* have a dragon," Tadeusz shrugged.

"Oh, does she?"

"Yes. It guards the fountain of life. That is why we are going, Sophie," Tadeusz's voice took on a pleading tone, softer than whining. "This fountain, I've been researching it, and I think it holds in some way the opposite of the Invisible. It is the source of all that is good in the world. The font of kindness and goodness and love."

"Than why is Jezda so fearsome?" Sophie asked. "If she's hanging out by this fountain all the time doesn't it rub off on her?"

"Jezda protects the fountain. She must be fearsome. So many people, beings under Kishka's influence, would try to destroy it. You must understand."

"So," said Sophie darkly, "if I unlock the gate and don't get my hand bitten off, then what?"

"We meet with Jezda. And if she likes you—if she believes in you—she will show you to the fountain, and she will give you gifts for your journey."

"Cool," Sophia nodded. "And if she doesn't?"

Tadeusz turned red in the face, and had to swallow a few times before he could get the words out. "She kills you and chops up your body for spells and stuff."

Sophie felt the doughy bagel and the crisp apple and every single tiny sunflower seed she'd eaten all rise up the back of her throat. Her eyes stung. "*Really?*" she choked.

Tadeusz nodded.

"Well, can't we skip it? I mean, it sounds risky. What if she's just in a bad mood today or something, and just decides she doesn't like me? Maybe she doesn't like young people. Or Americans. What if I smile at her by mistake?"

"Let us sit," Tadeusz said, collapsing onto the grass at the base of a tree. Sophie allowed her legs to give out beneath her. She plopped onto the ground besides Tadeusz.

"Listen," the boy began. "This is part of it. Part of your destiny, and your story. You are the visit with Jezda. This visit determines the next part of your story. I do not know why it should be this way, but it is so."

"My destiny," Sophie repeated.

"Yes," the boy nodded.

"Okay," the girl said, rallying some deep part of her. "Okay, okay, okay." She pulled herself up the trunk of the tree. "I know what I need," she said, half to herself and half to Tadeusz. She clapped her hands together—not because she needed to, but for effect—and before her appeared a mirror. She stood before it. There was her braid, strong as a rope. Her face had not exactly been fattened by her diet of mostly salt, but it did not look quite so gaunt, quite so haunted. The day, the sun, had flushed her cheeks. There she was, taller now. There she was, grown. *This is me*, she thought inside her heart. She stared herself down in the mirror, as if to memorize the vision. *I must understand who I am. I must not forget who I am and where I come from.*

The mirror vanished as if it had never been there. Tadeusz looked puzzled. "Just wanted to, um, fix your hair?"

"It is so weird when you make a joke," Sophie answered. "I can't tell if I like it or not."

"We should get our laughs where we can," said the boy, serious again. "While we can."

Sophie yanked him to his feet and they trudged deeper into the forest. "So all I have to do," she clarified, "is be myself?"

Tadeusz nodded.

"And because I am who I am, because of my destiny, my heart is pure enough to be admitted to Jezda's home."

"That's right."

"But there is just the eensiest, teensiest, itty-bittiest chance that there's been some terrible mistake, some glitch in the plan, and my heart *isn't* that pure, in which case I will be chopped up into little pieces."

"And used for spells," Tadeusz nodded. "That's what she does with the people she chops up."

"As a mathy sort of person," Sophie began, "what would you say the odds of my heart being impure are?"

Tadeusz tilted his head, knocking his glasses down his face. His eyes, right-sized, squinted in thought. "A fraction of a fraction, I would say."

"So there *is* a chance," Sophie dug in.

"I mean… there is always a chance of everything. Nothing in this universe is completely stable. We change things just by looking at them. But your odds could not be better. I promise you. If anything, I will get chopped up and thrown in her pot. And if I do—" the boy turned to Sophie, suddenly fierce, "then you must use me for a spell, to help you conquer Kishka."

"Tadeusz!" Sophie cried. "That's horrible! Nobody's going to chop you up! I'll kill this old witch—"

"You will do nothing of the sort. You will not risk everything by trying to harm Jezda. If I go I will be used for the battle. Like Krystyna. It will not be in vain. You will see to it."

"Well I just hate the way this conversation has turned." Sophie scowled, kicking her skate shoes through the lush forest grass. "It didn't occur to me that *you* might not be pure enough to get in. I mean, you seem pretty nice."

"Lots of people are nice," Tadeusz nodded. "But when terrible things happen, they turn terrible, too. Here in Poland. During the war. People turned their neighbors over to the Nazis. People helped the Nazis kill them. Jewish people. People moved into their homes and lived among their things. Nice people. You do not know what is in your own heart. If Jezda takes me it is because I am not worthy of the waters she protects. It will be my destiny. Just make magic of me, okay?"

Sophie gripped the boy's knobby shoulder. "Okay, Tadeusz."

THE SUN WAS low in the sky when Sophie and Tadeusz caught a glimpse of movement beyond the trees. The slightest breeze stirred the leaves, and the pair stood still and squinted into the distance, trying to get a better look at what lay ahead.

"Is it a bear?" Sophie asked, because she felt as if she were on the inside of a children's storybook. "Are there bears in this wood?"

"Not the regular part of the forest," Tadeusz said. "But feel the air here. I think we are in Jezda's woods. Anything can be here."

Sophie stilled herself, and indeed she could feel an energy prickling her skin. The hair at her scalp raised itself, as if reaching to meet a current. When Sophie reached for Tadeusz a bolt of electricity snapped her fingers.

"Whoa!" she gasped. Tadeusz rubbed the spot on his arm where she'd shocked him.

"Let's keep going," he said. "Bravely forward."

"Bravely forward," Sophie nodded. She was not the goofy girl in Chelsea, scared of jerky boys and bumbling klutzily around her grandmother's dump. She was the girl in the mirror. She was the girl on the salt wall, etched there, looking noble and strong and wise and pure and totally deserving of such a portrait, not to mention the kindness of a cannibal witch.

They heard the house before they saw it clearly. When it was still just a strange motion viewed between leaves they could hear its whir as it spun, heard the clatter of the chicken's claws where its feet had worn the earth to bedrock. How long had it spun there, Jezda's house? The trees grew closer as they approached, almost as if they were trying to block them from approaching. Wide, flat leaves whacked Sophie in the face and thin branches whipped her in the back, scratched at her face. She tore at them angrily, pulling fistfuls of green and mucking her palms with sticky sap.

"Hey, hey," Tadeusz calmed her. "They are only trying to help Jezda. Maybe you can talk to them?"

"Right," Sophie nodded. She looked forward to having a full and complete grasp on all her magical abilities. When using her powers was as natural to her as using her arms and legs. She believed that day would come. That was something, wasn't it? That was something new.

Sophie entered the warm, damp denseness of the tree. A thing without a heart, a thing made of heart. She traveled up it like the water being sucked through its roots. She showed herself to it. *Tell the others*, she requested, and felt something move back down to the roots, into the plush, ancient soil, up into all the other trees of the woods. And the trees relaxed. Their leaves drooped gently on their branches. "Thank you," Sophie said aloud. She did not want to leave the cool, sweet center of the tree. How marvelous it felt in there! Simple, and peaceful. She made a note to return to one sometime in the future. After defeating evil incarnate it would be nice to take a vacation inside a tree.

"Good job," Tadeusz nodded. "Are you always present when you go into a creature?"

"What do you mean?"

"I mean, you were here, with me, and you were inside the tree at the same time. Weren't you?"

Sophie nodded. "Yeah, I was both places."

"Are you always?"

Sophie remembered her trips into Bloo, into Syrena, into her mother and Angel. How overwhelming they were, how they knocked her out of herself. "No," she shook her head. "The trees are simpler. They don't toss me around. They're like a hammock."

"I see," Tadeusz said thoughtfully. "But—that must mean it's possible for you to enter others without losing yourself, too. Like, people."

"I guess so," Sophie said.

"We should practice," Tadeusz said. "Right now. With me."

"Here?" Sophie cried. She gestured to the spinning color in the distance, easily visible now through the trees' floppy leaves. "We're, like, there."

"Not yet, we're not. Let's try it. It feels important. Come on."

"Fine."

Sophie turned to the boy and with the slightest leap she was inside him. He wasn't Blooughadda's wild, red heart but he wasn't the mild, calming inside of a tree, either. For a moment Sophie was gone, thoroughly inside the boy, getting her footing within the environment of his heart. It was a sparkling place, surprisingly strong. It buzzed an electric buzz that distracted from the underlying pulse and thump, the painful grind of history inside him, the blood of his ancestors pooled within his own, all of it coursing through him, coursing around Sophie. It was a good heart. It was older than she had imagined, quite old, and unshakeable. Brave. Sophie found it simple enough to steady herself in such a place. Syncing her heart with Tadeusz, she opened an eye inside her soul and found herself beside him in the wood. Beside him and within him. For a moment, Sophie marveled that everyone had such a place inside them. *Everyone.* The jerkiest boys on the lost streets of Chelsea, the noblest pigeons soaring through the sky, every living thing had this place. Sophie was so grateful for her magic that let her see and feel such things."You're doing it," Tadeusz whispered, rousing her from her reverie.

"Does it feel okay?" she asked.

The boy nodded. It's strange. But it doesn't hurt or anything. He paused. "I wouldn't want you in there all the time or anything."

"It's nice in here, actually," Sophie nodded.

"Thank you."

"I suppose that is a compliment."

"Can you walk while you do this? Can you function normally? Let's try." The boy took a step forward.

"No," Sophie said. "Not toward Jezda. I'm not together enough."

"Okay." Tadeusz spun around and walked back where they had come. The trees swung down their branches and wove their leaves into a glossy, green barrier. Sophie pushed back into the tree, relishing the lovely feel of it. The tree was just doing its job. Once you got this deep into Jezda's woods there was no turning back. You must reckon with the witch. As the tree's knowledge flowed into Sophie, so it flowed into Tadeusz, whose heart she remained inside.

"Wow," Tadeusz nodded, receiving the information. "Wow, wow, wow. Sophie. There is a lot happening here."

Sophie pulled herself out of the tree and the boy, standing fully in the forest, whole. "I stayed," she said. "I was in your heart, and inside the tree, which is all heart, and I was here in the world."

"And you brought us together," Tadeusz marveled. He turned to the tree that Sophie had visited, and gently rubbed its bark. "I love this tree. Oh my goodness. Sophie. I have never been inside a tree before. I have never been anywhere but here." He touched at his heart. Sophie smiled.

"It is a good place to be," she said.

Tadeusz leaned his cheek against the tree. A breeze brought a leaf gently across his face. "I will never forget this tree," he promised.

Sophie wondered, briefly, if it wasn't only living things that had these places inside them. No—that was the wrong way to think of it. She felt her head wrapping itself around another strange truth. It was more that all things were alive. All things had their essence. If Sophie could move into a tree, she was sure she could move into, say, a crystal. And if she could move into a crystal, she could move into a stone. What was a city, if not wood and stone? What was Chelsea itself if not a living thing in its own right, with its own essence and its own complicated magic?

"Sophie, what is it?" Tad asked, letting go of his beloved tree. "Do you need salt?"

"No, no," Sophie snapped herself out of her revelation. "I'm here. I'm sorry. We have to keep working." The sun was all but gone from the sky, leaving but a slash of light in the deep purple heavens. Grasping at one another they moved forward, toward the scrape and whir that had echoed in their ears. Toward the blur of color they'd glimpsed in peeks. Toward the source of the electricity charging their skin. Toward Jezda's spinning home.

Chapter 17

Jezda's house smelled terrible. Not yet inside, not yet even certain they would be permitted inside, Sophie and Tadeusz could smell the stink of death as they beheld the terrible twirling hut. The whirl of the red cottage created a motion that blew the odor at them like a wind, smacking their faces and tossing their hair. The death stink was human and animal, things charred and things rotting. Heavy, oily smoke hung in the air, the slick wet stink of disintegration crawling beneath it. The pair hung back, adjusting to the smell, to the spectacle of the house jigging on six giant scaled chicken legs, the skin scaled and dirty, the claws sharp and cracked and caked with bits of rot.

"Oh, wow," Sophie breathed through laced fingers. "It is hard to imagine that anything about this situation could be helpful."

The sun was gone now, the purple sky deepening to black. Sophie reached out in the darkness, feeling for Tadeusz's hand, grasping it.

The bone-colored fence that bordered the witch's home was tipped in skulls, and as night came stronger their eye sockets began to glow, brighter and brighter until streams of white light poured out into the forest, crisscrossing each other like lasers. The windows of Jezda's house also began to glow, shooting beams through the forest as it turned.

"Okay, okay, okay," Sophie mumbled. Tadeusz was silent. Sophie could feel his hand pooling with sweat inside her own, and gave it a squeeze as she tugged the boy forward.

The bone-colored fence was indeed bone, bones of many shapes and sizes, carved and tied together to form posts stuck with skulls. Meat

clung here and there, to the posts and to the skulls, and to the meat clung the occasional maggot, inching whitely from morsel to morsel.

"I worked in my grandmother's dump," Sophie said quietly. "It was pretty gross. It smelled *really* bad. But the dump has nothing on this." Sophie bit her tongue, wondering if these comments were evidence of an impure heart. She decided they were simply the facts, and approached the spot where the bone fence became a bone gate. Set into it was a carefully notched keyhole, surrounded, as promised, by a ring of teeth, the jawbones of some chimera made of every fearsome creature ever to stalk human imagination. Vampire fangs and werewolf canines, capybara chompers, boogeyman teeth, the teeth of lions and sharks and long-dead dinosaurs. A single tooth possessing five sharpened fangs, ripped from the maw of a beast Sophie hoped she would never encounter. The molars of hellhounds. The milk teeth of a baby demon. Sophie was close enough to hear them chattering, waiting for a finger to devour. She turned to Tadeusz.

"The key?"

Tadeusz crouched low, his knees brushing the grass, peering at the keyhole. The teeth chattered louder, as if they could smell his skin. The clatter set Sophie's nerves on edge. "I think you're upsetting them. Back away. I'm afraid you'll get nipped."

"Hold on." Tadeusz stayed focused, then leaned back on his heels. From one pocket he removed a stick, and from the other a small knife. In the light of the skulls the boy unfolded the blade and deftly began to whittle.

"Really?" Sophie asked. "You're going to *whittle* a key?"

"Of course," Tadeusz said calmly. And whittle he did. Thin strips of wood flew off his knife, creating a tufty pile in the grass beneath him. He brought his face close to his work, both looking over his glasses and through his thick glasses. Sweat beaded on his forehead and dripped down his temples. Many times he caught his fingers in his work, and muttered what Sophie could only imagine were Polish curses. He sawed at the wood, and carved and stabbed. "I'm getting it," he promised. "I'm really getting it."

"From just *looking* at the keyhole?" Sophie said skeptically.

"I have that kind of mind," the boy said.

"Of course you do."

Tadeusz held the stick to his mouth and blew on it, picking away tiny bits of sawdust. He held it up to the beam of light arcing out of the nearest skull. It was no longer a stick. It was a skeleton key, pale and soft and intricately notched.

"I am seriously impressed," Sophie said.

The treetops behind them began to whip around as a new wind blew down upon them. Not the steady current the spinning house threw their way, but as if a giant bird were descending from the night sky, its feathered wings flapping. The pair bent back their heads, and, by skull-light and starlight, the lights of Jezda's windows and the milky light of the crescent moon, watched the witch fly through the trees in a great stone bowl, a blunt stone post in her hands, rowing the air as if through water.

"Jezda," Tadeusz whispered, straightening himself as if to meet a dignitary. Sophie did the same, brushing wisps of hair from her face only to have the winds blow them back.

"Children," the witch greeted them, landing her strange vessel beside them on the grass. Skulls banged against the stone, strung like a garland on heavy ropes. She slid the post behind her and clambered from the bowl. *Not a post,* Sophie thought, *a pestle.* A mortar and pestle. No broom for this witch; a different kitchen tool was her transportation. Sophie wondered if there were witches who flew on toasters, on cheese graters. Witches careening through the skies on electric mixers, hanging out of blenders, commandeering teakettles.

"Uh—hello," Tadeusz said simply, bringing Sophie out of her brain and into her manners.

"Hello," she said, with a tiny, awkward curtsy.

The witch laughed. "Am I the Queen of England?"

She lifted the raggedy hem of her long, black garment and dipped toward Sophie mockingly. Her white hair puffed about her wildly, a cloud that rose toward the treetops and spun back toward the city. The city. Hard for Sophie to remember there was a city, a real city, somewhere back through the trees. She felt like she had fallen into the pages of a terrible fairy tale, the kind used to frighten naughty children. Jezda wore a brightly colored patchwork vest over her ripped gown, and the small bones of animals ornamented her throat, her ears, her belt, her hair and fingers. At least Sophie hoped they'd been animals.

"I would say you are a queen of sorts," Sophie stammered.

"A queen of sorts. How about a queen out of sorts?" From a belt around her waist she lifted a rusty key, and undid the loop that held it there. She brandished it at the pair. "I was just going inside for a bit of supper," she told them. "But perhaps *you* might let me in?" She smirked at the wooden replica in Tadeusz's small hands. Small hands that trembled as he held it out to Sophie.

"Uh..." he stammered. "I believe it is... I mean... she's supposed to do it."

"Another brave man," Jezda snarked, loosing a gob of spit onto the ground by Tadeusz's feet.

"No, I mean, I would, of course, it's just—"

"It's my destiny," Sophie said, taking the wooden key. "I am your visitor. It's me who has come to see you. Tadeusz is just—he's my helper. My friend."

"Looks like he's never done a bit of hard work in his life," the witch said, sizing up the boy. She walked to him and took his arm in her hand, pinching his wobbly muscle with claws that looked like miniatures of the ones that spun her house. She clutched his soft hands. Tadeusz grimaced.

"He's very smart," Sophie defended the boy. "He works with his mind, mostly."

"That's fine by me," the witch said. "I like them tender. Much tastier." She smiled, revealing a mouth of teeth not unlike the ones circling the keyhole. "Come on now. I'm a hungry old woman."

Sophie approached the gate, fondling the smooth end of the key. The teeth tittered, as if laughing at her.

"Are you prepared?" Jezda called out behind her.

"I believe so," Sophie answered.

"Who is ever prepared?" the witch asked, tilting her face to the moon.

Sophie stopped, the key held close to the teeth. "Is that a question?" she asked nervously. "Like, a riddle? Am I supposed to answer that?"

"Oh, open the gate, for Hecate's sake! Do you believe yourself in a movie?"

"I mean, kind of," Sophie muttered, and jammed the key into the gate.

It slid in easily, and quickly the teeth became still. Sophie froze, her breath held in her lungs.

"You do know how to use a key, don't you?"

Sophie gave the wood a twist and the gate flung open. With the screech of nails on rock Jezda's hut came to a halt, swaying heavily atop its scrawny legs. A door swung open and unfurled a heavy red ramp, like a tongue lolling from a mouth. Sophie turned back to her company, and the gate slammed shut against them.

"Well done," Jezda said to Sophie. To Tadeusz she offered her own rusted key. "If you please," she said, sticking it into his palm when he hesitated.

At the gate, the teeth clicked and clacked in anticipation. Tadeusz looked up at Sophie, his eyes owlier than ever.

"Remember what I said," he instructed Sophie solemnly. "My request."

"Let me guess," hooted Jezda. "You request that your impure heart be used in the service of your friend's quest, eh? That we use your bones and hands and tender organs to add power to her spell? To be martyred for your mission?"

"Only if he is not admitted," Sophie said quickly. "And, I mean, Tadeusz is so *nice*, I can't imagine—"

"Fools, it is not for you to call how I use my materials!" The witch was mad. "You." she pointed a grimy claw at Sophie. "You have gotten in, but you have not proven yourself worthy of my assistance. And I am hungry. I feed my bones of the meat of nice boys whose hearts aren't worthy of my waters. So. What is your name, boy?"

"Tadeusz."

"Taddy. Tadpole. Should my wise gatekeeper sniff out the impurities in your soul, be sure I will cook them out before I eat you." The witch lifted from her belt a skull the size of a newborn baby and plucked away a bit of flesh that clung to the bone. "Come now," she said, chewing. "Let me in."

The rusted key clattered and clanged as Tadeusz's shaking hand bonked it into the jaw.

"Don't chip a tooth!" Jezda barked.

The key, with its layer of rust, was harder to stick into the lock, but Tadeusz did it. With a quick click the gate sprung open, and Tadeusz looked up at Sophie, his eyes wide and pink with tears. He entered the witch's yard, and the witch shuffled in behind him.

"Follow me, my esteemed guests," Jezda called as she made her way up the ramp. "Congratulations on not being rotten, on being capable enough to not waste my time. Thankfully, there are enough fools in the woods that my larder is full. Come in for supper."

Sophie and Tadeusz followed the witch up to her door, the ramp beneath their feet spongy as a tongue.

"Do you think we'll have to eat—people?" Sophie asked in a horrified whisper.

"I don't know," Tadeusz whispered back. "We shouldn't be rude."

"Eating people is rude," Sophie hissed. "What is wrong with you?"

Sophie took in the hut as they approached, noting the brown straw of the roof, the coarse hairs sprouting from the chicken feet at rest. As she stepped over the threshold, she realized that the witch's home was not red, as she'd first believed, but white. That red color was blood.

Chapter 18

Is that a foot? Sophie asked herself, peeking over the rim of Jezda's cauldron as she passed by, her arms heavy with stone plates. She set them down at the wooden table without grace, upsetting the jug of water Tadeusz had filled, splashing the bits of burlap he'd fashioned into napkins. Jezda set her dark gaze on the girl, eyes all pupil, no iris, and cocked a sparse eyebrow.

"You're a bit clumsy with the table settings. What do you do at home, eh? Your Mama must bite her fingers, watching you!"

"Uh, we don't really set the table at my house," Sophie said.

"Oh, you eat with your hands, like raccoons?"

Sophie found it odd to be defending her civility to a witch possibly cooking a stew of human toes, but she tried to explain what dinnertime was like back in Chelsea. "My mother works a lot. She's not home or else

she's tired. We mostly eat on our own. Like, cereal, or TV dinners or ramen."

"You don't think witches work a lot?" Jezda demanded. "Witches work harder than any woman. It is important to sit down and eat at the end of the day. I insist upon it. Tadeusz, very nice with the napkins. I'm impressed."

"Thank you," Tadeusz mumbled shyly.

Jezda directed her attention back to Sophie. "Well, I think my cooking is distracting you. So why don't you stir the pot and I'll help Tadeusz." The witch offered a hefty wooden spoon to Sophie. *Something* slid off the curve and into the broth with a *plop.*

"Sure... but I can't really cook," Sophie said uneasily.

"The cooking is done. Now you just stir." The witch smiled, showing off her deadly, mismatched teeth. Before abandoning her cauldron she removed what looked like the skull of a bird from her wrist and tossed it into the soup.

Sophie plunged the wooden spoon into the thick stew. Beneath the reddish broth—*tomatoes, right? Tomato soup like Andrea would make her with a grilled cheese, when she was younger*—the spoon bumped into mysterious things that sunk and bobbed and spun in the muck. *Not muck,* Sophie corrected herself. *The soup. It's just soup.* The steam from it rose up to her face, dampening her cheeks. It smelled good. It smelled like garlic, which always smelled good and was strong enough to mask the scent of anything else in the pot.

"It smells good," Sophie said to the witch, offering a weak smile.

"Of course it does," Jezda nodded. "It's been cooking for a long time. Best to bring out the flavors."

"Right."

Jezda joined her at the wide, metal cauldron, rubbing the mouth of a glass with a bit of burlap. "This particular stew has been going since, oh, I think 1945." She ducked her head into the steam and breathed it deeply.

Sophie stopped stirring. The spoon stood straight up in the thick broth. "You've been cooking this soup since 1945?" she asked.

"I began it in 1945," the witch said, reaching into a pocket in her skirts and withdrawing a fistful of herbs she sprinkled into the pot. "I add to it daily, of course. A little this, a little that. Whatever's around. There are lean times and fat times, but always my stew feeds me." She patted her belly, soft and wide.

"Jezda," Sophie grabbed the witch, her stomach roiling with fear and the sensation of being extremely grossed out. "I think it's great that you eat people. Really. Like, good for you! It makes sense that you would. You're a witch. But I'm a *person*. I can't eat other people. I don't want to be rude. It is so kind of you to have us for dinner. I mean, not have *us* for dinner—actually, it is so kind of you to *not* have us for dinner! I just—"

Jezda took the burlap rag and placed it over Sophie's mouth. "Do you think I would share a delicacy so rare, a taste so acquired, with a girl who sups on corn flakes and Lucky Charms?" She gestured to the stew. "There are no *people* in there, fool. I do not share my dark-hearted meats with anyone, especially not human children!"

"Phew!" Sophie's face cracked into a huge smile. She wiped her sweaty brow with the back of her hand. "Okay, great, that's great for everyone! Great plan, great plan." She took back up her task of stirring the stew, unafraid now of what lurked beneath the broth. What once was a heart was now but a turnip, a potato, a carrot. She flashed a smile of relief at Tadeusz, who had been made so nervous by the exchange he'd begun to absentmindedly chew on a napkin.

"And the 1945 thing, that's not, like, going to give us food poisoning or anything?" Sophie clarified.

"Well, it doesn't give *me* food poisoning," the witch cackled. "Magic is a capable preservative, I believe. See here—" She took the spoon away from Sophie and dredged the cauldron, struggling slightly to bring it back above the broth. "Oh, dear," she mumbled. Sophie assisted, and together they brought forth—*something*. Something puckered and red and white, stringy and fatty and *big*.

"Bear heart," the witch said, pulling a bit of meat free with her fingers and popping it into her mouth. "I took this one down thirty years ago, I believe. And here—" she dumped the heart with a splash and rummaged around the cauldron until she emerged with a what looked like an entire cat skeleton, held together with twine. "Bubula," she said fondly. "My familiar. Of course I would never share her meat, but her bones, her bones are good for soups."

"There's a cat in there," Sophie said dully.

"Just the bones, dearie. Just the bones. But the dogs, we have everything but the pelt in there." Jezda pat the sickened girl on the back cheerfully. "It's just a formality, the cooking. The stew is always ready, and is never finished. Let's eat." Grabbing a clay bowl marked with the witch's own fingerprints, Jezda served a deep spoonful of the stew and passed it to Sophie. "*Smacznego!*" she cried happily. Broth splashed over the top and wet Sophie's hoodie. She looked down into the bowl, not wanting to know what it was she was seeing. The aroma of the bowl wafted up to her face. Delicious. It really did smell delicious.

"SO. TELL ME why you are in my house." Jezda let loose a deep burp and patted her mouth daintily with a piece of burlap. "Compliments to the chef!" she cackled. "Which is me? Get it?"

The witch's laughter made Sophie dizzy. Or maybe it was the ancient stew made from a full menagerie of beasts. Or maybe it was the house, which had begun its spinning as they sat down to sup and gave no clue as to when it would stop. It was like eating atop a carnival ride, from one of those amusement parks that popped up in empty parking lots each summer back home. Like eating dog-bear-cat-rat stew in a spinning teacup with a witch who cackled at her own bad jokes. Sophie snapped her head as if she could shake it all from her brain, and rubbed the fog from her eyes.

"I am here for your help. My grandmother is Kishka. You may know her as another name, or creature. She is evil, *Odmieńce*, but she comes to me as my grandmother. She feeds off the dark matter that is destroying the universe, and I am meant to fight her. To win, I hope. And I believe you might help."

The witch pushed her rickety chair back from her rickety table. "And what made you think that, eh? Maybe I like there being evil in the world. Keeps things spicy. Makes my own place a bit secure. You know. Witches, evil. We are of a pair."

"That's not true," Sophie protested. "My Aunt Hennie is a witch and she is all good. The witches at the riverbank, who try to drive out the *Boginki*—"

"Wannabes," Jezda snorted. "These days, any human who ties a bundle of oregano to her ceiling claims to be a witch. Oh, you cook dinner? You're a witch! You brew tea? A witch! You like that pretty rock? You must be a witch! Where were all of them when we were being burned at the stake, run out of town? I had to move so deep into the forest I'm practically in the fairy lands. My house has legs so it can run me even deeper should the townsfolk show up with torches again." The witch sighed. "I do so miss city living."

"It is said that you guard the fountain of life," Sophie said.

"And so I do."

"There are springs on the planet where the dark matter enters,"

Sophie said. "And Tadeusz tells me that your spring seems to flow with the opposite. I would like to visit it."

"Would you."

"I visited the Invisible, near the swilkie, by the Ogresses. You know of them?"

Jezda snatched a bone from her plate and gnawed it petulantly. "You think all magic people know each other, eh? No, I don't know these 'Ogresses.' I don't know of this 'Invisible.'"

"Well—please," Sophie began to beg. This wasn't going as she'd hoped it would. The lock hadn't bitten her and the hag hadn't eaten her, so those parts worked out well, but Sophie was accustomed to her mentors being a bit more on their toes. "If you could just take me to it. Then we will be on our way, if it suits you."

Jezda stood up, gathering the wet plates and the stone cups.

"Please, let me help," Tadeusz asked eagerly. But the witch took her armful of dishes and hurled them to the floor. Tadeusz gave a little cry at the unexpected cacophony of stone shattering, and Sophie gripped the wooden table, slowing her breath and maintaining her calm as she stared down the witch.

"Put those back together," Jezda said. "And then I will take you to the fountain of life." The witch moved into an adjoining room, which Sophie spied was crawling with cats. Their eyes flashed like the skulls on the fence posts outside, and they alternately hissed and meowed, hopping to rub their heads against the witch as she entered. Sophie and Tadeusz stared at the mess.

"Well," Sophie sighed.

"I'll help you," Tadeusz said, dropping to his knees and gathering the larger chunks from the floor. He pointed to the tiny piles where the stone had become pulverized. "But what about this?" He was distraught.

"Oh please," Sophie muttered. "This is ridiculous." She let loose a quiet *zawolanie* and the cups and the bowls came together, lifted themselves into the cupboard, smooth as new, clean of stew.

"Jezda," Sophie called. "I am finished. May we see the fountain?"

"One moment." Jezda retuned to the kitchen, a cat upon her shoulders, twining her tail around the witch's neck. "I have some other tasks I hoped you could help me with." She nodded at the wall behind the table and with the noise of a small earthquake it crumbled to pieces, crushing the wooden tables and all the chairs, scaring the cat from her shoulder with a howl, and sending Tadeusz into a rolled-up ball on the floor, dust-covered and trembling. Sophie sighed.

This was ridiculous. But fine. If the witch needed to waste their time, fine. She gave the old woman a tight smile.

"Very well," Sophie nodded. "I will get to it. Thank you." Jezda left, and with a tensely uttered *zawolanie*, the walls came together, the table was mended, the chairs were sturdy once more, and poor, shaking Tadeusz was free of dust.

"Get up," Sophie hissed at him. "This is ridiculous. You need to be braver." She called out once more to the witch, who shuffled back into the kitchen.

"Very nice, very nice," Jezda nodded.

"Are we ready?" Sophie asked hopefully.

"I think not," the witch replied. With something like a sneeze coming out of the witch's wrinkled face the hut beneath their feet fell away. The walls and the floor, the ceiling, the cauldron of ancient animal stew, the fire in the fireplace, all were gone. The heart of the hut was revealed, a great, monstrous chicken, three-footed and two-headed, its four eyes flaring, its double beaks squawking. Its wide, feathered wings flapped widely as it continued its lunatic dance, spinning in the dirt on its six scabby feet.

The three of them had fallen to the ground, Jezda and Sophie and Tadeusz. Cats crawled over the lot of them, alarmed, hissing at the chicken. Jezda laughed wildly at the beast, seemingly oblivious to the clouds of dust its dance kicked up, the grime that floated down and stuck in their hair, coated their faces. Sophie noticed Tadeusz could not take his eyes off the giant, horrible bird. The corners of his eyes were wet and his mouth hung open. Perhaps he was in shock, Sophie considered.

"Tadeusz." She nudged him. "Close your mouth. You're eating dirt."

"You can see," Jezda cried cheerfully over the rumble and squawk, how such a beast is descended from dinosaurs, can you not? Their powerful ancestors live inside their bones. As do yours, my dearies." She smiled her crazy-toothed smile at her guests.

"What," Sophie asked wearily, "would you like me to do?"

"Why, put it back together, of course," the witch replied. She leaned back on a knoll of grass, and many cats moved to nestle themselves in her many soft places.

Sophie stared at the chicken. She took a step into its heart, making sure to leave a bit of herself outside, in the world, as she had just learned. Part of her stayed with wide-eyed Tadeusz and the mischievously grinning Jezda; the other part of her sank into the stormy heart of the giant chicken.

Oh, how its heart beat! Small for its body but large for the world, it clattered and clattered and rushed its body with life. The chicken was marvelously, monstrously *alive*. And without the shell of Jezda's hut it felt vulnerable and exposed, like a protective cloak had been ripped from it. The light of the sun, rising dimly beyond the trees, was too bright for it; even the pin-light of the final stars speckling the sky bothered it. It was panicked, and its spinning picked up anxious speed. Sophie dug in deeper, still binding herself to the real world, her eyes hooked into Tadeusz, who seemed to understand what she was doing and stayed with her. Beneath the chicken's animal panic Sophie felt something else. An abandoned feeling. A sadness. Did the witch not need him anymore? For hundreds of years he had kept her house strong, spun it safely out of reach of wanderers and ne'er-do-wells. Now the home that had been his second skin was gone, and the chicken wondered what he had done that the witch would strip him bare so violently.

Don't worry, Sophie soothed the beast. She had a quick flash of the first time she entered the heart of one of her beloved pigeons, how shocked she was to find such a wide landscape inside such a small body. Her love for them leached into her feelings for Jezda's chicken, and she did what she could to fill the beast with love. *Don't worry, it's all just a mistake, Jezda needs you, she maybe even loves you. Calm down, bird, Calm down. We're going to build you back up.*

And with one foot in the forest and one in the powerful, tender heart of the chicken, Sophie let scream a wild *zawolanie* thick as wood and stone and iron, wild as the wildest beast, ancient as dinosaur bones. She felt in her body the exact atomic fabric of the shreds of burlap, the water in the cats' many bowls, the squirrel carcass floating in the stew. She felt the walls and the little paintings that hung upon them, she felt the shelves and the stone dishes stacked within them. All of it rose up as if from the earth and arranged itself around the grateful bird, enclosing it from the fluff of its tail feathers to the peak of its rubbery comb, until only its many legs were visible, shuffling around on the dirt. The hut, fully assembled, stopped its movements briefly, and the entire structure seemed to dip ever so slightly, as if in curtsy. Then the sharp claws again began to click and clack as the bird took up its ancient twirl.

Sophie felt surprisingly exhausted. Sure, she had done bigger magic than this, but always in the sea, that womb of salt that just nurtured and nurtured her. The very thought of salt made her dry mouth unbearable. She remembered the crystals dotting the bagels they'd bought from the kiosk; the stone bowl the witch kept on her table, full of crunchy chunks. As if she knew what was in her mind, the witch smiled.

"Why don't you magic yourself some?" she asked teasingly. "Some of the salt I am sure you are drooling for right now, yes?"

Even nodding in assent drained the energy from Sophie's neck. She hadn't noticed the smaller drains the earlier *zawolanies* had taken on her, and now this trip inside the chicken's heart and the complete creation of Jezda's spinning hut had left her depleted. Tadeusz, alarmed at the sight of his friend, began slapping his pockets.

"Always I should have salt on me!" he cursed himself. "Sophia, I am so—"

"It's fine," Sophie dismissed him. "Jezda is right. I'll just magic some." With a small, sharp *zawolanie* Sophie commanded the very air around her to rearrange their molecules into a chunk of salt. And the air itself delivered, and a densely sparkling chunk of salt appeared on her lap. But the effort of it was triply exhausting. Sophie's weak hands lifted the rock to her lips, where she gnawed and slurped with all the grace and dignity of a starving beast. Jezda chuckled.

"Seems like you need a little more of that, eh? Conjuring it really took it out of you."

Sophie held up a finger, meaning *wait*. She devoured the salt, and raised her tingling face to the witch. She blurred, came into focus, and blurred again. The salt helped, but not enough. The witch was right, she would need more. She howled a larger *zawolanie*, commanding a larger hunk of salt from the ether. It arrived with a *plunk*. Now Sophie could hardly lift it, the effort of making it had so drained her. Tadeusz scuttled to her side and lifted the crystal to her mouth. Jezda leisurely stroked the cats that had piled themselves upon her lap.

"Hmmm," she mused. "It seems that this salt is not large enough to staunch the wound of its creation, eh? Perhaps try again, dear Sophie, and this time bring a bigger hunk!"

Desperately Sophie consumed the salt, breaking it with her teeth and swallowing shards so big they left her choking. Even as she ate this rock she knew that it also was not enough to restore her. She remembered the panicked heart of the chicken; it seemed to be inside her own ribs now.

"You're right," Sophie gasped over her coughing, the last of the salt making a wet trail down the back of her throat. She mustered up the strength to call a *zawolanie*, but felt herself falter. She lacked the strength to sound one even as loud as the last and feared the salt she would conjure would be even smaller than the last useless bit.

Chapter 19

Stop!" Tadeusz yelled suddenly, his eyes blazing beneath his owly specs. "Stop it! You're tricking her! Stop!"

The witch erupted in giggles, ducking her face into her bib of cats, smothering her cackles in their fur.

"It's not funny! She's sick! You've made her sick!"

"Eh, I made her learn," the witch shrugged. "Is that not why you came to me, girl? To learn?"

"What is she learning?" Tadeusz raged, not a question but an accusation. But Sophie knew.

"I can't," Sophie said. "I can't make salt."

"Yes, you can," Tadeusz encouraged her. "I saw you. Each one bigger and bigger."

"And none of it enough to heal her," Jezda said simply. "The more energy she expends to conjure it, the more she needs. The more she needs the more she makes and the making depletes her. On and on this could go, until it kills her."

"Sophie has magicked herself into sharks to battle Kishka." Tadeusz, offended, defended his friend. "She's made herself into mermaids. She rebuilt your home! She—"

"It's true, Tadeusz," Sophie said weakly. She lay upon the dirt, her body sickened with effort. The terrible smell of the place, which they had grown accustomed to, was suddenly strong inside her nose. She tilted her face into the dirt and let out a little spurt of vomit.

"Help her!" Tadeusz hollered. "Is she—you said she could—is she dying?"

"Hecate, you are a nervous one," Jezda snapped. "I don't know, why don't you ask her. Girl, are you dying? Do tell us."

Sophie felt her body, roiling with distress. It felt bad, but very alive. "No," Sophie spoke into the dirt. "I'm not dying." But still. She could feel in her sickened bones the truth of all the witch had said. The loop of salt-craving and salt-creating had only one end. Sophie felt as if she had been snapped from a terrible spell. She was still sickened, yes, and very in need of salt. But the whir of that cycle was gone, and she could think again.

"Thank you, Jezda," Sophie addressed the witch softly. "I hadn't known this. I understand now. Thank you for teaching me." Sophie felt humbled at the amount of help she had needed, from so many different creatures across the earth, and in such a short time! From Angel's persistent coaching to the guidance of her pigeon friends, to Syrena's epically patient impatience, to Tad and her three sisters flung across the globe, each needing help from their own mermaids and familiars. And now, witches.

Jezda nodded down at the girl, a small smile on her face. "It was my pleasure," she said.

"It seemed like your pleasure," Tadeusz snapped angrily. "Now, can we get her some salt? You have much in your cottage."

"Table salt? I can do her much better, my boy. Come. Help me lift her."

Sophie felt hands upon her, the gnarled claws of the witch and the soft palms of her friend. Together they lifted her and dumped her, rather rudely, into the witch's mortar. The rough stone abraded her; her feet kicked into a scattering of spices that made her sneeze. Her head bonked into the stone, slightly buffered by her disheveled braid. "Ow," she complained.

Soon the witch was beside her, seated on the edge of the mortar, her long black gown with the filthy, ragged hem dangling by Sophie's face. Beneath the garment poked out a pair of boots, the toes so long they curled, the heel run down to nails.

"You're magic," Sophie said to her. "Why don't you make yourself a new pair of boots?"

"I beg your pardon," Jezda said, setting her pestle into the air and lifting them into the sky. "These are the *perfect* witch boots." She made a scoffing sound as she clutched the heavy stone pestle, navigating the invisible currents of wind. Sophie gathered her strength and, bracing herself against the stone, pulled herself up so that her chin sat on the ledge. The mortar wobbled and dipped.

"Hello, excuse me!" Jezda snapped. "You are not small, and you are not steady. Please still yourself so that we arrive in one piece. I don't think you'd be able to help yourself with any magic were we to start to fall."

Sophie looked over the edge of the mortar, at the gorgeous, dark forest below. The tip-tops of trees blew this way and that as the witch manipulated the air around them. Tears stung the corners of the girl's eyes as she considered what the witch had just said.

"How," she whispered. "How am I to defeat Kishka if I get this messed up just trying to *zawolanie* a piece of salt?"

"Not the same thing, dearie," the witch said almost consolingly. "Not a measure of your capacity. This is one of your weaknesses. And better I show you than your grandmother." The witch began to land the mortar. "You do understand she is not really your grandmother, eh?"

Sophie understood, though the understanding made her sad. She already didn't have a dad, and she'd never known her grandfather as anything but a German shepherd. Now she was Nana-less as well.

"Poor me, poor me, pour me another drink!" the witch cackled. "Pity parties end poorly, girl. Let's see if we can get you out of my mortar. Can you stand on your own feet yet?"

Sophie checked in with her body and felt her legs, though still weak, were able to heft her up the side of the mortar. "Yeah," Sophie said. "Is there salt in this thing?"

"Maybe some remnants crushed on the floor," she said, "But not enough to cure you. Come. See what is helping you."

And Sophie heard it before she saw it, a sweet gurgling sound, a frothy giggle, a refreshing, wet noise. And before she heard it, she had smelled it. A brightness in the air that had cleaned away the stink of Jezda's house, that overpowered even the cool green perfume of the forest. This smell held the forest and also held the sea—Sophie could detect the tang of salt as well as the sweetness of watermelon and the bracing purity of lavender. It smelled of lilac and plumeria and also, somehow, of snow. It smelled crisp and luscious, like a cat whose back had been warmed by the sun, it smelled alive, like wet earth, the pale green smell of a tree stripped of bark, of sweet, spicy sap being pulled from its trunk. It was the fountain of life. Sophie pulled herself from the mortar and with a tumble landed on its bank.

"Oh," Sophie said, breathing it deeply.

"Drink from it," the witch urged. "Bathe in it. Become a part of it. All that is good in the world comes from this. Have a piece of it. There is always more."

A smooth dome of bedrock protruded from the earth, delivering the waters. From one main hole the spring flowed generously, while from assorted chinks and tears the water bubbled or sprayed. A halo of mist hung about it, and the rising sun shot it full of rainbows. The spring collected in a rippling pool before sliding away in a crystal-clear stream. Sophie thought it was the most beautiful thing she had ever seen. She dipped her face into the pool and let the waters cleanse her.

She opened her mouth and drank it in, its restorative powers immediately evident. Not only healed from her earlier efforts, she felt better than when she'd arrived at Jezda's spinning hut, better than when she'd lingered at the mermaid statue, better than when she'd woken up in her dilapidated castle. Beneath the waters she opened her eyes, and saw carved into the rock there a multitude of symbols, and though they were all foreign to her eye she understood them to be the grateful etchings of millennia of people who had sought its powers of beauty and been healed by its liquid mercies. Tears of wonder sprang to Sophie's eyes, were caught by the spring's gentle current and whisked downstream. Sophie remembered the witch's invitation and slid her whole body into the shallow pool, hugging her knees to her chest, immersing herself in the magic waters until she felt a palpable glow coming off her. When she could barely handle the surges of pure goodness coursing through her she rose from the spring, the water cascading from her, enveloped in dewy rainbows, indeed a glow rising from her being. Even Jezda, that witch, sucked in her breath at the girl's glory.

"My," she breathed, clutching her withered cheeks with her claws. "This is it. This is how religions begin, my dear. A witness to this would fall to their knees before you, would do your bidding for the rest of their days."

"I don't need that," Sophie said simply. She folded herself into the grass at the spring's banks. "Anyone touched by these waters knows they need nothing they haven't already been granted."

Sophie thought about her life, and a thankfulness as bright as the sun lit inside her. Syrena! Her deep and loyal friendship, that she should know a mermaid! Tadeusz, that this wise and humble boy would pledge himself to her assistance! That she had known the seas as no human ever could, had known the generosity of the Ogresses and the complexity of the Jottnar, the occult wisdom of the Vulcan and the tender, silent companionship of her octopus. The jolly tumbles of the dolphins, the belugas, the seals! That she would even have the acquaintance of the *Dola,* that mystical creep, made her swoon with wonder. Never mind her original family, way back in Chelsea—her vulnerable mother with her hard-working frizz of hair upon her head. Her grimy father, under a spell for now but perhaps not forever—no, Sophie felt it in her heart as her life flashed before her so pleasurably, maybe not

forever. Her beloved flock of pigeons and Dr. Chen who took care of them, her beloved Angel, her beloved Ella. That she had known any of them was cause for joy.

Sophie's heart and mind stretched in tandem to take in the love she was feeling. It washed over even the jerkiest boys of Chelsea, over the tough city itself, and finally, even onto Kishka. Because all of these people, these places, these phenomena, together they had built Sophie into the girl she was right then, they had given her the fantastically wonderful life she was living. No one and nothing could be pulled from the wild ball that was Sophie and her heart. She was lucky, so lucky, luckier than she had ever really known. It was as if the waters had washed away a film that had kept these truths from resonating, and now they echoed through her with a power that was almost disorienting.

"Jezda," Sophie breathed, trying to assimilate so much joy into her heart. "What this water does, it is what I am meant to do, to everyone."

The witch nodded her head, a bit of sadness in her face. "So it is, dearie." She could see in the girl the purity of inspiration, how she wanted to get to it *now*, share this bliss with the rest of the planet. And surely, she was meant to try. But others were meant to work against her, and Jezda was a simpler sort of witch, her vision limited, and no grand outcome was obvious to her right then. But the spray of the waters had affected even her, and a ghost of a heart hovered inside her and she hoped with all of it that this dear sweet girl would triumph, and that gloom would be lifted from all earth's creatures, even her, who held her gloom so tight she had made a practice of it.

From the trees behind the font waddled a new creature, green as the trees, stocky and strong, as if made from one strong muscle. It opened its mouth in greeting, and a bit of fire escaped its snout, licking the air. A pair of wings, webbed like a bat's, stretched upon its back as it plodded toward the witch who opened her arms cheerfully.

"Smok!" she greeted the dragon. He rubbed his scaly head into her lap, the way a dog or cat would, thought Sophie. "How's my boy?" Jezda reached deep into a pocket and pulled out a bone. "Fetch!" cried the witch, hurling it into the air with surprising force. Up leapt the dragon, his wings catching air, flapping, his eager neck reaching, reaching for the bone that landed in his jaws and vanished with a fiery *snap*.

"*Right*," Sophie nodded, breathless at the spectacle. "A dragon guards the fountain. Tadeusz told me."

"Poor Smok," Jezda shook her head. "He used to live down by the river, but once a month or so he'd eat someone." The witch shrugged. "He's a dragon. Finally one of the villagers tossed him a poisoned lamb and the dear crawled out here to die. I cared for him and brought him back to health. Partly with magic but mostly just herbs and water from the fountain."

The dragon landed upon the earth and crouched expectantly before the witch, who drew another bone from her garment and flung it high into the air.

"He is quite loyal to me for rescuing him. But I am loyal to him as well. It gets lonely out here for a witch. It's unusual to have friendly guests like you and your friend. Mostly people come here on dares, to try to slay me, return with my head or my heart for some prize. Smok is a good companion. I leave him by the waters and they have nice effect on his temperament. He becomes less fearsome. He eats woodland animals, roasts many for me to add to my stew." The witch paused. "Would you like to pet him?"

"Hmm," Sophie murmured, hesitating. "I mean, I probably shouldn't pass up the opportunity to pet a dragon."

"Surely not," Jezda grinned a toothsome grin. "Smok!" She held the dragon's face in her hands. "Go make a friend! Go see Sophie!"

The dragon regarded the girl with its yellowy eyes, then waddled in her direction, its fat tail flattening the grass in its wake. Sophie crouched to greet him. "Hello," she said. "Hello—"

"Smok," Jezda said cheerfully.

"Hello, Smok." Sophie cupped her hands and brought forth a bit of water from the fountain. She offered it to the dragon, who lapped it up, then rolled onto his back, wriggling on the ground, tiny flickers of fire escaping happily from his mouth.

"Pet his belly!" Jezda cried. "He loves it!" And so Sophie pet the dragon's belly, where the scales grew soft and pale. Smok's great, clawed paws rested gently in the air above him, and his long tongue lolled out of his fanged jaw, dangling in the dirt. Jezda joined them.

"Well, my dear," said the witch, "you have passed every test put forth, not only my tests but the test of my gate, of my home and dragon, and of the fountain itself. And now—"

Before her on the grass a wooden cart appeared, stocked with empty water jugs, heavy-bottomed, made of glass.

"Get to filling these," she instructed the girl. "And do not magic it. Work with the water, and work with the glass, which is blown from the sands that surround the Invisible."

Sophie moved toward the cart and touched the vessels, feeling for the profound sadness that marked those waters. "I can't feel anything," she said, and Jezda shook her head.

"The sand is neutral. It is more of a poetic spell. To fill the vessels of despair with the water of love. Fill them, and cork them, and bring them back to my hut. I will meet you there." The witch climbed into her mortar, and, rowing at the air with her pestle, disappeared above the trees.

Under Smok's watchful, golden eyes Sophie hefted a jug from the cart and waded into the pool. She held the glass beneath the water, she dipped its mouth toward the bubbling fountain, she splashed the liquid into it. All of it felt like play, like she was a child again, on a rare trip to the giant park in Boston, playing with the other children in the wide cement water fountain. Or in her own backyard, unraveling the green coil of the water hose, learning to squish her fingers into the tip so that the water sprayed into the air, making tiny rainbows and soaking her clothes. Sophie didn't know how much time passed this way, but when the jugs were full she wished for more, for another cart and then another. How lovely it would be to remain here with the witch, working by the fountain of life! She lay down in the shallow pool, the water coursing around her as it ran off into the woods in a tiny stream. Pure, radiant bliss.

A belch from Smok snapped her out of it, a fireball shot into the sky followed by the stink of charred meat. The beast batted a bashful eye at Sophie, who laughed. "I suppose it's time to go," she said, and rose from the waters. Leaving would have made her sad, if the fountain weren't making her so happy. She blew the spring a kiss. "Au revoir!" Sophie reconsidered. "*Do widzenia.*"

She turned to the cart, lifted its rope, and—nothing. Perhaps the vehicle shuddered slightly at the effort, but the wheels did not budge. She regarded the many jugs, thick and heavy. All full of water, wet and heavy.

Sophie giggled. "Really?" she asked Smok. "I can't magic this? I have to roll this all the way back to Jezda's?" The dragon drooped his eyes sleepily and chuffed a small puff of smoke before curling his long tail around himself and hunkering down for a snooze in the grass. Sophie sighed.

She supposed there could be good reason for her to *not* magic herself and her bundles back to the spinning chicken hut. Perhaps it was the witch's final test for her. Perhaps she had been so busy fine-tuning her magical aspects she'd neglected her human side, the very body meant to carry and conduct so much magic. Sophie figured this was true. All along, at every turn, her magic had been strong. It was only her body that had failed her, that fleshy, mortal thing. Sophie took a deep breath. She returned to the fountain for one final drink, one final dunk of her head, one final splash to her face. The optimism rolled from her skin in rivulets. "Let's do this," she said, and with one massive pull, began to roll the cart.

*   *   *

BY THE TIME Sophie could spy the revolution of color through the trees, by the time she heard the faint clacking of claws and smelled the terrible smell of the witch's cottage, she was busted. Her muscles burned and tore with the struggle forward. Her feet were crusted with dirt and poked sorely with pebbles. Her shoulders ached as if they carried the sun, the moon, and the earth upon them. She was no longer soaked in the waters of life but in her own salty, slightly funky sweat. Stray hairs stuck wetly to her face, tickling her, driving her so crazy she decided the first thing she would do upon reaching Jezda's would be to cut it all off. Maybe even shave it.

As she approached Jezda's gate the arc of teeth clicked and clacked and the bones flung open to welcome her. She heaved her last heave, pulling the cart into the yard, and the gate swung shut with a clatter. The chicken's feet stilled and the house's mouth opened, unfurling its long red tongues. Down slid Jezda, and behind her, Tadeusz.

"My dear girl," Jezda beamed. She pulled from her skirts a cloth moistened with an herbal brew and mopped Sophie down, her hot, hot head, her sore arms and legs. She picked the pebbles from the soles of her feet and washed the forest from her. Tadeusz smiled at her widely. Sophie thought that it felt like forever since they had seen one another, and her heart surged happily at the sight of him.

"Wow," he said simply, shaking his head so his glasses skidded down his nose. "I couldn't have done that."

"You would if you had to," Sophie said simply, opening her mouth to accept the hunk of salt the witch had pulled from a pouch on her belt.

"Very good," Jezda nodded. "Very good for you to know you had to. Good for you to feel your body, feel your strengths and its limitations." A tin was pulled from her skirts, and within it shone a disc of salve that Jezda scooped into her hands and massaged into Sophie's aching muscles.

"I know," Sophie said, nodding. "I understood." And as bad as she felt, she felt good, too. It was a good feeling, this worn-out pride. She flexed her muscles at Tadeusz and grinned. "Look, I'm so buff!"

"Now, to bring this home, back to your castle, you must use magic. Too dangerous to pull it through the city, with all the people, the cracked sidewalks, the officers and dogs and cars and whatnot. Too many possibilities for disaster. So, you magic it back to the cellar, where the salt and the water come together. You know this place?"

Sophie nodded. "Of course."

"Okay. I leave you to figure it out. Tadeusz and I will return in my mortar."

"Really?" the boy yelped with excitement.

"Certainly," she nodded.

"Oh, but I dislike heights," he remembered, his face falling. "I almost forgot."

"Forget again," quipped the witch.

"What do you mean?"

"Forget you dislike heights. Remember your love of heights."

"Okay," the boy said, confused. "But I—"

"Would you like a little help?" Jezda offered.

"Would that be okay? It's not cheating?"

"Witches are here to help," the old woman nodded, and quick as a flash found a pocket of dust in her skirts and flung a fist of it onto the boy. Swiftly they were in her mortar, rising into the sky.

"How wonderful!" cried Tadeusz, watching the forest grow wider and wider beneath him, spotting the Vistula winding like molten silver through Warsaw, even picking out their castle sitting grandly on its banks.

"You can't beat the view," Jezda agreed, pushing her pestle behind her, and they were off.

Chapter 20

Sophie sat in the chicken-scratched dirt outside the witch's house for quite some time, trying to conjure the best way to transport herself and the bottles and bottles of the waters of life back to the castle. Then she realized she was overthinking it. She seated herself uncomfortably atop the corked jugs, held the rope wound in her fists, sang a *zawolanie,* and found herself in the exact same configuration in the salt caves at the bottom of the castle. She ran her hand over the smooth, solid glass. The bottles were fine, not a crack nor a chink, no leaks. Sophie recalled the perfect feeling of being immersed in the water, and longed to tug free a cork and splash some pure happiness onto her face, but she did not. Like the salt walls that surrounded her, these jugs were meant to help her when she needed it most.

Sophie sat in the quiet, knowing that her life would not stay quiet for long. If she had learned anything since a mermaid swam into Chelsea

Creek, it was that. She thought back to the idea she'd had back at Jezda's tree, that a place, a city like Chelsea, might have its own heart to enter. The thought excited her, but it scared her, because it tempted her to walk inside the city's heart and she did not know if she wanted to visit such a place. But what she wanted and what she was meant to do were no longer the same things, if they had ever been. Sophie propped herself up against the jugs filled with the waters of the fountain of life and closed her eyes. She gave a push. And she was inside Chelsea.

The heart of a place is so different from the heart of a person. As people are made of so much dense red, so much muscle and bone, so their hearts feel that way, too. But cities have airy, dusty hearts, with weather and lights. A grit like glitter paved the streets of Chelsea's heart, it sparkled in the light of an ever-present moon, of a million miniature moons glowing from within street lamps, waxing and waning, the lamps' glow rising and falling like breath. And the heart of the city *did* breathe, Sophie stood inside its inhales and exhales, feeling the gentle winds fluff at her hair and cool her. It was warm, this place, and Sophie had the feeling that it always was, no matter how much snow lay upon its streets. Chelsea was hot-hearted. Its winds began to feel less like breath and more like an airy tide, a push and pull, push and pull. Sophie marveled at this place, where so many people from so many lands had been desperate to come. To come to and get out of, was that the tide pulled by this city's many moons? So many immigrants landing here with hope in their hearts, and the city was here for them, but then how the people ached to leave the city and climb deeper into the wide, wide world. Sophie felt a surge of love for Chelsea and the toughness people had brought along, packed into their steamer trunks and nylon suitcases, so many people over so many centuries, the toughest of the tough, to be able to leave the devil they knew and travel so precariously, to travel alongside death, for Sophie knew with a deep certainty how many had died along their journeys. There were the people who came, desperate, driven from their lands by poverty and greed and war and starvation. There were the people who were taken, shackled and sold, kidnapped, tortured; somehow they had found their way to Chelsea, or their children did, with all their parents' suffering etched upon their synapses. There were the people who were there at the beginning, infusing the land with their toughness, their ability to endure, and taking from the very earth of the place the land's own endurance. All who had ever been there had been a tough people and the city's heart was full of their trials and their survival. Tough people who had come together with other tough people and bred stones upon the town.

Sophie's heart softened and softened as she watched the city's heart calcify around her. It was like the sadness, she thought, it was one and the same, the toughness was a good thing, but it had grown out of balance and it was in Sophie's hands to restore it to its initial, noble strength, the strength of long winters and hungry bellies and hope. Of heat lightning that made night into day for but a minute, the noble strength of storms that whipped in wetly off the waters and called the townspeople to meet its fierceness. Sophie, who had always felt outside her town, now felt so deeply, unmistakably *of* it, its daughter, the electricity from its street lights running through her body, her blood nothing but the hot, molten glass of a million smashed bottles. Her mouth was wet with creek water. She knew then that not any girl could be what she was, and it was not a coincidence that she was born of this place. It had shaped her, and given her its magic. She felt it in her heart, and held it close there until she understood she didn't need to. For the city's ragged magic *was* her heart.

SOPHIE LEFT HER city's heart and sat quietly in the bottom of the castle. Her own heart beat differently within her, now that she understood of what it was made.

Smiling, she gathered herself to climb the stairs back to her quarters when a great splash sounded in the waters behind her. She spun around to see Syrena poking her ebony-tangled head above the dark waters, her white face like a crystal of salt, luminous in the dark. Her heart split open and she rushed to the edge.

"Syrena!" she cried. "Syrena, Syrena, Syrena!" The girl leapt into the water to better hug the creature, wrapping her human legs around her tail, burying her face in her epic snarl of hair.

"Okay, okay!" the mermaid cried. "I only away from you, what, a week? Calm down, I swear!"

Sophie let go of the mermaid and clambered back onto the salt ledge, kicking her feet in the water happily.

"I really really really *really really* missed you!" Sophie exploded.

"Let me guess," Syrena said dryly. "You find the waters of life. They make you little goofy, no?"

"Yeah," Sophie shrugged. "But I also just really really missed you!"

"How about Tadeusz," Syrena said. "He not good friend?"

"Tadeusz is a very good friend," Sophie nodded solemnly, as befitting Tadeusz's own solemn nature.

"And your friends, those pigeons. They fly all the way here from Chelsea. Is that not good friends?"

"The best," Sophie said. "I couldn't believe it when I saw them. That they would come so far for me. And the Polish pigeons, they're really great, too."

"Indeed," said Syrena. "Our pigeons are among the greatest, most noble pigeons anywhere."

"I believe it."

"And you make new friends, ya?"

"Do you mean the witch? Jezda?" Sophie considered the old woman, her strange ways and moods. "Yes," she decided. "I think Jezda is a great new friend. And her dragon Smok, too. And even her house. I became very close to that chicken, for a moment."

Syrena shuddered. "I only hear the stories. Not for me, a giant chicken. But I glad you have friends, Sophie. You need many friends, as many as you can get."

"Okay," Sophie said. "Those girls? The three girls? They're my friends, too?"

"Certainly."

"But you," Sophie said. "You are my best friend. My very best non-human friend in the entire world."

"World big place," Syrena said with a little smile. "You been to much of it now, yeah, but still even more you never see."

"Nobody could be a better friend than you," said Sophie, and again a tiny smile played at the edges of the mermaid's mouth.

"Is good," she nodded. "Is very good, Sophie. You my best friend as well. Best non-mermaid friend."

Sophie felt hot tears sting her eyes, and a feeling in her body like she was standing with one foot in the waters of life and one foot in the Invisible. Such a strange feeling to love so greatly, such a happy sadness!

Sophie searched for the words to put to her emotions when a commotion occurred behind her. She turned to find a procession funneling out from the narrow stairwell: Tadeusz, with the laptop tucked under his arm. Jezda, her skirts dragging dirtily on the ground. And pigeons. Pigeons and pigeons and pigeons and pigeons. Arthur stepped forward first, his wounded foot proud before him. Giddy and Roy snuggled up close, peeking at Sophie almost shyly between their feathers. The knowledgeable Loosha, eyes trained sternly oo the ground, not looking at Sophie. The air in the cave felt charged with something powerful and mysterious, something teetering. The birds were jostled with a fluttering of feathers, and Bix moved to the front, the only one of them to look Sophie dead in the eye.

"*How hard it is to smile again, to green, to spring, to the sun,*" he began.

"*We, the girls of bitter mouths, us girls on the shoulders of longing, / For we know that our own people will come back sometime...*" The bird gave a deep bow in Tadeusz's direction. "Krystyna Krahelska. Of course."

"What's up, you guys?" Sophie asked uneasily. "I mean, I'm happy to see you. But—what's up?"

The pack of them, human and bird, shuffled and looked at the ground. It was Syrena, on the outskirts, half submerged in the river, who spoke.

"Is time, Sophia," was all she said.

Chapter 21

Deep in the bowels of the castle, in some far-back part of the old salt mine, a shallow pit had been dug into the gray salt floor. It looked oddly like a snow angel to Sophie, little tufts of sand fluffing like snow around its edges. It *was* sort of angel-shaped. Girl-shaped. Sophie-shaped.

"Who did this?" she asked, and Tadeusz raised his hand, sheepish in the glare of anyone's attention, as usual. Sophie smiled thinking of noodly Tadeusz with a shovel or pickax, digging into the solid ground.

"Well—thank you?" she laughed nervously.

"We helped as much as we could," Arthur said regretfully. "But it was mostly a human job."

"They were great company," Tadeusz said quickly. "All the pigeons. They really kept my spirits up. I'm not so great at digging."

"I'm supposed to lie down here?" Sophie asked, but it wasn't really a question. She knew when she laid eyes on it that it was a little salt bed to hold her. *Salt grave*, some dark part of her brain worried. *Salt grave.*

"We want you to be as enclosed in salt as you can safely be," Tadeusz explained. "You will need to move some, and breathe of course. And we need to get to you, to care for you and feed you salt. To give you the waters. Whatever we have to do."

"So, you guys are all going to be here?" Sophie asked. A hundred pigeon heads bobbed *yes*.

"This is what we came here for," Giddy cooed sweetly. "This moment. To be with you."

Together Jezda and Tadeusz hefted a glass jug from the cart. The witch tugged the cork while Tadeusz caught his breath. Sophie tried not to laugh, then realized that laughter was exactly what the somber moment needed. She let out a belly laugh that made the witch smile. Tadeusz allowed a tiny, good-natured smirk.

"It's better to have a strong mind," Sophie said. "And yours is the strongest."

"No, Sophie," the boy said, intensity pulling the smile from his face. "Mine cannot be the strongest. Yours has to be. Please, do not even joke. It's not time for joking now." He took his trembling bottom lip in his teeth and chewed. Behind them, where the dark mine dropped into the Vistula, Syrena slapped the waters impatiently.

"I too far away!" she hollered. "Do not like missing jokes, missing everything!"

"Patience, fishy one!" Jezda cackled. "Let me set up the girl, then we will see about bringing you onto land."

Jezda tipped the jug into the ditch, filling it halfway with the waters of life. She motioned to the girl to get in, and Sophie laid herself down in the space.

"Oooh!" she cooed like the happiest pigeon in the world. "I would not have imagined that the waters lacked anything, but add some salt to it and—oh my god!" Sophie tilted her cheek to the wet and slurped some of it. An indescribable joy filled her heart, bubbled up into her brain, and frothed into her belly. She closed her eyes to savor the feeling.

"We will all be here," Tadeusz said, a promise and a fact. "Taking care of you throughout it all."

Sophie opened her eyes and was pleasantly startled to see the elegant, ageless face of the mermaid gazing down at her.

"You're out of the water!" Sophie laughed, like it was a marvelous joke. "You will be okay?"

"Of course. I am right by water. My tail get a little dry, no big deal. I oil it later." Her thin fingers with their opalescent fingernails reached out and stroked Sophie's face. "I be here to sing to you. Care for you. My sweet Sophia." The love in the mermaid's eyes was gorgeous to Sophie, and fascinating. She stared deep into the cool, silver orbs.

"Syrena, I love you very much."

The mermaid smiled a tight smile, a sad smile. "I love you too, *dziewczyna*."

Sophie reached up, her hands wet with salty water, and pushed the mermaid's wide mouth into a smile. "I'm coming for you first, Syrena," she joked, giddiness coursing through her.

"You better not," the mermaid said. "Remember last time you try to steal my sadness? Disaster!"

"I've gotten much better," Sophie promised.

A flock of pigeons clattered forward, tugging a large cloth sack in their collective beaks

"Thank you," Tadeusz said, receiving it. "Just keep bringing them, please."

"And if we run out?" asked a bird.

"I will be digging out more."

"Oy. Best hope we do not need more." The mermaid lifted a skeptical eyebrow.

"He's stronger than he looks," Sophie assured her. "We all are."

Tadeusz opened the heavy sack of salt and began packing it around Sophie. It dissolved slightly in the water, creating a slush that Sophie wriggled around in. "This feels *amazing*." She tilted her head to the side and slurped in a mouthful. "This is the very best I have ever felt in my entire life."

Sophie's friends, the boy and the witch and the mermaid, exchanged concerned looks, as did the flocks of pigeons, cooing amongst themselves.

"Is very good," Syrena said, nodding. "Means now time for starting."

*   *   *

SOPHIE SANK INTO the salty sludge, enjoying the heavy sensation of the wet crystals both weighing her down and floating her in her dugout. The vibrations of the waters filled her with love. She closed her eyes and felt a heavy, salt-soaked cloth being placed over it. After a moment she lost the feeling of being in a cellar, surrounded by friends. She was floating in utter darkness, the void of outer space, and was delighted to learn that instead of containing nothing it contained *everything*. Sophie could feel infinite joy, the specific infinite joy of a billion babies born, the joy of the people who birthed them receiving them into the world. The quieter joy of the enjoyment of food, or a close snuggle with a loved one, a parent, a puppy. All the major and minor joys of life coursed through her. The exhilaration of a ride on a roller coaster or a trip on the tip of a wave. The shimmering curtain of inspiration as it hits an artist, a poet, a painter, and envelops them, Sophie felt it just as it touched down within them. The selfless joy of watching those you love find a happiness, the way it lights its own mirror happiness within them, Sophie felt it. She felt the terror-joy of relief, people learning that something terrible had not happened after all, the bubbling font of gratitude that burst up into them, coming out through the tops of their heads. The simple, powerful joys of the smallest humans as they encountered first after first—first time standing on trembling legs, first wobbly step taken, first time understanding that a *sound* matched a *thing*. The joy of language taking root in them like a virus. Somewhere beneath this onslaught of feeling Sophie wondered how, when, did these experiences stop being joys. On the outskirts of her emotions was a whole other landscape; its shores were a numbness that thawed into increasingly terrible sensations. Sophie instinctively turned away from it, veering back to the wide bubble of joy that had illuminated her. But no. This was where she was meant to go. It was the place she was drifting toward, magnetized toward. She thought of the other girls, three of them, somewhere, doing what she was doing, and imagined stretching her hands through the darkness toward them. With a jolt like an electrical charge that ran up her arms, she could feel herself connect to them.

Chapter 22

Hello, Sophie communicated to them, wordless, drifting. She understood that part of her was lying in a ditch in a cellar in Poland, but this other part of her was elsewhere, able to reach into a simultaneous beyond she didn't quite comprehend. But that was okay: comprehension apparently wasn't required. Only this reaching feeling, thoughts that became their own actions.

Yaho, Sophie felt Isabelle greet her. Instinctively the girls swam into each other's hearts. Sophie understood Isabelle was buried in salty sand by the ocean in Japan, on an ancient salt farm. She was being tended to by a flock of zebra doves who had followed her from Hawaii, elegant birds with thin stripes on their feathers and electric blue rings around their eyes. Her witch, the Kitsune-mochi, meditated beside her, a fox curled in her lap. Isabelle's *ningyo* crouched beside her in the salty earth, so different from Sophie's mermaid! While her hair was long and dark and wild like Syrena's, and their tails were both sleek and powerful, the *ningyo* had long arms like a monkey's, covered with the same shining, golden scales that rippled the light on her tail. Fins feathered out above her ears, and a single tall fin rose along her back, from the nape of her neck to her tailbone. Sophie could have stared at this fascinating creature forever, but she understood it was not the time for such wonders. Sophie and Isabelle lingered in each other's hearts. She could feel Isabelle fighting off Michi, replenishing herself, being replenished by her team. She could also feel her softness and doubts, her true despair at the presence of so much pain in the world.

Sophie knew she owed her friends a magic. A Chelsea magic. What was a Chelsea magic, what could it be? When she thought of Chelsea she thought of grit and grime, her beloved pigeons and their sooty feathers. She thought of the library, the grand gray building and its wide steps, the old, yellow scent of books that invigorated her when the doors closed behind her. The safest place in Chelsea. The place where she could relax. So many things she learned under the warm lights, seated at a broad wooden table. Just as much she learned from the cracked concrete sidewalks, from the pigeons, from the boys who menaced her.

Intuitively, Sophie gathered it all together. The oily grime from the pigeons' iridescent wings. The crumble of long-pulverized side-walk, ground to dust. Pages from library books so old the nearly brown paper crumbled at the thought of touching it. The crumbs went into the magic, along with their beautiful smell, the smell of wisdom, of aging. Sophie shot it through with one electrifying bolt of fear, the essence of the anxiety so many in Chelsea felt. It kept you on your toes. You learned something from it, a good or bad lesson it was hard to say, maybe both. The only thing Sophie knew was that it was a knowledge. And her magic was a magic. And it was all she had to offer her sisters.

Sisters, Sophie thought, with a slight pang of betrayal. She had a sister, wasting away in a toxic garden in a toxic trailer in a toxic dump. Sophie reached out and into the bewildered, corrupt heart of her terribly innocent twin, and pulled out something essential. An innocence that remained beneath all else. She thanked her oblivious sister, and

tears came to her eyes. They went into the magic, too. The recipe was complete.

Yes! Isabelle cried as Sophie's magic swept through her. *Wow! I knew it, I knew it! And it's so you! Thank you, Sophie!*

Sophie could feel her magic invigorating the girl, healing her, affirming the fight inside her. *I needed this!*

So did I, Sophie smiled, and left. Sophie stretched out into the girl called Pipaluk, who had walked into the Arctic Ocean where it lapped icily at the shore of her town, Barrow, Alaska. Pipaluk's mermaid had brought her to Greenland, to a desolated town on the coast of the frozen island, an abandoned mine. Sophie entered Pipaluk's heart hesitantly, an icicle chamber, cold and hard, but shining and sharp. The Cryolite, the rare crystal that opened her heart and honed her intuition, gave her interior a toxic glow. Slowly Sophia waded into Pipaluk, her awe at the girl growing as she learned from her the lessons of the Cryolite, smooth and white, invisible in the water, streaked with spidery yellow cracks that sickened. Like humans, Sophie thought, so much of their luster shot through with sadness and pain. The Cryolite was a tough stone to work with, much trickier than salt, simple salt so eager to dissolve into you, to feed you its magic. Such a tough stone took a tough guide. Sophie could feel the mermaid Syrena called Arna, Arnakuagsak, the first mermaid, the one whose tears had given water its first salt. Who had created sea animals with the flesh of her body, her fingers chopped from her hands by the human father who had betrayed her so many millennia ago. Sophie learned that Pipaluk did know the powers of the salt, fed from the tears of her mermaid familiar; how Arna wept into the girl's face when the poison in the Cryolite overwhelmed her. She would do it all night, as they huddled together in the abandoned Cryolite mine in the Greenland ghost town. Pipaluk had a flock of snowy owls that had followed her from Alaska. She had her witch, the Witch Thorbjorg, adorned in stones, with pouches of magic around her waist. The Witch Thorbjorg sang a magic spell, the *varolokur*, like a *zawolanie* but different. And Arna, mother of all the witches, her fingerless hands, her wizened face lined with the etchings of time and the ink of her people, tattoos that arced up her cheekbones and down her brow. Pipaluk and Sophie hovered within each other's hearts, trading secrets of Cryolite and salt, of owls and pigeons.

I have magic for you, Sophie said, and gifted Pipaluk with her Chelsea brew. Inside the girl's heart, she felt it both harden and soften as it pumped the magic through her. It would give her what she needed, whatever it was. It would stay with her throughout their battle. Sophie felt proud, proud of her city's magic essence, which had unknowingly fed her all this time; proud of her friend Pipaluk, working her own hard magic, fighting her portion of the fight in this hardscrabble place. She offered the girl her love, and moved on.

Sophie reached out to her last sister, Lesia.

The African mermaid Mami Wata had come for Lesia where she lived in St. Martin, and together they swam to Africa, reversing the route that Lesia's ancestors had taken so many years ago, enslaved on a hulking ship, stolen from their village in Ghana. It was this village

Mami Wata had returned Lesia to, to the basement of a castle in the town of Elmina, where salt had long been extracted with the help of the burning sun. Like Sophie, Lesia rested in a room of salt, her flock of ground doves rustling their small bodies around her. Her witch, Obayifo, crouched beside her, her body wrapped in the torn skins of animals, marked with tattoos and emitting an eerie phosphorescence that lent a greenish glow to the salt room. As Sophie entered Lesia's heart she could feel the other girls there as well, and realized they were all in one another's hearts, in their minds and spirits, strengthening and encouraging each other. En-*couraging*, Sophie thought. Giving each other the courage they needed to do it, finally, this thing they'd all been training for, taken by mermaids and assisted by their winged friends, tested by witches and educated in the ways of helpful crystals and their own dormant powers. Together, the girls rested, briefly. With one foot in the world of the Polish castle and the stream of healing water being poured gently on her brow and the other in her sisters' hearts she felt a vibration rise inside her and she knew what it meant as it grew. She had to act fast.

Sophie cast her magic onto Lesia without introduction, causing Lesia to gasp and laugh. *Sorry!* Sophie said. *I just can feel—I can feel it. It's starting. Can you feel it?* There was a whirring within and without her. It felt like she might be torn from herself and flung out into the universe if she didn't take care to remain connected to her heart. Something like electricity danced upon her skin and made its way into her mind. Sophie thought and felt sparks. It was exhilarating. She laughed wildly.

I can feel it, too! Lesia cried, and Sophie could feel the others in their own knowing. *And this is just the shot I needed! Your magic is potent, Sophie! Wow!* She could feel Lesia's wild energy flickering around her, extra electric, brightened from the Chelsea magic.

It will stay with you, Sophie offered.

It sure will!

From within their shared heart, Sophie heard Pipaluk speak, her voice strong, and so filled with energy she thought it might burst, showering them with her essence.

Now, the girl spoke, giving the others chills. *It's time to fight.*

Chapter 22

Sophie began with those closest to her heart. Sophie felt herself enter her mother, Angel, and Ella as if magnetized to their darkly swirling interiors, as if plunging into a sinkhole, as if she had no choice. Once inside them she felt their pains and sadness, their hopeless places, their regrets, the soft parts that had been so chafed they grew calluses, patches hard as stone. Sophie felt their heaviness come into her, flood her body, and pass through into the salt earth beneath her. It entered the purifying stone and was gone. Sophie felt something buoyant like a bird fly from her heart—*yes!* This was how she would do it. It was as natural as walking, as eating, as commanding the waters to carry her through oceans. It was what she was built to do.

Sophie fell into the next group of people, then the next, then the next. It was as if people's spirits had caught wind of what was happening; Sophie could feel them gathering around her, an astral cloud that grew larger and larger, a swarm or galaxy. It would make her nervous to think about it, all these amorphous heart-places needing to be cleared, but she kept her courage focused and entered each spirit, one and then another, and then another, until they ceased being individuals, morphing into a landscape of tragedy that Sophie swept away as she passed, ducking deeply here and there as needed, always feeling the precious sadnesses, the sacred sadnesses that kept lost ones alive in the heart. Those she touched lightly with love as she passed, sliding through hearts as if through intricate tunnels of light and dark. She could do this forever, she understood, and it could take that long, couldn't it? Perhaps it had taken that long already. Time had turned into a haze, like something of a sunset in the distance, pretty to ponder but not very useful here. The ever-present tang of salt on her tongue, the watery weight of thick salt water upon her, these tactile sensations began to recede also as Sophie tunneled deeper and deeper into humanity's rocky interiors.

As Sophie purified these many hearts, so did Isabelle and Pipaluk and Lesia do the same. And back in the world of humans, people stopped in their tracks, woke in their beds, halted as they ate their breakfasts and lunches and dinners, a new understanding of their lives cracking over their heads, pouring into them like liquid sunshine. Something within them had broken, something they hadn't even known was there, and in its place bubbled a new feeling, gorgeous, like hope but rounder, a sensation that rendered even the sweetest hope obsolete because now there was nothing to hope for. Everything was here, everything was correct, everything was beautiful. Tiny tears of gratitude spritzed the corners of eyes and dried there. And the energy of these people, their hearts newly emptied of depression and anger and terrible longings, their energies rose up into the ether and helped the girls and their mermaids and witches and birds in the golden effort of clearing ever more hearts, and more and more.

Sophie felt herself at the bottom of the sea again, the lights of the luminescent creatures flashing against her eyelids. The unapproachable font that leached there, Sophie felt it. A razor-sharp shimmer, the bleeding edge of all pain cutting into this world, floating into the waters, evaporating and raining back down, drunk up by every living thing. *Maybe it's supposed to be this way*, Sophie thought as she drifted closer to the tremble. Like any mineral, like any element. Perhaps it is a true part of this world, perhaps even truer than most, perhaps, perhaps, perhaps. A weight came down on Sophie's chest, heavier than the salt bath her caretakers tended, a weight that crushed from the inside as the Invisible whispered its terrible truths to her.

It was older than the universe. It had been here before the psychedelic cataclysm that had led to all of this—fish and trees and spiders and humans, dogs and flowers and crystals and algae. Life. It was older than life and if life wanted to live it would have to live among this darkness. Was it such a terrible price to pay? Sophie wondered. Life was still good, was it not? The fish still glittered and the trees smelled good. The spiders' webs dazzled and the humans did their best and experienced joy, most of them anyway, some of the time at least. Why did anyone think they were entitled to more?

In a space free of time Sophie spent an eternity thinking these thoughts, floating around the Invisible's seductive spring. Sophie could stop this. She could cease this terrible effort. Everything, everyone, would be okay. And Sophie, she especially would be okay. Sophie was *magic*. She would always be fine in this place, regardless of how many wars sprung up, how many terrible things one human did to another. No matter how many scrawny children went to bed hungry. No matter how many parents went to bed crying for not being able to feed their scrawny children. No matter how many individuals languished in jail cells, chained to walls for having done nothing at all, born into the wrong time and place. No matter how many people lay in beds suffering sicknesses that needn't exist, if only this chemical or that chemical hadn't been created, Sophie saw how the chemicals created money that created freedom and beauty for some, and Sophie was like that some, but more so, for she was magic, and her grandmother was Kishka, a being more akin to an element, as natural as weather, a wind blowing through the universe, blowing her kiss onto Sophie.

Sophie was vaguely conscious of the heaviness of her chest growing denser, denser. The weight of salt upon her grew, the salt tumbled in tiny avalanches onto her face, her mouth stuffed with more salt than she could chew, it melted on her tongue and ran steadily down her throat, a subterranean river. She could not speak with so much salt in her mouth, could not get the breath to speak with the crystalline heap weighing in her lungs, if only she could, she would tell them to stop, the boy and the witch, those terrible birds, those filthy birds, *rats with wings,* and the mermaid, she would tell them all to stop, it was useless, to try to divide their hearts from this ancient heavy energy was useless. It was meant to crush them. The people, the children and the mothers and the men on the battlefields, the prisoners and the sick ones, the rich ones and the poor ones, they were all meant to be crushed.

But not you, my dearie, soothed the familiar voice. *Not you, not I.* It was Kishka, her grandmother. It felt good to be near something familiar. Sophie's own blood ran with the same stuff that made Kishka; she could feel something inside her ring with recognition. It felt good, a sort of joy. Sophie flashed on the joy, the pure joy, she had felt in the fountain of life. Somewhere above her, people who loved her dumped its waters onto her. Fools.

Exactly, Kishka cooed. Sophie could feel Kishka like a wind inside her, blowing her thoughts where she wanted them to be. The fountain of life. *You think you liked that, do you, dearie?* Of course Sophie did. The blissful, pure happiness. Some other part of Sophie, far away from her now, seemed to cry out at the memory of it. She felt a responsibility. She had to help people know that joy.

Oh, no you don't, Kishka snapped impatiently. *Forget that foolishness. What you* need *to do is help me bring the dark matter to that place. Replace the waters.* Then *I can truly thrive, my dearie! Ancient law prevents me from approaching it, but not you, my little girl. You have been there already. You can feel the darkness, can't you?*

I can, thought Sophie, swirling in it.

Think, Kishka hissed. *Go deep. Under the sands, beneath the earth. Pull the Invisible into the font. Contaminate it. That is all you need to do.*

That's all? Sophie wondered. *All this has been about—that? Just pull some of that—stuff—into the water of life? That's it?*

I told you you were making too big a deal of it, Kishka clucked. *Do your Nana one favor, why don't you? It's for your own good as well, you know. If I have everything you know I'll share a little with you.*

A dark glory bloomed in the distance, and it was Sophie's fate. She was moving toward it, through a web of threads that tried to pull her back from it. She could live there forever, in the dark heart of the universe. How it glowed, the closer she came to it! It seemed as though everything, every conceivable thing that existed and didn't exist whorled around this portal, an empty space that pulsed as if alive. As if more alive than anything Sophie had ever beheld. And though some caving part of Sophie's intelligence screamed out that this *thing,* this heart was certainly the cosmic source of the Invisibles on planet Earth, it was hard for Sophie to really hear it—or believe it? Or care?—with the lulling effect the rhythmic pulses had on her. This didn't send gloom over her, fill her with dread, or push her toward tears like that strange underwater flicker had. No, this energy calmed her, even as it filled her with a new and terrible inspiration, an energy that fed thoughts to her mind on tiny whispers.

Everything is as it should be, Sophie thought, or the thing thought for her. Either way was fine with Sophie; the thought felt *nice,* so nice, even as it was linked with so many flashes of suffering. What could any of that matter out here? *Meant to be, meant to be, meant to be*: the phrase took the form of a little song that Sophie hummed as she watched the ancient pulse inside the fiery tear at the center of all. Eventually she knew that she was not even seeing the fierce flames anymore; the primordial glow had burned her eyes. All she saw was the imprint of the glow on her scorched retinas.

You're going to go blind! A shrill, anxious thought, a last gasp before Sophie's old mind collapsed. She didn't need to see anyway. She could feel the pulse with every bit of her body, with her aura; whatever magic she carried on her was now tuned into this portal, and as she began to make her way toward it she could feel the centrifugal suck of it, the radioactive burn. Soon she would be one with the beating heart of the entire universe. What were eyes in the face of that?

Not heart, a voice broke through. *Not heart,* it echoed in a different voice. *Not heart.* It interfered with the mantra of *meant to be, meant to be* that had been swirling around Sophie's mind, simple yet mesmerizing. *Not heart, not heart, not heart!* Sophie felt herself distracted from the cocoon of sensation that had bedazzled her. She felt the heat of the portal intensify, but her eyes were shot with odd colors. Where was she? Was she moving? The fine hair on her arms began to singe.

You are the heart, you are the heart, you are the heart. The chant thudded against her like a drumbeat. She tried to pull away from the heat, the heat was making everything so difficult, it was hard to move, to see anything, hard to think. Think, think, think, Sophie needed to think. She closed her eyes and saw the outline of a million suns imploding seared onto the back of her lids.

We are the heart, we are the heart, we are the heart.

The chant kept changing, some voices going up, some down, some voices sounding choked with sorrow, others filled with joy.

It was the mermaids she saw first, as if in a vision. An army of them, their dizzying styles of tail and fin, their hair long or shorn, filled with trash or filled with ornament. They shone and they stomped, they waved their weapons. In the middle was Syrena, her mermaid, her narwhal tusk plunged into the air like calling down magic from the heavens.

The heat had lessened. Her mind struggled to remember something, something important. *We are the heart, we are the heart, we are the heart.*

SOPHIE! It was a cry as big as the world, and it took almost everything out of Isabelle to have made it. But it worked. Pipaluk and Lesia emanated shock and respect at the small girl's huge voice. And Sophie's own eyes widened at the sight of her, collapsed and crying. She rustled through herself for her Chelsea magic but couldn't find it. The girl brought her tear-streaked face up to Sophie, strands of long, glossy hair plastered to her face.

Sophie, WE are the heart. The heart of the universe. We are the universe's heart! That is Kishka!

And like a spell that names something, thus sucking away its power, Sophie looked to the blinding flare and saw instead a dragon's head, fire smoldering from its mouth, growing weaker, weaker, until in a flash of brilliance it collapsed upon itself, a star dying.

You're okay! Isabella cheered.

Are you? worried Lesia. *Are you okay?I think so,* Sophie said, a bit dazed, but growing clear. *You guys saved my life.*

Get it together, said Pipaluk sternly. *You let Grandmother in like that again and your whole quarter of humanity will be* gone. *Like* that. Sophie heard the crack of trees breaking in half as Pipaluk snapped her fingers. The sound bounced through her body, and she felt a wave of such fear and relief she cried out, then cried.

No time, Pipaluk said. *Get back to it. You are stronger now, for having been through it. Use it.*

She wants the fountain, she told the girls. *The fountain of life. She wants to divert the Invisible to flow through it.*

We have fountains to protect as well, Isabella shared. *She is doing the same with us all.*

She could strike us all as she struck Sophie, Pipaluk said darkly. *Be ready. Keep our hearts close.* And Sophie felt her heart swell, drawing near her sisters in this place beyond time, beyond space.

Sophie returned to her work, pulling strands of the Invisible's energy from the places it had lodged in humankind. And as she continued, methodically, lost in the beautiful rhythm of her work, so the hearts she rescued joined her, and in this way her army grew, and so grew the armies of her sisters, all of them with a growing flock of humans at their side, their simple, strong human magic buttressing the efforts of the magic girls, the whole world working together to clear the ancient energy of the Invisible, to shrink it back into the void, to tip the balance toward joy again.

We can't kill it, Sophie realized, speaking aloud to the other girls.

In that way it spoke the truth, Pipaluk agreed. *It is meant to be here. It is part of this place. But it is not meant to be so mighty.*

The girls hung together quietly, each considering the work they had done, each pushing and pressing on themselves—was it *enough?* Had they done *enough?* In the sudden stillness an ache and weariness that were incomprehensible filled them. *This is what the creator felt like after they created the world*, Sophie thought briefly. She longed to sleep the sleep of a planet, turning softly in space for millennia. But beyond her exhaustion, somewhere out there, was a tickle of joy. A pure, new, buoyant joy.

I think this is as small as it gets, Lesia mused. A bead in the vastness of space, but of such a weight that it ripped a hole in space-time for years in all directions. The thinnest trickle upwards through the sands, a leaky faucet letting out a drip every millennium.

We will have to do this again, Isabella realized. *In a million or two years.*

Sophie knew that it was true. The thought of tangling with Kishka—or whoever, or *whatever* would embody the dark matter in the future—would have filled her with a profound dread, but there was no room for profound dread in the universe right then. Only a charge of triumph, a bolt of joy. They had *done* it! All of them, the girls, yes, but their mermaids, too, their spell-casting witches and loving animal familiars. Their friends and their families and all of the magical creatures from myth still living just out of sight of human reality, and the humans themselves with their *want* of joy, all of them had come together and dried up the Invisible, balanced their joy and goodness against the mysterious force of the dark energy, and squeezed the evil from their grandmothers' hearts until they were simply grandmothers.

I've got to get out of here, Pipaluk said. *I mean, if we're done. My family needs me back in Alaska. I left my siblings to help with all the fishing, and they're lazy.*

I miss my mother, Isabella said, and Sophie could hear the tears in her voice. *I want to go back. To Hawaii.*

I have Carnival practice, Lesia said, remembering her old life, her costume of flash and feathers, the dance she'd studied until she could do the moves in her dreams. *I hope I'm not too late.*

Sophie felt her sisters slipping away, each into their own reality. *I hope I get to meet you all,* she hollered as they receded. *I mean, in real life!*

See you in a couple million years, Pipaluk said, and it took Sophie a moment to realize the girl had made a joke.

You guys saved me! she said quickly, remembering Kishka's grip on her soul. *Thank you, thank you so much!* But they were gone then, each back on their part of the earth, Isabella lying on the earth by the ocean in Japan, Lesia in a castle in Ghana, Pipaluk in an abandoned mine in freezing cold Greenland. And there was Sophie. She opened her eyes back into Poland, and was shocked to see not only her friends, the beloved friends who had kept her alive, but others, humans who had come down to the basement, their hearts cleared, to help Sophie fight. A crowd of Polish people, smiling at her.

Epilogue

ophie! I need your help!"

Sophie grabbed the hard-backed journal she was writing the story of her life into and shoved it into a desk drawer stuffed with similar books. Telling the story of your life took a long time, even if you'd only been around for thirteen or so years. She left her bedroom to find her mother hollering for her from the bathroom.

"What is it?"

"Just my hair again." Andrea scrunched up her nose at the madness of frizzy curls spiraling out from her head. "I was *certain* it was under a spell and that I would finally have perfect hair after you defeated evil, but no luck."

"Do you want me to magic it?" Sophie asked.

"If you don't mind."

Sophie sighed with light annoyance, and on her sigh floated a tiny spell that worked Andrea's hair into a glossy crown of chunky curls. "You know you could figure out how to do this with, like, hair product," she told her mother.

"Soph, you know I'm so bad at that sort of stuff. Thanks, Booboo, I love it!" Andrea gave her curls a pat and grabbed Sophie for a kiss. "You are the most amazing kid, do you know that?"

"Yeah, yeah."

"Not because of this," Andrea fingered a perfect ringlet. "Because of this." She tapped Sophie on her body, right above where her heart lay, beating. "Because of all the love you got in there, and all the smarts you got in there." Andrea gave Sophie's hair a ruffle.

"Ma! Don't mess up my braid!"

"Right. It would be terrible if you had to spend all of a second magicking it into place again."

"I'll have you know I did this with my *hands*," Sophie bragged. "I can't just magic my whole life, Ma. You know that."

"Go get your sister," Andrea said. "Get her head out of the clouds. We've got to get going."

Sophie found Belinda's door shut, as it always was, the tinkling of music faint inside the room. She knocked gingerly. "Lindy?"

The door cracked open and Sophie jumped a little as her own face peered through the crack at her. Belinda jumped a little too, and they both laughed. "It's still weird," Sophie shrugged.

"Which part?" Belinda asked. "Having a sister, or having an identical twin sister?"

"Both."

"The weirdest for me is living in a *house*," Belinda shared, opening her door to Sophie. Sophie gasped at the sight, though she'd seen it before. She stepped into the world her sister had made, the trees that stretched up to the ceiling, the shelves where vines cascaded from pots down onto her sister's bed.

"It's so beautiful," Sophie breathed. Belinda laughed.

"You could do it to your room," she shrugged. "It's just plants." But even as she said it, Belinda moved close to a ficus tree and rubbed its leaves with affectionate apology. They weren't just plants. They were Belinda's familiar, as individual and alive to her as the pigeons were to Sophie.

"I don't have a green thumb," Sophie grinned.

"Well, I said I'd help you. So let me know when you want to try something new."

"Are you ready? Sophie asked.

"Almost," Belinda said, and dashed around her room plucking a handful of blooms from the flowering plants.

"I can't believe you haven't done that yet! We're going to be late."

"I want them to be fresh," Belinda said, winding a ribbon around the stems. "See?"

"They're beautiful," Sophie said. "Of course."

Revere Beach looked *a lot* different than the last time Sophie had kicked up its sand. The first public beach in the USA, it had always had a lot of worn-out pride, but was not always the cleanest, or safest, place to visit. Sophie remembered trash in the sand, scummy foam in the waves, fistfights along the strip of pizza shops and fried food shacks and dive bars. Not anymore. The slight mist that glowed over the fountain of life glowed over all waters now, and created a bed of tiny rainbows in the sky. The sand glittered. The worldwide drive to clean the seas was working, and though the shores still harbored a stray piece of plastic here and there, there were now more crabs and seashells then there were chunks of Styrofoam.

"This is the perfect place to get married." Sophie heard a familiar voice behind her, and spun around to see Ella, a lovely dress swirling around her, jewels lifted from the cave of the Jottnar shining on her collarbone. Sophie and Ella hugged, and then Belinda and Ella hugged. Ella took in Belinda's dress. "Nice," she nodded approvingly. "At least I can always tell you two apart. Sophie always looks like a schlump, even on a day like today." She reached out and gave Sophie's shirt a little tug.

"What?" Sophie yelped. "I braided my hair!"

"You couldn't wear a dress?"

Sophie blanched. "Absolutely not." The three girls laughed.

"Well show some respect and at least magic your Vans clean?"

Sophie peered down at her shoes and with a thought wiped them clean. When she looked up, Ella's aunt was there, pulling baby Hector on a sled through the sand.

"A sled!" Sophie cracked up as Belinda crouched down and lifted the baby into the air. "That's genius."

"He can't walk yet," Ella shrugged.

"How is the littlest ring boy?" asked Belinda in a high-pitched coo. Sophie plugged her ears.

"Can't you just talk to him like he's a person?" she asked.

"He's not a person! He's a baby!"

"You're actually supposed to talk to them like that," Ella said. "They really like it. But sometimes I hear myself squealing at him and I want to stick a pen in my eye."

"I'm going to see if Hennie needs any help with the food," Belinda said, and Sophie and Ella followed her, baby Hector giggling as his sled slid along in the sand.

On a table covered with a cloth Hennie arranged bowls filled with watermelon and mango and pineapple, bowls filled with creamy guacamole and roasted corn salsa. In the center of it all towered a fluffy pink wedding cake.

"Mmm, I'm feeling snacky!" Ella cheered, chomping into a slice of mango and handing the rest to baby Hector.

"Hennie!" Sophie and Belinda cried in unison, wrapping themselves around the giggling witch.

"Hello, my girls!" she said, hugging them back tightly. "How are you this happy day?"

"Happy!" Sophie chirped.

"The happiest," nodded Belinda.

"Well, take care not to knock over the cake, I'd *hate* to have to magic another one." She gave a saucy wink.

"Hello, I'm here to deliver one flower girl!" Angel walked up to the table, her arm linked through the arm of Laurie LeClair, both of them pushing a very shy Alize forward.

"Oh, well look at this little honey!" Hennie said, clapping. Alize was a sight in her sparkled tutu and twinkling crown, her feet bare and her toes dotted with blobs of purple nail polish.

"She's been talking about this for *weeks*," Laurie said proudly. "It is just so sweet that she gets to do this."

"Well, I actually wanted to be flower girl, Alize!" Sophie said, teasing a smile out of the girl. "But I guess I'm too big, so I had to be the maid of honor."

"*Co*-maid of honor," Belinda interrupted, shoving her own arm through Sophie's. Angel watched them, a smile splitting her face.

"Never," Angel said, shaking her head, her shaggy hair shaking around her head. "Never did I think I'd see this day. High five, Swankowski." She offered her hand and Sophie clapped it.

"Aw, Belinda has her own magic, you know," Sophie said bashfully. "She was in there with her plants, scheming the whole time."

"Only once you cleared my heart, Sophie," said her twin, her eyes wide. "If you hadn't done that I would have been under Kishka—I mean, under the evil spell, probably forever."

"No more evil spells." Laurie smiled widely, and Sophie was struck by how cool-looking she was. Like a cat, with sleek eyes and her naturally black hair cascading down her shoulders. She nuzzled Angel happily, and Angel nuzzled her back.

"Mama, what's an evil spell?" Alize asked.

"Nothing you have to worry about," Laurie laughed. "Now, go check in with Kishka about what she wants you to do." Laurie gave the girl a little shove in the direction of Kishka, who stood among the white folding chairs, decorating them with beribboned sea dollars while giving Ella instructions for sledding baby Hector down the aisle during the procession. Sophie watched; her grandmother was in her element, conducting everyone, directing and decorating, the busy backbone of the wedding.

"At least she stopped smoking," Sophie said. She noticed Angel watching with her head cocked to the side like a nervous dog. She chewed her cheek.

"What is it?" Sophie asked.

"I don't know," Angel said uneasily. "Just... don't you ever worry?"

"Angel!" Laurie gasped. "Don't be rude!"

"Come on, you guys." Angel threw up her hands. "It's not like it's *crazy* for me to just be the tiniest bit worried."

"I get it," Sophie told Laurie, and to Angel, more tenderly, "I get it. But I've been in her heart. And, it's fine. It's not even fine, it's beautiful. It's all love in there—love for my mom, for me and Belinda. She wasn't the source of the evil after all. She was just a really, really good channel for it." Sophie shivered, remembering how close she had come to falling under its spell. "I understand. It almost happened to me, too."

Angel shook her head stubbornly. "No way. Not you."

"You don't know, Angel. It's very powerful. And by the time you're interacting with it you're so compromised—mentally, physically. All of it. I'm so grateful that I didn't fall down some terrible hole. And I'm so happy I was able to go into Kishka and get my grandmother back."

"Hmm." Angel looked unconvinced.

"Better get it together because here she comes," Laurie hissed, bumping Angel with her hip.

"Children!" Kishka called, hustling up the sandy aisle in a pair of flip flops. She wore her very best housedress, and instead of a pack of cigarettes her deep pockets held notebooks and pens, flowers and candy and seashells that struck her fancy as she dashed around the shore. "We are ready! Laurie, you and Angel sit in the front, in case Alize gets a bit of stage fright? You can coach her through it?"

"Sure," Laurie grinned.

"Sophie, you and Lindy will follow baby Hector down the aisle, okay?"

"Got it," Belinda nodded.

Kishka clapped her hands together, her nails painted red for the occasion flashing in the sun. She tucked a wisp of gray hair behind and ear and sighed. "We're ready."

AT THE FRONT of the chairs, with the Atlantic Ocean crashing behind them, Hennie and Kishka held one another around the waist and, swaying, sang a magic song. Tiny dust devils of sand spun along the shore to the sound of their tune, and out beyond the break a pod of dolphins leapt gleefully, charmed by the sound. Their music broke open

a sadly happy place in everyone's heart, a happily sad place, a lovingly tender place that held love and loss and everything dear. As their last notes trilled off, Ella made her way down the short aisle, Hector smacking the sand with his one hand, the other clutching a clamshell where the wedding rings were tucked away.

Alize skipped down the aisle next, holding a bouquet of Belinda's flowers. As she took her place beside Kishka, Sophie and Belinda made their way, holding hands.

"This is so weird," Sophie hissed, taking in the rows of relatives they hardly knew.

"It's sweet," Belinda hissed back.

"Totally. But it's weird, right?"

"Sophie, we are the weirdest people we will ever know. Get used to it already."

Sophie leaned over and kissed Belinda's cheek as they reached the others. Turning their backs to the sea, they settled in beside Hennie and watched their parents shyly walk down the aisle, hand in hand. The crowd erupted in applause, hoots and hollers that made Andrea and Ronald even shyer. Sophie watched her father's cheeks burn red, watched her mother tuck her face into her flowers. By the time they reached the front they were already teared up. Teared up and smiling.

Kishka and Hennie stepped forward, holding hands. Their free hands held in the air, they commanded the powers of all the seasons, of the sea and the land, the birds of land and air and ocean. They called upon the powers of the flowers and the skies, of the land beneath the dirt, where the tiniest creatures made their way, and they called upon the outer reaches of the universe, the vast unknowable places. And they let Andrea and Ronald know that in every way their love was like this—slow and steady, small in precious detail as the tiny spiders in the sand, and soaring and swift like the gulls above their heads, taking in the big picture of their shared destiny. It was fruitful as avocado trees and sweet as jasmine and formidable as a great Asian elephant. And there would be summers and winters and springs and falls and always they would grow and reap and bask and hibernate.

As Sophie could not get enough of the sight of her sister, so she could not get enough of Ronald, a vision. Ronald, wise and alert, snappy, witty, quick with a joke, always with a smile but quick also to shoot down to the depths if that was what the moment called for. When Sophie awoke from a dream of Kishka as a giant dragon about to set her face on fire, it was Ronald who offered her not just comfort but a mystical quip to help her grasp the strange magnitude of her life. When Belinda startled awake, certain her plants were killing her, he lingered behind after Andrea's hugs had soothed her emotions, with a riddle to calm her mind.

Sophie watched them gaze upon each other, all the love in their hearts freed up after the great growing, as people had begun referring to it, the great growing of their own hearts, of the love within themselves, of their potential. After they completed their vows to one another they turned to Sophie and Belinda and called their daughters to join them. Together they tumbled in a big, sloppy hug that turned into a silly dance, kicking up sand, Andrea shaking her bouquet in the air like a pom-pom.

"Ow!" she yelped, suddenly tossing the flowers.

"Hey, hey, we weren't prepared for the bouquet toss!" one of Ella's aunts hollered from her seat, laughing. Sophie caught her breath as she watched the blood drip from her mother's finger, catching the hem of her dress before it spattered on the sand.

"What happened?" Sophie demanded, grabbing her wrist.

"It—it—there must have been a bug in it. I felt something bite me!"

"But they're from my room," Belinda said, fetching the bouquet from the sand. She shook it out, peered into the petals.

"Perhaps a bee?" Kishka asked, patting her shoulder.

"More a bite than a sting. Look!" Andrea shook away the blood from the wound. It did look like a jagged bit of teeth had sunk into her finger.

"It's nothing!" Kishka called, grabbing the flowers from Belinda and shaking them until petals fluttered to the ground. "Come on, now! Hennie made a feast and this old lady is hungry! Three cheers for the newlyweds!"

Above them, the flock of pigeons swooped low, releasing confetti from their claws, trailing ribbons, cooing merrily. As they turned in the sky over Kishka, one let a wet, white pigeon turd splat onto the old woman's shoulder.

"Now, you!" she hollered up at them, her face a rage. Sophie's stomach lurched at the sight of it, the sight of the Kishka who'd terrorized her, the Kishka who'd wanted her dead.

Take a breath, take a breath, Sophie coached herself. PTSD from her supernatural experiences still flared up here and there, always unpredictable, often in situations you wished wouldn't, like your parents' own wedding.

"Holding a grudge, I suppose," Kishka muttered, looking after the birds as they flew off. Sophie started; it was unusual for Kishka to ever reference what had happened. Indeed, Sophie often wondered if she had no memory of it, if her time possessed by the Invisible had been wiped from her memory entirely, leaving her a blissfully ignorant little old lady.

"Sometime pigeons just poop on you," Sophie suggested. "It doesn't mean anything."

Kishka looked at her deeply, drawing her in. Sophie broke her gaze, looked over at her family, everyone she loved descending upon Hennie's feast. Her mother and father stood awkwardly by the teeter-tottering pink wedding cake, ready to cut into it.

"Get over here, Sophie!" Andrea hollered. "It's time for cake!

"Come on, Nana." Sophie tugged on Kishka. "I think you've been standing in the sun for too long. Let's get you lemonade."

"Two million years is a long time," Kishka said, quiet beneath the roar of the surf behind them.

"What?" Sophie asked

"I've been standing here a long time," Kishka said, gripping Sophie's arm tight as she shuffled through the sand.

"Yes," Sophie laughed nervously. "You really have."

"My offer will stand."

Overhead a gull screeched.

"What are you saying to me?" Sophie demanded. Kishka gazed at her granddaughter, full of admiration. She winked at Sophie and kissed her forehead, her lips lingering on Sophie's skin. Sophie smelled her powdery perfume, a scorched smell, cigarettes.

"My dear granddaughter. Take your Nana's hand."

Acknowledgments

The author would like to thank her entire team at McSweeney's, who have been so supportive of this collection, especially Andi Winette and Kristina Kearns. Thank you to Lindsay Edgecombe for all her diligent support and care. Thank you to her true love, Dashiell Lippman, and the offspring of their love, small Atticus Lippman, for their warmth and adoration, which she returns in buckets. Thank you to all the seekers and wishers and dreamers and radicals, to the pigeons and the poets and witches and mermaids, for making this planet livable.

About the Author

Michelle Tea is the author of the young adult novels *Mermaid in Chelsea Creek* and *Girl at the Bottom of the Sea*, as well as numerous books for grown-ups. She lives in Los Angeles, where she reads tarot cards, casts spells, and talks to birds.

About the Illustrator

Kelsey Short is an illustrator and cartoonist originally from Los Angeles now based in Queens, New York. She enjoys drawing empowered women, cats, snakes, and all things spooky.

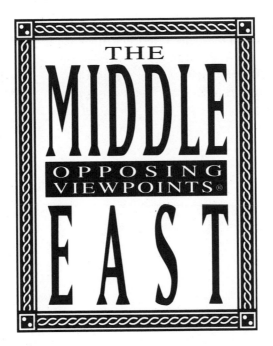

Other Books of Related Interest in the Opposing Viewpoints Series:

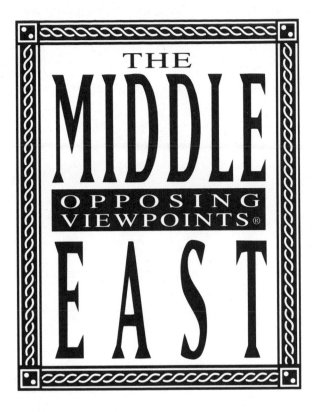

THE MIDDLE EAST

OPPOSING VIEWPOINTS®

David L. Bender & Bruno Leone, *Series Editors*

William Dudley, *Book Editor*

OPPOSING VIEWPOINTS SERIES ®

Greenhaven Press, Inc.   PO Box 289009   San Diego, CA 92198-0009

Library of Congress Cataloging-in-Publication Data

The Middle East : opposing viewpoints / William Dudley, book editor.
     p.   cm. — (Opposing viewpoints series)
   Includes bibliographical references and index.
   Summary: Presents articles for both sides of the questions: Why is the Middle East a conflict area? Are Palestinians treated justly? What role should the U.S. play in the Middle East? How does religion affect the Middle East? What is the Future of the Middle East?
   ISBN 0-89908-185-1 (lib. : acid-free paper). — ISBN 0-89908-160-6 (pap : acid-free paper).
   1. Middle East—Politics and government—1979-   2. Critical thinking.   [1. Middle East—Politics and government—1979-   2. Critical thinking.]   I. Dudley, William, 1964-   .
II. Series: Opposing viewpoints series (Unnumbered)
DS63.1.M5425   1992   91-43280
320.956—dc20

"Congress shall make no law . . .
abridging the freedom of speech,
or of the press."

First Amendment to the U.S. Constitution

The basic foundation of our democracy is the first amendment
guarantee of freedom of expression. The Opposing Viewpoints
Series is dedicated to the concept of this basic freedom and the
idea that it is more important to practice it than to enshrine it.

Contents

Why Consider Opposing Viewpoints?

The Importance of Examining Opposing Viewpoints

The purpose of the Opposing Viewpoints Series, and this book in particular, is to present balanced, and often difficult to find, opposing points of view on complex and sensitive issues.

Probably the best way to become informed is to analyze the positions of those who are regarded as experts and well studied on issues. It is important to consider every variety of opinion in an attempt to determine the truth. Opinions from the mainstream of society should be examined. But also important are opinions that are considered radical, reactionary, or minority as well as those stigmatized by some other uncomplimentary label. An important lesson of history is the eventual acceptance of many unpopular and even despised opinions. The ideas of Socrates, Jesus, and Galileo are good examples of this.

Readers will approach this book with their own opinions on the issues debated within it. However, to have a good grasp of one's own viewpoint, it is necessary to understand the arguments of those with whom one disagrees. It can be said that those who do not completely understand their adversary's point of view do not fully understand their own.

A persuasive case for considering opposing viewpoints has been presented by John Stuart Mill in his work *On Liberty*. When examining controversial issues it may be helpful to reflect on this suggestion:

9

The only way in which a human being can make some approach to knowing the whole of a subject, is by hearing what can be said about it by persons of every variety of opinion, and studying all modes in which it can be looked at by every character of mind. No wise man ever acquired his wisdom in any mode but this.

Analyzing Sources of Information

The Opposing Viewpoints Series includes diverse materials taken from magazines, journals, books, and newspapers, as well as statements and position papers from a wide range of individuals, organizations, and governments. This broad spectrum of sources helps to develop patterns of thinking which are open to the consideration of a variety of opinions.

Pitfalls to Avoid

A pitfall to avoid in considering opposing points of view is that of regarding one's own opinion as being common sense and the most rational stance, and the point of view of others as being only opinion and naturally wrong. It may be that another's opinion is correct and one's own is in error.

Another pitfall to avoid is that of closing one's mind to the opinions of those with whom one disagrees. The best way to approach a dialogue is to make one's primary purpose that of understanding the mind and arguments of the other person and not that of enlightening him or her with one's own solutions. More can be learned by listening than speaking.

It is my hope that after reading this book the reader will have a deeper understanding of the issues debated and will appreciate the complexity of even seemingly simple issues on which good and honest people disagree. This awareness is particularly important in a democratic society such as ours where people enter into public debate to determine the common good. Those with whom one disagrees should not necessarily be regarded as enemies, but perhaps simply as people who suggest different paths to a common goal.

Developing Basic Reading and Thinking Skills

In this book, carefully edited opposing viewpoints are purposely placed back to back to create a running debate; each viewpoint is preceded by a short quotation that best expresses the author's main argument. This format instantly plunges the reader into the midst of a controversial issue and greatly aids that reader in mastering the basic skill of recognizing an author's point of view.

A number of basic skills for critical thinking are practiced in the activities that appear throughout the books in the series. Some of the skills are:

Evaluating Sources of Information. The ability to choose from among alternative sources the most reliable and accurate source in relation to a given subject.

Separating Fact from Opinion. The ability to make the basic distinction between factual statements (those that can be demonstrated or verified empirically) and statements of opinion (those that are beliefs or attitudes that cannot be proved).

Identifying Stereotypes. The ability to identify oversimplified, exaggerated descriptions (favorable or unfavorable) about people and insulting statements about racial, religious, or national groups, based upon misinformation or lack of information.

Recognizing Ethnocentrism. The ability to recognize attitudes or opinions that express the view that one's own race, culture, or group is inherently superior, or those attitudes that judge another culture or group in terms of one's own.

It is important to consider opposing viewpoints and equally important to be able to critically analyze those viewpoints. The activities in this book are designed to help the reader master these thinking skills. Statements are taken from the book's viewpoints and the reader is asked to analyze them. This technique aids the reader in developing skills that not only can be applied to the viewpoints in this book, but also to situations where opinionated spokespersons comment on controversial issues. Although the activities are helpful to the solitary reader, they are most useful when the reader can benefit from the interaction of group discussion.

Using this book and others in the series should help readers develop basic reading and thinking skills. These skills should improve the reader's ability to understand what is read. Readers should be better able to separate fact from opinion, substance from rhetoric, and become better consumers of information in our media-centered culture.

This volume of the Opposing Viewpoints Series does not advocate a particular point of view. Quite the contrary! The very nature of the book leaves it to the reader to formulate the opinions he or she finds most suitable. My purpose as publisher is to see that this is made possible by offering a wide range of viewpoints that are fairly presented.

David L. Bender
Publisher

The Middle East

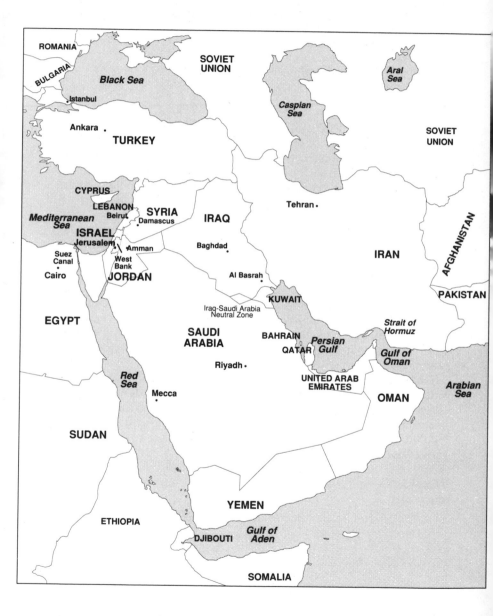

Introduction

For three days, beginning on October 31, 1991, delegations representing Israel, the Palestinians, Jordan, Syria, Egypt, and Lebanon met in Madrid, Spain. They sat across tables designed to be too wide to reach across for handshakes, and presented speeches blaming each other for the Arab-Israeli conflict. Their speeches and later meetings resulted in no peace treaties or formal agreements. The talks between them did not even deal directly with the issues, but instead focused on setting up the framework for future talks. Yet the occasion was quickly deemed not only successful, but historic. It was the first time that Israel and her Arab neighbors (excepting Egypt) had directly talked with each other. "Arab and Israeli delegates spent more time . . . talking *at* one another rather than *to* one another," wrote U.S. journalist Richard Z. Chesnoff. "But the mere act of getting the star players together on a single Spanish stage is an epic breakthrough."

Whether this breakthrough will be a major turning point in the road to Middle East peace, or whether it will only be a mirage leading to an ultimate dead end, remains to be seen. If one makes predictions purely on the issues separating the participants, there is little room for optimism. What hope there is comes from changes in the international situation—particularly in the demise of the Soviet Union and the subsequent preeminence of the United States.

For many years the Arab-Israeli conflict was enmeshed in the cold war rivalry between these two superpowers. U.S. military aid to Israel was counterbalanced by Soviet military aid to Syria and the Palestine Liberation Organization (PLO). With the support of opposing superpowers behind them, conflicting parties in the Middle East had no real incentive to work together to achieve peace.

The economic and military decline of the Soviet Union and its new rapprochement with the United States, however, left its former Middle East allies stranded without strategic backing. These allies now seek new links with the United States and the West. For example, Syria, no longer able to depend on the Soviet Union for aid and isolated from its neighbors, found that "improved relations with the United States were no longer a desirable option; they were a strategic necessity," according to Ronald D. McLaurin.

The end of the cold war also affected Israel. Instead of receiving nearly unconditional support from the United States, Israel, which depends on three billion dollars of annual U.S. assistance, faced strong American pressure not to obstruct peace. Israel attended the Madrid conference, according to McLaurin, because it did "not want to take actions that endanger its financial support or political relations with the United States."

It is largely due to the new influence of the United States, then, that the Madrid conference occurred. The work of the peace process, however, does not end with bringing these parties to the negotiating table. The parties have longstanding disputes that predate the cold war and have outlived its end. Most observers of the conference agree with foreign policy analyst William B. Quandt, who wrote that "left to their own, the Arabs and Israelis are very unlikely to negotiate peace agreements. Successful peace talks will require continual U.S. involvement." Whether or not the United States has the influence or the patience to achieve concrete results remains unclear. U.S. president George Bush expressed both realism and hope in his opening address to the Madrid conference:

> Let no one mistake the magnitude of this challenge. The struggle we seek to end has a long and violent history. Every life lost—every outrage, every act of violence—is etched deep in the hearts and history of the people of this region. Theirs is a history that weighs heavily against hope. And yet history need not be man's master. . . . Peace in the Middle East need not be a dream.

The issue of how to attain peace runs through *The Middle East: Opposing Viewpoints*, which replaces Greenhaven's 1988 book of the same title. The volume contains all new viewpoints and introduces several new topics. The questions examined are Why Is the Middle East a Conflict Area? Are Palestinian Rights Being Ignored? What Role Should the U.S. Play in the Middle East? How Does Religion Affect the Middle East? What is the Future of the Middle East? The wide-ranging viewpoints in this volume can help readers better understand the issues facing the Middle East and gain insight into the difficulty of attaining peace in the region.

Why Is the Middle East a Conflict Area?

Chapter Preface

The Middle East during the twentieth century has been a center of longstanding disputes that have resisted attempts at peacemaking. One issue that illustrates the persistent nature of Middle Eastern conflicts is the Arab-Israeli dispute. It was responsible for wars in 1948, 1956, 1967, 1973, and 1982. The issues that caused the wars remain unresolved, and Israel and the Arab countries still view each other with mutual distrust. The persistent failure of peace attempts suggests that the conflicts between these nations have deep roots in the culture and politics of the region.

While the Arab-Israeli conflict has received most of the world's attention, it is unfortunately not the only source of conflict in the Middle East. Longstanding animosities between Iran and Iraq culminated in the Iran-Iraq War, which took place from 1980 to 1988. That war was the region's bloodiest in the twentieth century, with about a million casualties. Other violence occurred in Lebanon, which was split by a fifteen-year civil war between its numerous ethnic groups. Yemen, too, was marred for almost thirty years by civil war. The Kurds, an ethnic group residing in Iraq and Turkey, have fought those countries intermittently for their own homeland for decades. The list goes on, which illustrates why the Middle East is considered one of the world's most violent regions.

Conflict in the Middle East has long been a concern of the rest of the world. During the height of the cold war between the United States and the Soviet Union, Middle East conflict was closely followed because it was considered one of the possible flashpoints that could draw the two superpowers into open confrontation. With the passing of the cold war, that particular threat is less likely. But Middle East conflict still carries large international repercussions. For example, Israel is believed to possess nuclear weapons, and other Middle Eastern nations, including Iraq and Iran, have worked to attain them. In addition, some countries in the region have tried to purchase and develop chemical and biological weapons. Iraq has been known to use chemical weapons against its own population, a development that has alarmed many outside observers. Finally, as a vital supplier of oil to the industrialized world, the Middle East has some control over the world economy. Massive disruptions of oil production could wreak havoc throughout the industrialized nations.

Both the persistence of Middle East conflicts and their repercussions on the wider world make the question of why the Middle East is a conflict area an important one. The following viewpoints examine some of the possible underlying causes of conflict in the Middle East.

"Israel's mass immigration policy and land acquisition goals constitute a serious threat to the peace and stability of the Middle East region."

Israel Is the Cause of Conflict

Sami Hadawi

Sami Hadawi is a Palestinian scholar who has written numerous books and pamphlets on the Middle East. He served as a government official under the British mandate over Palestine prior to Israel's founding in 1948. Hadawi later worked for the Jordanian government and the United Nations identifying and evaluating Arab property located in Israel. In the following viewpoint, he writes that conflict in the Middle East is caused by what he calls the unjust occupation of Palestinian land by Zionists. The 1948 United Nations partition of Palestine into Jewish and Arab homelands, the evacuation of Palestinians from their land by Israelis, and the continuing statelessness of Palestinians are all contributing causes of the central conflict of the Middle East, Hadawi argues. He concludes that peace can only be achieved when Israel gives up its aggressive posture.

As you read, consider the following questions:

1. How has world opinion over Israel and Palestine been distorted, according to Hadawi?
2. Why does the author believe Israel does not have peaceful intentions toward its neighbors?
3. What does Hadawi believe about the legitimacy of Israel's existence?

Excerpted, with permission, from *Bitter Harvest* by Sami Hadawi. Brooklyn: Olive Branch Press, 1990. Copyright © 1990 Sami Hadawi.

It is not the first time in history that partition has been resorted to as a solution to a problem. In ancient times, King Solomon ruled: If you cannot give one child to each of the two who claim to be the mother, then split the child into two and give half to one and the second half to the other.

The Division of Palestine

An analogous scene was re-enacted in Palestine three thousand years later, except that the wisdom of Solomon in the judgment was lacking in this case. Like the false mother who welcomed the bisection of the child who was not hers, the Zionists accepted partition of the Holy Land because it gave them something they did not own and to which they were not entitled in justice or in equity.

Partition of countries against the will of the people is not only wrong in principle; it has been proved to be inhuman too. Wherever applied, partition has brought tragedy, destruction and suffering to millions of human beings. War came to Korea only because of the partition of the land into North and South; and the fierce battles that raged for ten years in South Vietnam with the loss of hundreds of thousands of lives and considerable destruction, came to an end only after the North and South were reunited. . . .

The powers that resist the will of the people of these three countries to unity and impose upon them a partition that can only be maintained by force of arms, are the same powers that have inflicted the tragedy of partition on Palestine, with one additional iniquity—they first gave equal validity to the *claim* of the Zionists to Palestine and the *right* of the Arabs to their homeland in order to justify their plan of partition, then went to a step further by encouraging the dislodgement of the Arabs from their homes and property.

After thirty years of tribulation and suffering, the world has come to recognize the error of its judgment in partitioning the Holy Land in 1947; but there is nothing that can be done to remove the evil that has been unleashed upon a peaceful people and a land held sacred by the adherents of the three great faiths. The least that can now be done is to undo the injustice by recognizing that a wrong has been committed against an innocent people and to redress it in a just manner.

There is probably no subject fraught with so many distortions and misrepresentations as the Palestine problem. It has been widely discussed, debated, lectured upon and written about in the past six decades, but still it is far from being correctly understood.

World opinion has been led to believe that the Palestine problem is a conflict between Israel and the Arab States over the sovereignty of territory that the Arab States regard as part of the Arab homeland. The Israelis, on the other hand, claim Palestine as theirs by reason of the Balfour Declaration of 1917, the United Nations Partition Resolution of 1947, subsequent military conquests and what is commonly referred to as the "Biblical Promises." In other words, it is presumed to be a territorial dispute between nations, similar in some respects to the dispute between India and Pakistan over Kashmir.

Raeside/Victoria *Times-Colonist*. Reprinted with permission.

This Zionist approach is not without a motive. It is intended to confuse the issue and to obliterate the memories of the crimes committed against the Palestine Arabs—crimes which have been described by British historian Arnold Toynbee as no less heinous than the Nazi crimes against the Jews. Its purpose is also to by-pass standing United Nations resolutions calling upon the Israelis to surrender the extra territory they occupied by force of arms beyond the area assigned to the "Jewish State" under the Partition Plan of 1947; to give the refugees the choice between repatriation and compensation; and to permit the internationalization of Jerusalem. To label the conflict as a dispute between nations, divests it of its human and just elements and puts it in the same category as other world territorial issues where the parties proffer claims and counter-claims perhaps of equal strength.

The truth of the matter is that the Palestine problem must be called first and foremost a dispute between the Palestine Arabs and the Jews before it can be labelled as an Arab States-Israeli conflict. The issue is fundamentally one of individual rights and principles, as well as of territory, and must be treated as a moral and political issue.

No matter what language diplomacy uses in defining the rights of the Palestine Arabs, the fact remains that the major portion of the territory now called "Israel" is legitimately owned by individual Arabs. Their rights derive from the universally accepted principle that a country belongs to its indigenous inhabitants. The fact that the Arabs fled in terror, because of real fear of a repetition of the 1948 Zionist massacres, is no reason for denying them their homes, fields and livelihoods. Civilians caught in an area of military activity generally panic. But they have always been able to return to their homes when the danger subsides. Military conquest does not abolish private rights to property; nor does it entitle the victor to confiscate the homes, property and personal belongings of the non-combatant civilian population. The seizure of Arab property by the Israelis was an outrage. It was described by many distinguished writers as "robbery."

The position of the Arab States fully supports the Palestine Arabs' demand for rights to homes and country. Any solution agreed to by the Palestine Arabs would be acceptable to the Arab States. Conversely, the Arab States cannot conclude a settlement that is unacceptable to the Palestine Arabs.

Israeli Expansionism

A solution of the Palestine problem, however, does not necessarily mean a settlement of the Arab States-Israeli conflict. While the former may have some influence on the latter, the Arab States-Israeli conflict arises out of the danger that Zionist ambitions for expansion poses to the territorial integrity of the Arab States. Israel's mass immigration policy and land acquisition goals constitute a serious threat to the peace and stability of the Middle East region. Israeli leaders have repeatedly declared the need for a larger land area. Actions, such as the planned invasion of Egypt in 1956 and the attempted annexation of the Sinai Peninsula and the Gaza Strip territory—which inspired David Ben Gurion to proclaim the areas as having been "freed" and "liberated"—provide ample proof of Israeli future aspirations. This policy has been further confirmed by the June 1967 War and Israeli refusal since to withdraw from occupied territories.

It will be recalled that as early as 1948, the late UN mediator Count Folke Bernadotte—who was assassinated by the Israelis because of his recommendations for a solution of the Palestine problem not in conformity with Israeli policy—warned the Security Council: "It could not be ignored that unrestricted immigration to the Jewish area of Palestine might, over a period of years, give rise to a population pressure and to economic and political disturbances which would justify present Arab fears of ultimate Jewish expansion in the Near East." He added: "It can scarcely be ignored that Jewish immigration into the Jewish area of Palestine concerns not only the Jewish people and territory but also the neighboring Arab world."

It would, indeed, be suicidal for the Arab States to relax their vigilance and allow themselves to be deceived by the Jekyll and Hyde image of the Zionist-Israel character. While the Israelis claim they want peace, they are actually preparing all the time for war. If expansion is not their ultimate aim, what is the meaning of David Ben Gurion's statement: "To maintain the *status quo* will not do. We have set up a dynamic state, bent upon expansion"? This ambition he reiterated in 1952 when he said: "Israel . . . has been established in only a portion of the land of Israel. Even those who are dubious as to the restoration of the historical frontiers, as fixed and crystallized from the beginning of time, will hardly deny the anomaly of the boundaries of the new State."

If these statements by the architect of the "Jewish State" can be waved aside as pure fantasy, the declaration of the leader of the *Herut* Party—the second largest in the Israeli Parliament and which claimed credit for the ousting of the British from Palestine—confirms Zionist intentions that expansion is always their goal. He said: "I deeply believe in launching preventive war against the Arab states without further hesitation. By doing so, we will achieve two targets: firstly, the annihilation of Arab power; and secondly, the expansion of our territory."

This latter declaration by Menachem Begin was implemented in 1967 with the invasion and occupation of the Sinai Peninsula and the Gaza Strip, the Golan Heights and the West Bank of Jordan.

False Promises

Many were the Zionist promises and declarations that sought to lull the Arabs into a false sense of security and to mislead world opinion. When the Zionists promoted settlement of the Holy Land in 1920 as a result of the Balfour Declaration, they spoke lavishly of their goodwill toward their Arab neighbors and of the many skills and advantages they would bestow upon the country. For example, at the Zionist Congress in 1921, a resolution was passed that "solemnly declared the desire of the Jewish people to live with the Arab people in relations of friendship and mutual respect and, together with the Arab people, to develop the homeland common to both into a prosperous community which would ensure the growth of the peoples."

The world has seen how, thirty years later, the Arab people of

21

Palestine benefitted from Jewish immigration by expulsions and dispossessions under the most cruel conditions. Instead of peace and tranquility, the Holy Land has been turned into a battlefield; the Middle East is now a cauldron of unrest and instability; misery, hatred and bitterness prevail where previously there was harmony and friendship between Arab and Jew.

The Threat of Israel

Iraq and much of the Arab World face a serious threat from Israel. Israel occupies Arab territories—Palestinian, Syrian and Lebanese. In 1981, Israel bombed a French-supplied nuclear reactor near Baghdad. In 1985, Israel bombed the PLO headquarters in Tunis. Periodically, Israel attacks Palestinian and Lebanese targets in Lebanon, resulting in mostly civilian casualties. The threat of Israel looms large over the Arab World.

Bishara A. Bahbah, *The Return*, April/May 1990.

During this period, the Zionist-Israeli propaganda machine succeeded in convincing world public opinion that the Palestine tragedy was really a territorial dispute between the neighboring Arab States and Israel, with the latter determined to "push the Jews into the sea" and "annihilate the State of Israel." At the same time, it branded the Palestine Liberation Organization as a terrorist organization that murders innocent Jews to no advantage.

In this way, the Zionists have been able to divert attention from the crimes committed against the Palestinians first as Zionists during the period of the Mandate, and then as Israelis after the establishment of the Jewish State. Furthermore, they have been able to win sympathy for Israel as a so-called peace-loving nation that is a victim of Arab aggression; and to raise funds through the United Jewish Appeal and the sale of Israeli Bonds to exploit usurped Arab homes and Arab lands.

To the Israelis, peace means recognition by the Arab States of Israeli sovereignty over existing Israeli-occupied territory; the removal of the Arab boycott; the opening of the Suez Canal to Israeli shipping; and Arab acquiescence in the diversion of the waters of the River Jordan even though it is to the detriment of Arab rights and interests. By achieving these objectives, the Israelis hope to improve their economy and provide greater man-power through new immigrants, for ultimate realization of their dream of an "empire" from the "Nile to the Euphrates." As for the Palestine Arabs whom they expelled and dispossessed, this is a matter, they claim, which was the result of alleged Arab aggression against the Jewish state. Such being the case, they say, it is for the Arab governments, not Israel, to find a home for the Palestine Arabs.

Peace, in order to be real, has to be based on justice and equity. Ironically, Israel, while claiming to have a right to exist by reason of an act of the United Nations, refuses to honor her responsibilities to the organization that created it. According to a declaration by David Ben Gurion in 1953 Israel "considers the United Nations resolution of November 29, 1947, as null and void." If the Israelis are permitted to discard the United Nations resolution that gave birth to their state, by the same token Arab refusal to recognize the existence of the Jewish state is fully justified.

True and durable peace can come to the area only when the Israelis agree to withdraw entirely from occupied territories, including East Jerusalem; give adequate guarantees that they will no longer pose a threat to Arab lands; and sit and negotiate with the Palestine Liberation Organization as the representative of the Palestinian people on ways and means of settling their differences. . . .

Israel Must Change

More than forty years of claims and counter-claims and five wars over who historically owned Palestine, and who in this modern age is the rightful owner of the country, have gone by without the problem being solved. In the meantime, enmity and animosity have replaced the friendly and harmonious relations that existed between Arab and Jew for centuries. The extremists on both sides are increasing in number: The Zionists who will not be satisfied with less than the total expulsion of the Palestinian inhabitants from the territory of the whole of Palestine, and those in the Palestinian camp who believe that the only solution to end their homelessness is the total destruction of the state of Israel. If either side had its way, the end result would be catastrophic for the people of the Middle East and would affect the rest of the world.

For the state of Israel to survive, it must become a part of the Middle East, and the $3^1/_2$ million Jews must learn to live amicably among the 200 million Arabs. For Israel to continue to exist surrounded by enemies relying solely on the military and economic aid it receives from the U.S. government and world Jewry is short-sighted and unrealistic.

Various solutions for an equitable and just peaceful settlement have been suggested from time to time by people of goodwill and the time has come for the great powers to act jointly and seriously toward a solution that would conform with the principles of human justice and fundamental democratic freedoms.

"*Inter-Arab relations—and not Arab-Israeli relations—are the cause of political volatility in the Middle East.*"

Arab Rivalries Are the Cause of Conflict

Daniel Pipes

Daniel Pipes is director of the Foreign Policy Research Institute in Philadelphia and editor of its journal, *Orbis*. He has written numerous books and articles on the Middle East, including *The Long Shadow: Culture and Politics in the Middle East*. In the following viewpoint, excerpted from this book, Pipes argues that the center of conflict in the Middle East is not between Israel and the Palestinians, but between opposing Arab nations and groups over the fate of Palestine. Although Arabs blame Israel for the region's conflict, in reality, Pipes believes, the Arab world itself is deeply divided over who should control the Palestinians and how Israel should be treated.

As you read, consider the following questions:

1. What six Arab groups have competing claims over Palestine, according to Pipes?
2. Why does Pipes believe that peace in the Middle East will remain elusive?
3. How important are Israeli-Palestinian relations in examining the Middle East, according to the author?

Excerpted, with permission, from *The Long Shadow: Culture and Politics in the Middle East* by Daniel Pipes. New Brunswick, NJ: Transaction Publishers, 1989. Copyright © 1989 Daniel Pipes.

In Arab eyes, who should inherit Palestine? The leaders most directly concerned with this issue disagree, sometimes violently, among themselves as to who should rule Palestine and even where its rightful boundaries lie. . . .

These competing ambitions are not momentary breaches in an otherwise unified Arab position, but deep and abiding divisions that, more than the Arab confrontation with Israel itself, constitute the center of gravity in the Arab-Israeli conflict. The fact that so many Arab parties lay claim to Israel's territory renders accommodation unlikely and prolongs a conflict that otherwise might be settled. Indeed, relations between the Arab states determine the future course of that conflict far more than actions by Israel, the United States, or the Soviet Union.

Four Arab groups have had the longest and most important historical roles in the Arab struggle for Palestine: Palestinian separatists, Arab nationalists, the Jordanian government, and the Syrian government. Actors of secondary importance include fundamentalist Muslims and West Bank notables. . . .

Palestinian Separatists

The PLO has carried the standard of this group, often known as Palestinian nationalists, since 1964. Palestinian separatists envisage an independent state in the area that Israel now controls; this state of Palestine should possess all the conventional signs of sovereignty—borders, customs, embassies, a flag, an army, and membership in the United Nations. The Palestinian separatist claim dominated Arab efforts to control Palestine during two periods: from late 1920 to the declaration of Israeli statehood in 1948, and from the Six Day War of 1967 to the Battle for Beirut in 1982.

The Palestinian identity originates in the Jewish concept of Eretz Israel (Hebrew for "The Land of Israel"), the land promised by God to Abraham. Christians too have always seen this area as a special place, as Terra Sancta (the Holy Land), a hallowed, separate territory imbued with religious significance. Although Muslims inherited this concept, Palestine did not exist as a distinct political entity in the period of their rule, from A.D. 634 to 1917. During these centuries, Palestine was submerged within larger political units; it simply did not exist on the political map. Ten changes of Muslim dynasties never saw a Palestinian polity. Only when the region fell under the control of Christians coming from Europe did it acquire political form, once when the Crusaders ruled Palestine from 1099 to 1187, a second time when the British—who designated Palestine for the "national home for the Jewish people"—conquered it from the faltering Ottoman Empire in 1917. . . .

In drawing up plans for Palestine, the British and the U.N.

expected the local Arabs to form an independent nation. But with the proclamation of Jewish statehood in 1948, Jordan, Syria, and Egypt invaded Palestine and occupied portions of it. Settlements made after the war ignored the Palestinians as an independent political actor. As a result, Palestinian separatism weakened; by the late 1950s, it had become nearly defunct.

IN BEIRUT TODAY, THE PHALANGIST ATTACKED THE DRUSE WHO SIDED WITH THE SYRIAN-BACKED AMAL AGAINST THE IRANIAN-BACKED HEZBOLLAH WHICH ACCIDENTALLY DECLARED WAR ON ITSELF!!!

TV

Mike Peters. Reprinted with permission.

During this period the conflict with Israel was dominated by the Arab States. It was the Egyptian government, indeed, that revived the Palestinian separatist ideology in 1959 and five years later sponsored the PLO's establishment. Cairo's intent was to control and use the Palestinians—King Husayn observes that the PLO was created as "a tool to be used by this or that Arab state"—and it did so for some years. . . .

Palestinian separatism re-emerged as a significant force only in the aftermath of the 1967 war. The terrible military defeat suffered by Syria, Jordan, and Egypt prompted many Arabs, especially Arab nationalists, to seek an alternative approach to the struggle with Israel. In a supremely romantic move ("If we all die except for one pregnant woman, her child will liberate Palestine") they turned away from the established states and placed their faith in the unproven and undermanned Palestinian separatist guerrilla organization, the PLO. Although the PLO never lived up to expectations, Arab nationalist hopes for it were only withdrawn; what, after all, could replace it?

The PLO enjoyed fifteen years of unique prominence. No other irredentist movement has had its financial, military, and diplomatic backing. With an annual budget of several hundreds of millions of dollars, quasi-state authority in Beirut and south

26

Lebanon, and wide international support, the PLO acted as though it were the major opponent of Israel. Its claim to Palestine grew so strong, many observers, especially in the West, forgot that other Arab factions had different plans for Palestine. Politically, the Arab-Israeli conflict turned in those years into a Palestinian-Israeli conflict.

PLO strength, however, was always precarious. Although prominent in world politics, the organization always suffered from the lack of a secure base. Finally the PLO came crashing down in the summer of 1982, when Israel eliminated it from Beirut and south Lebanon. Syria finished the job in December 1983 when it drove the PLO from its remaining strongholds in north Lebanon. With these developments, the PLO lost its hold on the Arab claim for Palestine; as Jordan and Syria strengthened, the PLO had to cooperate with the one or other of them. . . .

Arab Nationalists

Palestinian separatism is often confused with Arab nationalism, though their goals are incompatible. The former aspires to make Palestine a fully independent country; the latter would integrate it into a much larger entity, the Arab nation. Arab nationalists (also called Pan-Arab nationalists or Pan-Arabists) hope to build a state that will eventually comprise all Arabic speakers between the Atlantic Ocean and the Persian Gulf, from Morocco to Oman. Palestinian separatists see Palestine as an independent state; Arab nationalists envision it as a province of a much larger unit. . . .

As Palestinian separatism faltered in the 1940s, Arab nationalists inherited some of its claim to Palestine. But they emerged as the dominant force only in the mid-1950s, when the president of Egypt, Jamal 'Abd an-Nasir, mesmerized Arabic-speakers with his vision of the grandeur and power of a united Arab people. Victory against Israel was to demonstrate that power; for 'Abd an-Nasir, Palestine would be the nucleus of a pan-Arab state. Palestine had only secondary importance in 'Abd an-Nasir's vision; more important was to make Cairo the capital of a unified Arab state. But he went to war against Israel too soon and suffered the repudiation of his dreams in June 1967. Military defeat provided an opening for all those, such as the Saudi royal family, who had been threatened by 'Abd an-Nasir's radical ideas and political ambitions; they gratefully turned to the Palestinian movement, which appeared less directly dangerous to their authority. In Egypt too, 'Abd an-Nasir's successors virtually abandoned the Arab stage to remedy the domestic ills he left behind.

Arab nationalism continues to have proponents, but none so popular or powerful as 'Abd an-Nasir. . . . Arab nationalism is in deep eclipse.

From the Roman period until 1920, the term "Syria" referred

to the area stretching from Turkey to Egypt and Iraq to the Mediterranean—a region that included all of Palestine. To the extent that the inhabitants of Palestine identified with a named place, they identified with Syria. The habit of considering Palestine a part of Syria almost died out in Palestine in the 1920s, when the Palestinian identity emerged. But Palestine was still seen as part of Syria elsewhere, especially in Amman and Damascus; to this day it remains an enduring political theme in those two capitals.

(To differentiate the modern state of Syria from the historic region that had made up Syria before 1918—which included the present states of Jordan, Syria, Lebanon, and Israel—the latter is known as Greater Syria. Pan-Syrian nationalism is the ideology calling for the creation of Greater Syria.)

Jordan

Jordan has had two major kings, 'Abdallah, who ruled from 1921 to 1951, and his grandson Husayn, who has ruled since 1953. Both of them aspired to Palestine. . . .

An opportunity to seize Palestinian territory came in 1948 when Great Britain gave up its mandate. With British cooperation, the Transjordanian army already occupied parts of Palestine by the time imperial troops evacuated in May 1948. It subsequently attacked the fledgling state of Israel and captured the territory that came to be known as the West Bank. Transjordan was renamed Jordan in June 1949 and the West Bank became part of Jordan in April 1950. Only Great Britain recognized this incorporation of the West Bank; the Arab states, unwilling to accept the Jordanian claim to Palestine, refused to sanction 'Abdallah's land grab.

Acting under pressure from the Arab rivals, 'Abdallah's grandson Husayn attacked Israel in June 1967. But his army failed and instead of winning more of Palestine, he lost the West Bank to Israel. Subsequent efforts by Husayn to regain the West Bank were thwarted by the Arab states, which remained reluctant to recognize Jordanian authority west of the Jordan River. At a meeting in October 1974, Jordan was compelled by the Arab rulers to accept the PLO as the "sole legitimate representative of the Palestinian people in any Palestinian territory that is liberated." King Husayn had no choice but to bite his tongue and pretend to recognize the PLO as rightful heir to the West Bank and Gaza Strip. To make matters worse, he had to agree to cooperate with the PLO, Syria, and Egypt to insure the implementation of this resolution. . . .

Certain characteristics have distinguished the Jordanian position over nearly seven decades: enmity toward the Palestinian separatists, friendship with the West, pragmatism, disagreement with the Arab consensus, and stable working relations with the

28

Jews. . . .

Syrians widely viewed the creation of a Palestinian polity after World War I as a rupture of their country, Greater Syria. . . .

After independence in 1946, the rulers of Syria, although weak and unstable, rejected their country's borders with vehemence. Syrian armies attacked the nascent Jewish state in 1948 and emerged from the war controlling the town of al-Hamma. Like Jordan, it annexed what it held in Palestine. Unlike the West Bank, however, its territory was so small, it had no political import other than to indicate the intentions of the Syrian regime. A Syrian delegate to the Armistice Conference between Syria and Israel made this explicit, announcing that "there is no international border between Israel and Syria."

A Culture of Hate

American policy largely papers over the root cause of the turmoil in the Middle East, which is the Arab culture of hate. Arab tribes hate each other. Arab sects hate each other. The poor hate the rich, who hate the poor. And they all hate Christians and Jews, who are seen as "infidels." The Koran tells them what to do with infidels: "Oh Prophet, make war upon infidels and unbelievers, and treat them with severity."

Cal Thomas, *The Washington Times*, May 2, 1991.

As the years passed, Syria's leaders continued not to reconcile themselves to their borders. Its own president in 1953 referred to Syria as "the current official name for that country which lies within the artificial borders drawn up by imperialism"—an extraordinary remark by a head of state. Syria's delegate to the U.N. Security Council observed in 1967 that it was Syria "from which Palestine was severed and from the territory of which Israel was created."

These assertions acquired additional force in 1974, when the Asad regime made Greater Syria a central foreign policy objective. Since then, Syrian officials repeatedly argued that Palestine is Southern Syria. . . .

Such talk may appeal to Syrians, but it arouses almost unanimous opposition outside Syria. Palestinians, other Arabs, Israelis, and the Great Powers all reject Syrian ambitions. Handicapped by a morally weak claim, Damascus must rely on a combination of dissimulation and military strength. In fact, the Syrian government usually downplays its Pan-Syrian goals by supporting one of the more acceptable claimants. When Arab nationalism predominated in the 1950s and 1960s, the Syrian government espoused a pan-Arabist solution for Palestine and

29

tried, without success, to dominate the Arab nationalist movement. When Palestinian separatism became the most acceptable solution, Syrian leaders changed their tune and quickly tried to take over that movement.

Military strength is the other major theme of Syria's claim. Long after Israel's other neighbors gave up hopes of taking on Israel, raw power remains a hallmark of Damascus' approach. . . .

Arab Disunity

Inter-Arab rivalry sheds light on many vexing questions of Middle Eastern politics. To begin with, there is no single unit called "the Arabs," at least with reference to the Arab-Israeli conflict. The perpetual incapacity of the Arabs to unify is not a problem of fractious personalities but of irreconcilable goals. Short of several actors withdrawing their claims to Palestine, Arab disunity will continue indefinitely.

Second, the prominent role of inter-Arab rivalries helps to understand the place of that most elusive institution, the PLO. Several points bear stressing here: As a rule, Arab leaders find it easier to mouth pieties about "Palestinian rights" than to defy the Palestinian claim. Muhammad Hasanayn Haykal, the Egyptian columnist, suggested that "the [Palestinian] guerrilla movement can be smothered with loving caresses." Similarly, the weaker an Arab leader, the more he tends to seek PLO legitimation. And a state's support for Palestinian separatism increases in proportion to the distance between its borders and Israel's. . . .

If the Arab states have their own designs on Israel, "Palestinian rights" have much less importance for the Arab-Israeli issue than it might appear. Most Arab leaders use the Palestinian cause as a screen behind which to pursue their real aspirations. Not only does this apply to pan-Arab, Jordanian, and Syrian leaders, but to some extent it even holds for PLO chieftains; they have often been accused, not without reason, of preferring the high life over concrete achievements. According to a Jordanian official, for example, "The PLO isn't a revolution. It's a corporation. After all these years, the paychecks keep coming and life is good. The PLO cares more about preserving its privilege than helping ordinary Palestinians.". . .

The Advantages of Conflict

The Arab claimants are not eager for the conflict to end quickly; each one would rather see Israel occupy the West Bank and Gaza than one of its rivals. Israeli control keeps alive the possibility of winning these territories, whereas rule by an Arab government would close the issue. As Ho Chi Minh observed in a related situation, "It is better to sniff the dung of France for a while than to eat China's all our lives." The contest must go on:

30

lose. At that point the benefits of conflict—a means to mobilize populations, make demands on other Arab states, and play a world role—would be forfeited.

The great number of Arab claimants keeps the Arabs and Israel at war. Their interminable conflict results not from a special viciousness or intractability but from the sheer quantity of participants. The confrontation continues even though several Arab parties seek to end it by accommodating Israel's existence. The Arab nationalist claim weakened after 1967, only to have its mantle passed to the Palestinian separatists. Egypt pulled out in the 1970s but its place was filled by Syria. Fundamentalist Muslims and West Bankers wait in the wings. As 'Arafat moves in the direction of a political resolution, other Palestinian groups fill the void, and the level of violence does not diminish. The rivalry fuels the conflict, the conflict provides a cover for the rivalry. . . .

For this reason, the impact of efforts by Arab leaders seeking to end the conflict—Mubarak, King Husayn, King Hasan, many of the Lebanese—will be limited so long as the Arab rivalry continues. Multiple actors prohibit a lasting peace with Israel. Resolution waits for the Arab positions to be whittled down. Although there is no prospect of this occurring soon, it could come about in one of three ways: by one actor dominating the others, by cooperation, or by all but one actor dropping their claims. A reduction in the multiplicity of Arab claims to Palestine would signal a beginning of the Arab-Israeli conflict's conclusion. . . .

The Causes of Conflict

Finally, inter-Arab relations—and not Arab-Israeli relations—are the cause of political volatility in the Middle East. The center of gravity lies in meetings of the Arab League, subsidies given to the PLO, press denunciations of Arab leaders who negotiate with Israel, terrorism against Arab diplomats, and the like. These drive the conflict far more than such factors as Israeli policy on the West Bank or U.S. willingness to sell arms to Saudi Arabia. Ironically, the state of relations between Arabs and Jews has only secondary importance; Israel's lack of diplomatic relations with the Arab states matters less than Egypt's.

Although Israeli-Palestinian relations receive massive attention, these have only tertiary importance. Were Arafat to accept Israel tomorrow, retire from the PLO, and move to a suburb of Haifa, hostilities would continue almost unabated. Indeed, the claims of other Palestinian leaders, the Arab nationalists, Amman, and Damascus would grow even stronger. The exaggerated attention paid in recent years to the Palestinian issue has distorted the issue by conflating the Arab struggle. To ignore the other Arab actors is dangerous for Israel and foolish for others.

31

"The Arabs have never forgotten the promises of freedom made to them in the First World War . . . and the subsequent betrayal of them."

A Legacy of Colonialism Causes Middle East Conflict

Phillip Knightley

Phillip Knightley writes in the following viewpoint that the root causes of Middle East conflict occurred after World War I when the Arab inhabitants of the Middle East were promised independence by Great Britain and France for fighting against the Turkish Ottoman empire, only to be betrayed when the two nations divided up the Middle East into colonies for themselves. Although these colonies no longer exist, Knightley concludes that the repercussions of British and French actions have continued to ensure conflict and Arab hatred of the West. Knightley is a journalist and author whose books include *The Secret Lives of Lawrence of Arabia* and *The First Casualty*, a study of war reporting and propaganda.

As you read, consider the following questions:

1. What is the importance of T.E. Lawrence in explaining the present situation in the Middle East, according to Knightley?
2. What two forces caused European nations to break their promise of granting Arab independence, according to the author?
3. Why is Knightley pessimistic about the chances for peace in the Middle East?

Adapted from "Desert Warriors: Why Are We in Saudi Arabia? Blame It on Lawrence" by Phillip Knightley, *M, Inc.*, November 1990. Copyright © 1990 Phillip Knightley. Reprinted with the author's permission.

The West lied to the Arabs in the First World War; it promised them independence but then imposed imperial mandates; this ensured Arab disunity at the very moment when the West created the state of Israel.

In January 1919, Paris was a city of pomp and splendor. The most ghastly war in history had ended two months earlier in triumph for the Allies: Britain, France, and the United States. Now diplomats from these countries, grave, impressive men flanked by their military advisers, had arrived for the peace conference that would decide the fate of Germany and divide the spoils of victory. . . .

T.E. Lawrence

In this colorful, cosmopolitan gathering, one delegate stood out. Restaurants grew quiet when he entered, and there was much behind-the-scenes jostling to meet him. For this was Lawrence of Arabia, the young Englishman who had helped persuade the Arabs to revolt against their Turkish masters, who were allies of Germany. This was the brilliant intelligence officer who had welded the warring tribes of the Middle East into a formidable guerrilla force. . . .

As a British political intelligence officer, Lawrence's job had been to find the Arab leaders most suited to run the revolt against the Turks, to keep them loyal to Britain by promises of freedom that he knew Britain would never keep and to risk this fraud "on my conviction that Arab help was necessary to our cheap and speedy victory in the East and that better we win and break our word than lose.". . .

The Arabs have never forgotten the promises of freedom made to them in the First World War by the likes of Lawrence and President Woodrow Wilson, and the subsequent betrayal of them at Paris. It will haunt them because history in the Middle East never favors the foreigner and always takes its revenge on those who insist on seeing the region through their own eyes.

The mess began soon after the turn of the century. Until then the Middle East had been under 400 years of domination by the Ottoman empire, a vast and powerful hegemony extending over northern Africa, Asia, and Europe. At one stage it had stretched from the Adriatic to Aden and from Morocco to the Persian Gulf, and the skill of its generals and the bravery of its soldiers once pushed its reach into Europe as far as the outskirts of Vienna.

But by the mid-nineteenth century the impact of Western technology had started to make itself felt, and the great empire began to flake at the edges. When in 1853 Czar Nicholas called Turkey "a sick man," Britain became worried. If Turkey collapsed, Britain would have a duty to protect her own military and economic lines of communication with India, where half the British army was stationed and which was unquestionably Britain's best customer.

Others also looked to their interests. Germany wanted to turn Iraq into "a German India"; France longed for Syria, a sentiment that dated back to the Crusades; and Russia yearned to dominate Constantinople, a terminus for all caravan routes in the Middle East.

By the early 1900s all these countries were pursuing their aims by covert action. In the regions now known as Afghanistan, Iran, Iraq, Syria, and the Persian Gulf, networks of Western intelligence agents—ostensibly consuls, travelers, merchants and archaeologists—were busy influencing chieftains, winning over tribes, settling disputes, and disparaging their rivals in the hope that they would benefit from the eventual disintegration of the Ottoman empire.

When the First World War broke out in August 1914, Turkey dithered and then chose the wrong side by joining Germany. Lawrence, working for the Arab Bureau in Cairo, was part of a plan to use Arab nationalism in the service of British war aims.

The scheme was simple. The British would encourage the Arabs to revolt against their Turkish masters by the promise of independence when Turkey was defeated. . . .

The more worldly Arab nationalists warned that helping France and Britain achieve victory over Turkey might well lead merely to an exchange of one form of foreign domination for another. But these words of warning went unheeded because the hopes of the Arab masses were raised by the United States' entry into the war in April 1917.

The Arabs thought that the American government might be more receptive than the British to their demands for self-determination. After all, the Americans knew what it was like to be under the thumb of a colonial power, and President Wilson's Fourteen Points, which advocated freedom and self-determination for races under the domination of the old multinational empires, was highly encouraging.

But the Arab skeptics turned out to be right. The Allies did not keep their promises. The Arabs did exchange one imperial ruler for another. There were forces at work of which they were ignorant. The two most powerful of these were oil and the Zionist hunger for a national home in Palestine.

The Scramble for Oil

The automobile had in 1919 not yet become the twentieth-century's most desirable object, but the war had made everyone realize the strategic importance of oil. Germany's oil-fired navy had been immobilized in port after the Battle of Jutland in May 1916, largely because the British blockade caused a shortage of fuel. German industrial production was hindered by a lack of lubricants, and its civilian transport almost came to a halt.

It was clear, then, that in any future conflict oil would be an essential weapon. Britain already had one source: British Petroleum, owned in part by the British government, had been pumping oil at Masjid-i-Salaman in Iran's Zagros Mountains since 1908. But it was not enough.

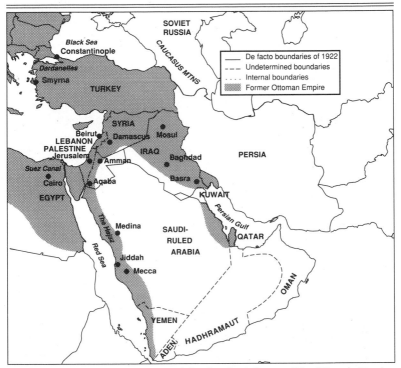

Map shows Middle East as of 1922, following the collapse of the Ottoman Empire. Britain took control over Iraq, Transjordan, and Palestine, while France took what is now Syria and Lebanon.

Source: *Smithsonian*, May 1991. Copyright © 1991, Bowring Cartographic. Reprinted with permission.

Even before the 1919 peace conference began to divide up the Middle East between Britain and France, some horse trading had taken place, making it unlikely that the promises made to the Arabs would be respected. France, for example, gave Britain the oil-rich area around Mosul, Iraq, in exchange for a share of the oil and a free hand in Syria. Unfortunately, Britain had already promised Syria to the Arabs. St. John Philby, the eccentric but perceptive English adviser to ibn Saud—and the man who eventually introduced American oil interests to Saudi Arabia—

understood that British explanations were mere pieties: "The real crux is oil."

At the peace conference, private oil concerns pushed their governments (in the national interest, of course) to renounce all wartime promises to the Arabs. For the oilmen saw only too well that oil concessions and royalties would be easier to negotiate with a series of rival Arab states lacking any sense of unity, than with a powerful independent Arab state in the Middle East. . . .

Zionism and Palestine

The second force that helped frustrate Arab aspirations was Zionism. While the European powers had seen the war with Turkey as an opportunity to divide the Ottoman empire and thus extend their imperial ambitions in the Middle East, the Zionists quickly realized that the future of Palestine was now open and that they might be able to play a large part in its future.

The British Zionists were led by Dr. Chaim Weizmann, a brilliant chemist who contributed to the war effort by discovering a new process for manufacturing acetone, a substance vital for TNT that was until then produced only in Germany. Weizmann saw a historic opening for Zionism and began to lobby influential British politicians. . . .

There was not much sympathy in the cabinet at first, but the Zionists did not let the matter lapse. Early in their talks with British politicians it became clear to them that the British government felt that only a British Palestine would be a reliable buffer for the Suez Canal. Weizmann therefore assured Britain that in exchange for its support, Zionists would work for the establishment of a British protectorate there. This suited Britain better than the agreement it had already made with France for an *international* administration for Palestine.

So on November 2, 1917, Foreign Secretary Arthur Balfour made his famous and deeply ambiguous declaration that Britain would "view with favor the establishment in Palestine of a national home for the Jewish people. . . ." How did the pledge to the Zionists square with what had already been promised to the Arabs in return for their support in the war against the Turks?

Never Resolved

This has been a matter of continuing controversy, but has never been satisfactorily resolved. The first agreement between the Arabs and the British was in correspondence between the British high commissioner in Egypt and King Hussein in Mecca. The Arabs say that these letters included Palestine in the area in which Britain promised to uphold Arab independence.

The Zionists deny this. The denial has also been the official British attitude, and it was endorsed by the Palestine Royal Commission report in 1937. But an Arab Bureau report, never rescinded or corrected, puts Palestine firmly in the area promised to the Arabs.

By the time of the peace conference, with a Zionist lobby led by Weizmann and Harvard Law School professor Felix Frankfurter (later U.S. Supreme Court justice) actively working for a national home in Palestine, the Arabs realized that they had been outmaneuvered. President Wilson, trying to be fair, insisted that a commission be dispatched to find out the wishes of the people in the whole area.

Their report made blunt reading: While there could be mandates for Palestine, Syria, and Iraq, they should only be for a limited term—independence was to be granted, as soon as possible. The idea of making Palestine into a Jewish commonwealth should be dropped. This suggestion that the Zionists should forget about Palestine must have seemed quite unrealistic—their aims were too close to realization for them to be abandoned—so it surprised only the Arabs when the report was ignored, even in Washington.

It took a further two years for the Allies to tidy up the arrangements they had made for the division of the Middle East. In April 1920, there was another conference, at San Remo, Italy, to ratify earlier agreements. The whole Arab rectangle lying between the Mediterranean and the Persian frontier, including Palestine, was placed under mandates allotted to suit the imperialist ambitions of Britain and France.

There was an outburst of bitter anger. The Arabs began raiding British establishments in Iraq and striking at the French in Syria. Both insurrections were ruthlessly put down. In Iraq the British army burnt any village from which an attack had been mounted, but the Iraqis were not deterred. . . .

Arab Nationalist leaders waited for American protests at this suppression in Iraq and Syria but nothing happened. What the Arabs failed to see was that with the Zionists already in the ascendancy in Palestine, America had lost interest in the sordid struggle of imperial powers in the Middle East.

Arab Humiliation

The humiliation suffered by those Arabs who had allied themselves with the imperial powers was encapsulated by the experiences of Faisal, the Arab leader Lawrence had "created" and then abandoned, the Arab he had chosen as military leader of the revolt, the man to whom he had conveyed all Britain's promises. When the French kicked Faisal out of Syria, an embarrassed delegation of British officials waited on him as he passed through Palestine. . . . It seems reasonable to assume that Lawrence felt guilty over the betrayal of the Arabs, both on a personal and a national level.

This would explain why he jumped at the chance to join Winston Churchill, who had by this time moved to the Colonial Office, and was determined to do something about the Middle East. Lawrence's first job was to make amends to Faisal by offering to make him king of Iraq.

The problem was that it was not clear that the Iraqis wanted Faisal. There were other popular claimants, including ibn Saud of Saudi Arabia, whom Churchill had rejected for fear that "he would plunge the whole country into religious pandemonium." Another candidate, the nationalist leader Sayid Taleb, gained enormous popular support after threatening to revolt if the British did not allow the Iraqis to choose their leader freely.

Ever resourceful, the British sabotaged Taleb's candidacy by arranging for an armored car to pick him up as he left the British high commissioner's house in Baghdad following afternoon tea. He was then whisked on board a British ship and sent for a long holiday in Ceylon. With Sayid Taleb out of the way, Faisal was elected king by a suspiciously large majority—96.8 percent.

British Influence

Because the British desired a quiet, stable state in Jordan to protect Palestine, Faisal's brother Abdullah was made king and provided with money and troops in return for his promise to suppress local anti-French and anti-Zionist activity. Their father, Hussein, the sharif of Mecca, the man who had started the Arab revolt, was offered £100,000 a year not to make a nuisance of himself. . . .

And that was that. Lawrence regarded this as redemption in full of Britain's promises to the Arabs. Unfortunately, the Arabs did not see it his way and have, in one way or another, been in revolt ever since.

In Iraq, Faisal managed to obtain some measure of independence by the time of his death in 1932. But British forces intervened again in 1942 to overthrow the pro-German nationalist government of Rashid Ali and restore the monarchy. Faisal's kingdom fell for the last time in 1958, a belated casualty of the Anglo-French invasion of Egypt two years earlier.

France hung on to Syria and Lebanon until 1946 before grudgingly evacuating its forces. In the same year Britain—then coming to terms with her diminished postwar status—gave up her claim on Jordan. Abdullah reigned until 1951 when he was shot dead while entering the mosque of El Aqsa in Jerusalem in the company of his grandson, the present King Hussein. The assassin was a follower of the ex-Mufti of Jerusalem, who had accused Abdullah of having betrayed the Arabs over Palestine.

In 1958 the American Sixth Fleet stood by to save Hussein from a repetition of the coup that had just ousted his cousin, Faisal II, in Iraq. Hussein and his kingdom, shorn of the West Bank, have survived—the lasting legacy of Lawrence.

"U.S. resistance to change has added fuel to the fires of ethnic and religious conflicts."

U.S. Involvement Is a Cause of Middle East Conflict

National Mobilization for Survival

The U.S. has been heavily involved in the Middle East since the 1940s. In the following viewpoint, taken from a pamphlet produced by National Mobilization for Survival, the authors argue that U.S. support of Israel and selling of arms to the Middle East have contributed to and exacerbated Middle East conflicts. The authors conclude that the U.S. must withdraw its military presence from the region and work harder on diplomatic efforts to attain peace in the Middle East. The National Mobilization for Survival advocates nuclear disarmament and other peace and social justice issues.

As you read, consider the following questions:

1. Why were the late 1980s a time of hope for peace in the Middle East, according to the authors?
2. Why do the authors believe that Middle Easterners distrust the U.S.?
3. According to the authors, what should guide U.S. policy in the Middle East?

Adapted from "Middle East Peace Alternative" by National Mobilization for Survival, January 1991. Reprinted with permission.

A broad international consensus seemed to exist in the late 1980s on the basis for peace in the Middle East. The Palestine Liberation Organization, seen by the great majority of the Palestinians as their leadership, proposed a political agenda based on negotiations through an international peace conference leading to the establishment of a Palestinian state alongside Israel. Many people in Israel and the Arab world joined the call for a negotiated solution. U.S.-Soviet detente seemed to make peace more likely.

New Violence

Yet the 1990s have brought new violence to the region. The endless wars in Lebanon and Afghanistan have been overshadowed by even bigger wars. Even before the Iraqi 1990 invasion of Kuwait, Israeli intransigence and the U.S. decision to break off dialogue with the P.L.O. were exacerbating the Israeli-Palestinian conflict. With the outbreak of the U.S.-Iraq war in 1991, the U.S. government once again chose war over peace, at the cost of death and devastation for thousands of people. A period of intensified conflict began across the Middle East.

The U.S. peace movement neither foresaw nor forestalled this new outbreak of violence. It has fallen short in influencing U.S. Middle East policy or even taking clear positions. This *Middle East Peace Alternative* is an attempt to explain the new descent into violence. It suggests why U.S. policy has been fruitless. It lays out principles for just and lasting peace in the Middle East, and specific goals that could bring peace closer.

Since the 1940s, U.S. policy in the Middle East has been designed to ensure U.S. economic and political control over the region. The U.S. has been willing to back repressive and unpopular regimes as long as they would protect U.S. investment, above all by U.S.-based oil companies. It has enlisted the state of Israel as a well-paid and useful junior partner in return for U.S. support.

As a result, the U.S. has seen movements for social change or national freedom in the Middle East as enemies. U.S. resistance to change has added fuel to the fires of ethnic and religious conflicts. Today these conflicts are fought with some of the world's most advanced bombers and missiles, many of them U.S.-supplied. On several occasions conflicts in the Middle East have brought the world perilously close to nuclear war.

Exacerbating Regional Tensions

When the Middle East entered the modern era, the multi-ethnic Ottoman empire that had dominated it was divided between European colonial powers, particularly the British and French. To win an initial foothold the European powers manipulated traditional religious and ethnic leaderships that had coexisted under Ottoman rule. After the First World War, Britain and France strengthened the role of sectarian movements and set them against one another in order to maintain the British and French empires. They saw the rise of nationalism and of independent Middle Eastern nations as a threat.

Failed Formulas

The United States has tried a variety of "formulas" aimed at protecting its interests in the region while "accommodating" Arab nationalism. The leaders of Jordan, Egypt, Morocco, and Lebanon have been protected (and spied upon) by CIA-trained security units, as Bob Woodward revealed in *Veil*; for twenty years Jordan's King Hussein even received annual stipends from the agency. Surrogates for U.S. power, like the shah of Iran and the Israelis, have been armed and given broad latitude. Practically everybody else with money—regardless of their despotic ways—was sold weapons as well, so long as they stayed out of the Soviet orbit. U.S. efforts to bar Soviet influence from the region combined with tilts toward favored clients had the effect of spurring deadly arms races and outbreaks of Arab-Israeli conflict.

Micah L. Sifry, *The Nation*, March 11, 1991.

After the Second World War the U.S. took over the role of the old colonial powers. U.S. policy has perpetuated the pattern of divide and rule. It has pitted communities against one another, primarily on the basis of their usefulness to U.S. power. The U.S. has backed efforts by reactionary movements in Lebanon to maintain a sectarian state structure in that country, sending in the Marines in 1958 and 1982. It gives the Israeli government the money and weapons it uses to push aside Palestinians in order to make room for Jewish settlers and new Jewish immigrants. It gives the Afghan mujahedin the money and weapons they use to impose their vision of Islam on both believers and non-believers. It has restored the power of the emir and the few who hold Kuwaiti citizenship over the disenfranchised majority in Kuwait.

Such U.S. actions contribute to a trend toward fragmentation and theocracy: the rise of "Islamic" states, the division of Lebanon and discrimination against non-Jews in Israel. They also make enemies of entire peoples. Most nations throughout the Middle East view the U.S. with suspicion. The U.S. has alienated not only the Palestinian and Lebanese peoples, but also peoples like the Kurds, whom it has used only to abandon them later to brutal Iraqi, Iranian and Turkish repression. To

41

many people in the region, the United States stands as a symbol of militaristic and racist forces supporting governments and movements that suppress them.

Blocking Palestinian Self-Determination

The Palestinian uprising is only one dramatic example of how current U.S. policy fosters conflict. The popular uprising (*Intifada*) grew out of decades of frustration with the status quo felt by the Palestinians in the territories Israel has occupied since 1967, who decided to take the issue into their own hands. The uprising has shown the inhumanity of the U.S.-funded Israeli occupation. It has also shown that Palestinians can organize and govern themselves. In 1988, the Palestinian National Council officially expressed Palestinians' will to govern themselves by proclaiming an independent Palestinian state. Almost in the same breath the PNC made unmistakably clear Palestinians' desire for a just peace with Israel.

The U.S. government's post-Gulf War gestures toward Arab-Israeli peace are doomed to failure as long as the U.S. has failed to acknowledge the Palestinians' right to national self-determination and failed to recognize the state the Palestinians are creating. Israel has remained the highest recipient of U.S. foreign aid throughout the uprising. Israel receives 20 percent of the U.S. foreign aid budget, amounting to more than $8 million per day or more than $7 million per Congressional District.

Reliance on Military Force

Every U.S. President since World War II has issued and endorsed doctrines stating U.S. determination to use military force to influence Middle East events. The U.S. Central Command includes hundreds of thousands of troops, nuclear-equipped naval battle groups in the Mediterranean, Gulf and Indian Ocean, and access to military bases in Bahrain, Diego Garcia, Egypt, Israel, Kenya, Morocco, Oman, United Arab Emirates, Saudi Arabia, Somalia and across southern Europe. The U.S.-Iraq war enabled the Pentagon to realize its long standing ambition of U.S. bases in the Arabian Peninsula.

Of the top ten recipients of U.S. military aid worldwide, four countries are in the Middle East: Israel, Egypt, Turkey and Pakistan. Three others, Portugal, Spain and Greece, host U.S. military bases which are used to support intervention in Middle East conflicts. The U.S. gives or sells billions of dollars worth of military hardware to Israel, Egypt, Saudi Arabia, Jordan and other countries in the region. Having armed the Shah of Iran before 1979, the U.S. built up Iraq as a barrier to Iranian power in the 1980s. Then to ensure victory in its war with Iraq, the U.S. sent billions of dollars worth of weapons to Saudi Arabia, and billions more to Israel. The spiral of armaments and violence continually escalates.

In the Middle East more than anywhere else in the world, the U.S. government has relied on deploying and threatening to use nuclear weapons. It has an extensive nuclear capability in the Middle East: on ships in its Mediterranean fleet, on planes based on aircraft carriers and on bases in nearby NATO countries. The U.S. has detailed contingency plans for escalation to nuclear war. At least five times during Middle East crises, up to and including the Gulf War, the U.S. has threatened to initiate nuclear war.

Due to a spiral of hostility to which U.S. policy has contributed, many Middle Eastern governments are turning to nuclear weapons as an imagined safeguard. Israel already has over 100 nuclear warheads. . . . . Several other Middle Eastern countries will develop the technology and raw materials needed to manufacture their own nuclear weapons during the 1990s. Nuclear technology, equipment and fuels supplied by the U.S. and its allies have helped create this perilous situation.

Principles for Peace

The peace and justice movement needs to present an alternative to current U.S. Middle East policy. We need a policy founded on principles genuinely compatible with lasting peace: the dignity and equality of peoples, social and economic justice, democracy and human rights.

Self-Determination. All people have the right to determine the political and social system under which they will live. . . . The United States must respect the right of all peoples in the Middle East to self-determination.

Nonintervention. We show our respect for self-determination by renouncing military interference in the affairs of other countries. . . . The United States must end its military intervention and its preparation for intervention in the Middle East.

Human Rights and Democracy. Any legitimate government must respect the full range of human rights for its citizens. The United States must end its backing and funding for governments that are undemocratic or violate human rights.

Equality of Peoples and Religions. In a region of many peoples and faiths, the only possible basis for coexistence is tolerance and guaranteed rights for all. . . . The United States must stop supporting or condoning ethnic or religious discrimination.

Equitable and Genuine Economic Development. Although domestic elites and multinational corporations have grown rich on oil, most people in the Middle East live in poverty. The United States must accept economic policies and assist development programs designed and controlled by the majority of people of the Middle East to meet their own needs.

"No institutions or political mechanisms, such as . . . free speech, exist to temper or moderate the use of force in a leader."

Lack of Democracy Creates Middle East Conflict

David Pryce-Jones

David Pryce-Jones is the author of fifteen books, including *The Closed Circle: An Interpretation of the Arabs*. In the following viewpoint, he argues that conflict persists in the Middle East because it is rooted in Arab culture. Arab states are ruled by dictators, he writes, who use force and military victory to justify their rule and status. Pryce-Jones maintains that Arabs respect power and will therefore follow powerful leaders, even though these leaders may be cruel and oppressive.

As you read, consider the following questions:

1. Why is military force useful to Arab leaders, according to Pryce-Jones?
2. How does the author contrast Western and Arab societies?
3. Why is negotiating for peace so difficult in the Middle East, according to Pryce-Jones?

Excerpted from "The Conquering Hero" by David Pryce-Jones, *The New Republic*, September 24, 1990. Reprinted by permission of *The New Republic*, © 1990, The New Republic, Inc.

Refusal to reflect upon the reality of the Arab world leads time and again to being disagreeably surprised by it. Anwar Sadat's crossing of the Suez Canal in 1973, the use of the oil weapon, the collapse of Lebanon and its invasion by Syria, the intifada, Saddam Hussein's attacks on Iran and Kuwait—all are presented in the West as unpredictable as acts of God. Their perpetrators are thought to be irrational or suicidal. Yet all are a natural part of the Arab social and political order. The violence is systemic, therefore self-repeating. . . .

According to Arab culture, power belongs to whoever has the will and strength to grasp it. Victory goes deservedly to the strong, while the vanquished and the weak are to be despised. Force is therefore a necessary instrument, the means by which the would-be leader eliminates his rivals. Once he has become an absolute power-holder at home, he finds some pretext to extend his reach by attacking abroad. Far from being considered a crime, the use of force establishes credentials in a leader, and determines the primacy of his status. So it happens that Arabs come to applaud a leader who is very obviously endangering them.

Western societies are based upon free association, government by consent under the rule of law—in a word, contract. Contract is incompatible with the Arab concept of absolute power sanctioned by status. The gap between status and contract was perfectly illustrated in the way the 1990 (Iraqi) invasion of Kuwait was answered by the legalities of the United Nations.

To Westerners, the use of force indicates social or political breakdown, and they can hardly conceive it in any positive connection with leadership and honor. It seems paradoxical that what looks like disorder and violence is actually a form of stability, a constant Darwinian testing of internal and external relationships. What puts an end to the ambitions of a leader is the arrival upon the scene of another who is more than his match. Communism in its heyday offered an approximation. The Party deemed that the promotion of its ends justified violence. The alleged class struggle of Nicolae Ceausescu resembled the careerist struggle of Saddam Hussein. Ceausescu's downfall is said to have jolted Hussein.

Culture, Not Character

Needless to say, Arabs are no more and no less disposed than other peoples to war and cruelty. The historic formula that "force is the only language they understand" is not a racist ascription of innate bad character, but a comment upon the absolutism built into their culture. No institutions or political mechanisms, such as genuine representation or free speech, exist to temper or moderate the use of force in a leader. *"L'état c'est moi"* is the total philosophy of every Arab ruler. Hussein put it clearly when he said that in Iraq the law is two lines on a sheet of paper with his signature below.

If the potential Arab leader is to succeed, he requires a heroic biography. Muammar Qaddafi, Yasir Arafat, Saddam Hussein, and others claim to have murdered with their own hands those who stood in their way. Hussein is sometimes credited with twenty-two murders carried out in person. These may well be only rumors or imaginative projections for purposes of enhancing status. Yet for these murders—as well as for ordering the gassing of the Kurds, Iraqi Shiites, and Iranians, and for practicing terrorism and waging wars of aggrandizement—Hussein can expect support from his culture. Many Arabs, of course, see him as a monster, but many more do indeed think he is making a hero of himself. Even those who fear him are compelled to admire in him an audacity they could not emulate.

No Opposition

Arab leaders have never faced the scrutiny of a fearless media or the heat of a truly free opposition. Arab leaders emerged unscathed from disasters they have personally inflicted on their own nations. Can anyone imagine Muammar Qaddafi facing a Libyan Ted Koppel in order to explain his unprovoked invasion of, and consequent humiliating withdrawal from, neighboring Chad? Hafez el-Assad sacrificed tens of thousands of Syrian soldiers in Lebanon and dwindled his national foreign currency reserves by impulsively purchasing arms. Syrians in line for food rations will never get to ask him: "Why?"

Amotz Asa-El, *The Christian Science Monitor*, November 11, 1990.

In the absence of any check on a leader's quest for power and status, he will press on until the test of experience reveals his limits. All the wars and coups in the Middle East of the past forty years are expressions of this quest on the part of one leader after another. In this latest example, Saudi Arabia and the other Gulf states understand that the next testing of Saddam Hussein's limits is likely to be at their expense. King Hussein daily demonstrates his fear of the same fate.

Little or nothing in Saddam Hussein's experience would have led him to anticipate that in invading Kuwait he might overreach the limit of his power. The international community had hardly complained at the use of forbidden forms of warfare against Iranians or about the tortures and executions in Iraq. When he was in danger of losing the war against Iran, the superpowers and other European states had, in fact, hastened to his rescue with arms, and until the attack on Kuwait had been offering financial credits, more arms, and overt encouragement. To Hussein, the world had granted him victory and status, which could only mean that it acknowledged him as the decisive arbiter of power in the Gulf and perhaps the entire Middle East. The embargo and sanctions of the U.N. may well have surprised Hussein as much as he had surprised others.

Arab leaders in search of power and status have made a practice of justifying their ambition by repeated claims to Arab unity, Islam, and supposed anti-Western sentiment. Hussein follows this well-worn path. Yet far from creating unity, he has raised up against himself a coalition of Egypt, Saudi Arabia, Syria, and others who dread his ambition, and for whom his downfall has become a political necessity. They have made a rational calculation that his idea of Arab unity involves their liquidation. Where Islam is concerned, in 1979 Hussein hanged the Iraqi Ayatollah Muhammad Al-Sadr as a warning that he was tolerating no fundamentalism, and he is already responsible for protracted intra-Muslim fighting. Demonstration of his power of life and death over Western hostages, and his repeated broadcasts in the rhetoric of honor about "burning" his enemies or cutting off parts of their bodies, are just self-enhancements typical of the culture and attempts to cover himself with doctrine.

The Palestinians

The Palestinians as usual are a special case. Kuwait had sheltered perhaps 350,000 of them, the majority of whom are probably still there. Its university was the last refuge of Palestinian intellectuals, among them some able PLO spokesmen. These Palestinians and their publications are now subjected to Iraqi control. Homes, businesses, and savings have been swept away. Tens of millions of dollars in subsidies from Kuwait, Saudi Arabia, and the rest of the Gulf will not be paid. Palestinians everywhere will be poorer, and their cause has suffered a disastrous setback.

Yet by and large the PLO leadership, and consequently the Palestinian masses, support Hussein. The motivation is instructive. Calculation counts for less than the recovery of honor and status. They feel humiliated by their history, and they are particularly aggrieved about unjust treatment in Kuwait, Jordan, and under Israeli occupation. Since Hussein threatens those responsible for such injustice, they overlook the fact that he is acting on his own behalf and is certain to retain all spoils for himself. New graffiti on the West Bank say, essentially, that chemical weapons mean strength (a play in Arabic on *qawii*, strong, and *kimawii*, chemical). In the event of chemical war, the rump of Palestine risks being lost forever, either through use of the weapon in the area or because an Israel at the end of its tether might drive the Arabs out. But so strong is the culture that the wish for violent revenge takes priority over self-interest.

No Room for Negotiations

In the old days the Ottoman sultan would have dispatched a pasha with a column of soldiers to hang someone like Hussein as a disturber of the peace. Faced with the same problem between the two world wars, the British and French decided to cut their losses and handed power to the disturbers, who of course described themselves as nationalist heroes. Gamal Abdel Nasser and his imitators, of whom Hussein is only the most recent, sought for themselves as much power as possible, creating conflicts of interest between Arabs and Westerners.

Irrespective of the rights and wrongs of those conflicts, the huge majority of Westerners each time called for solutions through negotiation. This too was a cultural response, but one that finds no correspondence in the Arab order. To be sure, Arabs have complex and satisfactory means of resolving disputes of low intensity through consensus. But once engaged in a conflict concerning a vital interest, an Arab leader has no choice but to give priority to status, and by definition status is not negotiable.

"If left unresolved, the problems of economic inequity . . . may cause future conflicts in the region."

Economic Inequality Causes Conflict

Mamoun Fandy

Mamoun Fandy is a U.S.-based Egyptian journalist whose articles have appeared in the *New York Times* and the *Christian Science Monitor*. In the following viewpoint, he argues that a primary cause of conflict in the Middle East is the stark contrast between rich and poor peoples in the region, both between and within countries. Fandy states that many Middle East political developments and conflicts, including the rise of Islamic fundamentalism, can be traced to the social unrest caused by poverty and economic inequality in the region.

As you read, consider the following questions:

1. Why does Fandy believe that the plight of poor Middle East nations cannot be viewed as separate from the situation of wealthy Middle East countries?
2. How does wealth relate to the growth of Islam, according to the author?
3. What possible future wars in the Middle East does Fandy believe might happen?

Mamoun Fandy, "The Rich Get Richer, the Poor Get Poorer." (A different version of this article appeared in the *Nuclear Times*, Autumn 1991.) Reprinted with permission.

During the 1991 Persian Gulf war, the Iraqi leadership brought to the forefront the hostilities between the haves and the have-nots of the Middle East. To those unfamiliar with the Arab world, these issues initially appeared to be merely a pretext for Iraq to invade Kuwait. But if left unresolved, the problems on economic inequity—both between and within Arab countries—may cause further conflicts in the region. And the Persian Gulf war has had the unfortunate effect of further aggravating these socioeconomic issues.

For years, wealthy Gulf countries have employed millions of "guest workers" from impoverished Arab countries to fill their work force. Now, however, the prosperous Arab countries that allied themselves with the United States during the war are expelling guest workers whose countries *failed to join the U.S.-led coalition.*

Most of these affluent Gulf countries have chosen to hire Americans and Asians, since they no longer fear the military strength *or political power* of the poorer nations. Moreover, the burden of the millions of displaced refugees will increase internal and ethnic conflict and cause greater economic inequity in the region. [In the absence of scientific solutions to complex problems, Islamic fundamentalists offer a simple solution: follow the Qur'an and God will solve the problem. For desperate and uneducated people, and most Arabs are both, this solution is appealing. Consequently, as the problem escalates and frustration builds, the Arab world may be swept by an Islamic revolution similar to that in Iran in 1979. This time, however, the fight may not merely be internal; it may also pit the poor Arab states against the rich ones. There is already enough resentment and hatred to trigger such a fight.]

Unearned Wealth

The *resentment* of the impoverished Arabs in such countries as Sudan, Yemen, Egypt, Syria, Tunisia, Morocco and Mauritania against the Arabs of the wealthy Gulf states is *rooted in history and arises from the perception that the now-rich families of the Gulf have stolen a wealth that should have belonged to all.* All of the Middle East and North Africa were once united under the caliphs. For thousands of years, nomadic tribes have travelled across what are now borders, and in fact continue to do this today between Saudi Arabia and Yemen, Morocco and Algeria, and Egypt and Libya.

Yet artificial boundaries contrived by colonial powers have separated the countries with oil from the countries without. In Arab eyes, the wealthy ruling families who profit from the oil revenues have no inherent right to this money, since they have done nothing to earn it. In the words of the poet Ahmed Mattar, gulf Arabs have a claim to the oil wells only because "their grandfathers' camels walked over them before ours did." Indeed, the Saud family doesn't even have that claim, since many of the oil deposits lie in the territory of the now dispossessed Shia tribesmen of Saudi Arabia's Eastern province or in land also claimed by Yemen.

Wealth and Poverty

The wealth that does exist in the Arab world is extremely concentrated. Figures for income distribution within countries, if they exist, are considered state secrets. Yet it is easy to see the disparities among countries as reflected in official national income accounts. Yemen's ambassador to the United Nations, Abdallah al-Ashtal, has observed that the region contains six of the richest (i.e., most cash-liquid) countries in the world and six of the poorest. Rami Khouri, the respected former editor of the *Jordan Times*, calculates that per-capita income in the Arab world, using 1986 figures, "ranged from $9,600 among the 15 million people of the oil-producing states, to $2,000 among the 60 million people of the middle-income Arab countries, to just $500 among the 113 million people of the low-income states."

Joe Stork, *World Policy Journal*, Spring 1991.

The plight of the poor Arab countries, moreover, cannot be viewed as separate from the good fortune of the prosperous ones, but rather as part of an interlocking system for maintaining the power of the ruling class in the rich and poor Arab countries alike. The poorer countries have an exportable worker class. The willingness of unemployed laborers, artisans, and even university graduates to work in the Gulf states relieves the poor countries of potential social agitators. Moreover, the "guest workers" are so ill-treated in the Gulf states that the repression in their own countries seems mild in comparison. (The repression ranges from harassment—like the case of an Egyptian teenager who was beaten and had his head shaved by Saudi Arabia's morality police because he was walking down the street singing a popular song—to false imprisonment and torture. One Lebanese cook was tortured for two weeks in a Saudi jail for admitting that he was a Shia Muslim.)

The Gulf rulers also benefit from the system of "guest workers." Since they hire foreigners to do all the work, they do not need their own citizens' services and can afford to ignore these citizens' requests for improved human rights and greater political participation. (Incidentally, human rights organizations are not allowed into most of the Gulf states, neither before the war nor now). The war has made this terrible situation worse, both politically and economically. Before the war, Arab workers stayed in the Gulf states because their only choices were to endure the maltreatment or risk the starvation of their families. When the war began, however, most of the workers fled for their lives. Some lost their life savings, others were robbed, and thousands, including many children, died on the road to Jordan or Iran or while waiting for the airplanes and ships to take them home.

These transportation efforts were stalled by many governments that realized the refugees could cause both economic and political conflict in their countries. Other Arab countries, such as Saudi Arabia, expelled workers from countries that failed to support the coalition. Many workers had no safe place to go. The Sudanese would be returning to an ongoing civil war, and Lebanese and Palestinians would be returning to occupied territories and the conflict with the Israelis in South Lebanon and the West Bank. The only alternative for many was to remain in poverty-stricken Jordan.

Also among the worse victims were the Yemenis. According to Saudi estimates, 800,000 Yemeni workers were expelled from Saudi Arabia as a punishment to the Yemeni government. Reports from Yemen indicate that the numbers were higher, since an entire Yemeni family frequently used the same passport. Before the crisis, about 1.5 million Yemenis were in Saudi Arabia. Now, most have gone back to Yemen, creating tremendous pressure on the ailing Yemeni economy. Yemen has a population of 11 million and a gross national product of $4 billion. Its per capita income is $500 a year, compared with Saudi Arabia's $12,180. Since the unification of the two Yemens, job opportunities have been limited and unemployment has doubled to 20%.

The economic crisis in Yemen and the ill-treatment of the expelled Yemeni workers, who were stripped of their belongings while they were being deported, are a potential source of conflict between Yemen and Saudi Arabia. Moreover, since the 1960's, the existence of a comparatively democratic government in Yemen has been seen as a threat to the stability of the Saudi monarchy and been a source of tension, as has the fact that many of the Saudi oil wells in the Asir, Jizan and Najran lie on what Yemenis believe is their land.

The Rise of Islamism

When secular leadership fails to establish a viable economy, people often look to religious solutions to their problems. Therefore it is no coincidence that the rise of what the West calls "Islamic Fundamentalism" can be traced directly to the terrible economic conditions in the poor Arab countries. (This "fundamentalism" is, incidentally, not to be confused with the "state Islam" of Saudi Arabia, where the ruling elite use Islam as a means of social control.)

Most of the violence in North Africa has centered around high prices for basic commodities such as bread, sugar, and rice. In 1977, there was the bread revolution in Egypt, which was followed by food riots that broke out in Morocco in 1984 and in Algeria in October 1988. Since then, Algeria became vulnerable to the influence of Islamic leadership and social turmoil became commonplace. The latest of these incidents has been the clashes between government forces and the supporters of Abbasi Madani's Islamic Front. According to most conservative estimates, this confrontation has led to the arrests of 5000, the deaths of 100, and the wounding of more than 1000 .

In Egypt, as in Algeria, Islam is appealing because the secular government has offered no solution to the economic problems there. Before the war, the economy was desperate. More than six million Egyptians suffer from bilharzia, a parasitic disease curable in its early stages but fatal if left untreated—as it often is among the poor. Three million homeless Egyptians have taken refuge in the cemeteries of Cairo.

Now, two million workers have returned from Iraq and Kuwait penniless, further straining the economy.

Currently, Egypt owes $45 billion in foreign debt and shows no signs of working towards economic reform. The United States has made this desperate situation worse by encouraging Egypt to buy arms. In May, the United States sold Egypt the equivalent of $1.6 billion in weapons. Many Egyptians and most Arabs believe the West is deliberately trying to impoverish them. . . .

The Poor Among the Wealthy

Few outsiders realize that living within the wealthy Gulf states are many destitute people. The prosperity in these Gulf states is not for all who live there, but rather for the chosen few.

Saudi Arabia, for example, belongs to two powerful families, Al Saud and Al Sudairi, and to their relatives among the Sunni population. The Shia of the Eastern province live in shanties above the oil deposits that made the Saud family rich. This is especially true in areas like Safwa and Al-Qatif. According to one Shia school teacher, students have no chairs and must sit on the floor and what little supplies there are have been purchased by the teachers.

An additional 1.5 million poor people are scattered throughout the Hijaz region of Saudi Arabia. Although these people came to the Haj generations ago, settling in the areas around Mecca and Jedda, they are still considered foreigners because they have no

Saudi tribal affiliation. Their situation is actually worse than that of the foreign workers because they are without citizenship, passports, or identification. Meanwhile, Saudi Arabia is spending 22% of its gross national product on the military.

Similar situations exist in Kuwait, Oman, Bahrain, the United Arab Emirates and Qatar. These millions are disenfranchised both politically and economically. Yet in the family-owned Gulf states that are protected by the most sophisticated security apparatus that the United States can supply, these poor cannot protest without risking their lives. Thus a region rich in both human and natural resources continues to live in poverty, tyranny, and the constant threat of war.

The Costs of War

Wars continue to drain the Middle East of its finances, and the recent Persian Gulf war was no exception. Initial estimates of the cost of the Gulf crisis to the Arab world range from $400 to $500 billion, while the gross domestic product of all of the Arab states combined is only $375 billion a year. As of 1986, Syria, Egypt, Yemen and Sudan all spent at least 100 times more on their militaries than on education and health combined. Tunisia, Morocco, and Mauritania spent over 50 times more on war making than on social welfare. If this money had been used in land reclamation and social reform, the Middle East would no longer be dependent on the outside world for food supplies. Instead, autocratic governments prevent reform and stifle discussion of their countries' problems while they squander their resources on Western weapons.

The Gulf war has made matters worse for all but the ruling elites of the Gulf states. Instead of ensuring democracy and the fair distribution of wealth, it has helped the Gulf families tighten their grip on the resources of the region. At the same time, it has created a nightmare for the impoverished Arab countries. Jordan's King Hussein has had to cope with the influx of Palestinians deported from both the Gulf states and Israel. Sudan must grapple with both civil war and famine. Egypt, Tunisia, Algeria, Yemen and Morocco are haunted by social chaos resulting from high rates of unemployment, malfunctioning economies and the upsurge of Islamic fundamentalism. Americans may think that they have won the war for democracy and freedom, but to the Arab world it looks like the victory of cruelty, poverty, and injustice over any semblance of human dignity and decency.

"While the oil sheikhs enjoy unprecedented luxury and splendor, overpopulated Arab countries continue to wallow in poverty."

Oil Causes Conflict

Shlomo Avineri

Shlomo Avineri is a professor of political science at the Hebrew University of Jerusalem and a former director-general of Israel's Ministry of Foreign Affairs. In the following viewpoint, he argues that the development of the Middle Eastern oil industry made some nations wealthy and left others desperately poor. The resentment of the poor nations toward the rich ones, he argues, is a contributing factor in Middle East conflicts. In addition, Avineri asserts, oil has been a destabilizing influence, even within oil-rich countries, by disrupting traditional life-styles and retarding social and political development.

As you read, consider the following questions:

1. How has the West affected the Arab world, in Avineri's opinion?
2. Why has oil wealth failed to benefit the lives of Middle East people, according to the author?
3. Why does Avineri call Arab society both divided and united?

Excerpted from "Beyond Saddam: The Arab Trauma" by Shlomo Avineri, translated by Barbara Harshav, *Dissent*, Spring 1991. Reprinted with permission.

In the 1991 Gulf War that Saddam Hussein forced on the whole world it was only natural that the Iraqi president should be portrayed as if he were the essential problem. If Iraq were routed, Saddam destroyed, and the Iraqi military machine demolished—according to conventional wisdom—a new world order could be created in the Middle East and stability restored to the region. But that is not the case.

Saddam Hussein is not the disease; he is only the symptom. With all his brutality, aggressiveness, and tyranny, he expresses a social phenomenon and a historical reality that are much more complex and threatening than the personality of this violent village thug who became a brutal ruler possessing weapons that endanger the region and the entire world. The problem is not Saddam. He is merely its most extreme and radical expression; hence, his personal disappearance—and it is hard to see how he will get out of this war alive—will not solve it. Although the solution of the problem itself is not at hand and is dependent on the outcome of the war, defining it and understanding it are possible and important even now. If we do not understand the problem, we shall end up being disappointed by the results of the war, even if it ends in a crushing victory over Saddam Hussein.

The Arab World and the West

The problem is the social, economic, political, and ideological structure of the Arab world. For over two hundred years, ever since Napoleon's invasion of Egypt and with the disintegration of the Ottoman Empire, this world has been coping with the West and its culture. The West conquered the Arab world and, in the process, became a symbol to be both imitated and hated. The West was both rejected by the Arab world and adopted by it. Even radical ideologies that intended to unite the Arab world against the West—secular nationalism à la Nasser, Arab socialism of one sort or another, or communism of the Soviet variety—all came from the West. Between this attraction toward the West and the repulsion from it, Arab society was pulverized and the Arab intelligentsia flung back and forth—an intelligentsia that sees Paris, London, New York, and Moscow as sources of inspiration and imitation but also of profound hatred. Thus, Saddam Hussein can carry on a war using purchased Western technology—and declare that the battle is between the Arabic-Islamic spirit and soulless Western technology. And thus, members of the Ba'ath party—secular Arab modernists—can turn into Islamic extremists. Islamic fundamentalism is now nourished by this love-hate relation. Israel forms its focus and symbolizes the Western ethos the Arab world detests and wants to emulate, unsuccessfully and with intense yearning.

For the last hundred years, in the process of its failed modernization, Arab society has taken from the Western world all forms of government that it wanted to adopt. First, the Arab elites, educated in English and French schools, tried to adopt parliamentary-constitutional models, resulting in regimes like those of King Farouk in Egypt and Nuri Said in Iraq. Movements influenced by fascism and nazism emerged on the periphery of Arab society and produced such widely diverse phenomena as the Lebanese Phalangist movement and the Syrian and Iraqi branches of the Ba'ath party. Nasser's pan-Arab radicalism also wanted to take over secular nationalist ideas of the West and adapt them to the complex Arab reality. All these attempts failed; and the latest developments in Jordan and Algeria, responding to the demands of democracy, have also paradoxically promoted the forces of Islamic fundamentalism in both these divergent instances.

Only in this light is it possible to understand Islamic fundamentalism as a cry of protest for the despair of a hundred years of attempts to emulate the West and draw encouragement and inspiration from it. Except for Egypt, which, with a delicate and fragile balance, has managed to preserve a stable and valid form of government that is not overly oppressive, the political map of the Arab world knows only military-ideological dictatorships like Iraq's and Syria's on the one hand, and conservative monarchical regimes like Saudi Arabia's and Kuwait's on the other. Egypt's ability to preserve its internal balance while making peace with Israel—and there is a connection between the form of government in Egypt and its willingness to reconcile itself to the reality of Israel—is even more impressive in light of the ugly alternatives all around, including the Lebanese horror and the Libyan absurdity.

The failure of the Arab world is not unique and must be seen within the framework of the failures of modernization of the Third World in general. But the Arab failure is perhaps more profound and more searing because it occurs against a background of a rich Arabic-Islamic cultural legacy. On the one hand, this legacy is a cause of pride and high expectations; on the other hand, the legacy itself appears to constitute an obstacle to modernization. Moreover, this Arab failure is accompanied by an additional factor: the blessing—or curse—of oil.

The Legacy of Oil

In the last twenty years oil has brought an indescribable accumulation of wealth in those Arab countries where it exists in abundance. In Iraq, for example, it has helped the Ba'ath regime to advance impressively the standard of living of Iraqi society; but at the same time it has also enabled the construction of the Iraqi war machine and involvement in the war against Iran. Now Iraq and the entire area have been pushed into a major war.

But most of the countries where there is oil—Saudi Arabia, Kuwait, the Gulf Emirates—are underpopulated and have leapt within less than a generation from the standard of life of Bedouin tribes into one of the most astounding accumulations of wealth in the world. Kuwait, which was merely a group of clans of marginal tribes up to the time of British control just before World War I, has become one of the richest countries in the world and a central investor in the money markets. Its financial position—above and beyond its oil wealth—influences the investment policies of the Western world more than any investment company or industrial giant.

However, as a consequence of the traditionalist, old-fashioned structure of these oil countries, they went through an accelerated process of economic modernization without any significant change in their political and social forms of government. Thus the Saud dynasty in Saudi Arabia and the al-Sabah family in Kuwait (and other families of sheikhs in the Gulf) were transformed from heads of tribes to heads of the richest countries in the world. Economic and political control remained in the hands of those same traditional strata (as their base was broadened and their life-styles were changed); and while some of those dynasties, as in Kuwait, managed to carry on a relatively enlightened policy of social investment, control and supervision of resources remained in the hands of the traditional rulers.

A Source of Envy

The wealth of oil sheiks has always been a source of envy and resentment for other Arabs. . . .

Two main factors have determined the disparity in wealth of the Arab world: oil and population. The nations of the Arabian peninsula control 46 percent of world oil resources. Within the Arab world, per capita income varies from $600 in overpopulated Egypt to $17,000 in the United Arab Emirates.

Karim Pakravan, *The Christian Science Monitor*, February 19, 1991.

Two things characterized this accumulation of wealth in the hands of the traditional dynasties. First, as in another case of an amassing of wealth not originating in production (Spain and Portugal, which plundered their colonies in America over hundreds of years), this accumulation did not create a base for local industrial and economic development. It is the nature of wealth that does not originate in production to result only in consumption. Industrialization is created only by hard work, as in the West (and today Japan, Korea, and other areas of the Far East). Second, the Arab masses in the Middle East do not share this wealth, which is concentrated mainly in the Arabian Peninsula. While the oil sheikhs enjoy unprecedented luxury and splendor, overpopulated Arab countries continue to wallow in poverty and the problems of the population explosion. Meanwhile, their rich relations throw them crumbs and leftovers from time to time, half as charity, half as bribery to keep them from upsetting the status quo that enables the rich to go on enjoying their riches.

Reality and Rhetoric

This polarization in the Arab world occurred against a background of an Arab ideology which has claimed—since the rise of Arab nationalism at the beginning of the century—that the Arab world is one world, united in solidarity and lending institutional and political expression to this unity through the Arab League and the unified effort for the liberation of Palestine. Thus, on the one hand, the ideology, symbols, and language of solidarity emerged in the Arab world and, on the other hand, there is the reality of a growing social and economic gap between unimaginable wealth and unending poverty. The Palestinians and their singular problem also widened this gap between the ideal and the real; there is not a single Arab leader who has not raised the problem of Palestine to the top of his list of rhetorical concerns, but the practical willingness of Arab rulers for sacrifice—especially the conservative oil princes but also leaders like Assad and ultimately also Sadat and Mubarak—is limited and marginal. The leaders of Saudi Arabia did support the Palestinian Liberation Organization economically and politically, but, at the same time, they continued the good life, and are careful not to sacrifice the slightest iota of their wealth and position for their Palestinian brethren.

Never has there been a society like Arab society, so united by the ideal of unity and solidarity and so divided, fragmented, and polarized in reality. The Arab reality, as reflected in the consciousness of the masses and the intellectuals, is the oil emirates squandering their wealth—the wealth of the Arab nation—in the casinos and brothels of the West, while opposite them are the millions suffering deprivation as well as the distress of the Palestinians, which is not even close to a solution—even after three years of the intifada, twenty-four years after the Six-Day War, and forty-three years after the founding of the State of Israel.

Into this vacuum between ideal and reality, between the vision of unity and sacrifice and the reality of lying and demoralization, came Saddam Hussein. By invading Kuwait he captured the imagination of the Arab masses in most Arab countries and the Palestinians as well. In this respect, there is a similarity between him and Hitler, not in the propagandistic sense used by many Western (and Israeli) observers, but rather as a factual assessment. Hitler achieved so much support among the German people during the thirties because, after World War I and the Versailles Treaty, Germany and the Germans had a great many just claims against the West, in economics, politics, and ideas. Hitler took these just claims and turned them into darts poisoned by the filth of his ideology, which saw Bolsheviks, capitalists, and Jews as responsible for all of Germany's woes.

Arab Grievances

In a similar way, Saddam plays on the just grievances and frustrations that fill the Arab world. Imagine an average Arab intellectual who wants to see the progress of the entire Arab nation in terms of political unity and economic development—a goal that, in itself, is certainly decent and hard to oppose. What does he find in reality? An Arab politics of deceit; kings and presidents, with none of whom he can identify; Arab wealth, which, if not squandered on conspicuous consumption in the West, is well invested in the stock markets of the West; princes and emirs who are strict about torturing all those who drink beer in their kingdom and who drink fine whiskey themselves in sexually mixed company in the West; and Palestinians who have become at best hewers of wood and drawers of water (albeit for fat salaries) in the courts of the rulers of Kuwait and Saudi Arabia, while no one is willing to give up even a crumb of comfort to really help them either economically or politically.

Saddam Hussein burst into his arena, brutally ousted one of the richest and most despised rulers in the Arab world, stood up to the admired-and-hated West with a historic bravado, and promised the Arab world everything that Arab ideology had always promised: a pan-Arab solidarity that would bring about a just and equal division of the enormous wealth buried under the sands of the Arabian Desert, the destruction of the reactionary regimes and the artificial borders drawn (in fact) by Western imperialism and perpetuated by all Arab rulers without ideological distinction or social origin—by presidents as well as kings, emirs as well as military tyrants, and that he would also solve the Palestinian problem—as every Arab ruler (including the King of Saudi Arabia and the Emir of Kuwait) had always promised to solve it—through the destruction of Israel. . . .

In this way, and only in this way, can we understand the enormous resonance Saddam Hussein has in the Arab world. Only the liquidation of these factors of frustration—and not just the end of Saddam—can create a more stable Middle East. The failure of modernization, the love-hate relationship with the West, the failure to deal with Israel, the despair with Western democracy and with communism, and the enmity toward the oil rulers—for every person who respects himself and his nation must feel degraded by their existence (especially if he relies on their charity, as do many Palestinians in Kuwait and the Gulf)—all these combine into the situation where a cruel despot finds himself becoming a symbol of the downtrodden and persecuted. Without the frustration and humiliation of the Germans, Hitler would not have risen to power; and without the genuine and profound frustrations of the Arab world, Saddam would not have risen either. . . .

Western Myopia

In the last twenty years, the attention of Western policy has been devoted solely to two aspects of Middle Eastern reality: guaranteeing the flow of oil at reasonable prices for the Western economy and the investment of petro-dollars in the Western economy, for one, and the Palestinian problem, for another. These were the only problems that seemed important to the West; the crisis of the structure of Arab society was of absolutely no interest whatsoever. As a result, the West was not capable of understanding the Iraqi threat or its scope.

There were good reasons for the West to focus on those two points: the guarantee of oil at reasonable prices for the oil-dependent Western economy is a legitimate, vital, and justified interest. Those who sneer at a "war for oil" ignore the fact that without oil the culture and economy of the West cannot exist. For good or for bad, the culture of Western civilization as we know it relies on this oil, and a considerable part of it comes from the Middle East. The fear that the non-solution of the Palestinian problem is a factor in regional instability is also correct and justified.

But what did not interest Western society was who ruled the Arab world. As long as the oil flowed, the West was willing to get along with any Arab ruler, whether he was a feudal sheikh or a Ba'athist military tyrant, and to rake in as much wealth as possible from wheeling and dealing with him and his regime. Atomic reactors for Iraq—fine; AWACS planes for Saudi Arabia—why not? The possibility that the social imbalance would create a dangerous explosive did not interest anyone. In recent years, anyone who claimed that the Arab world was based on social injustice and terrifying inequality that could one day explode was considered by statesmen and sober scholars in the West as an ivory-tower intellectual, a bleeding heart, and perhaps (who knows?) even a communist, God forbid. And anyone who tried to argue that it was hard to guarantee stability in the region solely with the establishment of a Palestinian state, and that such a state could not contribute to regional stability if the region as a whole was based on a gap between emirs and tyrants, was considered an apologist for the status quo and perhaps a lobbyist for the Likud and an adherent of the Greater Israel Movement. . . .

The world will have to deal with the real and complicated problem: how to encourage the creation in the Arab world of a social, economic, and political order that will allow the Arabs, including the Palestinians, to express their uniqueness and their culture and that will guarantee oil at reasonable prices for the world economy—all that along with the creation of a more just and equitable Arab society, which will not be limited to the choice between sheikhs and corrupt rulers on the one hand and brutal dictators on the other. Such a regime cannot be imposed from outside, but it will by no means be achieved merely by a return to the status quo prior to August 2, 1990. . . .

A Missed Opportunity

The past several years saw sharp outbreaks of unrest, provoked by economic crisis, in Jordan, Algeria, Morocco, and Tunisia, and economic deterioration played no small part in sparking the Palestinian *intifada*. A generalized resentment at the concentration of wealth in the small oil sheikhdoms of the Gulf was aggravated by a strong sense that the oil-producing countries (including Iraq) had squandered a historic opportunity for regional development—an opportunity that would not come again.

Joe Stork, *World Policy Journal*, Spring 1991.

The best Arab and Western (and Soviet and Israeli) minds will have to deal with this problem, which will perhaps be similar to what happened in Europe (and Japan) after 1945. There is no magic solution to this problem; the path to it will be strewn with trial and error, with failures and conflicts, and no one today can envision the shape of the new Middle East, just as in 1939, no one could have imagined the shape of Europe after 1945.

It is important to remember that the problem is not only Saddam Hussein and his military might, just as the solution is not the restoration of the al-Sabah dynasty to its feudal estate or the safety of the royal Saudi government. The challenge will be the creation of a more just and equal Arab society in the Middle East, a goal that Western imperviousness and greed, Soviet aggressive interests, and Arab social gaps and the frustrations that grew out of them have not yet been able to achieve.

"The Middle East is on the verge of an explosive crisis, some experts and officials say, over . . . water."

Water Shortages Create Middle East Conflict

Caryle Murphy

The Middle East is primarily an arid region that faces increasing pressure to provide water for its growing population. In the following viewpoint, Caryle Murphy writes that impending water shortages coupled with political and ethnic conflicts in the Middle East could perhaps lead to future wars in the region. The author describes three areas where water shortages and control over water supplies are a concern: the Nile, the Jordan, and the Euphrates rivers. Murphy reports on the Middle East for the *Washington Post*.

As you read, consider the following questions:

1. What are some of the signs of the Middle East water crisis, according to Murphy?
2. What kinds of water strategies and policies have Middle East countries devised, according to Murphy?
3. How have the actions of specific countries, including Israel and Turkey, exacerbated tensions in the Middle East, according to the author?

Caryle Murphy, "Could a Water Shortage Cause a War?" *The Washington Post National Weekly Edition*, March 19-21, 1990, © 1990 The Washington Post. Reprinted with permission.

The Middle East is on the verge of an explosive crisis, some experts and officials say, over a commodity that could become more precious than oil: water.

From the Euphrates to the Nile—and especially in the volatile Jordan River basin, where the intertwined water resources of Jordan, Israel and the occupied West Bank add a complex dimension to peace efforts—governments face growing water demands from swelling populations, increasing urbanization and rising agricultural and industrial requirements.

To satisfy these needs, officials are racing to draw on rivers shared with neighbors who have competing demands, and on underground water supplies that are being depleted at alarming rates.

Signs of the crisis are many. In Egypt, which imports half of its food, the biggest constraint on new agricultural production is water.

In the Israeli-occupied Gaza Strip, drinking water is salty because sea water has tainted the drawn-down underground water source, or aquifer.

In Jordan, the government recently installed an irrigation system for 6,000 acres, but has no water to supply it. In Damascus, residential water taps go dry every day from 2 p.m. until 6 the next morning.

Water Shortages

Experts foresee critical water shortages in this decade in several countries of the Middle East, which averages 3 percent population growth annually.

"If that rate [of growth] continues undiminished," says Philadelphia-based water expert Thomas Naff, "then within 30 years, for the entire region, all the advances they are making in water conservation will be wiped out. There will not be enough water supplies to support a population of that magnitude."

A Worldwatch Institute study issued by Sandra Postel said that if current consumption patterns continue, "water demands in Israel, Jordan and the occupied West Bank will exceed all renewable supplies within six years."

In this rain-poor region, which is armed to the teeth and infused with political, religious and national rivalries, some water experts and political analysts warn of possible military conflict over water rights in the future.

"Before the 21st century, the struggle over limited and threatened water resources could sunder already fragile ties among regional states and lead to unprecedented upheaval," according to a report issued by the Center for Strategic and International Studies (CSIS) in Washington.

Water experts from 11 Arab states meeting in Amman in April

1989 declared that "water security in the Arab world is as essential as national and military security."

Yet Middle East leaders have given scant attention to future water needs.

"There is a shortage in information" about resources, the Arabs' report said, a "deficiency in qualified specialists," and "very little concern about water research and studies on the academic and national levels."

"We don't have a strategy or policy for water," Jordan University hydrologist Elias Salameh says. "We just have projects. Nobody is really concentrating on, or pushing for, a policy or strategy."

Even if countries adopted national long-range policies, their mutual dependence on shared water sources requires far-reaching political cooperation in a region where, in the words of the CSIS report, "neighborly good will has seldom existed in the past and may become even more elusive in the future."

An overriding problem is that none of the Middle East's major rivers and aquifers is governed by a negotiated accord accepted by all parties who claim rights.

"Water to my mind is the main resource priority of the '90s," says Joyce R. Starr, a coauthor of the CSIS report, "but in Washington, it's invisible."

Points of Conflict

The scope of the problem is apparent in these points of conflict over water:

• The Jordan River Basin. Israeli journalist Zeev Schiff, writing of Israeli-Palestinian interdependence on water resources, warns that water-sharing agreements that satisfy the needs of both parties must figure in any future peace arrangement because "to disregard this sensitive question is to ensure a future" cause of war.

By 2000, Israeli and West Bank water demands will outstrip resources by 20 percent if no alternatives are found, according to water expert Naff. Israel takes up to 40 percent of its water supply from sources in the occupied territories, he says.

Israeli authorities severely restrict Palestinians from drilling new wells, to prevent the aquifers from being drained and then contaminated by sea water. This practice has blocked Arab agricultural development.

In the overcrowded Gaza Strip, consumption from the Gaza aquifer was outpacing its natural replenishment by almost 50 percent as of 1985, and Naff warns that the reservoir is nearing irreversible damage from sea water seepage.

Linked to the Israeli-Palestinian dispute are the conflicting water needs of Israel and Jordan.

Israel's extensive use of the Jordan River and Sea of Galilee has left the remaining river water south of the sea so polluted that Jordan cannot use it, according to Salameh and Naff.

In addition, Israel takes 100 million cubic meters of water annually from the Yarmuk River, which feeds into the Jordan and forms the border between Syria and Jordan.

If Israel, which has access to the Yarmuk through a sliver of land seized in 1967, continues this practice, Jordan will not be able to use fully the so-called Unity Dam it hopes to build with Syria on the Yarmuk.

Water and War

Middle Eastern leaders are acutely conscious of the potential for conflict stemming from chronic water shortages. "The only matter that could take Egypt to war again is water," declared President Anwar Sadat in the spring of 1979, only days after signing the historic peace treaty with Israel. His unveiled threat was not directed at Israel, but at Ethiopia, the upstream neighbor that controls 85 percent of the headwaters of Egypt's life line, the Nile River. In 1990 Jordan's King Hussein issued similar warlike declarations.

Most countries in the Middle East are linked to one another by common aquifers subject to overwithdrawal or overcontamination. Iraqi leader Saddam Hussein's rationale for invading Kuwait in August 1990 was the latter's overpumping of shared oil reserves. How long will it be before aquifer conflict becomes common terminology in the lexicon of Middle East specialists?

Joyce R. Starr, *Foreign Policy*, Spring 1991.

Naff and Jordanian officials say the dam is needed by 1995 to avert a major crisis in Jordan.

• The Nile. When reports reached Cairo recently that Ethiopia, where the Blue Nile headwaters supply 85 percent of the river's flow, was surveying possible dam sites, there were swift Egyptian protests.

Ethiopia denied any plan to harm Egypt, but the incident underlined the absence of a formal agreement between the two countries to protect Egypt's interests in the face of upstream development projects.

Egypt, under a 1959 pact with Sudan, is guaranteed an annual quota of 55.5 billion cubic meters of water.

Egypt hopes this quota can be increased by the construction of canals in Sudan's southern swamps to reduce evaporation losses on the White Nile, which joins the Blue Nile, but this project has been stalled indefinitely by Sudan's civil war.

Egypt, which depends on the river to supply water and electricity to a population of 56 million, expects demand to double in the next decade, according to Mahmoud Abu Zeid, chairman of Egypt's Water Resources Institute. The population grows by 1 million each nine months.

To meet these needs, the government is increasing its irrigation efficiency and tapping underground water in the desert by drilling 3,000 wells.

If everything works out, Zeid says, "we are safe until 2010."

• The Euphrates. Straddling the swift, turquoise waters of the Euphrates, the 12-year-old Thawra Dam in north-central Syria has created the country's largest lake, irrigated thousands of acres of farmland and, in 1988, supplied more than half of the nation's electrical power.

But on Jan. 13, 1990, Turkey cut the Euphrates' flow to one-tenth its normal volume for 27 days to begin filling its massive new Ataturk Dam reservoir.

Syrian officials say they were forced to draw on reserves to keep their dam's eight turbines from shutting down entirely.

New Dams

The Ataturk is the centerpiece of Turkey's Southeast Anatolia project, a $56 billion undertaking to build 21 dams on the headwaters of the Euphrates and Tigris rivers for irrigation and electrical power.

If Turkey fully realizes these plans, water expert Naff estimates, the Euphrates's flow into Syria could be permanently reduced by up to 40 percent, and by up to 80 percent into Iraq.

Turkish President Turgut Ozal has promised to "never threaten anyone" through his country's control of the rivers. Turkey periodically briefed Syrian and Iraqi engineers on the project, and for two months before the recent cut it increased the water flow so it could be stored downstream for future use.

But Turkey has expressed no interest in a negotiated accord governing water-sharing among the three countries, according to Turkish and Arab officials, even though "there is enough water in the Euphrates for all three countries, provided they come to basin-wide agreement on sharing it," Naff says.

Locating Scapegoats

During World War II, the Nazis in Germany systematically killed millions of Jews. The Nazis continually propagandized the outrageous lie that Jews were responsible for many of Germany's social problems. Jews became the victims of irrational leaders who glorified force, violence, and the doctrine of racial supremacy. One of the principal propaganda weapons used against the Jews by Germany's leaders was the tactic of scapegoating.

On an individual level, scapegoating involves the process of transferring personal blame or anger to another individual or object. Most people, for example, have kicked their table or chair as an outlet for anger and frustration over a mistake or failure. *On a group level, scapegoating involves the placement of blame on entire groups of people or objects for social problems that they have not caused.* Scapegoats may be totally or only partially innocent, but they always receive more blame than can be rationally justified.

Because human societies are so complex, problems are often not completely understood by any single citizen. Yet people always demand answers, and there exists a human tendency to create imaginary and simplistic explanations for complex racial, social, economic, and political problems that defy easy understanding and solution. The Middle East, with its many conflicts and tensions, falls into this category. Middle East conflict has so far defied any equitable and peaceful solution. In such a frustrating and emotionally charged situation, scapegoating can occur.

Examine the following statements. *Mark an S by any statement that you believe is an example of scapegoating. Mark NS by any statement you believe is not an example of scapegoating. Mark a U by any statement that you are unsure is an example of scapegoating.*

$$S = \textit{an example of scapegoating}$$
$$NS = \textit{not an example of scapegoating}$$
$$U = \textit{unsure or undecided}$$

1. Saddam Hussein is a bloodthirsty dictator who is solely responsible for starting two major wars in the Middle East.

2. Religious differences between Jews and Muslims have tragically contributed to instability in the Middle East.

3. The Middle East will remain violent as long as Palestinians remain committed to terrorism.

4. As more countries in the Middle East face the prospect of water shortages, the chances for war increase.

5. Middle East wars are a direct result of U.S. meddling.

6. Arabs are poor because U.S. oil companies conspire to deprive Middle Eastern countries of their fair share of oil receipts.

7. Israel's occupation of Palestinian territory may be unjust, but it is not the sole cause of Middle East conflict.

8. With the exception of Egypt, no Arab nation has signed a peace treaty with Israel.

9. Many Arab leaders refuse to pursue peace in the Middle East because such a development would threaten their nondemocratic ruling powers.

10. British imperialists such as Winston Churchill and T.E. Lawrence are the reason millions of Middle Easterners have died in twentieth-century wars.

11. After Israel was founded in 1948, thousands of Palestinians fled to other countries. Their continuing existence as stateless people contributes to Middle East instability.

12. Conflict will remain in the Middle East as long as religious fanatics have political clout in the region.

13. By selling billions of dollars in arms to the Middle East, the U.S. and other nations have increased the potential risks of Middle East wars.

Periodical Bibliography

The following articles have been selected to supplement the diverse views presented in this chapter.

Feroz Ahmad	"Arab Nationalism, Radicalism, and the Specter of Neocolonialism," *Monthly Review*, February 1991.
Lisa Beyer	"Let the Game Begin," *Time*, October 28, 1991.
David Fromkin	"How the Modern Middle East Map Came to Be Drawn," *Smithsonian*, May 1991.
Dilip Hiro	"Uneasy Lie the Oil Kings' Heads," *The Nation*, September 17, 1990.
Robert A. Licht	"Israel Among the Nationalisms," *First Things*, April 1991.
Fouad Moughrabi	"The Crisis of Leadership," *The World & I*, December 1990. Available from 2800 New York Ave. NE, Washington, DC 20002
Muhammad Muslih and Augustus Richard Norton	"The Need for Arab Democracy," *Foreign Policy*, no. 83, Summer 1991.
Douglas Pasternak	"A Guide to the Issues," *U.S. News & World Report*, October 28, 1991.
Martin Peretz	"Unpromised Lands," *The New Republic*, June 3, 1991.
Amos Perlmutter	"Can Glasnost Bring Peace to the Middle East?" *The World & I*, July 1990.
Daniel Pipes	"Israel, America & Arab Delusions," *Commentary*, March 1991.
Carla Anne Robbins et al.	"Hopes vs. History," *U.S. News & World Report*, November 11, 1991.
Yahya Sadowski and Martha Wenger	"Rich and Poor in the Arab World," *Middle East Report*, May/June 1991.
Yezid Sayigh	"The Gulf Crisis: Why the Arab Regional Order Failed," *International Affairs*, July 1991.
Joyce R. Starr	"Water Wars," *Foreign Policy*, no. 82, Spring 1991.
David Twersky	"The Arab-Israeli Knot," *Nuclear Times*, Summer 1991.

Are Palestinian Rights Being Ignored?

Chapter Preface

The status and treatment of Palestinians has been a source of conflict and tension in the Middle East for decades. Ironically, the controversy can be traced to a settlement originally meant to rectify grave injustices committed against another persecuted group, the Jews. After six million Jews were killed in Nazi concentration camps during World War II, international concern focused on the creation of a homeland for the survivors. The region called Palestine seemed a natural choice because Jews had historic ties to the land and because Zionist Jews had been immigrating to Palestine since the 1880s. The issue came before the newly created United Nations (UN) in 1947 and the state of Israel was proclaimed in 1948. This solution, however, created a new problem: there was a large population of Palestinian Arabs in Palestine. More than a half million of them were displaced at the end of a civil war between Arabs and Jews. Those that remained in Israel were denied the full status and rights of citizenship reserved for Jews. Since then, there has been constant conflict, often bloody, between Israel and the Palestinian Arabs who feel they have been driven from their land.

In 1967, a war broke out between Israel and its Arab neighbors that dramatically changed the Palestinian issue. In six days, Israel defeated the Egyptian, Syrian, and Jordanian armies and took territory three times its own size from all three countries. It gained the Sinai Peninsula and Gaza Strip from Egypt, the West Bank from Jordan, and the Golan Heights from Syria. (Israel later returned the Sinai Peninsula to Egypt.) It also, consequently, acquired an even larger Palestinian population. Today, Palestinians continue to struggle against Israeli rule over these areas, especially the West Bank and Gaza Strip. In 1988 the Palestine National Council, a Palestinian parliament-in-exile, declared the establishment of an independent Palestinian state to be located in these territories. Yet to many Jews, these territories and Jerusalem in particular are integral parts of Israel.

The range of opinion regarding the Palestinian-Israeli conflict is diverse. Some Palestinians believe the state of Israel is an illegitimate entity and should be replaced by a Palestinian state. Some Israelis believe that Palestinians should be expelled from Israel, Gaza, and the West Bank. Between these two extremes are many proposals and arguments over how Palestinians should be treated as a people, and how peace between Palestinians and Jews can be achieved. This chapter explores these issues.

"It is clear that Israel has committed grave breaches . . . of the most elemental norms of human rights."

Israel Violates Palestinian Human Rights

Tom Farer

Tom Farer is a professor and director of the joint program in law and international relations at American University in Washington, D.C., and is a former chairman of the Inter-American Commission on Human Rights. In the following viewpoint, he argues that Israel has extensively violated the civil rights of Palestinians living in the West Bank and Gaza Strip, including the rights of free speech and a free press, and the right to a fair trial. In addition, Farer argues that Palestinians are being deprived economically by the Israelis, and are being denied the right to create their own state. He argues that Israel should be held accountable by other nations for its treatment of Palestinians.

As you read, consider the following questions:

1. How has Israel's response to the *intifada* violated Palestinian human rights, according to Farer?
2. What human rights violations in addition to those mentioned above does the author describe?
3. How does Farer respond to arguments that Israel is being held to a tougher human rights standard than other countries?

Excerpted from "Israel's Unlawful Occupation" by Tom Farer. Reprinted with permission from *Foreign Policy* 82 (Spring 1991). Copyright © 1991 by the Carnegie Endowment for International Peace.

The 1991 confrontation in the Persian Gulf between Iraq and the grand coalition of states defending Kuwait is swollen with potential for either the further unraveling or the refurbishment of international order. That the United States, whether alone or with other states, can pulverize Iraq and thereby restore Kuwait's sovereignty is not in serious doubt. But the rout of the Iraqi army will not necessarily enhance political stability in the Middle East or induce more orderly and cooperative relations among states generally. In order to realize the confrontation's positive potential and to limit its risks, the United States must act in defense of broad principles beneficial to most peoples and must avoid the perception that the primary reason for crushing Iraq is to keep the Arab world divided and weak. . . .

Israel's Transgressions

Iraq's transgressions, being blatant, require neither enumeration nor analysis. Israel's, however, are often veiled: veiled by the skill and meticulously legal rhetoric of its advocates, by the penumbra surrounding its legitimate acts of self-defense, by the numbing effect of repetition, by the unclean hands of many of its Arab accusers, by a generalized presumption of good conduct stemming from condign Western guilt for the Holocaust, and by a Western perception of Israel as an open, democratic, rule-of-law society.

This latter perception mutes response even when the veil is pierced. Since Israel has an elected government, its behavior is deemed self-correcting. Yet, freely elected governments have at various times in the past century and a half committed great crimes and injustices. Democracies can be as cruel as other forms of government in their treatment of those who stand beyond the racial, cultural, religious, or geographic boundaries defined by dominant groups. Where the alien is also seen as a material threat, the likelihood of atrocity expands. In Israeli-occupied territories, the logic of atrocity has prevailed. . . .

At an absolute minimum, states are prohibited from practicing, encouraging, or condoning murder, torture, or other cruel, inhuman, or degrading treatment or punishment, prolonged arbitrary detention, or a consistent pattern of gross violations of such internationally recognized human rights as freedom of conscience, association, expression, participation in government, and departure from and return to the place of one's residence. States are prohibited as well from treating persons under its jurisdiction in any way that amounts (in the language of the [fourth] Geneva Convention) to an "adverse distinction founded on race, colour, religion or faith, sex, birth or wealth, or any other similar criteria."

Considering only those actions officially acknowledged by

74

Israeli authorities, it is clear that Israel has committed grave breaches of the Geneva Conventions and of the most elemental norms of human rights. If one looks deeper, and considers allegations supported by persuasive evidence, the situation appears considerably grimmer. Among the acts either acknowledged or confirmed by persuasive evidence are the following:

Collective Punishment. The Israeli administration employs house sealings and demolitions both to punish families for alleged violations of Israeli security regulations by family members and to punish groups of people residing in areas that have been scenes of violent acts. A notorious example was the demolition of 14 homes in Beita village following the April 1988 killing of an Israeli girl. No one in any of the homes was even accused of the crime. Before the demolition was completed, an official Israeli investigation established that the death had been inadvertently caused by an Israeli settler.

Ramirez/Copley News Service. Reprinted with permission.

Exact figures are difficult to obtain. The human rights organization Middle East Watch states that 462 houses were sealed or destroyed since the beginning of the *intifada*, as the Palestinian uprising is known. Despite appeals, the Israeli Supreme Court has not blocked a single demolition order. . . .

Another form of collective punishment is the imposition of curfews in areas where there has been no imminent threat of violence. In fall 1989, for example, the West Bank village of Beit Sahur was under round-the-clock curfew almost continuously for 40 days because its inhabitants refused to pay taxes (protesting, among other things, taxation without representation). The punitive, as opposed to preventive, character of many curfews is evidenced by the concurrent disconnection of power, water, and telephone lines to all homes in curfewed villages—including those of the sick and persons tending them.

Prolonged closure of all universities is yet another form of Israeli collective punishment. If its only purpose were to pre-empt violence, there would be no satisfactory reason for preventing professors from using libraries and laboratories.

Attacks Against Individual Autonomy

The demolitions, curfews, and university closings constitute punishment without due process of law and are culpable on that ground alone. But more than that they are affronts to the very idea of individual autonomy—the rock on which the whole edifice of political and civil rights is built. As noted above, in deference to the awful necessities of war, international law allows certain limited trespass on individual rights. Once armed conflict has ceased, however, the more demanding law of human rights springs back into place, leaving the law of war simply as a supplementary source of protection for persons in territory that remains occupied.

Coercive Interrogation. Article 31 of the Fourth Convention outlaws "physical or moral coercion . . . in particular to obtain information." Yet for years Israeli security forces have been accused of torturing detainees. . . .

In testimony submitted to the U.S. House of Representatives Foreign Affairs Committee in May 1990, Amnesty International USA concluded on the basis of its inquiries that "thousands of Palestinians have been beaten while in the hands of Israeli forces or tortured or ill-treated in detention centers. . . . Wounded Palestinians have been dragged out of hospitals against the advice of doctors and beaten before being taken to detention centers." The 1989 State Department Report on the condition of human rights in various countries states that in the occupied territories "at least 10 deaths can be attributed to beatings" and that "physical and psychological pressures are particularly severe in incommunicado detention during investigation and interrogation."

Murder. Murder includes the use of force not only with specific intent to kill but also with wanton indifference to human life, as U.S. courts have consistently confirmed. Since the *intifada's* beginning three years ago, more than 700 Palestinians have been

76

killed and many thousands wounded by troops firing live ammunition or plastic bullets at lethally close range. Of those killed as of May 1990, close to 150 were aged 16 or younger. . . .

The carnage in the occupied territories is clearly the result of wanton indifference to the crippling and death of the territories' non-Jewish inhabitants. If Israeli behavior is driven by the conviction that the episodic use of deadly force serves as a deterrent and is therefore a relatively efficient means for suppressing resistance to Israeli rule, then that behavior may properly be described as a form of state terrorism: the employment of force or the threat thereof against a limited set of targets for the purpose of engendering fear in a larger audience and thereby advancing political ends.

Illicit internment under illicit conditions. To assist in repressing the *intifada*, the Israeli government has empowered military authorities to imprison individuals without formal charge or trial for renewable periods of up to 12 months each. An individual may be detained whenever a commander has "reasonable cause to believe that reasons of state security or public security require [it]." For reasons of security the commander may also refuse to reveal the basis for his belief and to specify the acts imputed to the detainee. According to a June-July 1989 report by the International Commission of Jurists, since the beginning of the *intifada*, some 5,500 Palestinians have been subjected to detention orders; some 1,500 were still in custody two years later. . . .

Exile and Deportation. The West Bank Data Base Project, organized by former Jerusalem Deputy Mayor Meron Benvenisti, puts the figure of those expelled since 1967 under formal deportation orders at just under 2,000. Whatever the actual number, the practice violates the Fourth Convention's requirement that punishment never be inflicted without due process of law. According to the State Department's 1989 Country Report, "the deportation process is characterized by a lack of formal charges and the use of secret evidence not disclosed to the suspect or his attorney." And while Palestinians under deportation orders can appeal to the Israel High Court, according to the U.S. State Department no appeal has yet been successful. . . .

Violating Human Rights

For the past 23 years, the Arab inhabitants of the occupied territories have continued to live under what amounts to an authoritarian government that exercises close supervision over many aspects of their social and working lives. The Israeli government has formally annexed a part of the territories, namely old East Jerusalem and substantial adjoining land. Seizing privately held land through various legal and administrative guises is practiced throughout the West Bank. And while refraining from formal annexation of the remainder of the territories,

Israel has declared that it will not relinquish control and that it has a superior claim to such possession. Meanwhile, through subsidies, public works, and other incentives, Israel has fostered the settlement of its Jewish citizens in the territories. And it has in effect set aside the preponderance of the land for the continued expansion of such settlements. . . .

Israeli Cruelties

Israel is killing Palestinians in the Occupied Lands at a rate, adjusted for time-period and population, much greater than our own death-rate in the Korean and the Vietnam Wars. Thousands of Palestinians have been (and are still being) cruelly beaten, with serious injury and some deaths as the result—often beaten quite at random, with no charge and with no disclosed grounds for any definite suspicion, except as the mere fact of being Palestinian may be thought such a ground. . . .

Thousands have been arrested and confined in prison without charge or trial or after a mockery of trial, under conditions so grossly inhumane that our own legal system would hold these to be in violation of our own constitutional guarantee against cruel and unusual punishments.

Charles L. Black Jr., *Let Us Rethink Our "Special Relationship" with Israel*, 1989.

Other aspects of Israeli rule arguably violate one or another convention provision and indisputably violate human rights norms. In its 1989 Country Report, the State Department identifies ongoing violations of the following rights:

• *The right of citizens to form political parties and to elect their government.* Israel bans Palestinian political parties and has not allowed even municipal elections in the territories since 1976. Most mayors elected then were later dismissed on security grounds.

• *The right to peaceful assembly and association.* Aside from the ban on political parties as such, the Israeli administration uses its compulsory registration requirement (among other means) to prevent the formation of charitable, community, professional, and self-help organizations if their activities are viewed as overtly political. Additionally, military orders ban public gatherings of 10 or more people without a permit.

Trampled Human Rights

• *Freedom of speech and press.* The indigenous Arab press is subject to tight restrictions and censorship. Articles and editorials relating to Palestinian political goals or the uprising, though sometimes permitted, are routinely censored. The State

Department reports that "Arabic translations of uprising-related news stories which had previously appeared in the Hebrew language press were routinely expurgated from the Arabic press. . . . A military order closing a prominent Palestinian press service was renewed, and two other Palestinian services were closed."

In addition, "the display of Palestinian political symbols, such as flags, national colors, and graffiti is punishable by fines, detention, or imprisonment."

• *The right to a fair trial.* Palestinians accused of "security offenses"—a term that covers nationalist activity of a nonviolent character—are tried in military courts. Acquittals, according to the State Department, are "very rare" since most convictions are based on confessions. The State Department says that "the absence of bail, long pretrial delays, and physical and psychological pressures increase the likelihood of confessions. These are usually recorded in Hebrew, which many defendants are unable to read." Further, arrests require no warrant and can be executed by any soldier. Once arrested, individuals may be held for 96 hours without a warrant from any judicial authority and may be, and routinely are, held for up to 18 days without formal charges and without access to counsel. Finally, cases are heard by a single judge, who can impose prison sentences of up to five years, and may be appealed only with the permission of the court.

No Fair Trials

These procedures considered as a whole are flagrantly inconsistent with the paradigm of a fair trial delineated in Article 14 of the International Covenant on Civil and Political Rights and fail to meet the more precarious requirements of Article 3 of the Fourth Convention, which prohibits the passing of sentences other than by "a regularly constituted court, affording all the judicial guarantees which are recognized as indispensable by civilized peoples."

• *The right not to be the object of discrimination based on race, sex, religion, language, or social status.* The 1989 State Department report declares that

> under the dual system of governance applied to Palestinians— both Muslim and Christian—and Israelis, Palestinians are treated less favorably than Israeli settlers on a broad range of issues, including the right to due process, right of residency, freedom of movement, sale of crops and goods, land and water use, and access to health and social services. . . .

The second basic parallel between the Gulf and the Israeli-Palestinian conflicts concerns the right to self-determination. The U.N. General Assembly's Consensus Declaration on Principles of International Law Concerning Friendly Relations and Cooperation Among States declares that all peoples have a right to self-determination and "that subjection of peoples to alien subjugation, domination and exploitation constitutes a violation of the principle [of self-determination], as well as a denial of fundamental human rights, and is contrary to the Charter.". . .

The Palestinians have a *conditional* legal right to self-determination, a right to form an independent political community in some part of the territory that was granted to them in the U.N. partition of 1947. If the Israelis conceded the right of Palestinian self-determination but claimed that it cannot be exercised under existing conditions because the Palestinians do not provide sufficient guarantees for the identical right of the Jewish people, then the Israelis would be on firm ground. Moving to that ground, however, involves conceding that the Arab population of the occupied territories, including the formally annexed areas, is there by legal right. It is inconsistent, moreover, with the policy of denying political expression to the Arab population. And it is incompatible with the Israeli policy of freezing Arab society while encouraging the settlement of Jews on land in the occupied territories. . . .

Defying the World

The third parallel is quickly stated. Israel has repeatedly defied requests, proposals, and decisions of the General Assembly and the Security Council. It has done so when decisions were driven over Western opposition by the sheer numerical weight of the nonaligned bloc; it has done so when decisions were virtually unanimous.

The U.N. has recognized a Palestinian right to self-determination; Israel denies it. The Security Council has called for application of the Fourth Geneva Convention to the occupied territories; Israel refuses to apply it. The U.N. has found the unilateral annexation of East Jerusalem to be unlawful; Israel says the status of Jerusalem is non-negotiable and hastens to alter the religious/ethnic balance of East Jerusalem's population. The Security Council has called on Israel to end the deportation of Palestinians; Israel continues to deport them.

"The steps taken by Israel against extremist elements who promote violence and turmoil are fully in keeping with international law."

Israel Does Not Violate Palestinian Human Rights

Israel Ministry of Foreign Affairs

Israel has been frequently criticized for its treatment of Palestinians in the West Bank and Gaza Strip, territories it has occupied since 1967. In the following viewpoint, the Israel Ministry of Foreign Affairs defends Israel's human rights record in Gaza and Judea-Samaria, or the West Bank. Considering the violence that Israel faces from the Palestinians, the authors believe that Israel has effectively protected human rights in the territories.

As you read, consider the following questions:

1. Which Palestinians do the authors blame for most of the violence in the West Bank and Gaza?
2. What measures has the Israeli military taken to safeguard human rights, according to the authors?
3. According to the authors, how does Israel compare with its neighboring states in the area of human rights?

Israel Ministry of Foreign Affairs, "Israel's Measures in the Territories and Human Rights," January 1990. Reprinted with permission.

The riots and violence in Judea-Samaria and the Gaza District are the most recent link in a chain of violence and hostility against Israel. The disturbances since December 1987 have posed serious problems and challenges for Israel, which is duty-bound to take all necessary measures to restore calm and stability. The steps taken by Israel against extremist elements who promote violence and turmoil are fully in keeping with international law.

Since the Six Day War of 1967, a war that Israel was compelled to fight for its very survival, Israel is the authority responsible for security and stability in Judea-Samaria and the Gaza District, and for the welfare of the residents there, Arabs and Jews. In the last 22 years, Israel has exerted efforts in numerous areas to improve the living standards of the local Palestinian Arab inhabitants.

Moreover, with the signing of the Camp David Accords, Israel agreed to an interim phase of autonomy for the local Palestinian Arab inhabitants and negotiations to determine the final status of Judea-Samaria and the Gaza District. Unfortunately, the PLO and other Arab rejectionists exerted heavy pressure, including the brutal murder of several Palestinian Arabs from the territories, thereby undermining prospects for moving towards implementation of the Camp David Accords. . . .

PLO Violence

Israel's actions have been directed against violence, frequently incited and instigated by extremist elements. Scores of leaflets and numerous PLO radio broadcasts have exhorted and instructed local operatives to carry out attacks against Arabs and Jews. The violence of the intifada has been characterized by riots, terrorist attacks, and assaults against the life and property of Arabs and Jews.

The participants in riots and other acts of violence have resorted to a variety of implements: rocks, concrete blocks, slings, iron bars, slingshots, zip-guns, nail-studded potatoes, knives, hatchets, Molotov cocktails, and even on occasion firearms. This violence is meant to kill, as illustrated by an incident on February 24, 1989: a young paratrooper was struck dead by a 33 lb/15 kilo concrete block which was hurled at his patrol from atop a four-story building in Shechem (Nablus). During the first 20 months of the intifada, some 1,836 Molotov cocktails were thrown at civilians and soldiers, maiming and disfiguring some of the victims, killing others. . . .

The Palestinian Arab extremists have also launched attacks against civilians inside Israel's pre-1967 lines. Israelis have been stabbed to death, as seen in the knife attack in Jerusalem on May 3, 1989: two elderly Jews were killed and three were wounded. Two Israeli soldiers were kidnapped near Ashdod, in the south of Israel, and brutally murdered by members of HAMAS [an Islamic Palestinian group]. A Tel Aviv-Jerusalem bus was forced into a ravine on July 6, 1989, killing 16 passengers, including an American citizen, and wounding 25 others.

Israel at War

For Israelis, the basic fact is that the Palestinians are waging a war, no less a war for being pursued by teenagers and women who are being put out front by the Palestinian opposition to throw rocks and gasoline bombs, at little risk, given the relative restraint of the Israelis. Tear gas, curfews, demolition, detention and deportation are less onerous than massive shootings and deaths by which the Arab states suppress their own insurrections. Israel is portrayed as immoral for thus acting in self-defense, but no country faced with comparable threats, internal and external, has ever accorded the human rights to those who oppose it as Israel has to Palestinians during the *intifada.*

Mortimer B. Zuckerman, *U.S. News & World Report,* January 22, 1990.

By January 1990, 51 Israelis had lost their lives. That more Israelis have not died during the intifada has not been due to any lack of trying by the PLO-affiliated and Islamic fundamentalist extremists: since the outbreak of the intifada in December 1987, more than 2500 Israelis—more than 1700 soldiers and 800 civilians—have been injured, some of them critically.

The Palestinian Arab population has also felt the hand of intifada extremism. Coercion is one of the tactics used to promote confrontation. Local PLO and HAMAS operatives have pressured local shopkeepers to close businesses under threat of violence and vandalism, and have forcibly prevented Arab workers from commuting to their jobs within Israel by causing damage to their vehicles, attacking public transportation and even burning buses. Extremists have tried to force local Arab administrative personnel to quit their jobs, in most cases without success. Local youths are encouraged and instructed by adult activists to take part in the rioting, block the roads with burning tires and other obstacles, and throw rocks.

The ultimate form of pressure—physical assaults on specific individuals and their families—has also been used by Palestinian Arab extremists. Since the intifada began, nearly 170 Palestinians, from all walks of life, were murdered by fellow Palestinians. Many of these killings, often preceded by torture, were carried out by PLO and HAMAS hit squads. . . .

Israel is empowered, indeed obligated, by international law to maintain order and public safety in the territories, for the benefit of Arabs and Jews alike. Article 43 of the Hague regulations stipulates that the controlling authority "shall take all the measures in his power to restore and ensure, as far as possible, public order and safety, while respecting, unless absolutely prevented, the laws in force in the country." As the authority currently responsible for maintaining order and public safety in Judea-Samaria and the Gaza District, Israel constantly seeks to find the proper balance between security and humanitarian requirements.

Those residents of the territories who are suspected of having committed security offenses are dealt with in full accordance with international law and the humanitarian provisions of the Geneva Conventions.

The access which the residents of the territories have to the Israeli legal system—even to the highest court in the land, the Israel Supreme Court sitting as the High Court of Justice—is unprecedented in international practice. Such access serves as a unique safeguard of the rule of law. Moreover, Israel fully cooperates with organizations such as the International Red Cross which is given full access to every location in the territories.

Force Precautions

By involving large numbers of people and incidents, the general unrest has compounded the difficulties faced by Israel in its efforts to deal with the situation and restore stability. The violent nature of the intifada necessitates a response entailing the use of force. At the same time, special efforts have been undertaken to make clear to Israeli security personnel that, however great the provocation, their behavior must conform to strict regulations and standards, and that restraint must be exercised.

The limitations on the use of force have been conveyed through strict rules of engagement, stringent directives concerning the use of live ammunition and plastic or rubber bullets, other IDF [Israel Defense Forces] standing orders, and a dispatch from the IDF Chief of Staff summarizing these orders. The security personnel are instructed in these rules before entering the territories and prior to specific duty. According to regulations force may be used to stop violent activity and to overcome resistance to arrest. Force is prohibited as a form of punishment or to deliberately inflict injuries; similarly the use of force is forbidden against a person who, after having been arrested, shows no resistance or makes no attempt to escape.

A soldier who is suspected of improper or excessive use of force is subject to military trial and punishment. While some excesses have occurred, these have been unacceptable departures from policy, and have been dealt with accordingly. IDF commanders and soldiers have themselves reported violations of orders by fellow soldiers. Moreover, a special team, commanded by a reserve officer with the rank of colonel and a lawyer by profession, has been established in the Central Command to investigate complaints. . . .

Banning Pamphlets

The instigators of the disturbances in Judea-Samaria and the Gaza District have made extensive use of printed materials, in the form of leaflets and pamphlets, to incite violence and unrest. Therefore, such material is banned, a policy that is in keeping with international law. IDF units are ordered to confiscate incitement material, and legal measures are taken especially against those who write and produce this material. Only in a few cases are legal proceedings held against a person solely for possessing banned incitement material. These usually possessed a large quantity of such documents.

Since the beginning of the intifada, the residents of the territories have continuously been urged by the instigators of the disturbances to display the PLO flag on a wide scale. Display of the flag is intended to provide a backdrop and encouragement to acts of violence, assaults on soldiers and Palestinian inhabitants, roadblocks and attacks on moving vehicles.

Regulations in the territories prohibit the display of flags or political emblems, unless permitted by the IDF Commander. These regulations are intended to prevent incitement to rioting and mob violence. In 1989, the number of cases in which suspects were tried solely for displaying PLO flags was negligible. Even in those cases where individuals were tried solely for this violation, the maximum penalty was a fine.

Trials for security offenses are heard before a military court, and are held in accordance with the procedures and rules of evidence obtaining in the courts of common law in western countries. Convictions in such trials cannot be based on written confessions alone. Indeed, defendants were released from custody following their arraignment, because the court had not been presented with sufficient evidence against them. The suspect has the right to be represented by an attorney, to request a review of his sentence by petitioning a military court of appeals in accordance with the law, and then the Israel Supreme Court, sitting as the High Court of Justice. Throughout the period of imprisonment, inmates may turn to an attorney of their own choice, and a legal adviser is present at the facility. . . .

Conditions at Prison Facilities

The parameters for detention and the rights of prisoners are strictly defined by security regulations. Within 96 hours after an arrest, a written warrant must be issued by a police officer. The period of arrest may not exceed seven days. Detention may be extended for another seven days by a police officer whose rank is not less than captain. An additional period of detention is possible only if so decided by a military court, which also has the authority to order the release of a prisoner, on bail or unconditionally, at any stage of the arrest. A doctor must examine the prisoner to determine whether he is medically fit for detention.

The Israeli authorities make every effort to provide prisoners with appropriate conditions. A proper supply of fresh foodstuffs, water, and personal requirements is provided. In deference to the inmates' dietary preferences, meals are prepared by cooks chosen from among the inmates. A doctor and medical staff are present at every facility, and every inmate is entitled to receive free medical and dental care. Family visits are permitted. . . .

Expulsion

Expulsion is not a general policy, but a measure of last resort. The expulsion of particular agitators or terrorists is fully in keeping with Israel's responsibilities in Judea-Samaria and the Gaza District. Expulsion orders have rarely been issued; they have been carried out only in extreme cases where other measures have not succeeded in stopping hostile activity.

Those expelled were neither innocent activists nor peaceful demonstrators, but individuals prominent in instigating and perpetrating violence-related acts. Many of them were leaders of local PLO groups, and some even bear direct responsibility for acts of terror and murder committed under PLO orders. Several were tried and convicted of terrorism, and later released from prison as a result of the 1985 prisoner exchange with the PLO Jibril faction; although, as a condition of their release, these convicts committed themselves to refrain from all terrorist activities, they afterwards disregarded this pledge. Others were prominent in local extremist Islamic fundamentalist organizations. . . .

Freedom of Movement

In accordance with international law, entry into and departure from Judea-Samaria and the Gaza District require a permit. However, immediately after the Six Day War in June 1967, a liberal "Open Bridges" policy was put into effect. Under this policy, travel permits are routinely given to the residents of the territories who wish to travel to Arab countries. They are also permitted to invite and host relatives and guests from abroad, including from the Arab states.

Moreover, movement between the territories and Israel is permitted, and every effort has been made to avoid restricting movement within the territories, although some restrictions are necessary due to security considerations involving the curbing of violent activity and rioting. . . .

Israel's policy in Judea-Samaria and the Gaza District since

1967 has always been to encourage academic and normal school activity and to improve the educational system there. Within this framework, many new institutions of learning were opened, including five universities where none existed before. . . .

Since December 1987, however, the schools have frequently served as one of the centers for organizing and launching violent activity in the territories. PLO extremists have on numerous occasions entered the classrooms to encourage and compel the pupils to join the rioting in the streets.

Israeli Restraint

We must remember that Israel has shown far more restraint towards violent demonstrations than any hostile neighboring Arab state has ever shown toward peaceful demonstrations against government policy. Israel remains the only country in the entire Middle East in which Arabs can enjoy any measure of political freedom.

Daniel Patrick Moynihan, letter, May 3, 1988.

The use of schools and educational facilities as centers for inciting and engaging in violence is unacceptable, and would not be tolerated by any democratic country. Therefore, Israel had no choice but to close schools which had ceased to be places for study, but had instead become foci for promoting violence. . . .

Israel's policy has always been to uphold religious freedom and the sanctity of religious sites. Free access to places of worship is a cardinal principle of this policy.

Since the beginning of the intifada, the Israel Police, responsible for public order in the State of Israel, has not restricted or prevented the access of worshipers to the Al-Aqsa Mosque on Fridays or on Islamic holidays.

In order to ensure public order in the area and in deference to the sensitivity of the Moslem worshipers, access to the Al-Aqsa Mosque is banned to non-Moslem tourists and other visitors, often Israeli Jews, during times of prayer. . . .

The Palestinian extremists have exploited the special status of mosques and have turned them into instruments of the intifada. In many places, mosques and places of worship have become operational headquarters and centers for organizing, planning, and inciting violent activity. Intifada activists seize control of mosques, prevent worship, and proceed to incite the crowd of worshipers to go out into the streets, riot, and engage in other forms of violent activity. The loudspeaker systems at the mosques are used to read the content of intifada leaflets distributed among the local population. Because of the general immunity of these premises, mosques have become hiding places and shelters for rioters and instigators, as well as places for storing equipment used in the intifada, such as explosives, Molotov cocktails, masks, and manuals on how to incite the local population and make explosives. Mosques are used as sites for recruiting new members to the extremist Islamic organizations. Mosques are also used as sites for "purging" Palestinian Arabs who have "repented" their departure from extremist Palestinian dictates.

As a result of these abuses, the IDF has on a number of occasions had to act against those who have turned the mosques into tools of the intifada. In keeping with Israel's policy regarding the sanctity of places of worship, special orders have been issued regarding the conduct of security personnel at the holy sites in the territories. As a rule, soldiers may not approach such a site and may not enter except when conducting a search, and even then only after having received special approval from a senior military commander. Soldiers are ordered to show respect at the mosques and other holy sites; they must not interfere with religious observance. . . .

A Double Standard

When considering the question of human rights in the context of Israel and the territories, it is advisable that consideration be given to the enormous difficulties and dilemmas which Israel, committed to democratic principles, has had to face in Judea-Samaria and the Gaza District. The threat to Israel's vital security interests should not be ignored, nor should the violent character of the intifada. Israel's measures, in keeping with international standards, have not differed from those of other democratic countries when facing violence in the form of riots, armed assaults, murder, and terror.

Nor is it fair when the media focuses mainly on Israel, instead of devoting attention to the massive abuse of human rights in many countries of the world, e.g. the Arab states, where dictatorial regimes use every means at their disposal to silence and crush all potential and actual dissent.

These other countries, as seen in the Middle East, lack the most basic elements of human rights—freedom of speech, freedom of the press, free elections, equality for women, freedom of religion, freedom of association—and opponents, instead of facing television cameras, face execution. These countries do not have to defend themselves against self-declared foes who continue to aim for their demise. Yet, these nations do not draw the enormous degree of attention that Israel receives for measures taken in defense of its security needs and in accordance with international law.

"Most people in the world support the need of the Palestinian people to freedom and independence."

The Palestinians Have a Right to an Independent State

Ali Kazak

Ali Kazak is a Palestinian Liberation Organization (PLO) representative. The PLO consists of several Palestinian guerrilla, political, and refugee groups working to establish a homeland for Palestinians in areas now under Israeli control. Israel has refused to negotiate with the PLO because factions of the PLO have engaged in terrorism and have called for the elimination of Israel. In the following viewpoint, Kazak states that Palestinians should have their own independent country in the West Bank and Gaza Strip, territories that since 1967 have been occupied by Israel. He argues that more than one hundred nations have recognized the independent state of Palestine, and urges Israel and the U.S. to do the same.

As you read, consider the following questions:

1. What is the central obstacle to Middle East peace, according to Kazak?
2. Why does Kazak call the PLO's declaration of an independent Palestinian state a huge compromise?
3. What should the U.S. do to resolve the Israel/Palestinian conflict besides recognize the state of Palestine, in Kazak's opinion?

Excerpted from "Urgent Need to Address Palestinian Question," by Ali Kazak, *Al-Fajr*, April 1, 1991. Reprinted with permission.

As each new dispute arises in the Middle East, Israel quickly labels it the principal issue in the region. Yet time always reveals the falsity of these claims, as solutions are found and the disputes settled, while the Palestinian question, the central issue and main obstacle to achieving stability in the Middle East, dangerously festers on for its fifth decade.

In the post-Gulf war period the utmost urgency of the Palestine question must now be addressed in all its aspects by the United States and the Western world to avoid further destabilization, upheavals and wars, of which no one can predict their destructive and disastrous outcome, and which may affect the whole world, considering Israel's threat of mass destructive weapons, such as its nuclear, biological and chemical warheads. Israel is today the world's sixth nuclear power and fourth in the world in terms of military striking power.

Declaration of Independence

In November 1988, the Palestine National Council, the Palestinian parliament in exile and the highest authoritative body in the Palestine Liberation Organization, launched the Declaration of Independence of the State of Palestine and a peace initiative, which proposed two states in the historic land of Palestine and expressed the PLO's readiness for talks without preconditions.

The PLO stated its acceptance of all U.N. resolutions relevant to the Palestine question, taken as a whole, including Security Council resolutions 242 and 338. The present proposal by President Yasser Arafat involves an Israeli withdrawal from the occupied territories to allow free and democratic U.N.-supervised elections, including PLO participation, to select Palestinian representatives who would then attend the international peace conference leading to self-determination for the Palestinians in their own state.

All Arab countries and the international community, with the exception of two countries only—the United States and Israel—supported this initiative, which still stands despite Israel's rejectionism, continued massacres and atrocities.

The Palestinian peace initiative shows the huge compromise the PLO made for the sake of peace; it accepted to establish a Palestinian state in the 1967 occupied territories—East Jerusalem, the West Bank and the Gaza Strip, which amounts to 23 percent of Palestine, a compromise of 77 percent of the Palestinian people's homeland.

While the PLO has expressed its readiness for talks without preconditions and recognized Israel's right to exist, Israeli intransigence has only hardened. Israel to date has refused all Palestinian peace initiatives including the convening of the international peace conference. Its policy since 1948 confirms that it rules out any compromise or negotiations, attempting instead to settle the issue by force of arms. . . .

"I can't understand this obsession for their very own homeland. . . ."

Corky Trinidad/*Honolulu Star Bulletin*. Reprinted with permission.

The PLO welcomed the positive elements contained in President George Bush's speech to a joint session of the U.S. Congress on March 6, 1991, regarding a solution to the Arab, Palestinian-Israeli conflict, in accordance with U.N. Security Council resolutions 242 and 338.

In its statement the PLO said it believes, however, that the position expressed by President Bush needs continuing serious efforts for the implementation of all U.N. resolutions relevant to the Palestine question and the Middle East which will guarantee the end of Israel's occupation of the Palestinian and Arab occupied territories and the exercise of the Palestinian people's right to self-determination and independence.

Most people in the world support the need of the Palestinian people to freedom and independence and the international consensus favors an international conference, attended by all relevant Middle East parties and the five permanent members of the U.N. Security Council, to work out a comprehensive and lasting peace based on justice for all nations in the area.

Yet one party stands defiantly against the international consensus. Israeli Prime Minister Yitzhak Shamir has for years been repeatedly quoted as saying he would never agree to talk to Palestinian delegates named by the PLO, would not accept a Palestinian state in any part of Palestine and saw no point in holding the international peace conference. Mr. Shamir's stated reason for opposing the peace conference is that Israel would have to make compromises at such a gathering.

Further to this Mr. Shamir stood on Nov. 19, 1990, and stated publicly once more his and the Israeli government's position on the so-called "Greater Israel" saying, "It is our duty to maintain the land of Israel from the sea to the Jordan River for the generations to come and for the great immigration."

This was affirmed by the announcement of Israel's minister of housing, Mr. Ariel Sharon, better known as the Butcher of Beirut, that Israel is building 15,000 housing units in Jerusalem and other occupied Palestinian territories to settle new Jewish settlers and to Judaize the Holy City.

The Five Noes

Indeed, both the Israeli Likud government and the face on the other side of the coin, the Labor Party, have repeatedly stated their well-known five "Noes":

No to recognition of the PLO;

No to recognition of the right of the Palestinian people to self-determination;

No to recognition of the Palestinians' right to return;

No to withdrawal from the Arab and Palestinian territories occupied in 1967; and

No to the establishment of an independent Palestinian state.

The PLO is recognized by every segment of the Palestinian people as their sole legitimate representative and is recognized internationally as such by more than 140 governments, as well as the United Nations, the Non-Aligned Movement, the Islamic Summit and the Organization of African Unity.

And nobody besides the PLO even claims to speak for the Palestinians. Yet Israel and the United States continue to veto talks with the PLO. This has caused many people to ask that if the Israelis and the Americans can choose their own representatives, why can't the Palestinians?

Furthermore, since the declaration of the State of Palestine on Nov. 15, 1988, more than 100 countries have recognized Palestine and established full diplomatic relations with it.

Why then, does Israel continually refuse to sit down and talk to the Palestinian leadership? Simply because the present Israeli leadership knows that this would imply recognition of the Palestinian nation and its concomitant right to a state. . . .

The PLO's representation, legitimacy and credibility come first and foremost from the Palestinian people themselves; it is their democratic right to choose their own representatives and the Palestinians have paid dearly to legitimize their representative, the PLO. It is a well-known fact, to the foe before the friends, that the PLO and President Arafat enjoy overwhelming support from the Palestinian people in occupied Palestine and the diaspora. All Israeli and other attempts to bypass the PLO and create a puppet leadership have failed. . . .

Israel and its lobby are now attempting to renew their old and unsuccessful campaign against the PLO to draw the international community's attention away from addressing the real question, which remains Israel's illegal occupation, denial of the Palestinians' national and human rights and refusal to adhere to numerous U.N. resolutions in this regard.

Israel's aim is to free itself from the pressure it is under to reciprocate the PLO's recognition and peace initiative, to prevent the convening of an international peace conference, and to gain the time it needs, as always, to create more facts on the ground and make the world face these newly-created facts, especially now with regard to Soviet Jewish settlements and its hopes to annex the remainder of occupied Palestine.

One of the other facts exposed by the Gulf war is the myth of secure borders. In his speech to the joint session of Congress, President Bush acknowledged this myth once and for all when he said, "We have learned in the modern age, geography cannot guarantee security and security does not come from military power alone." Nor can there be secure borders based on occupation, dispossession and oppression.

True Security

However, true security for Israel cannot be separated from the security of Palestine and the Arab region as a whole; it must be multilateral and reciprocal. This would allow all the peoples in the Middle East to live in peace with stable, flourishing and secure economies.

President Bush's and Secretary of State Baker's repeated line that they can't force peace in the Middle East reminds one of the Arab saying: "Angelic words aiming for devilish results." Of course no one is asking the United States to force peace. But what the United States can do and is required to do is to force the implementation of international legality and the U.N. resolutions relevant to the question of Palestine.

The right to self-determination and independence is one of the most basic human rights, and its denial to the Palestinians by Israeli occupation is the direct cause of the uprising.

Twenty-three years of subjugation and misery will no longer be tolerated by the Palestinians, and they have shown that they are willing to lay down their lives rather than accept further oppression and racism.

The claim that there could be democracy under Israeli military occupation and rule, puts in question the concept of such a democracy. It is a contradiction in terms.

The current uprising by the Palestinians . . . and the brutal response by the Israeli military forces has once again underlined the tragedy of the Palestinian people and the urgent need for a peaceful settlement.

Human Rights Abuses

Israel's human rights abuses have been repeatedly condemned by world governments, and the United Nations and its agencies, but Western indifference and a soft approach toward Israel's crimes have made the Israeli occupation authorities safe from the possibility of punishment or deterrence, which has only served to encourage it to continue its crimes, described in international law as war crimes and crimes against humanity.

Israeli minister Mr. Rehavam Ze'evi and a number of other ministers are now openly calling for the mass expulsion of the remaining Palestinian people from their homeland and the Israeli prime minister, Mr. Shamir, has also openly called for the destruction and disappearance of the PLO. Would we have witnessed the same deafening silence from the Western countries if members of the PLO Executive Committee had called for the expulsion of the Israelis back to Poland, the Soviet Union and other countries they came from, and if President Arafat had called for the destruction and disappearance of Israel?

Under the racist Israeli "Law of Return," any Jew of any nationality, anywhere in the world, is automatically granted Israeli citizenship on arriving in Israel. In 1990, Israel brought more than 200,000 Soviet Jews and plans to bring another 800,000 in the next two years according to the World Jewish Congress.

Yet the dispossessed Palestinians and their families are still not allowed to return to their homeland.

It is expected, and it is time, for those who believe that Jews have no more rights than non-Jews, to speak out in support of the rights of the Palestinian Christians and Muslims, dispossessed by the Israelis in 1948 and 1967, to return to their homeland, rights which have been supported by U.N. Resolution 194, the Universal Declaration of Human Rights and repeatedly called for by numerous other U.N. resolutions.

During the Gulf war, the Israeli minister for myths and propaganda, Mr. Binyamin Netanyahu, who is also deputy foreign minister, frequently repeated the myths to the gullible Western media that it was the Arabs that attacked Israel in 1967 and started the fighting, and that Israel was in danger of annihilation. Both are false and were refuted by none other than Israeli leaders themselves.

Even while Israel was launching its Pearl Harbor-type of attack on Egypt's airfields, it announced to a believing Western world that in the early hours of June 5, 1967, its radar screens had picked up large numbers of Egyptian planes flying toward Israel. This was a complete fabrication and was shown to be so by the fact that the Israeli Air Force trapped and destroyed most of the Egyptian Air Force on the ground. It was some days before the West learned the truth and by then the fighting was over.

General Matityahu Peled, one of the architects of the Israeli victory, committed what the Israeli public considered blasphemy when he admitted the true thinking of the Israeli leadership: "The thesis that the danger of genocide was hanging over us in June 1967 and that Israel was fighting for its physical existence is only a bluff, which was born and developed after the war."

Declaration of Independence

By virtue of the natural, historical and legal right of the Palestinian Arab people to its homeland, Palestine, and of the sacrifices of its succeeding generations in defence of the freedom and independence of that homeland.

Pursuant to the resolutions of the Arab Summit Conferences and on the basis of the international legitimacy embodied in the resolutions of the United Nations since 1947, and

Through the exercise by the Palestinian Arab people of its right to self-determination, political independence and sovereignty over its territory:

The Palestine National Council hereby declares, in the Name of God and on behalf of the Palestinian Arab people, the establishment of the State of Palestine in the land of Palestine with its capital at Jerusalem.

Palestine National Council, Declaration of Independence of the State of Palestine, November 15, 1988.

Israeli Air Force General Ezer Weizmann declared bluntly that "there was never any danger of extermination," while a former Israeli minister, Mordechai Bentov, dismissed the theory with the words: "All this story about the danger of extermination had been a complete invention and had been blown up *a posteriori* to justify the annexation of new Arab territories." As to the threat to Israel's security, this plainly was non-existent. According to *The Observer*, Nasser's purpose was clearly "to deter Israel rather than provoke it to a fight." In 1982, the Israelis finally admitted that they had started the war. Prime Minister Menachem Begin in a speech at the Israeli National Defense College said, "The Egyptian army concentrations in the Sinai approaches do not prove that Nasser was really about to attack us. We must be honest with ourselves. We decided to attack him."

The repeated myths and misquotations of PLO leaders by Mr. Netanyahu and his colleagues, which are designed to mislead the Western audience, make one wonder whether there are limits to their lies and linguistic acrobatics, and whether there are limits to how much the West can take of such insults to their intelligence and the falsification of history in such an undignified way.

The New World Order

In the same address to the joint session of Congress, President Bush did answer the question of whether, in the New World Order, international legality applies to Israel and whether the Palestinian people are entitled to their rights to self-determination, freedom, independence and return to their homeland, by saying, "Now we can see a new world coming into view. A world in which there is a very real prospect of a new world order. In the words of Winston Churchill, a 'world order' in which 'the principles of justice and fair play . . . protect the weak against the strong. . . .' A world where the United Nations, freed from Cold War stalemate, is poised to fulfill the historic vision of its founders. A world in which freedom and respect for human rights find a home among all nations."

Fine words indeed, but what the United States needs to do is put substance into them in order to retain the credibility it lost much of in the pre-New World Order, where it applied one set of principles to Israel and another to the rest of the world.

Furthermore, it is laughable in the post-Gulf war period with the mass destruction of Iraq and Kuwait by the United States and the coalition, to return to the old argument that Israel does not respond to pressure because that will antagonize the extremists.

The United States arms, finances and protects Israel's occupation of Palestine and other Arab territories. The United States does not need to send half a million troops to force Israel to implement U.N. resolutions and withdraw from the 1967 occupied territories. Israel would be brought to its knees in one month if the United States stopped its economic aid to Israel.

Mr. Bush must lead the way for Israel by bringing about the United States' recognition of the Palestinian people's right to self-determination and the State of Palestine, and the establishment of full diplomatic relations with it. There are no more excuses for more delay and waiting.

"I guarantee you: No one will work harder for a stable peace in the region than we will," said Mr. Bush in his speech. The world is watching and will judge the United States by its deeds and not by its words alone.

96

"There is no group of . . . distinct Arabs that is eligible on the basis of the principle of self-determination to establish an additional Arab state."

The Palestinians Do Not Have a Right to an Independent State

Ze'ev B. Begin

Ze'ev B. Begin is a member of the Israeli Knesset, the governing body of Israel, and chairman of its subcommittee on National Security Policy. In the following viewpoint, he argues that Judea-Samaria, or the West Bank, and Gaza should not be made into an independent Palestinian state. He maintains that the original land of Palestine has already been divided into two states: one Jewish (Israel) and one Arab (Jordan), and that there is no need for another state in the region. Establishing such a state, he asserts, would endanger Israel.

As you read, consider the following questions:

1. What Zionist goals must not be compromised, in Begin's opinion?
2. Why does the author believe that UN resolutions 242 and 338 do not require Israel to give up territory to the Palestinians?
3. What does Begin think Palestinians should do?

Excerpted from "The Likud Vision for Israel at Peace," by Ze'ev B. Begin, *Foreign Affairs*, Fall 1991. Copyright © 1991 by the Council on Foreign Relations, Inc. Reprinted with permission.

Those who call for a "new order" in the Middle East are very generous in their regard for our troubled region, as if we ever had an "old order." The grim truth of the matter is that the Middle East is characterized by numerous political volcanoes, distributed randomly in space, which erupt violently, randomly in time. This is a textbook definition of disorder. Whether in cellular biology, solid state physics, social structure or political systems, the transformation of disorder into order entails the investment of energy for the application of a set of rules.

We in Israel have our concept of the relevant rules that we believe is shared by the international community, and we are ready to spend all needed energy toward transforming our region from chaos to order. My stand and that of the Likud Party is a Zionist position. . . .

Our Zionist stand is based on the Zionist goal: the creation of a safe haven for the Jewish nation in the Land of Israel. It rests on two pillars: the right of the Jewish nation to the Land of Israel; and the right of the Jewish state to national security, to allow its sons and daughters to live in freedom. Upon these pillars rests the three-pronged policy of the Israeli government: the prevention of foreign rule west of the Jordan River, an initiative to establish understanding and mutual respect between Israelis and their Arab neighbors, and efforts to reach peace treaties between Israel and the Arab countries.

There are those who dismiss this Zionist stand as founded on aspirations of the past, not on a rational examination of difficulties in the present. I sometimes find myself envious of those of other nations, not as ancient as ours, not as rich with spiritual treasures, not as tied to the cradle of their heritage who, nevertheless, have deep feelings toward their country and express those feelings as "self-evident."

The Jewish Heritage

Early in my service as a member of the Knesset, I hosted a delegation of visitors headed by a member of the U.S. Congress from Alaska, which had been transferred to American sovereignty from the Russian tsars in the Alaska purchase some 125 years ago. For my guests it was self-evident that Alaska is part and parcel of the United States. I reminded my visitors that the "Hebron purchase" had taken place some four thousand years ago, between Abraham the Hebrew and Ephron the Hittite; that the "Jerusalem purchase" was sealed three thousand years ago between David the Jew and Aravna the Jebusite, and that we can present a document proving that in both cases our forefathers paid for those lands in cash—a document called the Bible.

North of Jerusalem the Arab village of Anata now stands

where 2,600 years ago Jeremiah was born and raised in the village then called Anatot. Since his prophecy, and that of the other Hebrew prophets of that era, no one has surpassed them in spiritual achievement. In every realm of life new generations improve upon their predecessors, but in this case the Hebrew prophets peaked, both in literary style and in moral values. If there are universal values, they are reflected best in the writings of these sons of the Jewish nation. Therefore we believe that our quest for a natural, open, straightforward connection to these sources of our heritage should be taken as "self-evident.". . .

Thompson/Copley News Service. Reprinted with permission.

These assertions seem, to some people, to conflict with the right of the Arab inhabitants of Judea, Samaria and Gaza to establish their own state. I would like, however, to challenge such a wrong impression. In order for a group of people to be considered a separate nation, to have the right to self-determination, that people must be different from other groups to such an extent that would justify its separation from them. In the Land of Israel, on both sides of the Jordan River, within the boundaries of Palestine, only two such groups live: the children of the Arab nation and the children of the Jewish nation. The Palestinian Arabs on both sides of the Jordan River are claimed as an integral part of the Arab nation even under the Palestinian charter of the Palestine Liberation Organization (PLO). But the Syrian government, for instance, has for past decades considered the Palestinian Arabs to be "South Syrians"; the lack of distinguishing national qualities is one of the reasons why Syrian leaders have long been reserved about the need for a unique Palestinian Arab state.

Yet people still insist that the Arabs in the Land of Israel, that is the Arabs of Palestine, are distinguished in their traits and dialect from their Arab brethren in Syria, Iraq and Saudi Arabia.

For the sake of argument let us accept that position, although many would agree that the differences between an Italian from Milan and an Italian from Naples are deeper than the differences between an Arab from Baghdad and an Arab from Amman. But now, after we distinguish this group from the Arab nation and after we refer to them in a linguistic exercise as a "people," the proposition is imposed upon us that out of this "people" we should still distinguish the Arabs of Samaria-Judea-Gaza as a separate "people." This artificial distinction must lead, however, to the far-reaching conclusion that the Palestinian-Arab people is now separated into three different peoples: the Samarian-Judean-Gazan Arab people in the center, the Trans-Jordanian Arab people to the east and the Israeli Galilean Arab people to the west. If the first has a right to self-determination, so have the other two. In other words: one becomes three, and the result is nonsensical.

No Need for Another Arab State

Rhetorical positions aside, the Arab nation of all the nations on earth has enjoyed the fullest expression of its right to self-determination, in 20 independent states where 95 percent of the sons and daughters of the Arab nation live. The need for a unique Palestinian Arab state west of the Jordan River was not heard before 1967 in the years when Jordan occupied Judea and Samaria.

In the Land of Israel, which some call Palestine, two states were established: one Arab, one Jewish. There is no group of different and distinct Arabs that is eligible on the basis of the principle of self-determination to establish an additional Arab state west of the Jordan River.

It is true that the 1978 Camp David accords state that negotiations on the final status of Samaria, Judea and the Gaza district will address the "legitimate rights" of its Arab inhabitants. But these legitimate rights do not include the right to establish another Arab state, especially as we know that such a state would eventually be established upon the ruins of the state of Israel.

100

We must make every effort to reach an agreement with our Arab neighbors based on mutual respect, but we must not yield to the false claim that such an agreement must be based on the fictitious recognition of a "symmetry" between the rights of the Jewish nation and that small portion—one percent—of the Arab nation in the western Land of Israel.

UN Resolutions

The set of rules pertaining to the Arab-Israeli dispute are contained in three familiar international documents. First, U.N. resolution 242, adopted on November 22, 1967, called for "withdrawal of Israeli armed forces from territories occupied" and, at the same time, "acknowledgment of the sovereignty, territorial integrity and political independence of every state in the area, and their right to live in peace within secure and recognized boundaries." The resolution is "a balanced whole," said Lord Caradon of Britain, its sponsor, in 1967. "To add to it or to detract from it would destroy the balance. . . . It must be considered as a whole and as it stands."

Six years later the U.N. Security Council ordered in resolution 338 that "negotiations start between the parties concerned under appropriate auspices, aimed at establishing a just and lasting peace in the Middle East." Thus, resolution 242 offers guidelines toward the desired goal, and resolution 338 describes the method for getting there. . . .

Up to now the Arab states, with the exception of Egypt, have paid only lip service to their acceptance of resolutions 242 and 338, and this set of rules has been severely distorted, both by addition and by omission. The "right of self-determination of the Palestinians" does not appear in the text; an international parley is not mentioned; the parties appearing in the text only include states, and no "organization," or terrorist syndicate such as the PLO, is mentioned. The phrase "territories occupied" is neither preceded by "the," nor is it followed by "on all fronts." Moreover resolution 242 specifically mentions withdrawal of Israel's armed forces, and not its administration or any other aspect of its sovereignty.

Concurrent with undue additions, a major omission has become habitual in discussion: few remember that the crux of resolutions 242 and 338 is negotiations between parties aimed at establishing a just and durable peace. The rest of the texts, as important as they may be, are details, and since some of these significant details are disputed, the differences must be resolved through direct negotiations without prior conditions. . . .

We know of course that geography does not guarantee security, but we also know that in the Middle East a lack of minimum geography guarantees defeat. If a government of Israel declares, as some people expect it to, that it would be ready to

101

shrink itself back to the pre-1967 lines "in exchange for peace," shortsightedness will triumph and peace will be defeated. The temptation to eliminate the ten-mile-wide Jewish democracy in one quick blow would be irresistible for Middle Eastern dictators, whether radical Arab nationalists such as those in Syria and Iraq, or Islamic fundamentalists in Iran or Algeria. . . .

Jordan Is Palestine

There already exists a Palestinian Arab State. It is called Jordan.

Jordan spans the whole of eastern Palestine, up to the Jordan River. A majority of its citizens east of the Jordan River are Palestinian Arabs, not to mention the West Bankers, who hold Jordanian citizenship. All Jordanians are, by geographic definition, "Palestinians," as are all Israelis. Movement of the Arab population, including the Palestinian refugees, took place *inside the historic area of Palestine.*

Leonard J. Davis, *Myths and Facts 1989,* 1988.

Our Zionist conclusion is, therefore, logical and plausible. It is vital for Israeli security to control the Golan Heights as well as the entire area west of the Jordan River. By defending our land we will protect our people. . . .

The Camp David Approach

The Arab-Israeli dispute is so deeply rooted—in both the historical and psychological senses—that one should not expect it to be solved in a single short diplomatic move. With this realization in mind the participants in the Camp David accords agreed on a gradual approach. This in turn was translated to a "partial agreement," in two different meanings. First, it is an interim agreement, defining a transitional period of five years, which will enable the parties to examine carefully the developments in the Middle East, in particular, those west of the Jordan River. Second, the agreement is partial also in terms of substance. The parties are asked to seek agreement on the "softer" issues, on which they can hopefully agree, while addressing the harder issues would be deferred to a later phase (but still within the transitional period). It is understood that the hardest-to-solve point of contention is the final status of Samaria, Judea and the Gaza district.

The wisdom of Camp David dictated that the five transitional years should not be wasted, but instead should become a source for confidence building between Arabs and Jews west of the Jordan River. This approach was translated to the need to decrease to a minimum possible sources of friction between the

Arab inhabitants and branches of the Israeli government. The tool proposed for that was a self-governing authority. Accordingly the Arab inhabitants of Samaria, Judea and Gaza will run their own affairs through an Arab administrative council to be elected by them, while Israel takes care of its security through means determined by the government. . . .

It should be stressed that the agreement between Egypt and Israel concerning Arab autonomy pertains not to the territory of Samaria, Judea and Gaza, but to its Arab inhabitants. In early 1982, before the Egyptian delegation withdrew from the negotiations, Israel proposed an extensive, detailed list of powers and responsibilities to be transferred to the Arab administrative council. These include: administration of justice, including supervision of the administrative and prosecution systems; administration of finance—budgeting and allocation, taxation; and local police, with the operation of a strong police force and maintenance of prisons for criminal offenders. This far-reaching proposal is still on the table, and was included in Prime Minister Yitzhak Shamir's letter to President Bush in April 1990. . . .

An Existential Issue

The Camp David framework is the only practical diplomatic vehicle that carries any hope for progress toward a workable solution, containing the necessary and the sufficient elements for beginning negotiations. It is important that our Arab neighbors examine these documents and assess their advantages without prejudice. They must give up the illusion that violence, from within or without, shall force us into more far-reaching proposals, such as a commitment to accept a future 21st Arab state west of the Jordan River. All of us will have to find a way to live side by side west of the Jordan River—and when our neighbors understand that, there is a possibility that they will sit with us, negotiate and agree, for their sake. We shall be there too, for our sake. . . .

When people demand "Peace Now," it is our responsibility to ask them, "And what then?" The conflict between Israel and the Arab nations has deep historical and psychological roots pertaining not only to Samaria, Judea and Gaza but also to the Israeli coastal plain. What is Hebron to us, they call el-Halil; Ashkelon for us is Majdal to them; our Jerusalem is their Urshulim-el-Kuds, and our Haifa is for them also Haifa. This is not "just another" border dispute on acid rain, sardine fishing rights or even drug smuggling. For Israel it is an existential issue, and such a conflict cannot be ended by a quick fix.

"The intifada [has] brought new hope for challenging the occupation. "

The *Intifada* Has Helped the Palestinians' Campaign for Rights

Phyllis Bennis

In December 1987 the Israeli/Palestinian conflict intensified when Palestinians in the West Bank and Gaza engaged in both violent and nonviolent demonstrations of unprecedented size and organization. The uprising, which became known as the *intifada*, gained momentum in organization and leadership, and became the most sustained and intense revolt of Palestinians in decades. In the following viewpoint, Phyllis Bennis examines the *intifada* and argues that it has given Palestinian residents of the Israeli-occupied territories new inspiration and unity in their quest for independence, as well as giving their cause renewed international attention. Bennis is a United Nations and Middle East correspondent for Pacifica radio and co-editor of *Beyond the Storm: A Gulf Crisis Reader*. She wrote *From Stones to Statehood*, a book on the *intifada*, from which this viewpoint is excerpted.

As you read, consider the following questions:

1. Who are the leaders of the *intifada*, according to Bennis?
2. What cultural changes has the *intifada* made among Palestinians, according to the author?
3. How has the *intifada* changed the international standing of the Palestinian cause, in Bennis's opinion?

On December 8, 1987, near the densely crowded checkpoint at the entrance to the occupied Gaza Strip, an incident occurred. It involved an Israeli truck—some say an army truck—that swerved, and struck and killed four Palestinians: a doctor, an engineer and two workers. Some say it was deliberate. What makes this incident different from the hundreds, perhaps thousands, of similar incidents during the 20 years of Israeli occupation was its outcome.

The incident was different, this time, because it sparked an uprising that swept across the Gaza Strip, jumped like a roaring forest fire across Israeli territory to the occupied West Bank, and set into motion a blaze of nationalist resistance that has not yet been extinguished.

The uprising ignited in a specific time and a specific place. The time was now, only now, at the confluence of years of smoldering and waiting, and the immediate spark of the moment's crisis.

In some ways, the real surprise was not that the uprising began, but that it did not begin earlier. The occupation, after all, had been going on for more than 20 years. The denial of national rights, the disorientation of Palestinians being made refugees in their own land, the constant repression, all led to widespread despair—and for many living under Israeli military control, to passivity.

The Palestinians living in the West Bank and Gaza are a young community; more than half the population grew up knowing nothing but Israeli occupation. Only now, has the intifada brought new hope for challenging the occupation; only now, especially since the Declaration of an independent State of Palestine on November 15, 1988, is there a glimmer of what a Palestine free from occupation could look like.

One community leader in Beit Sahour, near Bethlehem, said "Palestine has become the intifada. And the intifada is transforming Palestine."

New Leadership

But however the uprising began, if it had been strictly spontaneous, it would have collapsed in just a few weeks. The ferocity of Israel's counter-attack left little hope for an ad-libbed resistance movement.

But this resistance was not ad-libbed. A popular committee representative from the small northern village of Qabatiya described how "the intifada was spontaneous at first. But after about one month, our earlier organizing efforts took root, and gained control of the political motion of the intifada. That is what allowed the uprising to continue."

Existing grass-roots organizations inside occupied Palestine

105

quickly mobilized their resources to respond to the new challenges posed every day. Their leaders met to assess, and try to answer, the needs of the population as institutions of the occupation authority crumbled.

One El Bireh leader described how "the reasons for the intifada are both objective and subjective. The objective reason, of course, is the 21 years of occupation, of repression. The subjective side is the Palestinian resistance movement we have built over those same 21 years, increasing the participation of every sector of society. It was the accumulation of those objective and subjective factors together that created the intifada. Nothing is spontaneous here any more."

Wider Implications

The *intifada* has had a profound effect on the course and dynamics of the Palestinian-Israeli conflict. Its implications have been greatest, of course, for Palestinians under occupation and the broader process of Palestinian nation-building, and for Israeli politics and Israel's own future course as a society. Yet the Palestinian uprising has also had wider repercussions than these, in the arena of regional and international politics. The Palestine Liberation Organization, by its declaration of independence and statehood in November 1988, signaled its hope that a diplomatic settlement to the conflict might be found. Within Israel, many have pointed to the need for a political, rather than military, solution to the Palestinian issue (however differently this may be defined). The *intifada* has created new regional pressures, constraints and opportunities, and an altered political environment for Egypt, Jordan, Syria and other regional actors.

Rex Brynen and Neil Caplan, *Echoes of the Intifada*, 1991.

At the same time, the clandestine local branches of the PLO's main constituent groups, already well positioned inside the broader local organizations, emerged to play a more public role. Public, that is, as integral and acknowledged parts of the emerging infrastructure of the new Palestinian community life. The individual leaders of these movements collectively soon joined with representatives of the local organizations to form the Unified National Leadership of the Uprising (UNLU). . . .

The UNLU itself remains underground. Despite frequent Israeli claims of having destroyed the leadership core, UNLU has been consistently visible through its regular communiques. Those numbered leaflets, appearing suddenly on street corners throughout the West Bank and Gaza about every two weeks, identify the new stages of the uprising, and coordinate the various aspects of resistance. Each leaflet, eagerly awaited, outlines the specific tasks for each day of the coming period. Which are the days for complete commercial strikes, which to protest the condition of prisoners in administrative detention, which to work on the land, which to highlight women's roles in the uprising, which to confront the occupation's military forces, which to spend in commemorating the legacy of the intifada's martyrs. . . .

"We have to say," an activist from one of the women's committees in Ramallah said, "that the Unified Leadership, in whose name the Calls have been issued, is the voice of the PLO in the West Bank and Gaza, in all the occupied land. Really, we are not disconnected from the PLO, we are one people outside and inside the territories. We have one aim, and the PLO is our representative. . . . Whether we talk about the grassroots committees or the leadership, the UNLU, they are actually representing groups which are part of the PLO. We are one, and the PLO is our sole representative, and they fulfill our aspirations.". . .

Grassroots Organizations

The grassroots organizations are of two distinct but inter-related types. Some form the basis for mobilizing and energizing Palestinians on the basis of social factors. Thus the women's associations, trade unions, student and professional groups, farmers' and merchants' organizations all play a critical role in involving those sectors in the uprising.

Other groups, some with a history many years older than the intifada, function as alternative social service organizations, providing for food production and distribution, health needs, financial assistance and education on a society-wide basis. Some form the basis for an increasingly independent Palestinian economy—including the merchants' organizations that determine the character of the intifada's commercial strikes, agricultural cooperatives, and trade unions forging new relations with Palestinian factory owners.

The role of these new institutions grows as the status and power of the occupation authorities weaken. The astonishing multiplicity and consolidation of these popular organizations, a key part of the uprising's strategy, set the conditions for a kind of dual power in the West Bank and Gaza, in which Palestinian national institutions contend directly with the military-controlled structures of Israeli occupation.

According to a women's association leader, "this dual power is what we are aiming at with the uprising, to create a gap between the Palestinians under occupation and the Israeli authorities. For the last 20 years, Israel was able to create this connection between the Palestinian population and the occupation authority. There is the economic link, for example. We have been completely dependent on the Israeli economy. We were without an infrastructure of our own, or an economy, or a state. We had nothing, so we had to be dependent on their economy. And many people were really collaborating with them. Now what the uprising is doing is disconnecting, creating a complete disconnection, by going to the policemen, asking them to resign, asking people not to pay taxes, all these things. . . . You can feel that a Palestinian authority has somehow been created during this uprising. You can feel it in the neighborhood committees, where everybody in a neighborhood gets together, to form a guard committee, agricultural committee, food storage, education, sort of a small government in the street. And really, the Israelis cannot do anything about it."

Taken together, the two kinds of popular institutions weave a tight fabric of Palestinian resistance, self-reliance, and an extraordinary level of unity, across class, sex, geographic, occupational, and age lines. When joined with the PLO's vision for the creation of an independent Palestine, the result is the nascent apparatus of a state. The popularly chosen leadership of the neighborhood, city, and national institutions of the intifada, the emerging structures for governing a new society, coalesce in the Unified National Leadership of the Uprising. . . .

New People

"We are creating a different kind of person now," the village leader in Beit Sahour mused one day, "even as we build the uprising. In the past, sometimes there was selfishness, or a lack of cooperation. People wanted to build their own castle, alone, to say 'I want my wife, my children, to be better off.' Now it's different, now people are cooperating. We all have the same feelings toward the future, because we had the same problems in the past. We share the same dreams now."

Those shared dreams are part of the changes going on inside Palestinian society as a result of the uprising. The outside world, watching the intifada through a prism of media-defined headlines, sees mostly the most direct forms of resistance against the occupying army: Palestinian children throwing stones at well-armed Israeli troops.

And certainly that stone-throwing has been, and remains, a critical component of this multifaceted intifada. But the children of the stones are part of a larger process as well. Their stones and slingshots have become catalysts for far-reaching changes within Palestinian life.

The Arabic root for "intifada," the word "nafada," focuses more on the internal aspects of the process than on its impact on the external world—Palestinian scholar Shukri Abed writes that nafada means to shudder or tremble, to shake off or shake out, to recover or jump to one's feet.

Knowing the importance of what something is called to determine how it is viewed, Palestinians chose "uprising" as the closest English equivalent for intifada. And though it pinpoints direct resistance to Israeli occupation as the key characteristic, "uprising" still misses some of the layers of meaning. In part, this might be attributable to the rich complexity of Arabic compared to the more precise and linear English. But whatever word is used, the internal consequences of the intifada within Palestinian public and private life, may well prove to be as revolutionary and long-lasting as its task of ending the occupation. The "shaking off" of passivity, of old ideas constrained by feudal traditions, or the "jumping to their feet" of newly mobilized sectors of society, all are part of the ongoing intifada.

Female Leadership

The cultural changes began to emerge as early as the first months of the uprising. The visible leadership role of many Palestinian women directly challenged—although it did not yet entirely end—the legacy of women being kept at home and out of public life. The popularity of Arabic and Western pop music declined. It was replaced by smuggled in and widely distributed cassettes of nationalist and revolutionary "intifada music." Wedding customs began to change, as once-extravagant celebrations were pared down to more modest family-based affairs, and traditional lavish dowries were supplanted by collections of money to support the uprising. The traditional three-day mourning period has been recast for martyrs of the intifada: from days of prayer and keening, to three-day strikes with shuttered shops and soldiers challenged, with funeral processions transformed into protest marches.

A popular committee leader in Qabatiya described how "social organization here used to be based on tribal and clan affiliation, with status determined by family ties. Now it is based on our new democracy, with respect based on how much each person participates. We are changing our culture and consciousness.". . .

In Geneva, on the night of Yasir Arafat's 1988 address to the United Nations, Akram Haniyeh reflected on the impact of the uprising on Palestinian society. A noted journalist and short story writer, Haniyeh was expelled from his birthplace in the West Bank in 1986. He is now part of the PLO's committee on the occupied territories.

"No one should be surprised by the intifada," Haniyeh told me, "except we were all surprised by our people's ability to sacrifice. The intifada has taught all of us. It has educated our people. The *nida'at* [communiques of the UNLU] are not an invention of the national movement, their outcome comes from the people. The intifada has built a new model, something entirely new to the international heritage of revolution. The people have revolutionary initiative now. They have the ability to face the new needs of the uprising as those needs escalate.". . .

A Sense of Community

What is most impressive is the sense that the intifada demonstrated of a collectivity or community finding its way together. The source of this is the organic nationhood that today underlies Palestinian life. For the first time Palestinians exposed themselves to it, allowed themselves to be guided by it directly, offered themselves to its imperatives. Instead of individuals and private interests, the public good and the collective will predominated. Leaders were never identified. Personalities were submerged in the group.

The intifada therefore accomplished a number of unprecedented things. In my opinion, the future of the Middle East as a whole is going to be influenced by them, and Palestine and Israel will never be the same again because of them.

Edward W. Said, *Intifada*, 1989.

Eighteen months into the intifada, a doctor from one of the popular health committees told me how "this new generation, that grew up during the occupation, they have now said they would not wait any longer. It used to be a question in the rest of the world whether we Palestinians even had the right to talk about freedom; now we have a new kind of self-respect. The intifada has brought an earthquake to our society. . . ."

The results of this earthquake, this "shaking loose," can be seen on both the internal and international levels.

Palestinians living under occupation, living the intifada, claim credit for the changing international conditions and the growing acceptance throughout the world of Palestine as a national entity. They see those changes as a direct result of the strength of the uprising itself.

The international shifts are easier to see and quantify. They began during the summer of 1988, eight months into the intifada, and they first emerged visibly within the Arab world.

In that first summer of the uprising, Jordan's King Hussein severed all administrative and economic ties with the West Bank. Hussein described the cutting of ties as an expression of support for Palestinian independence and the PLO. For the Palestinians, his act represented a crucial victory for the intifada, derailing longstanding Jordanian efforts to act as interlocutor for the Palestinians in any international arena. . . .

The next visible international accomplishment came three and a half months later. The Palestine National Council, the legislative and highest branch of the Palestinian national movement, convened in Algiers. Its extraordinary session acted on behalf of the entire Palestinian people, those living inside occupied Palestine and those living in scattered exile.

With the unanimous support of the delegates, and the power of the intifada behind him, PLO Chairman Yasir Arafat declared that, "in exercise by the Palestinian people of its right to self-determination, political independence, and sovereignty over its territory, the Palestine National Council, in the name of God, and in the name of the Palestinian Arab people, hereby proclaims the establishment of the State of Palestine on our Palestinian territory with its capital Jerusalem." A thunderous ovation welcomed Arafat's reading of the Declaration of Independence, written by Palestine's national poet, Mahmoud Darwish. . . .

Five months after PLO Chairman—now Palestinian President—Arafat read the Declaration of Independence, Hanan Mikhail Ashrawi visited the United States. She is the Dean of the Faculty of Arts at Bir Zeit University, closed by the Israelis since before the beginning of the uprising. . . .

An Act of Pride

Ashrawi delivered the keynote address to the Washington convention of the American-Arab Anti-Discrimination Committee. "The intifada's pride is the pride of a people who have forged national unity in the searing kiln of determination and sacrifice," she said, "welding together a oneness of purpose, a oneness of being, and a holistic vision of peace and justice. The health of our nation, the integrity of its identity, and the authenticity of its fabric are all indivisible from its collective commitment to the intifada as a self-generating, self-sustaining act of rejuvenation and pride. . . .

"Our rights are not to be reduced to mere 'legitimate political rights,'" she went on, "for we clearly aim and proclaim those universal rights of all nations which no colonial or occupying power can eradicate. We claim our birthright and the truth of our vision, for the intifada is our national epiphany, and the inevitable birth of our state is its fulfillment. . . .

"For once, the authentic resonance of the Palestinian voice has filled the world's ears. It does not seek to silence others, but it will not be silenced, nor deflected."

111

"Palestinians are waging a war against themselves."

The *Intifada* Has Harmed the Palestinians' Campaign for Rights

Daniel Williams

The *intifada* is the name for the Palestinian uprising in the West Bank and Gaza strip which began in December 1987. In the following viewpoint, Daniel Williams argues that the movement, once a goal-oriented uprising against Israeli occupation, has degenerated into purposeless violence dominated by criminal youths and gangs. Palestinians are becoming increasingly divided into rival factions, and are victimizing each other, he asserts. Besides harming the Palestinian community, he writes, the *intifada* has hurt the Palestinian standing in the international community. Williams is a reporter for the *Los Angeles Times*.

As you read, consider the following questions:

1. What has caused increased *intifada*-related violence, according to Williams?
2. According to the author, what are the two main factions within the *intifada* movement?
3. Why have moderates lost influence within the *intifada*, in Williams's opinion?

Some say the trouble began after some 6- and 7-year-olds taunted a column of teen-age Muslim nationalists parading through the winding Old City of Nablus. The Muslims boxed the ears of some of the toddlers and offended their big brothers, who belonged to a rival gang from the Palestine Liberation Organization. Others say the conflict stemmed from simple turf battles between the Muslims and the secular PLO youths.

Gang Warfare

No matter. Things quickly got out of hand on a recent afternoon in Nablus' Old City. The rival gangs met, and exchanged pistol and machine-gun shots. Six Palestinian militants were wounded. In a sordid finale, Muslim youths stormed a local hospital and stabbed a wounded PLO rival five times as he lay on the operating table. The youth survived, but the surprise and bitterness is unfading.

"This was a shock," said Said Kanaan, a Nablus merchant and mainline Palestinian activist. "When I heard the shooting, I thought it was Israeli soldiers firing on Palestinians. Unfortunately, it was among ourselves."

After 3 1/2 years of the Arab uprising against Israeli rule in the West Bank and Gaza Strip, pride in the struggle has turned into embarrassment. Palestinians are waging a war against themselves.

Public and clandestine leaders of the revolt, known as the *intifada*, express helplessness in the face of intramural squabbles among directionless youth and their brutal attacks on collaborators.

The deepening concern is reflected in frequent appeals for self-control and especially for an end to collaborator killings, which totaled more than 40 between April 1 and June 12, 1991.

Out of Control

The appeals more often than not fall on deaf ears. Much *intifada* activity is in the hands of hardened youths who answer only to themselves. "Things are definitely out of control," said Mahdi Abdel Hadi, a Jerusalem-based political analyst.

Adnan Damiri, a Palestinian journalist for the Al Fajr newspaper, wrote: "The fear relates to everyone. To the writer, the peasant, farmer, the clerk, the laborer and academician. This is a fear which encompasses all strata of the population. We fear for ourselves and from ourselves, from our dream which has become a nightmare."

Damiri's words made a special impact on Palestinian readers because he had spent eight years in Israeli prisons on charges of anti-Israeli subversion. He called the *intifada* "the beast that devours its children."

113

The drumbeat of Arab-on-Arab violence has sounded almost without letup since the end of the Persian Gulf War. In one week, a suspected informer in the Gaza Strip was stabbed and hacked with knives and axes and left to die in a car trunk; three masked men fatally stabbed a school janitor in the West Bank town of Hebron on suspicion of fingering young militants to Israeli secret police; masked gunmen fatally shot a woman, and when masked raiders assaulted the home of a suspected collaborator in Gaza, the target struck back by tossing a grenade that killed one attacker. (Informers in Israel's service often are armed by authorities for protection.)

The Intifadah

Danziger/*The Christian Science Monitor*. Reprinted with permission.

All the incidents occurred after the clandestine *intifada* leadership issued a leaflet calling for an end to "kidnapings, interrogations and killings, except those agreed upon by all factions."

Killings

When such slayings first became a prominent feature of the *intifada* many activists just shrugged. The killings seemed justified as a means of weeding out criminals and informers. Now, many Palestinian activists say the effort to distinguish between executions and random vengeance attacks only fuels a spiral of violence. "These killings can in no way be excused as housecleaning," one underground activist said.

Public leaders have blamed the step-up in violence on the uprising's inconclusive results. Failed diplomacy has bred bitterness among many teen-agers and men in their 20s whose educations have been interrupted and who are mainly skilled at playing at dangerous cat-and-mouse street chases with Israeli soldiers. The population at large is tired and struggling to get by; these youths have no future except revolt—even if it means taking on each other.

The Palestinians' deteriorating economic condition also plays a role, Palestinians insist. Money from outside has dried up as the Gulf War disrupted the livelihoods of exiles in Kuwait. Israel is cutting off Palestinians from jobs in Israel, where jobless Soviet immigrants are taking their places.

The unwillingness of the young street toughs to curb their conduct throws light on the weakness of Palestinian leadership in the West Bank and Gaza Strip. Unable to deliver gains from their express willingness to compromise with Israel, moderates hold little sway with the gangs, which dominate political life in many towns and villages. Meantime, some local activists vocally challenge the primacy of PLO chief Yasser Arafat. A day after he made an appeal for an end to collaborator killings, another body was found in Gaza.

With U.S.-brokered peace talks hanging in the balance, the violence raises the question of how, in the end, fractious, hotheaded rebels will accept negotiations that might take years to produce results—and perhaps fall short of the most radical goals of many Palestinians.

"If the peace process stops, the young cadres will say, 'Enough is enough.' Even Arafat himself will be unable to stop armed attacks," Said Kanaan predicted.

Desperate Men

Many gangs are made up of desperate men on the run from the Israeli army. They arm themselves, contending that Israeli hit squads have gunned down militants on the West Bank and in Gaza and they need to defend themselves. Their actions also receive a political color, provided by disputes among PLO factions; there are, of course, factions within factions of the PLO. PLO groups with secular orientations and Muslim nationalists imbued with religious fervor have clashed repeatedly in several places, including Nablus.

Whatever the differences, the political dimension is inevitably overwhelmed by a gangland, Sharks vs. Jets flavor.

Mahmoud—a slender, swaggering 22-year-old Nablus man—blamed the recent violence on Hamas, an acronym that stands for the Islamic Resistance Movement. Hamas is a PLO rival throughout the West Bank and Gaza Strip. Mahmoud belongs to the Shabiba, or "Guys," one of four Nablus wings of Fatah,

115

which is the main faction of the four-sided PLO.

Hamas, Mahmoud said, attacked some second-graders and some Shabiba members after hearing insults in a schoolyard. Shabiba and Hamas representatives tried to soothe feelings by agreeing to pull members of each group off the streets of the Old City.

Palestinian Killings

Overall, more than 400 Palestinians have been killed by other Arabs, compared to more than 830 who have been slain by the army or Israeli civilians since the uprising began in December 1987. But while the rate of killings of Palestinians by the army has shrunk every year, the internecine killings have steadily mounted in both frequency and ferocity.

Most of those killed were accused of being "collaborators" who spied for Israel's security services in the territories. But a growing number of Palestinian leaders concede that the army is correct in its claim that many of the dead had nothing to do with Israeli authorities.

Jackson Diehl, *The Washington Post National Weekly Edition*, June 17-23, 1991.

In defiance of the agreement, Hamas paraded its forces Saturday—black-hooded masks are the group's trademark. Shabiba, wearing their customary black-checked scarves, confronted them, and harsh words turned to gunfire. A Hamas shot a Shabiba in the back; a friend of his responded by pulling out a submachine gun and firing on Hamas.

"They forced us to fight back," said Mahmoud, with an odd blend of bluster and sheepishness. Two bodyguards, about Mahmoud's age, smiled at the tale.

Hamas members put a different spin on the affair, although with the same insistence that they were not to blame, claiming they had been framed. "One of the Shabiba came to us in the street and called us" a profanity and "waved his machine gun," said the Hamas militant who talked to reporters in a building not far away.

Asked about the attack on the Shabiba victim in the hospital, the young man admitted reluctantly, "Yeah, it was probably Hamas that did it."

Nablus citizens appear to be fed up. A sandwich shop owner, hearing that two reporters had visited the Old City, asked in disbelief, "In there? You have to be crazy."

The story of the *intifada* in Nablus is a tale of decaying discipline and fulsome acts of brutality. When the uprising began, the streets were in the hands of toughened former convicts who had been jailed for anti-Israeli plotting. The street captains were taught methods of organization in jail and were able to discipline new recruits to the cause. Hokey uniforms and homemade masks were viewed as a means of giving gangs a sense of cohesiveness. Their homemade axes and swords drew naive laughter from onlookers.

At first, youths limited themselves to warning collaborators to stop cooperating with Israelis in the police and government, refrain from selling them land and, most gravely, to never finger activists to Israeli agents.

The warnings soon gave way to killings, which have snowballed since. The numbers of dead tell only part of the story.

The gruesome trademarks of the executions portray a growing brutality. Suspected collaborators have been dismembered, hung from meat hooks, thrown dead into garbage dumps, stabbed and axed.

The yen for spectacle is evident even in relatively mild cases of punishment. The other day in Nablus, a Fatah faction called Revolutionary Security hauled a suspected thief to the Old City's main square and flogged him 50 times.

The masks, once viewed as a badge of courage, became sinister emblems of vengeance and ferocity.

Executions

Abroad, the PLO boasted that it controlled the "executions" of collaborators. As the toll mounted, the PLO itself ordered a halt, a call widely ignored. In Nablus, a group called the Black Panthers openly paraded with machine guns in hand and boasted of their executions. In 1990, the Panthers met their downfall when plainclothes Israeli commandos raided a barbershop where five of them hung out and shot them to death.

Some groups directly attacked veteran PLO sympathizers. Said Kanaan's general store was ransacked and a relative's car burned in the street.

Finally, the public leaders could turn a blind eye no more. In June 1991, in an unusual display of chagrin, a group of pro-PLO journalists and professors met at a Jerusalem theater to discuss the turmoil. A subject once only whispered became the topic of an open seminar.

Several participants criticized the PLO for unleashing the killings. Others said the West Bank and Gaza leadership had grown out of touch with the youthful militants.

Admitted Yahiya abu Sharif, a reporter from the Arabic *Al Ittihad* newspaper: "There is a crisis in the *intifada*. It is not enough for leaders outside and inside the West Bank and Gaza just to give orders."

Distinguishing Between Fact and Opinion

This activity is designed to help develop the basic reading and thinking skill of distinguishing between fact and opinion. Consider the following statement as an example: "Israel took the Golan Heights from Syria during the 1967 Six-Day War." This is a factual statement that could be checked by looking up historical accounts of that war. But the statement "Israel should immediately return the Golan Heights to Syria" is an opinion. Many Israelis believe that returning the land to Syria would jeopardize Israel's security.

When investigating controversial issues, it is important that one be able to distinguish between statements of fact and statements of opinion. It is also important to recognize that not all statements of fact are true. They may appear to be true, but some are based on inaccurate or false information. For this activity, however, we are concerned with understanding the difference between those statements that appear to be factual and those that appear to be based primarily on opinion.

Most of the following statements are taken from the viewpoints in this chapter. Consider each statement carefully. *Mark O for any statement you believe is an opinion or interpretation of facts. Mark F for any statement you believe is a fact. Mark I for any statement you believe is impossible to judge.*

If you are doing this activity as a member of a class or group, compare your answers with those of other class or group members. Be able to defend your answers. You may discover that others come to different conclusions than you do. Listening to the reasons others present for their answers may give you valuable insights into distinguishing between fact and opinion.

O = opinion
F = fact
I = impossible to judge

1. The Palestine Liberation Organization is headquartered in Tunisia.

2. The Israeli-Palestinian dispute is the cause of all conflict in the Middle East.

3. Most of the people of the world support independence for the Palestinians.

4. United Nations Resolution 242 calls for the "withdrawal of Israeli armed forces from territories occupied," and the right of every state in the region "to live in peace within secure and recognized boundaries."

5. United Nations Resolution 242 does not necessarily call for total Israeli withdrawal from the West Bank.

6. Withdrawal from the West Bank will leave Israel with a section of territory only ten miles wide.

7. Some Israeli leaders call the West Bank Judea/Samaria.

8. It is vital for Israel's security to control the West Bank.

9. Under the Fourth Geneva Convention, countries are prohibited from practicing or condoning murder and torture.

10. More than seven hundred Palestinians have been killed by Israeli troops since the beginning of the *intifada* in 1987.

11. The *intifada* is an inspiring grassroots movement for independence.

12. Israel has formally deported more than two thousand Palestinians from the West Bank since 1967.

13. Israel bans Palestinian political parties in the occupied territories.

14. The United Nations is biased against Israel.

15. Israel has a better human rights record than its neighbors.

16. Israel is held to a higher human rights standard than other countries.

17. The word *intifada* means uprising.

18. The *intifada* began from an incident on December 8, 1987, when an Israeli truck swerved and killed four Palestinians.

19. The Palestinian *intifada* has degenerated into gang warfare.

20. It is obvious that Israel, in its treatment of Palestinians, has massively violated the Fourth Geneva Convention.

Periodical Bibliography

The following articles have been selected to supplement the diverse views presented in this chapter.

Joel Brinkley "A Price for Security," *The New York Times Magazine*, September 8, 1991.

Norman G. Finkelstein "Israel and Iraq: A Double Standard in the Application of International Law," *Monthly Review*, July/August 1991.

Jonathan Frankel "Into Year Four of the *Intifada*," *Dissent*, Summer 1991.

Martin Indyk "Peace Without the PLO," *Foreign Policy*, no. 83, Summer 1991.

Michael Kelly "Losing Faith in the Holy Land," *Esquire*, February 1991.

David Kupelian "Israel's Most Dangerous Hour," *New Dimensions*, January 1991.

Andrea Levin "CNN vs. Israel," *Commentary*, July 1991.

Louise Lief and David Makovsky "Juggling Guns and Butter," *U.S. News & World Report*, October 14, 1991.

Lance Morrow "An *Intifadeh* of the Soul," *Time*, July 23, 1990.

Aryeh Neier "Watching Rights," *The Nation*, June 24, 1991.

Eugene V. Rostow "Resolved," *The New Republic*, October 21, 1991.

Hillel Schenker "A Nation Living on the Edge," *The Nation*, January 21, 1991.

Ze'ev Schiff "Israel After the War," *Foreign Affairs*, Spring 1991.

Jerome M. Segal "The Missing Peace," *Mother Jones*, May/June 1991.

Hanna S. Siniora "Twenty-Four Years of Occupation," *Mediterranean Quarterly*, Summer 1991. Available from Duke University Press, PO Box 6697, College Station, Durham, NC 27708.

Tikkun "The Wrong Arm of the Law: Torture Disclosed and Deflected in Israeli Politics," September/October 1991.

Patrick White "Making Facts, Not Peace," *Commonweal*, June 14, 1991.

Ehud Ya'ari "Intafading," *The New Republic*, November 11, 1991.

Mortimer B. Zuckerman "The PLO as Image Maker," *U.S. News & World Report*, January 22, 1990.

What Role Should the U.S. Play in the Middle East?

THE MIDDLE EAST

Chapter Preface

In 1948, the United States became the first country to recognize the state of Israel. Since then, the United States has been more involved in Middle Eastern affairs than any other country outside the region. This involvement can be seen in several areas. Militarily, the United States provided leadership and more than a half-million troops in the 1991 Persian Gulf War against Iraq. In addition, the United States has provided arms and military aid to many Middle Eastern countries, especially Israel. Economically, almost half of the total U.S. foreign aid budget goes to countries in the Middle East, with Israel and Egypt receiving more than 40 percent of all U.S. aid. Diplomatically, U.S. leaders have been heavily involved in peace efforts, with special attention to the Arab-Israeli conflict.

Why does the United States take such an interest in the Middle East? Most analysts identify two primary reasons: oil and Israel. The United States is the world's largest importer of oil, and the Middle East holds two-thirds of the world's known oil reserves—reserves that can be extracted with less cost than anywhere else in the world. The 1973 oil embargo, in which Saudi Arabia and other Middle Eastern countries withheld their oil from the United States, sharply raised oil prices and demonstrated the potential power of Middle Eastern countries to dominate the world oil market in ways detrimental to the United States and other oil-consuming nations. Much U.S. foreign policy is designed to maintain friendly relations with these countries to ensure a stable supply of oil.

While America's interest in oil is based on economics, its support of Israel is based on historical, moral, and strategic reasons. After the Holocaust, in which millions of Jews were killed by Nazi Germany during World War II, many Americans viewed the Jews' desire for a homeland as one way to prevent future Jewish persecution. In addition, Israel, "as the only democracy in an inherently unstable region," according to political analyst Alon Ben-Meir, provided the United States with a strategic military ally in the Middle East.

America's need for oil and its support of Israel are often in conflict. For example, U.S. attempts to cultivate good relations with oil-rich Arab states have been complicated by the unresolved hostilities between the Arabs and Israel. Thus, debates within the United States have focused not only on the extent of U.S. involvement in the Middle East, but also on whether the United States is fair in its involvement in the Arab-Israeli conflict. The viewpoints in this chapter debate these and other issues of U.S. foreign policy in the Middle East.

"The risks of engagement in the Middle East are substantial. . . . But so are the risks of retreat."

The U.S. Should Take an Active Role in the Middle East

Henry R. Nau

The United States demonstrated its commitment to the Middle East during the 1991 Persian Gulf War. Following that conflict, debate arose within the U.S. as to what extent it should participate in Middle East affairs. In the following viewpoint, Henry R. Nau argues that the U.S. should remain involved in the Middle East. He writes that the U.S. should take an active and leading role in guaranteeing the security of Middle East states, promoting diplomatic solutions to conflicts, and encouraging democracy in the region. Nau is associate dean of the Elliott School of International Affairs at George Washington University and the author of the book *The Myth of America's Decline*.

As you read, consider the following questions:

1. What three lessons from the Cold War apply to the Middle East, according to Nau?
2. What does the author believe is the significance of oil in U.S. relations with the Middle East?
3. Why is America ideally suited for leadership in Middle East diplomacy, in Nau's opinion?

Henry R. Nau, "Winning the Peace," *National Review*, April 1, 1991. Copyright © 1991 by National Review, Inc., 150 E. 35th St., New York, NY 10016. Reprinted by permission.

The conventional wisdom in the fall of 1990 was that the United States could not fight a shooting war to liberate Kuwait without breaking up the Arab-American coalition and alienating a good portion of the Moslem world. That conventional wisdom was wrong. Today the conventional wisdom is that the United States cannot lead a long-term peace effort in the Middle East without falling prey to the psychotic politics of that region and exhausting its own economic resources. That wisdom too is wrong.

The U.S. and Europe

Those considering the question of American leadership in the Gulf can profitably begin by studying America's peace-making role in Europe after World War II. The Middle East is not Europe, to be sure, but three lessons can be learned from the cold war that do apply to the Middle East: War never ensures peace. Peace is not possible without either an armed balance or a political community. And the best road to political community, behind a shield of defense, is open commerce, both within a region and between the states of that region and like-minded states elsewhere.

America left Europe in 1945 thinking that World War II had resolved the issues of peace. It had to go back in 1948 at far greater expense than if it had asked the right questions in the first place. Today, America and its allies have won a lightning war in the Persian Gulf. They will not win the peace so quickly. Yet already pundits are urging that America come home, that peacekeeping duties be taken over by UN forces, that political dialogue be left to Arab-Israeli interlocutors, and that economic reconstruction be initiated by oil-rich Arab sheikhdoms. In short, America can go back to its old over-the-horizon role, confident that war has won the peace.

These pundits repeat the mistakes of 1945. They assume that force is the *ultimate ratio* in international disputes, the so-called final argument of kings. In fact, force is the beginning, not the end, of the resolution of disputes. War creates an opportunity to alter the conditions that led to war. Either that opportunity is seized or war will be repeated. Have we forgotten that the United States lost 240 Marines in Lebanon in 1984—three times the number of dead in the war just concluded?

Having made the supreme engagement for war, America should now do no less for peace. This engagement is necessary not just because of oil. Some commentators chase the illusion that if America only eliminated its energy dependence on the Middle East, it could escape the political clutches of this region. In fact, America is not in the Middle East only or even primarily for oil. It is in the Middle East to contest which political values

124

oil will be used for in the world community. Will oil support the extremist values of fascist or totalitarian regimes, as would have been the case if Iraq (or for that matter Khomeini's Iran or Assad's Syria) had dominated the region? Or will oil promote the needs and aspirations of more moderate Middle Eastern regimes, which, if they are not now democracies, at least have a chance to become so and are willing in the meantime to cooperate with Western democracies. Sure, oil will be sold to anyone at the right price. But economic relations between adversaries are not very stable. Have we forgotten the cold-war experience with East-West trade?

To What End?

Cynics like to reduce international politics to mere struggles for wealth and power. They ignore the different political purposes for which states use wealth and power. Europe's importance to the United States after World War II did not derive from its resources. Indeed, after sharing resources with Europe to build peace, the United States is relatively less powerful today than it was in 1945. But it succeeded in building a community of shared political purposes with Europe (and Japan). That community so magnified the collective resources of the West that the West eventually persuaded Communist governments in Eastern Europe to turn to more market-oriented and democratic policies.

U.S. Influence

What tasks should the U.S. now shoulder, bearing morality and geopolitics in mind? The point of departure for any answer must be the recognition that the U.S. now has unprecedented influence on the fate of an entire region.

After World War II, Harry S. Truman recognized America's moral and political responsibility for the future of Europe. He rose to that challenge through a firm commitment to large-scale relief, reconstruction and reconciliation. Today, the Persian Gulf and Middle East needs all three.

Zbigniew Brzezinski, *The New York Times*, April 21, 1991.

The objective of America's engagement in the Middle East, therefore, has to be the development of greater political community in this region. Political community does not now exist in the Middle East, as it did not in Europe in 1945. The last significant steps toward peace—Egyptian-Israeli *rapprochement*—came in the wake of the 1973 Arab-Israeli war. The Gulf War provides another historic opportunity.

In the absence of shared political community, the first requirement is security. The United States must lead an effort to establish viable military balances within the region and constraints on arms transfers to the region. To do this, the United States need not provide large military forces of its own. But it will have to provide enough manpower and direction to midwife credible military arrangements. After all, it was American military power and leadership that liberated Kuwait, with politically important but militarily modest help from coalition allies. It is illogical to argue that UN peacekeeping forces or Egyptian and Saudi troops, without a significant American presence, are sufficient to safeguard the peace.

The United States should not return to an over-the-horizon role, positioning military equipment in Saudi Arabia but pulling out all significant military personnel. Such a role would not be sufficient to build confidence among moderate Arab states and Israel. And without such confidence, these states will not take the political and economic risks needed to build peace in this region on a basis eventually going beyond military balances. Moreover, the Gulf Arabs have crossed the line in terms of siding with Western power to defend their security. They cannot and do not want to go back to the fiction of buying their security from radical Arabs.

Security Guarantees

A U.S. presence in the moderate Arab states gives Israel stronger security guarantees than it has ever had. Israel may come to see that now is the time for decisive discussions with the Palestinians. With Iraq on the ropes, Iran still recovering from war, Syria neutralized (at least for a year or so) following its alliance with the West in the war against Iraq, and Jordan looking for some way to rejoin the moderate Arab community, significant threats to Israel in the short to medium term do not exist. Psychologically, the Israelis may not see it that way, especially after the Scud missile attacks and the carnage wreaked by Iraqi power in Kuwait. But the reality is nevertheless so.

While strong security arrangements are the first step, economic initiatives must follow quickly if the Middle East is to move over the next decade toward a more stable peace. Here the oil-rich Gulf states have a special responsibility. Saudi Arabia, Kuwait, and the Gulf emirates should redirect the uses of their oil resources, away from bankrupt policies of jousting with the West in OPEC [Organization of Petroleum Exporting Countries] and paying off radical Arabs, toward a massive program of reconstruction and economic cooperation in the Middle East. Such an Arab-launched "Marshall Plan" would aim, in the

126

first instance, to benefit the poor Arab states such as Egypt and Jordan, but also to influence the use of oil resources in radical states such as Iran and Iraq. It might be coupled with a strengthened set of economic ties with Israel, the United States, Europe, and Japan, beginning perhaps with a multilateralization of the free-trade agreement between the United States and Israel.

Past U.S. Roles

Progress toward peace will be made only if the United States engages itself at the highest level and provides substantial inducements for progress. We may deplore this fact, but that changes nothing. Arabs and Israelis alike remember that after the 1973 war, Nixon and Kissinger made an all-out effort to reach partial agreements. And from 1977 to 1979 Jimmy Carter devoted much of his time to Arab-Israeli issues. In each case, the United States played multiple roles—catalyst, mediator, bully, friend—as it tried to persuade the parties to the conflict to make compromises for the sake of peace.

William B. Quandt, *The Brookings Review*, Summer 1991.

Germany and Japan also have special responsibilities in the economic area. They too benefited from allied military power without in their case contributing any combat forces, unlike the Gulf Arab states. If they are struggling to find peaceful ways to exercise influence in world affairs, what better way than to put their money and people into the task of economic reconstruction in the Gulf?

Taking the Lead

In all of this, America's role is crucial. It is the only country whose military power engenders confidence, not threat, and whose political leadership is acceptable to all the parties involved. As the framework outlined above suggests, it does not have to provide the major economic means, as it did in Europe in 1948. The Middle East has the resources to earn immediate wealth, and Germany and Japan can help. But the United States has to supply the political vision, the military stability, and the diplomatic direction.

The United States did this and more to win the peace in Europe after World War II. Of course, the circumstances are different today. But so is the world. The major nations of the world, including the rival superpowers of the cold-war era, stood politically united behind the effort to liberate Kuwait. The Western world today enjoys unprecedented economic riches.

Democracy does not exist in the Persian Gulf, to be sure, but it does exist in two-thirds of the rest of the world, unlike in 1945, and more and more countries, especially in the Third World, are experimenting with more democratic forms of government. In the wake of this war, Kuwait, Saudi Arabia, and other Arab states will almost certainly seek to strengthen democratic procedures in their countries.

For the United States the risks of engagement in the Middle East are substantial—anti-Westernism, unstable governments, and terrorism flourish there. But so are the risks of retreat. Losing the peace can have only one outcome: another costly war. America learned in Europe that winning the peace takes much longer, but in the end is less costly.

"The United States should refrain from entering a new cycle of military commitment and diplomatic hyperactivity."

The U.S. Should Reduce Its Role in the Middle East

Leon T. Hadar

Leon T. Hadar, former bureau chief for the *Jerusalem Post*, is an adjunct professor of international relations at American University in Washington, D.C. In the following viewpoint, he argues that the U.S. should withdraw its military commitments and diplomatic activity from the Middle East. The U.S. has much to lose and no compelling reason to play a dominant role in the region, he asserts. Hadar writes that Europe and the Middle East countries themselves should take over the management of their affairs and work for peace in the region.

As you read, consider the following questions:

1. Why is U.S. involvement in the Middle East a no-win situation, according to Hadar?
2. What does the author assert to be the real lessons of the Persian Gulf War?
3. What dubious assumption underlies U.S. efforts to solve the Arab-Israeli conflict, according to Hadar?

Excerpted from "Extricating America from Its Middle Eastern Entanglement," by Leon T. Hadar, in the Cato Institute's *Policy Analysis*, no. 154, June 12, 1991. Reprinted with permission.

The successful outcome of a war tends to create unrealistic expectations. World War I was supposed to have been the war to end all wars. World War II was expected to usher in a new era of permanent peace. There was in the United States, in the days following the military victory in the Persian Gulf, a sense of omnipotence similar to the euphoria that dominated Israel after the Six-Day war in 1967, a feeling that everything was possible in arranging the political cards of the Middle East; that after Saddam Hussein, an Iraqi Thomas Jefferson would come to power in Baghdad and a window of opportunity would be opened for democracy, stability, and peace in the Middle East.

As the decadent Kuwaiti emir returned to his liberated city-state, American policy experts and pundits discussed plans for establishing a constitutional monarchy in Kuwait and a democracy in Iraq, and for launching a Marshall Plan for economic development in the region to close the gap between the "have" and the "have not" states. Others called for structuring a NATO-type security arrangement in the gulf and in the entire Middle East and for using American leadership to bring peace between Israelis and Arabs.

Making the Middle East Safe for Democracy?

One source of those high expectations was the misconceived attempt to apply the post-World War II script to the post-Gulf War Middle East. We forget, however, that the reconstruction of Germany and Japan was successful because it was based on existing and very powerful civil societies, strong national identities, large educated middle classes, and previous experience with political and economic freedom. Some or all of those ingredients are missing in most Middle Eastern societies today.

Indeed, as the immediate post-Gulf War developments in Kuwait and Iraq suggest, those states and most other Middle Eastern countries lack the political culture necessary to deal with one of the major dilemmas of politics: how to reconcile order and stability on the one hand and freedom and justice on the other. Those countries lack agreed-upon mechanisms for the peaceful transfer of power and, as a result, either produce central and somewhat heavy-handed governmental authorities or deteriorate into political and social chaos.

The region's governments, like other governments in the Third World, face a pervasive crisis of political legitimacy. They are unable to mobilize domestic support except by invoking a dream that could undermine them: a unified Arab nation or an Islamic empire. That action, in turn, invites other regional powers to meddle in their domestic problems and to create more sources of instability.

Hence, the oil-rich regimes of Saudi Arabia and Kuwait face

Catch-22 dilemmas. Those countries declare their commitments to Arab and Islamic solidarity to lend political legitimacy to their rulers. However, that very commitment encourages their resource-poor Arab brothers, such as Yemen and Jordan, to demand that they share their oil revenues. Indeed, the Arab solidarity argument was one justification for Iraq's invasion of Kuwait. . . .

Reprinted by permission of *Middle East International*, Washington, D.C. & London.

Notwithstanding official American rhetoric encouraging moves toward democracy in the gulf region, Washington, bearing in mind the alternatives, will continue to tolerate the autocratic rule of sheiks. The Gulf War pointed to the long-term problem facing traditional Middle Eastern monarchies: To survive politically, they must continue to rely on direct and indirect American aid and military support. That dependency exposes their populations to competing Western political and economic models and creates politically explosive expectations. The discrepancy between the traditional ruling elites' pretensions of resisting the influence of outside "infidels" and those elites' alliances with those very infidels is revealed. Opposition from both modernizing and fundamentalist forces is quite likely at some point.

Those developments reflect the larger picture: neoconservative intellectuals in the United States insist that the global spread of democracy will also produce an increase in pro-American sentiment. That is not the case in the Middle East. Anti-Americanism pervades the Arab and Moslem worlds and stems from resentment of both the tacit U.S.-Israeli alliance and direct American intervention in the region. Indeed, such states as Jordan, Algeria, and Yemen, which have experimented in recent years with quasi-free elections, have seen the forces of the more fundamentalist and anti-Western groups gain strength. . . .

The chances for making the Middle East safe for democracy, along with Washington's power to move the region's states in that direction, are therefore extremely limited. Actually, American efforts can create a backlash and produce major political costs for perceived American interests in the area since such efforts are bound to unleash anti-Western, authoritarian forces. At the same time, an alliance with the status quo regimes in the Arab world, such as those in Saudi Arabia and Kuwait, will inevitably turn Washington into a symbol of repression in the eyes of democratic and revolutionary factions.

The United States faces a no-win situation in its relationship with existing political regimes. Attempting to democratize them produces political and social instability and creates a vacuum that entices militant domestic and outside forces. Trying to secure the power of existing regimes creates conditions that will lead to the inevitable rise of anti-American successor governments. . . .

Establishing a Middle Eastern NATO?

Competing with the goal of promoting democracy is what seems to be the more realistic goal of creating (through regional balance-of-power arrangements and American military commitments) a regional zone of stability and security. That effort also reflects a desire to produce in the Middle East a rerun of post-World War II Europe or post-1953 Korea. However, those security structures were based on a clear perception of an external threat and a set of rules of the game, which resulted from—among other things—the nuclear balance of terror, that produced a certain stability and predictability in the relationships among the major cold-war players. Those elements are missing in the Middle East. . . .

The problem is that Israel and the Arab states are not just nation-states striving for security. They represent powerful ideologies: Zionism and Pan-Arabism. Only a solution to the Palestinian-Israeli problem—the recognition on both sides of the other's legitimate rights in the land they share—can lead to a political accommodation between the two. A political accommodation, and serious consideration of core issues such as the political legitimacy of existing regimes in the Middle East, can perhaps help the region move toward normal international relationships. Without a solution to the Arab-Israeli conflicts, the danger exists that the most extreme nationalist and religious-fundamentalist groups on both sides will gain power and will lead the region toward an inevitable religious zero-sum-game conflict.

Until core political change occurs, the Middle East after the Gulf War will be the same Middle East, a place that is not hospitable to a new Wilsonian regional order with its search for democracy and "good guys." Instead, the region will be dominated by the old Hobbesian regional chaos—in which a mishmash of ethnic, religious, national, regional, and international players combines and divides in shifting alliances and conflicts. There, the United States finds itself operating in a kind of political and military kaleidoscope. Every turn of the kaleidoscope, like the Gulf War, creates new and unpredictable configurations. . . .

The U.S. and the Israeli-Palestinian Conflict

When it comes to dealing with the kaleidoscopic problems of the Middle East, Washington's power to reshape the region and to solve the Israeli-Palestinian conflict will be extremely limited. Actually, the higher the expectations, the greater the disappointments. . . .

Since 1948 the driving force behind U.S. efforts to reach peace between Israel and the Arabs has been the desire to bridge the gap between U.S. interests in the Arab gulf states and the moral commitment of the United States to Israel. Indeed, finding a way to solve the Arab-Israeli-Persian Gulf "linkage" problem has dominated U.S. polices toward the area. . . .

The limited American power to affect Arab-Israeli relationships and the increasing irrelevancy of those relationships to American interests, should lead to a reassessment of the hyperactive American diplomatic approach toward Arab-Israeli peace. The activist approach has been based on a perverted assumption: Washington should pay the financial and diplomatic costs of helping Arabs and Israelis to stop killing each other, since by so doing they are supposedly doing more of a favor for the United States than for themselves.

That assumption derived from Washington's Middle Eastern policy paradigm, which assumed that unless Americans helped make peace between Israel and its Arab neighbors, there would be several unpleasant results. First, Washington, as a result of Arab resentments, would find it difficult to safeguard Western oil and strategic interests in the gulf. Second, the United States would endanger its moral commitment to Israel, since that state's security can be guaranteed in the long run only by recognition and acceptance by its neighbors. Finally, U.S. failure to

secure peace would produce regional instability that would invite Soviet meddling and expansionism.

The end of the cold war has largely eliminated the third factor
from the overall American calculation, although Washington
will have to recognize the legitimate Soviet interests in
Moscow's Middle Eastern geopolitical back yard and should not
exclude the Soviets from regional diplomatic efforts. As noted,
the Gulf War at least weakened, if not removed, the first factor:
the linkage between the Arab-Israeli issue and American interests in the gulf.

America Has Little Influence

Whatever influence America has to shape events in the Middle
East is a rapidly wasting asset. The Soviet Union, Iran, and the
countries of Western Europe have their own views about the political and security arrangements that should be put in place in
the region. Moreover, Washington is likely to have little leverage
over its Middle East clients, notwithstanding America's wartime
exertions on their behalf, on any regional issues—including the
Arab-Israeli problem and a postwar Gulf security regime. These
nations will be resistant to U.S. pressures because the matters at
stake in the Middle East are far more important to them than
they are to the United States.

Christopher Layne, *The Atlantic*, July 1991.

Continued Israeli occupation of the West Bank and Gaza
raises major questions about the second element in America's
Middle Eastern paradigm: Washington's moral commitment to
the Jewish state. American support and aid keep a repressive
militant government and a bankrupt socialist economy in
Jerusalem. If Israel wants to maintain American public support,
which was based on the argument that Israel is a democratic nation and is different from the surrounding Arab authoritarian
and dictatorial regimes, it will have no future choice (in its own
interest) but to decouple itself from the occupied Arab territories, reach some modus vivendi with its Arab neighbors, and reform its political and economic systems. Then it could focus on
its real challenge—the absorption of hundreds of thousands of
Soviet-Jewish immigrants. Israel could become a major trading
state, a kind of a Middle Eastern Singapore.

By perpetuating its Middle Eastern paradigm, Washington is
actually removing incentives for diplomatic and economic
changes on both the Israeli and the Arab sides. Washington's
high-profile involvement in trying to bring peace between Arabs
and Israelis creates the impression that the diplomatic stakes in

solving the conflict are higher for Washington than for the regional adversaries—that it owes them diplomatic support or financial compensation if they are willing to make concessions. The United States also ends up a party to domestic political battles in the Middle East as Israelis and Arabs opposed to its moves begin to direct their frustration against Washington. Moreover, by creating the expectation that it can deliver a solution, the United States is bound to produce an eventual backlash when its commitments to each side are not fulfilled.

A Policy of Benign Neglect

Washington should consider a new approach: an attitude of neglect toward the Palestinian-Israeli conflict, the kind of attitude it has adopted toward other regional conflicts such as that between India and Pakistan. That approach might actually persuade more Israelis and Palestinians that unless they move seriously to solve their conflict they will be the ones to bear the costs of their own intransigence. . . .

It is essential to . . . create a new U.S. policy. Soon the discrepancy between the growing diplomatic and military costs of U.S. regional commitments and the meager benefits to the United States will become apparent. At that point, more Americans will begin to search for more attractive policies. One important change should be to begin shifting more security and economic responsibilities in the region to other parties—especially the European Community.

A European Role

Americans have been complaining about Europe's free-rider position in the gulf, that is, its lack of willingness to pay the costs of containing security threats there. However, Europeans respond by suggesting that there is no taxation without representation and that they also want to share in making decisions about the Middle East.

Since the victory in the Gulf War, Europe seems willing to accept American leadership in the region. However, as Washington faces increasing diplomatic and military problems in shaping security arrangements in the gulf and in maintaining the Israeli-Arab peace momentum, new acrimonies between the United States and Great Britain on the one hand and the rest of Europe (particularly the Mediterranean states—France, Italy, and Spain) on the other will resurface.

France would like to play a more independent security role in the region, perhaps as part of a new military undertaking of the Western European Union, which would put Paris in conflict with Washington and London, who want any European "out of area" security policy firmly anchored in an American-led NATO. Italy and Spain, with French support, have begun push-

135

ing their plan for establishment of a Conference on Security and Cooperation in the Mediterranean. The Mediterranean European states with their geographic, economic, demographic, and cultural ties with the Middle East and North Africa have been stressing the need to deal with the Palestinian issue as part of an international conference on the Middle East, an idea that has not been received with great enthusiasm in Washington and London. France also indicated that the PLO should play an important role in any Middle Eastern peace process. The disagreements over those issues are bound to become more apparent, especially if Israeli opposition to withdrawal from the West Bank and Gaza becomes obvious.

Washington should welcome the possibility that France and the European Community will return to play a more active diplomatic and military role. And Washington should be prepared, if asked by all sides of the Arab-Israeli conflict, to offer its diplomatic services as an honest broker, while making it clear to both Arabs and Israelis that such a move will depend on their willingness to reach an agreement. Furthermore, it should be clearly understood that the United States will not be willing to incur major financial costs or to undertake military commitments in the region as part of a final peace agreement. . . .

Needed: A More Cautious Approach

The United States should refrain from entering a new cycle of military commitment and diplomatic hyperactivity, which would lead political elites in the region to look to Washington to solve their domestic and political problems and to contain regional threats. By renewing military and diplomatic commitments, the United States would remove the incentives for those regimes to reform their political and economic systems, to create stable balance-of-power systems and viable security arrangements, and to reach diplomatic solutions to their conflicts. Instead of becoming a symbol of political and economic freedom (a model to be imitated), the United States would be identified with repressive regimes and become a symbol of evil in the eyes of new, rising elites. Washington would also risk becoming a party to regional conflicts and being drawn into one military intervention after another. . . .

Instead of letting itself be lured into such a morass, the United States should seize the opportunity provided by the end of the cold war and the completion of the Gulf War to replace its decaying Middle Eastern paradigm with a more cautious approach toward the region. Washington should maintain friendly relationships with Middle Eastern countries that share its values and should increase its economic ties with those who want to trade. But the United States cannot hope to impose stability on that fractious region or to solve its multifaceted problems.

136

VIEWPOINT

"Israel is the only state in the Middle East that is not a potential enemy of the United States."

The U.S. Should Maintain a Strong Relationship with Israel

Steven R. David

The U.S. and Israel have been closely linked since Israel's founding in 1948, and in 1987 the U.S. declared Israel to be one of its foremost allies. In support of this alliance, the U.S. annually provides Israel with between $3 billion and $4 billion in economic and military aid. In the following viewpoint, Steven R. David argues that Israel is America's only dependable friend in the Middle East, and that the two countries should maintain their close relationship. David is an associate professor of political science at Johns Hopkins University in Baltimore, Maryland.

As you read, consider the following questions:

1. Why can the U.S. depend on Israel, according to David?
2. According to the author, what values do Israel and the U.S. share?
3. Why does the U.S. hold Israel to a higher human rights standard than neighboring countries, according to David?

Excerpted from "Bosom of Abraham: America's Enduring Affection for Israel," by Steven R. David. Reprinted, with permission, from the Winter 1991 issue of *Policy Review*, the flagship publication of The Heritage Foundation, 214 Massachusetts Ave. NE, Washington, DC 20002.

Neither the end of the Cold War nor the involvement of most of the Arab world in the coalition against Iraq diminishes the strategic and moral importance of Israel to the United States. America and Israel enjoy a deep friendship based on shared democratic values and a common commitment to religious freedom. By virtue of this friendship and its military strength, Israel remains the only country in the Middle East with the power and willingness to consistently defend American interests in the region. . . .

Unique Dependability

Israel is the only state in the Middle East that is not a potential enemy of the United States. The interests of Israel and the United States are not identical, and disputes will arise between the two countries. But it is unthinkable that Israel would ever engage in anti-American terrorism, support countries that threaten the United States, or confront American forces directly, as have so many of America's Arab allies. In terms of fundamental interests—promoting stability in the Middle East, bolstering moderate Arab regimes, and countering terrorism—Israel and the U.S. are now and will remain in essential agreement.

The United States can depend on Israel for two fundamental reasons. First, Israel is not subject to the coups and rebellions that have bedeviled virtually every other Middle Eastern country. Groups that have seized power have often turned against Washington, as has occurred in Egypt (1955), Syria (1955), Iraq, (1958), Libya (1969), and Iran (1979). Second, Israel's pro-American orientation is rooted in the democratic values of its society. In no other Middle Eastern state are the roots of pro-American support so deep, widespread, and immutable.

The consistency and durability of Israel's pro-American commitment is especially important in light of the many shifts of allegiance of regimes in the Middle East and in neighboring Third World States. In the early 1970s, Egypt, Somalia, and the Sudan were strongly pro-Soviet, and Ethiopia was the closest friend of the United States in sub-Saharan Africa. Within 10 years, each of these countries had switched superpower patrons. Because the political orientation of these countries is determined by a narrow leadership elite—sometimes by one leader—a change of government or even a change of mind is enough to alter the country's allegiance.

Israeli support for U.S. interests is independent of the vagaries of inter-Arab politics. Even regimes friendly to the United States will go against American interest if there is strong Arab sentiment to do so. Following the 1973 War, Saudi Arabia, one of America's closest allies, embargoed critically needed oil to the

138

United States. In 1991, Jordan's King Hussein, responding in part to domestic pressure . . . tilted toward Iraq in that country's confrontation with the United States. The Jordanian response demonstrates the fragility of Arab support for the U.S. . . .

Israel as a Just Society

As important and reliable as Israel is to the United States strategically, it is the moral ties based on ideological and cultural affinity that best explain and justify the relationship between the two countries.

Even at the height of the Cold War, Americans were never driven by a narrow vision of realpolitik. Nevertheless, when the Soviet Union presented a direct and pressing threat to American security, other interests had to be subordinated to meeting that threat. This often resulted in U.S. support for countries whose values failed to meet the standards of the American people. Now, with the diminishment of the Soviet threat, the United States has the luxury of allowing moral and ideological concerns to play a major role in determining policy. So long as Israel continues to reflect American values to a far greater extent than any other country in the Middle East, close ties between the two countries will be maintained.

Aid to Israel Benefits U.S.

If one understands the nature of the dynamics propelling U.S. policy of extended containment of the Soviet Union, the Israeli case has fit snugly into overall American strategy, and has been an important component of the scaffolding of the U.S. international order. Assistance to Israel has been cost-effective, and more important, in view of what American leaders judged American interests to be, it has brought success.

A.F.K. Orshanski, *The $36 Billion Bargain*, 1990.

Israel is a society informed by a sense of justice that Americans recognize and rightfully admire. It is the only democracy in the Middle East. Israel is the only country in the region that provides (however imperfectly) the basic rights of freedom of speech, press, religion, and emigration that Americans hold so dear. It is a society in which dissent is not only allowed—it is a way of life. It is a society that fosters the formation of human rights commissions that scrutinize every aspect of governmental policy.

None of this is meant to suggest that Israel is without faults. Its continuing occupation of the West Bank and Gaza has resulted in abuses of power that have been well documented. Moreover, as the killing of some 17 Palestinians on the Temple Mount, or Haram al-Sharif, has shown, Israeli security forces at times act irresponsibly to suppress unrest.

Without excusing Israeli excesses, however, it must be remembered that the Israeli occupation results from a war of aggression launched by Jordan in 1967. If King Hussein had responded to Israeli requests not to attack during Israel's war with Egypt and Syria, the West Bank would have remained in Arab hands and a Palestinian state could have been established there.

Disputes Among Friends

As for other Israeli transgressions, at least Israel makes an effort to determine when it has behaved wrongly and punishes those responsible. Following the 1982 Sabra and Shatila massacres (in which Christian militiamen slaughtered Palestinians in Lebanese refugee camps under Israeli control) and the Temple Mount shootings, it is noteworthy that Israel established commissions of inquiry. These commissions found some Israeli fault in both episodes. Many in the world community complained that Israel did not go far enough in admitting blame and punishing the wrong-doers, but where else in the Middle East would remotely similar assessments of conduct have taken place?

Americans also feel a special affinity with Israel as the birthplace of Judaism and Christianity. While the support of American Jews for Israel is well documented and understandable, far too little attention has been given to American Christian, especially Evangelical Protestant, support of Israel. Some of this support stems from religious beliefs that Israel has a major role in the fulfillment of biblical prophecy. More generally, religious Americans, Christian as well as Jewish, have an emotional attachment to the land of Israel and the cities of Scripture—Nazareth, Beersheba, Jerusalem. Christian backing also arises from a recognition that freedom of access to the holy sites in Israel—Moslem, Christian, and Jewish—has been assured only by the Israeli state. Along with American Jews, these Christians remember that under King Hussein's rule, access to the Western Wall (the holiest place in Judaism) was denied to the Jewish people. Concerns for justice, fears that one prohibition could spawn others, and the recognition that the demise of Israel would end any hopes of Jews, Moslems, and Christians living together peacefully, explain much of this Christian support for Israel.

These common values linking the United States to Israel have helped keep Israeli-American relations strong even when our strategic interests have diverged. Examples of intense disagreements between the U.S. and Israel are many. In the 1956 War the United States condemned Israel's attack on Egypt and forced an Israeli withdrawal from the Sinai. In the early 1970s the United States criticized Israel for not being forthcoming enough in establishing peace negotiations. Following the 1973 War, Henry Kissinger's "shuttle diplomacy" included many bitter exchanges with Israel over its alleged intransigence. In 1982 the United States strongly condemned the Israeli invasion of Lebanon. At present it is clear that the Bush administration would prefer more flexibility from Israel on the issues of the occupied territories and negotiations with the Palestinians. And more recently America has condemned Israel for the killing of the Palestinians on the Temple Mount. What is remarkable is not that we have had so many problems with Israel, but that in spite of these disputes American ties with Israel have remained fundamentally close.

Historical Ties

The U.S. commitment to Israel, while not rooted in concrete economic interests, is at least as compelling as our Persian Gulf interests. For historical, moral, and political reasons, the United States finds itself tied to the existence and well-being of a Jewish state in at least part of the former British mandate of Palestine. No U.S. president would turn his back on Israel if its vital security were endangered.

William B. Quandt, *The Brookings Review*, Summer 1991.

America's admiration for Israel does not prevent it from frequently criticizing Jerusalem, leading many to charge that Washington is employing a double standard. Such complaints miss the point. Of course, the United States holds Israel to a much higher level of accountability than it does Syria, Iraq, or even Saudi Arabia and Egypt. Of course, Israeli transgressions have never approached the massacre of tens of thousands of Syrians by Hafez al-Assad, the killing of hundreds of Moslems during the pilgrimage to Mecca in 1991, or Saddam Hussein's gassing of thousands of Kurds and commitment of atrocities against the Kuwaitis. And American criticism of Israel often fails to take into account the neighborhood in which Israel lives and the often unsavory actions it must undertake in order to survive.

It is to Israel's benefit, however, that it is subject to tougher U.S. moral standards than its neighbors. Precisely because Israel is seen as morally superior to its neighbors, it receives more

American political, economic, and military assistance than they do. The price Israel must pay for this largesse is an intense American scrutiny of its behavior and the need to justify its actions to an extent far greater than its neighbors. It is a high price to pay, but so long as Israel expects U.S. backing, it is a price that must be met.

A Double Standard

America's double standard toward Israel thus has a different origin than does the double standard of the world community. The disproportionate censure and vilification that Israel receives from the United Nations and other international organizations is hypocritical, particularly when many of the same countries that seek to delegitimate Israel on moral grounds are themselves among the worst abusers of human rights. This constant and one-sided condemnation of Israel serves only to create a siege mentality that encourages the Israelis to ignore even justified international criticisms. By usually refusing to join this disgraceful bandwagon the United States shows its respect to the international community by holding it to a high standard of fairness.

The central role of shared values in determining the American-Israeli friendship carries an important warning. The most likely way the United States' relationship with Israel will be undermined is not through demonstrating that the Arab states are more important strategically than Israel, or that American support for Israel hurts other, more significant American interests. Rather, if the relationship is undermined it will be through the perception that Israel is no longer committed to the values that drew American support in the first place. Despite the many problems of Israeli society, events have not yet reached that level. But if they should, no demonstration of Israeli strategic worth would be enough to stave off an American abandonment of the Jewish state.

"The argument that US interests require support for Israel has never been more questionable."

The U.S. Should Decrease Its Ties to Israel

Jerome Slater and Terry Nardin

Many people have questioned America's relationship with Israel, and argue that it has harmed U.S. relations with other countries in the Middle East. In the following viewpoint, Jerome Slater and Terry Nardin state that close U.S.-Israeli ties, which include U.S. aid to Israel, have set back U.S. interests in the Middle East and have impeded progress toward a settlement of the Arab-Israeli conflict. They write that the moral reasons for U.S. support of the establishment of Israel have been undercut by Israel's subsequent repression of the Palestinians. They conclude that because the U.S. does not benefit from its relationship to Israel, the U.S. should reassess the alliance. Slater and Nardin are both professors of political science. Slater teaches at the State University of New York at Buffalo. Nardin teaches at the University of Wisconsin at Milwaukee.

As you read, consider the following questions:

1. What moral obligations caused the U.S. to support the creation of Israel, according to Slater and Nardin?
2. According to the authors, how have U.S.-Israeli ties harmed U.S. relations with the Middle East nations?
3. What actions by Israel threaten to erode U.S. support, in Slater's and Nardin's opinion?

Excerpted from "Interests vs. Principles: Reassessing the U.S. Commitment to Israel," by Jerome Slater and Terry Nardin, *The Jerusalem Journal of International Relations*, vol. 13, no. 3, September 1991. Reprinted with permission.

It is commonly argued that since its emergence as a global power in 1945 the United States has had a number of important interests in the Middle East. These include containing Soviet expansion, maintaining Western access to oil at favorable prices, helping to ensure the security of Israel, and promoting peace and stability in the region. Beneath this consensus, however, there is considerable confusion and disagreement. Are these real interests or just slogans? Are the objectives mutually rein- forcing or are they in tension with one another? By what means should they be pursued? And what has been the impact on these objectives of the recent dramatic changes in international politics in general and in the Middle East in particular?

Our aim is to examine the US commitment to the security of Israel in relation to the other major American objectives in the Middle East. This commitment has been an enduring concern of American foreign policy since the founding of the state of Israel in 1948. It is bipartisan, cuts across liberal-conservative ideological lines, and has survived a number of substantial disagreements between the governments of the United States and Israel. What accounts for the remarkable stability and depth of this commitment? Has it been based primarily on US national interests, or even on domestic politics? And, above all, what is the soundest basis in the future for this commitment? . . .

Interests and Principles

Most American policymakers have believed that *both* national interests and moral principles have required US support for Israel. We shall contend, however, that US "interests," understood properly, have always been undercut more than furthered by support for Israel, even at the height of the Cold War, and therefore that it is the argument from principle that is more persuasive.

In any case, however one assesses the past, the foundations of the US commitment to Israel are now eroding. To be sure, in the war against Iraq there was a brief convergence of US and Israeli interests and a surge of American sympathy for Israel, but now that the war is over the two nations are once again diverging in their approach to a settlement of the Arab-Israeli and Israeli-Palestinian conflicts, a divergence that could precipitate a crisis in the relationship. Although such crises have often been predicted in the past and have not materialized, the prognosis is especially grave now, because both the interest-based and principle-based arguments for the US commitment are subject to serious challenge. As a result of changes in the international arena as well as Israel's continuing intransigence on the Palestinian issue, the argument that US interests require support for Israel has never been more questionable; simultaneously, Israeli repression of the Palestinians and the effects of that repression on

144

Israeli society and democracy are undermining the bases of the moral commitment.

During the events of 1947-1948, the US government was divided on whether to support the creation of a Jewish state in Palestine. Whereas President Truman favored recognition of the proposed state immediately following the termination of the British Mandate, the State Department was skeptical because it feared the consequences for the American interest in access to Persian Gulf oil as well as, more generally, for US influence in the Arab Middle East. Indeed, the entire foreign policy establishment bitterly opposed Truman on this issue. The State Department's argument that US interests precluded active US support for a Jewish state was not seriously challenged at the time; rather, it was simply overridden by the widespread conviction in public opinion, in Congress and, especially, of Truman himself that America had a moral obligation to support the creation—and, later, the continuation—of the state of Israel.

'Shut up and pass the mortar!'

Dennis Renault/*Sacramento Bee*. Reprinted with permission.

This conviction that America had a moral obligation to Israel rested on several grounds. In part it derived from a sense of guilt that the Christian West in general and the United States in particular had done nothing to prevent the Nazi destruction of European Jewry and little even to mitigate its effects by accepting large numbers of Jewish refugees or by making the survival of the European Jews a major priority of the military strategy of the war against Germany. Beyond that, Israel quickly captured the imagination and sympathy of American public opinion, Congress, and a succession of presidents. This involved partly the belief that American principles required support for Israel as a Western liberal democracy in a region dominated by despotic and violent regimes; and partly the traditional American sympathy for the victims or underdogs. Not only was Israel seen as David vs. the Arab Goliath, it was widely accepted that the root of the Arab-Israeli conflict was the uncompromising refusal of the Arabs to accept the existence of Israel. . . .

The view that Israel could be an important ally in containing Soviet expansion began emerging in the early 1950s, following Israel's unexpected victory in the 1948 war and the decision of the Ben-Gurion government to align Israel with the West rather than remain neutral in the Cold War. These developments convinced the State Department that Israel could play a useful role in the anticommunist struggle, balancing its potential liabilities.

From about 1970, following the brief Syrian-Jordanian conflict in which Israel and the United States threatened a joint military intervention to force Syrian troops to withdraw from Jordan, through the end of the Cold War in the late 1980s, the American perception of Israel as a vital "strategic asset" in the Cold War led to a vast increase in economic and military assistance. The strategic asset concept was based not only on Israel's anti-Soviet stand in the Middle East and its provision of military intelligence and captured Soviet weaponry to the United States, but also on its covert cooperation with US interventions in the Third World, in which Israel stood ready to do "America's dirty work" in Africa and, especially, Central America. . . .

A Vital Ally?

The argument that Israel is a vital strategic ally of the United States, helping serve American interests, is almost certain to weaken over time. Even at the height of the Cold War this argument was questionable: both the extent of Soviet influence in the Middle East and the threat such influence posed to US interests were considerably exaggerated. As one of us has argued elsewhere, Soviet Middle Eastern policies in the postwar era were best understood in terms of traditional Russian geopolitical objectives, reaction to US efforts to expand its influence in the area, and Soviet aspirations to be recognized as a superpower equal in influence and prestige to the United States—rather than in terms of "expansionism." In any case, such influence as it had was limited and ephemeral, as was made evident in the early 1970s by the sudden Soviet expulsion from Egypt, until then the major Soviet ally and the site of its most important bases.

146

Moreover, to the extent that the Soviets gained influence in the Middle East, it was a consequence of the US decision to extend the containment policy to the region, of Israel's decision to ally itself with the United States in the early 1950s, and of the subsequent growing US political, economic, and military support for Israel in the Arab-Israeli conflict. The creation of Israel and its alliance with the US opened rather than barred the door to the Soviet Union, for it gave the Arab world the perceived need for its own superpower protector and supplier, while simultaneously giving the Soviets a good reason to join forces with the Arabs. . . .

In sum, even at the height of the Cold War and of Soviet influence in the area, it was the strategic alliance of the US with Israel that facilitated rather than contained Soviet "penetration" of the Middle East, for it gave the Soviets both the motive and the opportunity to acquire allies in the region, in an essentially defensive and reactive effort to balance US influence. Put differently, if Israel had not existed, there would have been no need for an American strategic ally in the Middle East.

A Strategic Liability

Some supporters of Israel did concede that Israel was more of a strategic liability than an asset of the United States, but argued that for moral reasons the United States nonetheless should support Israel—that is, *despite* rather than because of its "interests." But even this argument was undercut by the connection between the ever-expanding and essentially unconditional nature of US political, economic, and military support for Israel and Israel's unwillingness to compromise in the Arab-Israeli conflict. Indeed, Israel's reluctance to negotiate a political settlement not only undercut the moral basis for US support, it also harmed US interests. A settlement of the Arab-Israeli conflict would have furthered general US interests in regional and global order; lessened if not eliminated the chances of a superpower confrontation in the Middle East; and eliminated one (not all) of the causes of Arab political instability, which in turn threatened the moderate Arab regimes that provided most of the oil imported by the US from the region. . . .

In any case, the end of the Cold War has made this history increasingly moot. The United States does not seek to block Soviet access to the Middle East any longer. . . .

To be sure, Israel and its supporters recently have been arguing that Israel is still a strategic asset to the United States, despite the end of the Cold War, for it can deter Middle Eastern radicalism and shore up shaky moderate Arab regimes, thereby helping the US and its allies preserve their access to oil. The argument is not persuasive, however. Regardless of their ideologies, oil-producing regimes have powerful economic reasons to sell oil to whoever will buy it; moreover, they have powerful prudential reasons not to challenge the US interest in maintaining Western access to oil. Only an overriding emotional or ideological motivation, such as anger at American support for Israel, could conceivably lead the Arab states to ignore their own interests in order to punish the United States. So long as it occupies the West Bank and Gaza and rejects Palestinian self-determination, Israel feeds, even though it is not the primary cause, the forces of Arab nationalism and fundamentalism that potentially endanger the moderate Arab regimes that control most of the oil.

Cutting Ties

The strategic interests of no one—not America, Israel, or the Arabs—are served over the long run by the maintenance of the U.S.-Israeli strategic alliance. The United States wishes to operate freely, unhindered by Israel's refusal to consider land for peace—an agenda that drifts ever further away from the rest of the world. Israel itself needs to operate as an independent state in the region, and not as somebody's strategic instrument. The Arab states need to begin working with each other in the region without constant obsession with the Palestinian problem that so plagues their every move even today. Cutting the binding and usually conflicting ties of the present alliance will better serve everyone's interest.

Graham E. Fuller, *The National Interest*, Winter 1990/1991.

Moreover, not only is it the case that US support for Israel creates the potential oil problem for the United States, but the military power of Israel is not likely to be available to "solve" it. What is it that Israel can or is likely to do to deter radicalism or shore up moderate Arab regimes? Since Lebanon, it is implausible that Israeli military power would be used in an attempt to avert or reverse the fall of Arab governments, save perhaps in Jordan (which in any case has no oil)—and if even the attempt was made, success in countries such as Egypt and Saudi Arabia would be highly unlikely.

In short, even on the premise that national policies should be judged only by their contributions to national interests, it has never been in the "interest" of the United States to support Israel—even at the height of the Cold War, let alone today. If the United States had not supported Israel and not extended the containment policy to the Middle East, there would have been little or no Soviet "expansionism" in the Middle East, no reason for Arab nationalism to be anti-American, and no threat to US access to oil.

This leaves only the moral argument as a persuasive basis for

American support for Israel, and it too is less compelling than it once was. To begin with, Israel cannot indefinitely count on Western guilt over past antisemitism and the Holocaust; as time passes new generations will surely—and rightly—feel less direct moral responsibility, and therefore less reason to atone for the failures of an earlier generation.

More important, though, is the Israeli occupation of the West Bank and Gaza, the growing Jewish settlement of the West Bank, and the repressive means that Israel must now resort to in order to suppress Palestinian resistance. The David-vs.-Goliath image that previously benefited the Israelis has been reversed, at least in terms of Israel's conflict with the Palestinians as opposed to Arab states. Moreover, it is now Israel, not the Palestinians or even most of the Arab states, that is unwilling to compromise and is therefore increasingly culpable for the continuing strife in the territories. Much of the moral strength of Israel's position derived from its status as a victim of implacable Arab hostility and from its right to security. If a now much strengthened and secure Israel continues to provoke hostility by its own religious and nationalist expansionism, its moral claim on the United States is obviously weakened.

Weakened Moral Claims

The Israeli refusal to consider a genuine compromise settlement with the Palestinians, based on Israeli withdrawal from the West Bank and Gaza and the creation of a limited, demilitarized Palestinian state in these areas, also threatens to undermine another concern, moral as well as prudential, of the United States: maintaining peace and stability in the Middle East. Until the 1967 war it was widely accepted that the primary threat to stability was the Arab refusal to accept the existence of Israel, but today the matter is considerably more complicated. Indeed, it now appears that the matter was always more complicated, for recent Israeli scholarship suggests that during the 1930-1967 period the Jews were not merely victims of Arab hostility and intransigence, for their *own* intransigence and violence played an important role in deepening the cycle of conflict.

In any case, today there is hardly a monolithic Arab rejection of Israel: Jordan has sought a compromise settlement since 1948; Egypt reached one with Israel in the 1970s that has held firm since; there are indications that Saudi Arabia will acquiesce in a settlement if Israel withdraws from lands occupied since the 1967 war and allows the creation of a Palestinian state; and even Syria has recently moved toward a more moderate position, indicating it would agree to a de facto settlement in exchange for the return of a demilitarized Golan Heights to Syria and Israel's withdrawal from the West Bank and Gaza.

The responsibility of the PLO and the Palestinians for the ongoing conflict with Israel is more complicated. In the initial decades after the creation of Israel the Palestinians sought to overturn the results of the 1948 war and to regain all of Palestine from the Jews. The futility of this position became increasingly clear to many Palestinian leaders, however, and from the end of the 1970s until the Persian Gulf crisis the PLO position gradually evolved toward a more realistic one, culminating in the 1989 official PLO acceptance of a compromise settlement based on Israeli acceptance of a demilitarized Palestinian state in the West Bank and Gaza and Palestinian acceptance of Israel within its pre-1967 borders. Whatever ambiguities may have remained in the Palestinian position, the real cause for the breakdown of any prospect for a settlement based on mutual Israeli-Palestinian political recognition and nonaggression was the hard-line position of the Israeli government, which was determined to allow no Palestinian state in "Judea and Samaria," far more for ideological than genuine security reasons. . . .

Yet another threat to US moral support for Israel is the continuing decline of liberal democracy in Israel. In the first twenty years of Israel's history, the stark contrast between Israel and its adversaries had much to do with enthusiasm for Israel as a bastion of Western civilization amid so many barbaric Arab regimes. The contrast still exists, but it is no longer so stark. To be sure, despite its flaws, Israel is certainly no Lebanon, Syria, Iraq, or Iran. But the Israeli repression of Arabs in the occupied territories, the clearly unequal treatment of Arabs within Israel itself, and the rise of Israeli anti-Arab racism, religious fundamentalism, and extremist nationalism are undermining Israel's claim to moral distinctiveness.

A Higher Standard

Israelis often complain of a Western "double standard," bitterly citing the failure of the West to criticize, say, the brutality of the Syrian regime. If the media focuses on Israeli shootings of Palestinians in the occupied territories, Israelis are sure to point out that the Syrians killed ten thousand people to suppress a domestic uprising in the 1970s. But there is no double standard here. Rather (as Abba Eban has pointed out), the world is only comparing Israel to the standards it has set for itself. . . .

But there is a still more important reason why Israel has been and ought to be held to higher standards than prevail elsewhere in the Middle East. Precisely because the real foundation of US support for Israel is moral, and because that support involves serious costs and risks to US national interests—including, as the Iraqi crisis has demonstrated, the costs and risks of outright war—it is not sufficient that Israel be only *relatively* superior to its enemies, particularly given the typically dreary standards of those enemies.

"U.S. officials should be wary of transferring more arms to the Middle East."

The U.S. Should Limit Arms Sales to the Middle East

Michael T. Klare

The U.S. and other nations sell billions of dollars' worth of arms to countries in the Middle East. In the following viewpoint, Michael T. Klare argues that such arms sales destabilize the region and encourage leaders such as Iraq's Saddam Hussein to take aggressive military action. He argues that the U.S. should reduce its arms sales to the Middle East and use its international influence to encourage other nations to do the same. Klare is an associate professor of peace and world security studies at Hampshire College in Amherst, Massachusetts. He is the author of several books analyzing international politics, including *American Arms Supermarket.*

As you read, consider the following questions:

1. What countries sell the most arms to the Middle East, according to Klare?
2. How has the sale of arms affected the Middle East region, in the author's opinion?
3. Why does the U.S. sell arms to countries in the Middle East according to Klare?

Excerpted from "Fueling the Fire: How We Armed the Middle East," by Michael T. Klare, *Bulletin of the Atomic Scientists*, January/February 1991. Copyright © 1991 by the Educational Foundation for Nuclear Science, 6042 S. Kimbark, Chicago, IL 60637 USA. A one-year subscription is $30. Reprinted with permission.

Warning that "the virtually unrestrained spread of conventional weaponry threatens stability in every region of the world," President Jimmy Carter attempted in the mid-1970s to constrain U.S. military sales to the Third World and to negotiate a mutual curb on arms exports with the Soviets. These efforts failed. Carter's attempt to limit U.S. military sales collided with the use of arms transfers as an instrument of diplomacy—especially in the Middle East—and his overtures to Moscow were forestalled by a resurgence of Cold War tensions. Since then, no serious effort has been made to curb international arms trafficking, and sales to the Third World have skyrocketed. As Carter predicted, unrestrained commerce in conventional arms has fueled local arms races and inspired aggressive powers like Iraq to employ their bulging arsenals in unprovoked attacks on neighboring countries. If the 1990-1991 crisis in the Persian Gulf is to have any positive outcome, therefore, it should be to demonstrate the urgent need to curtail the global arms trade.

Iraq's Military Buildup

The arms-trade danger is underscored by the relative ease with which Saddam Hussein was able to assemble a massive arsenal of conventional weapons. Between 1981 and 1988, Iraq purchased an estimated $46.7 billion worth of arms and military equipment from foreign suppliers, the largest accumulation ever of modern weapons by a Third World country. . . .

On the basis of this experience, U.S. officials should be wary of transferring more arms to the Middle East—at least until some multilateral constraints are in place. Instead, the Bush administration has decided to proceed with a new round of multibillion-dollar sales to friendly nations in the region. . . .

The intended beneficiaries of these sales will continue to pursue their own political and military objectives—often risking armed combat with their neighbors in the process. The most likely outcome of fresh arms deliveries to the Middle East will thus be intensified regional tensions and a heightened risk of armed conflict. . . .

The risk of escalating conflicts in volatile Third World areas has led nations to agree on the need to prevent sales of chemical and nuclear weapons and to curb the diffusion of ballistic missile delivery systems. Despite repeated crises, however, there are no such constraints on conventional weapons. . . .

Many countries offer some type of weapon for sale, but the trade in major combat systems is highly concentrated. According to the Congressional Research Service of the Library of Congress, in the 1980s the United States and Soviet Union accounted for three-fifths of all arms sales to the Third World, and five other nations—France, Great Britain, West Germany, Italy, and China—shared another 22 percent. These nations remain the source of most heavy weapons supplied to Middle Eastern countries, and it is their sales policies that must be addressed if the flow of combat gear is to be constrained.

New world orders

Dick Adair/*Honolulu Advertiser.* Reprinted with permission.

Many factors—political, economic, and military—figure in these nations' arms export behavior. For the superpowers, economic considerations have generally played a secondary role to political and strategic considerations. Samuel Huntington suggested in 1987 that U.S. and Soviet involvement in the Third World reflects "the bipolar structure of world politics and the competitive relationship they have with each other." In their mutual quest for strategic advantage, each superpower has sought to expand its own perimeter of influence while "minimizing the power and influence of the other." As part of this process, each side has used arms transfers to lure new allies into its own camp or to discourage existing allies from breaking away.

This use of arms transfers began in the Middle East in 1955, when President Gamal Abdel Nasser of Egypt turned to Moscow for the modern weapons the West had denied him. By giving Egypt advanced weapons, Moscow forged a *de facto* alliance with Cairo, and succeeded, for the first time, in leaping over the ring of hostile states organized by the United States to contain Soviet power in Eurasia. This feat prompted Washington to establish arms-supply relationships with other countries in the region, including Iran, Israel, Jordan, and Saudi Arabia. These moves, in turn, aroused anxiety among the more radical Arab regimes, leading Syria, and then Iraq, to forge military ties with the Soviet bloc. Egypt switched sides following the October War of 1973, but the Middle Eastern arms acquisition patterns established in the mid-to-late 1950s have remained essentially intact to this day.

Different Motives

In justifying U.S. arms transfers to the Middle East, U.S. leaders repeatedly asserted that supplier and recipient were bound by common opposition to communist expansionism. For their part, Soviet leaders stressed the common struggle against imperialism. However, the recipients' principal motive for acquiring arms was not the struggle between communism and imperialism, but rather a desire to offset the military might of their regional rivals or to deter attack by an antagonistic neighbor. As Stephen M. Walt suggested in his masterful study of Middle East alliance patterns, "The superpowers sought to balance each other, [while] their clients sought outside support to counter threats from other regional states."

At first glance, this system has a certain logic: each party receives something it wants, and the various arms deliveries balance each other out. In reality, however, the system is fundamentally unstable. No recipient is content with balancing its rivals, but seeks a margin of advantage—either to allow for a preemptive strike (should that be deemed necessary), or to compensate for the other side's perceived advantages. Any major weapons delivery to one side automatically triggers a comparable but larger delivery to the other, prompting a new round of deliveries to the first party, and so on. The only break in this grim pattern occurs when one side or the other seeks to forestall an imminent shift in military advantage to the opposing side by launching a preemptive attack—as has occurred again and again in the Middle East.

This instability is mirrored in the relations between client and supplier. By agreeing to provide arms to a client, the supplier seeks a local ally for its ongoing struggle against the other superpower. Once the relationship has been forged, however, the recipient comes to expect continuing and even expanded arms deliveries in exchange for its continued loyalty to the supplier—and any reluctance on the part of the supplier will be condemned as evidence of inconstancy and unreliability. Such charges usually have the effect of prying additional or more advanced weapons out of the supplier's hands.

The result is "reverse dependency." The patron finds itself be-

154

holden to the good will of the client, and must satisfy the client's appetite for modern arms. As Walt points out, "A large [military] aid relationship may actually be a reflection of the client's ability to extort support from its patron, rather than being a sign of the patron's ability to control its client." For the Soviet Union, the principal beneficiaries of reverse dependency were Egypt (until 1973), Syria, and Iraq; for the United States, they were Iran (until 1978), Israel, and Saudi Arabia. . . .

Both superpowers also sought to woo away each other's allies and clients, often using arms transfers in the process. . . .

Large Armies

As a result of these deeply entrenched arms-supply patterns, many Middle Eastern nations now possess arsenals comparable or superior to those found among the front-line states in NATO [North Atlantic Treaty Organization] and the Warsaw Pact. But if the genesis of these arms-supply relationships was the early Cold War, it would seem logical for them to fade as the Cold War draws to a close. U.S. and Soviet leaders have lent some credence to this assumption. . . .

Despite progress on the rhetorical front, however, the superpowers have taken no steps to curb their exports of conventional arms to the Third World. As noted above, the United States has announced record-breaking sales to Saudi Arabia, and sales of sophisticated arms to Egypt, Israel, Turkey, and the United Arab Emirates are in the offing. The Soviet Union continues to supply major equipment to India, Libya, and Syria, and was pouring arms into Iraq until the moment Saddam Hussein ordered the invasion of Kuwait.

Economic conditions have something to do with this. The Soviet Union is desperately in need of hard currency for its industrial rehabilitation, and weapons are among the few commodities it can successfully market abroad. Arms exports give U.S. weapons manufacturers an attractive "safety valve" at a time of declining military spending at home. But political factors remain a major determinant of the superpowers' arms transfer policies. Moscow and Washington once sought Third World allies in their struggle with one another; today they seek allies in order to better position themselves for global influence in an uncertain, polycentric era.

In the view of senior U.S. strategists, this era is likely to witness the emergence of regional powers, many of which will be armed with weapons of mass destruction, and some will be hostile to long-term U.S. interests. "The emergence of regional powers is rapidly changing the strategic landscape," President Bush noted in an address to the U.S. Coast Guard Academy in May 1989. "In the Middle East, in South Asia, in our own hemisphere, a growing number of nations are acquiring advanced

155

and highly destructive capabilities," posing a significant threat to U.S. security. In this environment, any effort by the United States to protect its overseas interests through military means . . . will require the cooperation of friendly Third World powers. "Where American intervention seems necessary," the U.S. Commission on Integrated Long-Term Strategy affirmed in 1988, "it will generally require far more cooperation with Third World countries than has been required in the past."

And cooperation is secured through arms transfers. In other words, arms sales are the essential glue for the "regional security structure" that Secretary of State James Baker told the House Foreign Affairs Committee on September 4, 1990 the administration wants to establish in the Middle East.

Whether the Soviet Union has similar intentions cannot be determined. It is clear that Soviet leaders want to maintain close ties with regional powers like Syria and India, and to establish new ties—cemented by arms transfers if necessary—with other powers in the region. Potential buyers are still able to play one suitor off against the other, obtaining favorable conditions for the acquisition of ever more capable weapons. Whatever impact the end of the Cold War may have in other areas, it has not diminished the intensity of local arms races—or the likelihood of regional conflict—in the Middle East.

No Escape

There is no escape from this pattern if the major powers continue to view arms exports as tools of convenience in their quest for political advantage, and if regional powers continue to rely on military means to resolve disputes with their neighbors. U.S. and Soviet leaders—and subsequently, the leaders of France, Britain, and China—must be convinced that a stable international order cannot be achieved in a world of uncontrolled arms transfers, and that curbs on arms are essential to post-Cold War stability. At the same time, Middle Eastern leaders must be persuaded that the best hope for long-term protection against dissension and bloodshed lies with a regional peace agreement that respects the national aspirations of unrepresented peoples, eliminates nuclear and chemical weapons, and limits the acquisition of offensively oriented conventional weapons.

"The United States is in for an exercise in frustration if it chooses to embark on a . . . plan for arms control in the Middle East."

U.S. Attempts to Limit Middle East Arms Sales Are Futile

Amos Perlmutter

Amos Perlmutter is a professor of political science and sociology at American University in Washington, D.C., and editor of the *Journal of Strategic Studies*. In the following viewpoint, he argues that U.S. efforts to control arms sales to the Middle East would be futile as long as conflicts remain in that region. There are too many countries that sell arms, Perlmutter writes, for the U.S. to have much effectiveness in controlling the arms trade.

As you read, consider the following questions:

1. What factors does Perlmutter believe are necessary for successful arms control plans?
2. How does the Middle East situation differ from the U.S.-Soviet confrontation, according to the author?
3. Why are many countries hesitant to limit their arms sales to the Middle East, according to Perlmutter?

Amos Perlmutter, "Arms Control for the Middle East," *The Washington Times*, May 23, 1991. Reprinted with permission.

Both the Bush administration and the Congress are buzzing with ideas on . . . arms control and reduction policy in the Middle East and the Persian Gulf.

The administration and Congress differ in their approach, however. The president wants to focus on the users of weapons in the Middle East and Persian Gulf, while Congress wants to put a ban on the suppliers, which would include the United States, the Soviet Union, China, France, Germany, Italy, Great Britain, Brazil and all those nations involved in the multi-billion dollar global arms industry operating in the area.

On the surface, the aim seems noble, but the approach is almost certainly to be doomed. This is not the first time in this century that arms-control efforts, both limited and general, have been attempted.

The successful arms limitations programs had in the end little to do with weapons but more to do with politics, perceptions, alliances and moods of the time. For an arms-reduction plan to succeed, several factors have to be at work. To begin with, there is the role of the parties to the arrangements. Are they politically, psychologically and diplomatically ready to make the sacrifices necessary for success? Then there are the issues of enforcement, verification and control. Who will enforce the agreements reached? Who will be the adjudicator of complaints and who will right wrongs? Will it be the United States or the Soviet Union, the politically influential powers, the economically wealthy? Can one or several powers be trusted? Is the United Nations capable of enforcement or could the European Economic Community do it?

Impractical Goals

President Bush appears to be proposing the elimination of biological, chemical and other lethal weapons employed by the Arabs while Israel freezes its nuclear production. On the surface, this seems a fine goal meant to stabilize, to bring about a more quiescent political atmosphere. It is also an impractical goal, because what's needed to make it achievable is a political will to make concessions and compromise on the part of the belligerents.

Israel and Syria, the major military powers in the area now that Iraq's force and power have been decimated and Egypt is no longer at war with Israel, are both unwilling to make the barest of concessions. Saudi Arabia appears incapable of even altering the smallest word in the Arab economic boycott against Israel. How can one expect a climate to exist for disarmament if there is no climate for peace?

The United States and the Soviet Union reached an arms-control agreement only after the Soviets realized that they could not keep up in the arms race without totally destroying their already overburdened economy. But the Arab states still retain the hope that their financial strength and good relations with the United States can keep them from the negotiations table, and therefore are hardly ready to talk about peace or arms control. On the other hand, it's unthinkable for Israel to surrender the only weapon, next to its superb force of 2,000 pilots, which guarantees its security—that is, its nuclear supremacy. The Arabs, meanwhile, rely on the poor man's nuclear bomb, their arsenal of chemical and biological weapons.

Even at the highest point of the Cold War, the United States and the Soviet Union never came to the point of war, nor did they threaten each other with military or nuclear annihilation. Israel, on the other hand, can hear the Arab annihilatory threat and its echoes daily and thus remains unwilling to halt, let alone relinquish, its nuclear arsenal.

Arms Control Impossible

It will be impossible, even with the best intentions (assuming they exist), to curtail arms sales to the region in the long run. The complex and secretive arms trade environment and the availability of billions of petro-dollars on the demand side virtually guarantee continued activity. The cooling of U.S.-Soviet relations as a result of the Gulf War and the new repression in the Soviet Union make it difficult to envision Moscow's extensive cooperation in new Middle East arms control efforts. Israel, Turkey, and the moderate Arab states will request more weapons to defend themselves against "new Saddams," and Washington, pressured by Israeli and Arab lobbies and encouraged by the now-rejuvenated military-industrial complex, will find it difficult not to provide those weapons.

Leon T. Hadar, Cato Institute *Policy Analysis*, no. 154, June 12, 1991.

The arms race in the Middle East is not just a matter of the constant Arab-Israeli conflict, but also extends to inter-Arab rivalries. Syria, for instance, confronts not only Israel but also a still surviving and vengeful Saddam Hussein in Iraq to the east.

Arms reduction is no substitute for political and diplomatic movement in the direction of negotiations and conflict resolution. But Israel remains inherently distrustful of the United Nations. The United Nations as a guarantor of peace and faithful negotiations is a myth and fiction. Every party in the Middle East is aware of its political impotence. Nor does Israel trust the Soviet Union, which once again has shown its support for Arab positions, instead of adopting an evenhanded approach.

That leaves the United States, with its restricted diplomatic

Blairsville High School Library.

capabilities, that wields a two-edged sword when it comes to arms control in the Middle East and the Gulf. In order to assure a successful arms-control policy, it must, in effect, police the aggressive arms salesmen practically all over the world, especially among its allies. The business of arms manufacture and sale is after all a $50 billion to $70 billion industry. Tiny and impoverished as well as democratic Czechoslovakia, political friend of Israel, will nevertheless sell weapons to Arab regimes to ensure that its 80,000 workers stay employed. Who can police Czechoslovakia and its finely tuned military, weapons and explosive industry? (It was Czech-made plastics, incidentally, that helped Arab terrorists blow up Pan Am Flight 107 in 1989.)

How can the traditional sources of arms in Europe be curbed? There is also to be considered the $30 billion in weapons that goes yearly from the United States to the Persian Gulf.

The most politically dangerous and difficult part of arms control for the United States would come in the area of enforcing restrictions on the manufacturing, selling, transporting and supplying of weapons to the regimes in the area. An arms moratorium plan would meet the stiffest resistance not from the area involved but from our closest allies in Europe. The French would never accept any limits on their authority over their highly profitable and extensive arms industry, which sells more than $5 billion in weapons annually.

For that matter, what if a Middle East country would say it would not buy weapon X unless it could also get weapon Y? So interconnected is the arms industry today that every country of note engages in it. North Korea sells Scuds to Syria. The arms export business is the Soviet Union's lone remaining profitable industry.

Weapons Systems

Today, weapons are matters of systems. In each system, there is always some critical part or other, usually electronic, that sells on the open market and therefore is almost impossible to control. It would amount to having to tell the Japanese to stop selling computers, or American companies to stop selling software critical for missile delivery systems.

Weapons systems today are so sophisticated and complex that they have produced what amounts to an international and multinational arms industry. And the major obstacles to an arms freeze are not the buyers but the sellers. The arms market is a seller's market. The buyer could be curbed only if the sellers can be prevented from selling, which is next to impossible.

The United States is in for an exercise in frustration if it chooses to embark on a policy or a plan for arms control in the Middle East and the Gulf.

Ranking American Foreign Policy Concerns

This activity will allow you to explore the values you consider important in making foreign policy decisions. In studying world politics you will discover that countries, depending on their location, military strength, and economic power, have different priorities for their foreign policies. Consider the difference in foreign policy concerns between Canada, which is bounded only by the U.S. and three oceans, and Israel, which is geographically bounded by hostile nations. Since Canada is relatively isolated, the likelihood of surprise attack is fairly small, allowing national security to be secondary to some other foreign policy concerns such as trade. Israel, on the other hand, must continually be on guard against its aggressive neighbors. For Israel, maintaining national security is its main priority.

"Do you think we'd be here if all the Middle East produced was broccoli?"

Conrad. Copyright, 1991, Los Angeles Times Syndicate. Reprinted with permission.

In the viewpoints in this chapter, the authors have given many different reasons why the U.S. should or should not be involved in the Middle East.

Consider the above cartoon. The cartoonist implies that oil is the primary reason the U.S. was involved in the 1991 Persian Gulf conflict. The cartoonist suggests that this is not a good reason for the U.S. to send troops to the Middle East. Others would argue that ensuring a consistent and inexpensive oil supply *is* essential and warrants the deployment of U.S. troops.

In this activity, you will be asked to decide which concerns you think are the most important to justify U.S. involvement in the Middle East.

Step 1. Rank the concerns listed below. Use number 1 to designate the most important concern, number 2 for the second most important concern, and so on.

_____ ensuring a steady flow of oil to the U.S.

_____ having a military ally in the Middle East

_____ freeing U.S. hostages

_____ establishing a country or homeland for Palestinians

_____ maintaining America's historical commitment to Israel

_____ preventing nuclear proliferation

_____ promoting democracy and human rights

_____ preventing the spread of Islamic fundamentalism

Step 2. Review the list of concerns, starting with what you marked to be most important. Ask yourself if this concern justifies deploying American troops in the Middle East. Then mark *T* next to each concern you believe justifies such action.

Step 3. After students have completed their individual rankings, the class should break into groups. Students should compare their rankings with those of others in the group, giving reasons for their choices.

Step 4. Students should compare which concerns they believe justify U.S. military action. Then the students should make a new list that reflects the concerns of the group as a whole.

Step 5. Have the entire class discuss the following questions:

1. Did your individual rankings change after comparing your answers with the answers of others in the group?

2. How did your reasons differ from those of others in the group?

3. Do your highest-ranking priorities always justify military action? Why or why not?

4. Do you think U.S. military involvement was justified in the case of Iraq's 1990 invasion of Kuwait? Why or why not?

Periodical Bibliography

The following articles have been selected to supplement the diverse views presented in this chapter.

Amy Borrus et al.	"Shut Down the Mideast Arms Bazaar? Forget It," *Business Week*, March 11, 1991.
Stuart Eizenstat	"Loving Israel—Warts and All," *Foreign Policy*, no. 81, Winter 1990/1991.
Graham E. Fuller	"Respecting Regional Realities," *Foreign Policy*, no. 83, Summer 1991.
Mark A. Heller	"Coping with Missile Proliferation in the Middle East," *Orbis*, Winter 1991.
Martin Indyk	"Half-Bakered," *The New Republic*, May 27, 1991.
June Jordan	"Intifada, U.S.A.," *The Progressive*, December 1990.
Elie Kedourie	"Iraq: The Mystery of American Policy," *Commentary*, June 1991.
Geoffrey Kemp	"The Middle East Arms Race: Can It Be Controlled?" *The Middle East Journal*, Summer 1991.
Morton Kondracke	"Unsettling," *The New Republic*, July 29, 1991.
Charles Lane et al.	"A Marriage on the Rocks," *Newsweek*, September 30, 1991.
Roger Matthews	"Washington's New Chance to Make Peace," *World Press Review*, May 1991.
Tom Mayer	"Imperialism and the Gulf War," *Monthly Review*, April 1991.
National Review	"Can America Bring Peace?" Part I: August 26, 1991; Part II: October 7, 1991.
Janne E. Nolan	"The Global Arms Market After the Gulf War: Prospects for Control," *The Washington Quarterly*, Summer 1991.
Daniel Pipes	"What Kind of Peace?" *The National Interest*, Spring 1991.
Steven V. Roberts	"Brawl in the Family," *U.S. News & World Report*, September 30, 1991.
Peter W. Rodman	"Middle East Diplomacy After the Gulf War," *Foreign Affairs*, Spring 1991.
Jill Smolowe	"Why Should Americans Care?" *Time*, November 11, 1991.
Mortimer B. Zuckerman	"Playing Games with Israel," *U.S. News & World Report*, September 30, 1991.

4 CHAPTER

How Does Religion Affect the Middle East?

Chapter Preface

The Middle East has been the birthplace of three of the world's great religions: Judaism, Christianity, and Islam. Of the three religions, which share some common elements, Islam is both the newest and the most dominant in the Middle East, where it is followed by more than 90 percent of the population.

While this figure may suggest religious unity among Middle Eastern peoples, in fact the region is marked by complex religious divisions. As philosophy professor Habib C. Malik writes:

> Few outsiders may realize it but there are innumerable religious minority groups throughout the Middle East. . . . There are the Coptic Christians of Egypt; the many Jewish communities still remaining in the Arab world; the Jews of historic Palestine: the Christians of Lebanon, Syria, Israel, Jordan, Iraq, and southern Sudan—including Greek Orthodox, Syrian Orthodox (Jacobites), Assyrians (Nestorians), Greek Catholics (Melkites), Chaldaeans, Maronites, Latins, and Protestants; the Druze of Syria, Lebanon and Israel; the Armenians of Lebanon; and others. Even the Muslim majority is itself divided into two main groups of Sunnis and Shiites, along with a host of esoteric offshoot sects of these two branches.

This religious diversity makes religious conflict almost inevitable. Religious differences have been an underlying cause of many Middle Eastern disputes. For example, violence in Lebanon often occurs between religious groups. And the Israeli-Palestinian conflict has been affected by religion as partisans on all sides of the conflict espouse Jewish, Christian, and Islamic beliefs in their refusal to compromise with each other.

In spite of the problems religious conflicts cause in the Middle East, German theologian Hans Küng believes the Middle East religions could point the way to peace. He writes that Judaism, Christianity, and Islam "have much in common. All three of these religions are of Eastern Semitic origin, all are prophetic in character, and all three trace themselves back to a common progenitor, Abraham. Were they to reflect upon this common origin, these religions could perhaps make a vital contribution to world peace." The viewpoints in this chapter examine this and other aspects of how religion affects the Middle East.

"A rising tide of Islamic fundamentalists . . . are using democratic openings . . . to try to purge the Arab world of Western corruption and install the Holy Koran as its highest authority."

Islam Threatens Democracy in the Middle East

Louise Lief

One of the main beneficiaries of elections held in Jordan, Algeria, and other Middle East countries has been the Islamic fundamentalist movement. In the following viewpoint, journalist Louise Lief examines the role of Islam in Middle East politics and argues that it poses a threat to emerging democratic trends. Many people in Islamic movements, she writes, do not want to establish democracies in their countries, and are opposed to such values as the separation of church and state and equal rights for women. Lief is an associate editor of *U.S. News & World Report*, a weekly newsmagazine.

As you read, consider the following questions:

1. What do the Arabic words *shura* and *Umma* mean, and why are they important to the Islamic movement, according to Lief?
2. What examples of discrimination against women in Islamic countries does the author describe?

Excerpted from "Battling for the Arab Mind" by Louise Lief, *U.S. News & World Report*, January 21, 1991. Copyright © 1991 U.S. News & World Report. Reprinted with permission.

Just off the harbor, in the Martyr's Square in downtown Algiers, 5,000 young, mostly bearded men have assembled for a Friday campaign rally of the Islamic Salvation Front (FIS), an Islamic party that could win the largest plurality in elections for the National Assembly this spring. Men are perched in the treetops, hanging off the railings and crushed together in the square to hear the spellbinding oratory of Ali Belhadj, one of the movement's two principal leaders.

"For 14 centuries, Islam worked alone, without infidels and unbelievers," Belhadj intones in Arabic from the gazebo at the center of the square. He is dressed in a long white tunic with a knitted skullcap on his head, a group of white-robed sheiks seated at his feet like disciples. One, with a beard hennaed bright orange, raises his hand to the heavens. "Are you afraid of authority? The president? The prime minister?" Belhadj asks, his voice dripping with scorn. "Allahu Akbar!" the crowd roars. God is great! A man in the crowd goes into hysterics, faints and is rushed out by the white-robed attendants. Belhadj's voice rises to a shriek. "Muslims will take over and put in the government of God. We are going to establish an Islamic state in this country."

Officially, the Arab Organization for Human Rights, a tiny first-floor office in a run-down building at 17 Aswan Square in Cairo, near a pleasant but neglected garden of rubber trees, does not exist. Inside, a young woman in a canary-yellow hijab, *or veil, clips newspapers. Other volunteers answer phones and do typing. Barely tolerated by the Egyptian government, they dwell in a kind of bureaucratic limbo, their newsletter classified as a "nonperiodical."*

A Battle for the Mind

The human-rights group in Cairo and the fundamentalists massed in Algiers represent the opposing forces in a hidden battle for the Arab mind—a struggle that will endure and intensify long after the 1991 Persian Gulf crisis has ended. On one front, democracy-minded human-rights activists have launched a growing campaign to promote individual rights and to protest torture and other abuses of state power that are commonplace throughout the Arab world. On another, a rising tide of Islamic fundamentalists, financed largely by Saudi Arabia, are using democratic openings in Egypt, Jordan, Algeria and elsewhere to try to purge the Arab world of Western corruption and install the Holy Koran as its highest authority.

While the dual assaults on the traditional Arab state system gather momentum, the world remains understandably transfixed by the gulf crisis, and by the battle between Israelis and Palestinians. The United States continues to ignore a lesson it should have learned in Muslim but non-Arab Iran: The greatest dangers in the Mideast may come from the fraying relations between friendly governments and their own people, not from the hostilities between rich and poor Arab states or between Muslims and Jews.

Though their visions of the future differ sharply, liberal reformers and fundamentalists are allied in attacking the status quo. All across the Arab world, governments headed by kings, military dictators and political strongmen rest uneasily on eroding political and economic foundations. Even before Saddam Hussein's grab for Kuwait, the veneer of legitimacy on other Arab regimes was cracking, and defeating Iraq, militarily or diplomatically, will not stop the spreading disaffection. "The gulf crisis was the catalyst for exposing all these regimes," says Mona Makram Obeid, a petite, energetic member of the Egyptian human-rights organization and the opposition Wafd Party. "Iraq is not the only one that is despotic. Others are obsolete or illegitimate or tepid about advancing the democratic process."

Incompatible Philosophies

Islam has no monopoly on oppression. Many a dictator is doing quite well for himself with no help from Allah. But Islam and democracy are rarely good bedfellows. Only two of the 43 Moslem countries are democracies. Moslem theology does not tend to nurture pluralism, and the Islamists deprecate democracy all the more because it comes from the West.

Jean-Pierre Langellier, *World Press Review*, July 1989.

In fact, all the Arab regimes, to varying degrees, are clinging to some form of authoritarianism. By far the worst offenders are Iraq and Syria. Syrian Baathism is a cover for brutal military rule by President Hafez Assad's minority Alawite sect. In Iraq, Saddam Hussein has created a totalitarian regime controlled by his local clan and held in place by torture and summary executions.

For many Arab rulers, charges of Western imperialism, Zionism and neo-colonialism have become convenient excuses for maintaining tight control at home. Says Lebanese human-rights activist Ghassan Salameh, "The Arab-Israeli conflict legitimized military rule, military expenditures and repression at home. People said, 'It is not the time to fight Assad's policies while he is busy fighting Israel.'"

"The Arab world has no answers to contemporary problems," admits Algerian Prime Minister Mouloud Hamrouche, whose National Liberation Front (FLN) government is fighting for survival in the run-up to elections this spring. "It is at an impasse. There's no democracy, no freedom of expression. Regimes can maintain order, yes. But what is the societal base of these regimes? Today we want to build real power on the basis of the popular will."

U.S. officials argue that some Arab regimes are moving toward democracy, and there are signs of nascent democratic sentiment across the region. Many of the Arab lawyers, professors, journalists and feminists who once looked to leftist ideologies have gravitated to a creed of human rights as the best way to bring democracy, development and social justice to the region. . . .

Reformers in the Mideast argue that the existing Arab state system is bankrupt. The Algerian desperate for foreign currency to buy medicine for his sick daughter and the Egyptian villager leaving his family for years to work in Iraq or Saudi Arabia both are proof that Arab authoritarian regimes outside the oil-rich Persian Gulf don't work much better than the totalitarian ones that have been overthrown in Eastern Europe.

Until the early 1980s, says Mideast expert Yahya Sadowski of Washington's Brookings Institution, in a booming petrodollar economy poor Arab governments "were able to buy a measure of popularity among their citizens by offering consumer subsidies, public employment programs and lucrative state contracts." But during the last decade, he argues, a combination of growing populations, falling oil prices, unwise economic policies and official corruption have been draining even some wealthy gulf states and fueling popular unrest.

The Fundamentalists

While human-rights activists and other crusaders look to Western liberalism for answers to the Arab world's problems, many fundamentalists argue that Western values are threatening the Islamic community, or *Umma*. "When the colonialists went, they left their agents behind," says a young Algerian doctor. "Their job was to make sure the politics and culture of colonialism continued."

The Islamic fervor rising in the Arab world, unlike Iran's 1979 Shiite revolution, is within the rival Sunni branch of Islam and based on the writings of Egypt's Sheik Hassan al-Banna, who in 1928 founded the Muslim Brotherhood.

Today Islamic groups are the best organized nongovernmental political movement in the Arab world and the loudest voice calling for free elections. They are in a strong position now to exploit economic unrest and anti-Western sentiments fueled by a war in the gulf. "Every Iraqi our troops kill will provide fresh ammunition for the Islamist campaign to expunge Western influence in the region," argues Yahya Sadowski.

While each group has developed locally, they are in frequent contact with each other and with their supporters in Europe and the United States. Sermons by charismatic sheiks recorded on tape cassettes circulate throughout the region. Unlike other political parties, the Islamic fundamentalists work at the grass roots. During a strike in Algeria, the fundamentalists picked up the garbage. In Egypt they run low-cost medical clinics and provide tutors to students.

Although the fundamentalists use Western technology to spread their message, their views of democracy, human rights and civil liberties often differ sharply from those in the West. Many Islamic fundamentalists point out that the word "democracy" is a Western one of Greek origin. They prefer the Arabic word *shura*, a somewhat vague term meaning consultation. "When you have democracy, it runs beautifully in England, but this same democracy looks down on the other nations it colonizes," says Leith Shbeilat, a member of the Jordanian parliament. In the Arab world, he argues, democracy should "serve our Islamic values."

A Democratic Dilemma

A new wave of Islamic activism surging through the Middle East . . . is forcing moderate governments to confront an essential dilemma of the new Arab democracy: How do you keep the most popular party from winning?. . .

Political pluralism in the Middle East increasingly is coming to mean a voice for anti-Western Islamic fundamentalists, groups that often seek through strict religious practices to limit the very democratic freedoms that have allowed their rise to power.

Kim Murphy, *Los Angeles Times*, July 7, 1991.

Western culture stresses individual rights, but Islam emphasizes the *Umma*, the Islamic community. "The family and not the individual is the primary unit of society," says Seif al-Banna, son of Hassan al-Banna, founder of the Muslim Brotherhood. "To guard over the family is society's most important obligation."

The Woman's Role

What is considered discrimination in the West is doctrine in the Islamic fundamentalist's world. Muslim women inherit half the amount men do, Islamic fundamentalists say, because men have the primary obligation to support the family. The testimony of a woman is worth half that of a man, says Seif al-Banna in Egypt, because women "are made of weaker material and can be influenced more easily." In Algeria's municipal elections in

June 1990, women who supported the FIS gave a proxy ballot to their husbands or male relatives, since they felt it was not a woman's role to vote. "I don't prohibit alcohol," says Sheik Abassi Madani, one of the leaders of Algeria's Islamic Salvation Front (FIS). "It's God who forbids it, not me."

Islamic fundamentalists oppose the separation of church and state: *Sharia*, or Islamic law, is the essence of the governments they want to establish. "We don't need to be secular because we don't have many religions, like France or England," says Abassi Madani.

In the eastern Middle East, where there are sizable Christian minorities, Islamic fundamentalists argue that these communities have coexisted peacefully for thousands of years and can do so in an Islamic state. They do insist, however, that Christians will have to conform in public places to Islamic values. "Doesn't the majority make the laws everywhere in the world?" asks Ma'amoun Odeibi, a Muslim Brother and former member of parliament in Egypt who refuses to speak to unveiled women.

The platform of Algeria's FIS, one of the few explicit Islamic political programs, says the group aims "to protect the community against all cultural invasions and the schemings of unfavorable civilizations." Control of information is an important tool in "the struggle that is unfolding on a planetary level," and an Islamic press "will permit us to face the detractors of our religion and the schemers who try to mislead and intoxicate public opinion and set it against Islam." The FIS also encourages the formation of a military industry and military research "capable of taking up the civilizational challenge that awaits us." The party plainly has won converts: It got 55 percent of the votes in municipal elections in 1990.

Strange Bedfellows

In some countries, Islamic fundamentalists and human-rights activists are uneasily allied against authoritarian regimes that meet neither the fundamentalists' tests of Islamic purity nor the liberals' standards of democratic behavior. The new Arab human-rights groups defend imprisoned fundamentalists, but the fundamentalists often reject their allies' definition of human rights because the United Nations' Universal Declaration of Human Rights, on which it is based, is not always in accordance with Islamic law.

Some Muslim Brothers in Egypt and Sudan have refused to collaborate with Amnesty because it opposes corporal punishment and the death penalty. Other fundamentalists oppose human-rights groups that advocate freedom of religion or the right of Muslim women to marry non-Muslim men.

The fundamentalists' hostility to the West is not born of igno-

171

rance: Jordanian parliamentarian Leith Shbeilat has a master's degree in civil engineering from George Washington University. Abdel Latif Arabiyat, a Muslim Brother and the newly elected speaker of the Jordanian Parliament, has a Ph.D. in education from Texas A&M University. Sheik Abassi Madani of Algeria's FIS studied English literature for three years in London. Rachid al Gannouchi, head of the Nahda movement in Tunisia, was a Ph.D. candidate at the Sorbonne in Paris.

Many fundamentalists were impressed by Western scientific and economic prowess but repelled by aspects of Western culture—pornography, alcoholism and drug abuse, materialism and old age homes. "There's a lack of compassion in the West," says Jbali. "In our poor society, we have that."

Skepticism About Democracy

But even many Arabs who do not share the fundamentalists' hostility to the West are skeptical that democracy is the answer to their problems. Mindful of their countries' turbulent histories, middle-class Cairene grocers in their dark, narrow shops selling dusty canned goods, prosperous Tunisian pharmacists and the haberdashers of Damascus all fear that giving real power to the people might endanger stability and even bring Islamic fundamentalist governments to power. "There are a sizable number of middle-class people in the Arab world," says Mustapha Kamel Said, a political science professor at Cairo University, "who feel that democracy doesn't promise them anything."

Such frustrations notwithstanding, many Arab intellectuals and professionals now feel that fighting for human rights is a necessary first step on the long road to democracy, an idea they believe now has a chance of winning widespread public support. A new order in the Arab world is beginning to take shape, but it remains to be seen whether God's government or democratic pluralism will rule it.

> *"Islamic groups may be the most democratic, sincere, and popularly supported."*

Islam Does Not Threaten Democracy in the Middle East

Sonia Shah

Many Americans stereotype Islamic groups and activists in the Middle East, Sonia Shah states in the following viewpoint. She argues that Islamic activists are not violent religious fanatics automatically opposed to democracy, but instead have been at the forefront of the movement toward democratization in the Middle East. Shah is managing editor of *Nuclear Times*, a quarterly publication that covers war and peace issues.

As you read, consider the following questions:

1. How does Shah describe the government of Iran?
2. What are the main differences between Islamic and secular political groups in the Middle East, according to the author?
3. How does Islam impact upon Middle East politics, according to Shah?

Excerpted from "Allahu Akbar!" by Sonia Shah, *Nuclear Times*, Summer 1991. Reprinted with permission.

A high school teacher in Riverdale, New York, reportedly asked her tenth-grade students to write down what entered their minds when they thought of Islam. "Warmongers," "religious fanatics," "intolerant," "militaristic," and "stubborn and ignorant," they wrote.

These youth represent the opinion of the American public. Ever since the Iranian revolution in 1979, most modern-day Westerners have dismissed Islam as violent religious fanaticism. Most probably, there are reasons to be wary of Islamicism, reasons that have been expounded on in countless books and articles, such as its potential for intolerance, militance, and patriarchy.

False Fears

Although some of these fears may be legitimate, many of them are the result of xenophobia and ignorance. For example, the press and Western policy makers portray Iran—the paradigm of the West's concept of backward "Islamic fundamentalism"—as rigid, repressive, and authoritarian. The Iranian government operates within a religious framework, but insofar as people accept Islam, says Eric Hoogland, an editor of *Middle East Report*, "Iran is more democratic than authoritarian." What we don't hear about is Iran's parliament, where serious debates on government policy are held, its relatively free elections, and free press that is frequently critical of public policy, Hoogland says. The news media and politicians are not entirely to blame. Most of us don't ask.

In recent years, Islamic activists have gained governmental power in many more Muslim countries, such as Algeria, Jordan, Pakistan, and Tunisia, and are gathering strength in other countries in opposition to their government. By dismissing Islam as a nation of fanatics, we have missed Islamic activists' calls for social justice and liberalization. In fact, "in recent years, Islamic movements have been at the forefront in the movement toward democratization," says John L. Esposito, director of the center of international studies at the College of the Holy Cross in Worcester, Massachusetts. "People come to the topic of Islamic politics in terms of radicalism and terrorism. But that outlook misses the significant thrust of the next few years" of politics in the Muslim world, he says. The instability and humiliation of the gulf war will probably lead to heightened activism—Islamic, anti-imperialist, pan-Arabist, and *democratic* activism, he says.

Repressive regimes squash these opposition groups, forcing them underground, and in many cases, to arms. What has been happening in recent years is that the governmental repression has fostered a growing demand for democratic pluralism among Islamic opposition groups and their supporters. "The regimes they are confronting are highly nondemocratic," says Hoogland.

174

"These opposition parties are diverse, but the one thing they have in common is that they all advocate a pluralistic society," he says, "because that is the only way they could hope to operate in authoritarian societies."

U.S. Religious Groups

Certainly, to Americans, it should be believable that repressed religious groups may be sincere about pluralism. The Puritans figure prominently in our own democratic heritage. Modernization does not necessarily lead to radical secularization. The Roman Catholic Church, for example, played an important role in the revolutions of 1989 in Eastern and Central Europe. Latin American politics hinge on issues of religion. Religious values dominate political forces in South Asia.

Some would argue that Islam now has the most powerful political impact of any religion in the world. Muslim scholars are developing Koranic theories of religious tolerance and of what we would call civil society.

Islam and Democracy

What the peoples of the Middle East are groping for is a sociopolitical-intellectual culture of their own, drawn from Islam and parts of other complete traditions and systems but uniquely theirs nevertheless.

The argument that Islam is not Islam unless it conforms to what it was at some particular time and in some particular place should be seriously challenged, since it is demonstrably false. Equally fallacious is the notion that liberal democracy and nationalism can only function in the West. They can operate and have operated elsewhere. They are not the exclusive property of special people. The only requirement is that the necessary institutional structures be in place, and even when they are, they have to be constantly reviewed and reinforced. There is consequently no reason to believe that a satisfactory synthesis cannot be achieved in the Middle East.

Alan R. Taylor, *The Islamic Question in Middle East Politics*, 1988.

The shape of postwar Middle East will be at least outlined by the movements in Iraq and Kuwait, including the Islamic movements agitating for democratic reform. The American public, including those concerned with peace in the Middle East, cannot continue to view Islam as monolithically fanatical and antithetical to democratic pluralism. We run the risk of neglecting to see the possibility that Islamic groups may be the most democratic, sincere, and popularly supported. Our government will be able to rationalize support for authoritarianism rather than liberalization, in the name of anti-fanaticism—just as it was able in the name of anticommunism. Militant Islamic groups are potent forces, but both the U.S. government and the Middle Eastern people stand to lose if, in our government's inevitable meddling, we fail to push for the support of Islamic liberalization movements because of our fear of "Islamic fundamentalism."

Islam vs. Secularism

What delineates Islamic groups from secular political groups mainly is their language, symbolism, and purported authority, not necessarily their political platforms.

While secular activists speak of the working class, the exploited, the proletariat, and the oppressors, Islamic activists speak of the poor, wretched, weak on earth, and corrupt on earth. Secular groups seek legitimacy through the authority of independent intellectual thought; Islamic groups seek legitimacy through the authority of the Koran and other religious teachings.

In terms of platform, secular movements encompass much diversity, and similarly, so do religious movements. Although there are many political theories and only one Islam, Islam is a vast and complex body of thought, open to countless interpretations. Some groups claim their program is directly derived from the *shari'a* (the Koran and other religious teachings); others believe their program is reflective of the essence of the *shari'a* or inspired by the *shari'a*.

In many cases, secular and Islamic activists advocate similar platforms. Some are radical, others moderate. Even the most militant, such as members of the Egyptian Military Academy, who were responsible for the murder of a former minister and profess Islamic teachings as the first and last authority, advocate equal education for women, ownership of private property, free enterprise, democratic elections, and a classless society, according to the *Middle East Report*. Members of the Muslim Brotherhood, a large, moderate Islamic political organization, "talk about moral economy and equity," like communist leaders do, says James Gelvin, a lecturer at Boston College. "The symbols are different but the content is very similar," he says.

In many predominantly Muslim countries, Islamic groups are, arguably, more appealing than secular ones. Embracing Islam, particularly in the post-colonialist era, signifies pride and self-esteem, since Islam characterizes a part of Middle Eastern identity distinct from the influence of Western imperialists who had colonized much of the region. In the post-colonial era, secular politics have failed to resolve what Muslims see as the most pressing and recurrent economic and social problems of the region, such as the foreign encroachment embodied in Israel, the displacement of the Palestinian people, and the unequal distribution of sudden oil wealth.

The staleness of secular leftist movements in the region further bolsters the potential dynamism of Islamic movements. Marxist revolutionaries and secular movements in general have always suffered a dubious legitimacy, leaving them vulnerable to sudden withdrawals of popular support. Gamal Abdul Nasser's secular regime in Egypt from 1954 to 1970, for instance, although widely supported and embraced for a time, was denounced after his defeat in the 1967 war against Israel, sparking a wave of Islamic political activity. Now, the Soviet Union is busy with domestic problems and Third World governments have little to gain from playing the Soviet Union off the United States. Consequently, Marxist movements stand even less chance of gaining momentum.

Islam in the Mainstream

The growing popularity and political activism of Islamic movements have altered the balance of power in several countries, particularly in Egypt, North Africa and Jordan. By and large, however, these groups have pressed their demands through conventional channels of the party system, electoral competition and parliamentary debate. Assuming more prominent roles as part of the loyal opposition, they have shown considerable skill and flexibility in forging alliances with longtime rivals who share a common commitment to human rights and political reform. Even where their long-term objectives include controversial visions of an Islamic state, they have focused on more modest and incremental goals that place them squarely in the political mainstream.

Robert Bianchi, *American-Arab Affairs*, Spring 1991.

Ultimately, nonreligiously aligned politics seem foreign in many Muslim countries, and suspiciously Western. Islam—its concepts, images, symbols, and language—is the medium of political expression in predominantly Muslim countries. This is not a new development. "There always were strong Islamic images and symbols in Middle Eastern society, since ages ago," says Gelvin, such as the concepts of religious community, social justice, equity, and just war, which are largely derived from Islamic teachings. "They have been modified and changed over time, so they have become part of people's value systems and symbols, much like Judeo-Christian images have become part of American life," he says. Many political movements act within the broad framework of Islam, explains Bruce B. Lawrence of Duke University, because "it is the only means by which dissidents of any sort can express themselves in most Muslim countries."

While America saw the Middle East only in terms of its oil market, "Islamic fundamentalism," and the spread of Soviet-style communism, Islamic movements slowly came into more power, says Rami G. Khouri, former editor of the *Jordan Times*. Within the past three years, Islamic movements have had significant impact in many parts of the world.

• In Algeria, the Islamic Salvation Front swept the municipal elections throughout the country. National elections have been postponed, but many experts gamble that Islamic candidates will win when the elections are held.

• In Jordan, Islamic candidates won 38 out of 80 parliamentary seats, as well as five cabinet posts and speaker of the house.

• In Tunisia, Islamic groups comprise the leading opposition to the government.

• In Pakistan, the Islamic Democratic Alliance defeated Prime Minister Benazhir Bhutto.

Before and during the gulf war, in countries like Egypt, Syria, and Iraq, repressive political and military machinery crushed the activities of these Islamic movements, yet they have rebounded, remaining strong and active opposition whether underground or in exile. Since the war, and the demolition of Iraq and Kuwait, oppositionists in those countries have risen up, outraged. . . .

This (Iraqi) opposition movement is not a "monolithically united community," says Esposito. The commonly used delineation between Shi'ite Muslims in the south and Kurdish nationalists in the north shows little more than ethnicity, he says. The recently united opposition movement is diverse politically, and faces not only the inevitable tensions between religious and secular groups, but tensions between the different religious groups. Most experts dismiss the simplistic fear of an Iranian-style revolution, but worry about whether the alliance will withstand the challenge of democratic pluralism if and when they fall their common enemy. This opposition alliance comprises groups not only willing but accustomed to using force as a means to power. Another area of concern is that there are few if any democratic structures in Iraq or Kuwait. And, although most of the allied groups call for democracy, some Western experts wonder to what extent they are using liberalization as a means to power, rather than an end.

Islamic Democracy

Many of these groups, both Islamic and secular, are calling for democracy, however, and since Islamicism may be most successful on a popular level and would not preclude liberalization, spaces for democratic change do exist. Westerners must be sensitive and attentive to the growth and powers of these groups, even if they are Islamic; or perhaps *especially* if they are Islamic.

"The misery and desperation that have marked the history of Palestine . . . are the direct result of the biblical and religious character of the land."

Judeo-Christian Beliefs Make Peace Impossible

Hassan S. Haddad

Israel is a sacred and holy land to many Jews and Christians. In the following viewpoint, Hassan S. Haddad argues that these religious beliefs prevent diplomatic or political settlements in the Middle East. The belief that the land of Israel belongs especially and exclusively to the Jews, Haddad asserts, creates and maintains conflict between Israelis and Palestinians, who also claim the land. Haddad concludes that Judeo-Christian beliefs concerning Israel must be rethought. Haddad is a professor of history at Saint Xavier College in Chicago.

As you read, consider the following questions:

1. What is the religious basis for the Israeli refusal to give up the West Bank and Golan Heights, according to Haddad?
2. Why does the author refuse to call Israel/Palestine a holy land?
3. What solutions to Middle East conflict does Haddad propose?

Excerpted from "The Scandal of the Holy Land" by Hassan S. Haddad, *Arab-American Affairs*, Spring 1991. Reprinted with permission.

The religious dimensions of the Palestinian problem have complicated the continuous efforts towards a solution. The holiness of the land seems to have been its main calamity. Speaking as a student of history, I am appalled by the torrent of blood spilled for the sake of a small piece of land just because it is called holy, promised, Yahweh's own, or the third holiest shrine. I am also concerned about the promise of more blood to be shed, more homes to be demolished, more injustice done, and the prospect of the specter of Armageddon finally emerging from the biblical nightmare to become a historical reality.

The events in Jerusalem, the locus of the problem of Holy Geography, point to the urgency and magnitude of the question. No matter how much some Jews, Israelis, Christians, and Palestinians try to think of the conflict in secular political terms, events such as the massacre on the Haram al-Sharif, or Temple Mount, keep reminding us that the religious and biblical dimensions of the conflict remain predominant. In fact, I am more and more convinced that the misery and desperation that have marked the history of Palestine since the burning bush appeared on Mt. Sinai, up to and including the massacre on that sacred hill in Jerusalem, are the direct result of the biblical and religious character of the land.

The Curse of Holiness

From the biblical sanctification of the Promised Land, the consecration of Jerusalem as the holy abode of Yahweh to the present Zionist movement, the holiness of that particular place has been its curse. It will remain so as long as secular things are called sacred and as long as the sacred justifies the profanity of particularism. In fact the problem of Palestine is becoming more complex and dangerous because it is regarded as holy not only by one group but by three. Now that Christians and Muslims subscribe to the sacredness of Jerusalem and Palestine, the chances for continued strife have tripled, and the chance for a peaceful solution has all but vanished. In Jerusalem, there is a sacred rock for Muslims, a holy tomb for Christians and an ancient wall for Jews. They are all sacred. Wars have been fought around them and over them. More wars are foreseen for the future. Two groups identify one hill as the most sacred place on earth and are willing to fight and die for it. This means that Jerusalem, and the holiest spots in that holiest of cities, are candidates for eternal strife, atrocious behavior, and sacrificial human victims.

Jerusalem is the prime candidate for the fuse that will ignite the fury of an extensive war in the future. Is it worth it?

The idolatry of the Land, like the idolatry of the Chosen Tribe and the idolatry of the Strict Text have, in the past, been respon-

O, Israel, thou bleeding piece of Earth. . .

sible for many of man's wars and massacres. They will remain with us as long as we remain faithful to them. I am not naive enough to think that the secularization of the Palestine problem will purge it completely from violence and injustice. But I submit to you that the holiness of a place narrows the possibilities of pluralistic sharing. I also know, from the study of history, that a war over a secular problem is not as hot and ugly as a religious war which uses sacralized weapons for a holy cause. . . .

The modern conquests of Zionism have already claimed many victims and committed many crimes. But what is awaited may be more than the civilized world has bargained for and probably more than civilization could withstand.

The Land of Promise is one of the most prominent doctrines of the Old Testament. It is the cornerstone of the Zionist movement. The territorial element of Zionism is the least ambiguous of all the issues that confront Jewish nationalism. While the question of peoplehood (who is a Jew?) may be open to complex biblical interpretations, and the problem of dealing with the indigenous population is subject to some moral considerations from certain groups, the right to the land is so basic that it is hardly contested.

Although there are different delineations of the boundaries of the Promised Land in the Bible, the locus of *Eretz Yisrael* is clear and constant. Whether it is defined as "from Dan to Beersheba" and "from the desert to the sea" or, more often, from the Nile to the Euphrates, Jerusalem is the center around which these circles of varying size are drawn.

Territoriality in the Bible is raised beyond political, economic, and strategic considerations. It is made a theological imperative. Under the influence of the Bible, Jerusalem has acquired an importance far beyond its reality. "God will not come to the heavenly Jerusalem," goes a rabbinical saying, "till Israel has come to the earthly Jerusalem.". . .

Christian Views

This rabbinical view is parallelled by one held by Christian fundamentalists. Both groups hold that the possession of the land by the Jews is a theological mandate. Jews have to come to the earthly Jerusalem, say the fundamentalist preachers, as a condition for the establishment of the Kingdom of God. A temporal act in a physical location is made to be the key to God's Kingdom.

The Gift of Land becomes the cornerstone of Zionist expectations and demands of the Christian Churches: to recognize that Palestine belongs to the Jews by divine title found in the Bible. Rabbi Wolfe Kelman, chief executive officer of the International Association of Conservative Rabbis, commenting on a proposed Vatican document concerning Judaism, welcomed in particular the document's "recognition of the reality, of the State of Israel," its assertion that Jewish fidelity to the Old Covenant between God and the people Israel is "linked to the gift of land, which, in the Jewish soul, has endured as the object of aspiration that Christians should strive to understand and respect."

In view of this Jewish attitude toward the land of Palestine, settlement in it becomes an act of piety, of righteousness, of religious fulfillment, placed above legal and humanistic considerations. . . .

Having studied the dimensions of the territorial imperative in the Bible, and having surmised that the policies of Israel, especially its territorial policies, conform to the biblical record, I wrote in 1973 the following:

> It is against this biblical background that one can see why Israel is quite categorical about not withdrawing from Jerusalem, and highly intransigent on the West Bank and the Golan Heights (they both fall within the biblical boundaries of the Promised Land). Although [Israel] may reluctantly pull out partially or even totally if forced from Sinai, which is not clearly included in the biblical promise. Certainly the great resistance of the Israeli government to pressure, even after the October War and disengagement with Egypt and Syria, to pull out of occupied Arab lands cannot be explained in terms of strategic considerations and security alone. . . .

All people of goodwill and perception should ask themselves if the belief in the eternal value of the Sinaitic covenant is worth all the suffering and the injustice that it has caused both Jews and non-Jews. The fear of denying the eternal value of the covenant should be allayed by recourse to human compassion, fairness and decency. Christianity has already rejected some very fundamental rules and conditions of that God-given covenant. Important elements such as circumcision, the seal of the relationship between Yahweh and his people; the commandments against making graven images and keeping the Sabbath; basic tenets of the Torah and the covenant, have been discarded easily by Christians and by many Jews as well. . . .

Theological Beliefs

The problem with the doctrine of land is not so much in the collective desire of the Jews of the world to have a land base for their nationalism (although it can be argued that this emphasis on Jewish nationalism and ingathering in the Holy Land is a historical archaism that can be detrimental to Jewish life). The problem lies in the belief among Jews and among many more Christians, that the possession of the land, in this case, is a theological, not a historical category. It is the insistence on describing the land as a specific piece of holy real estate, eternally consecrated and promised to a certain people, also consecrated and elected. This question becomes, in the modern historical context, and from a common-sense point of view, a discriminatory, racist endeavor condoned and encouraged by a biblical religious establishment. The insistence on covenant is a commitment to ethnic racism. In addition, the concentration on the specific role of the land (the gift, the promise) strengthens further the racist tendencies and adds another dimension to ethnic racism, that of geographic racism. This is a form of discrimination no less reprehensible because it promotes the holy war, justifies conquest, and sanctions injustice and brutality. . . .

I have become so convinced of the subliminal effect of the Bible on the minds of most Christians and Jews that I have developed a strong objection to calling Palestine a holy land. I see in this biblical designation one of the causes for the misery of that land all through its history, a misery that might continue if the world fails to desacralize the land and the conflict that plagues it. Calling Palestine a holy land and Jerusalem a holy city is an acquiescence in the scandal of particularism which is the essence of the biblical covenant. Those who claim to inherit the covenant (Jews, Christians, and Muslims) have always claimed control by divine revelation and direction, from the time of the ancient Hebrews to the Christian Crusaders, to the modern Zionists. Ironically, because Jerusalem has been regarded as a distinctly holy city it has never been a city of peace. . . .

The Right to Conquer

The right to conquer, to acquire land by force, to exercise one's lust for possession, has always been justified by religion, by reference to a higher authority in heaven, and by mystification of the goals. The overwhelming biblical concern with the conquest of the land of Canaan, holding it, returning to it, colonizing it, has been thus attributed to a divine intervention. The conquest of Canaan and the recommended massacre of the indigenous population is justified as a means to a higher end, a way to prevent the pollution of the holy land by "inferior races."

The American conquest of the West and the Southwest was similarly transformed into a divinely preordained matter, Manifest Destiny. To the early settlers, armed with biblical texts asserting the promise of land, and calling themselves the new Israel, the killing of the native Americans was seen as parallel to the divine order to kill the Canaanites.

Yet the particularism of Manifest Destiny has almost disappeared because it had no sacred writ to support it. But the subjugation of Palestine and the Palestinians to conquest, deportation, disenfranchisement, and abuse remains, up to the present, anchored firmly to biblical religion.

In spite of the pronouncement by Jesus, "My Kingdom is not of this world," the Church and its theologians still place emphasis on the kingdom of David and Solomon as expressions of the divine will. They link that ancient, highly legendary state, to present and future political entities. The biblical value of Israel, the temporal and the spiritual, (for there is hardly any distinction between them in most Old Testament writing), remains the monkey on the back of Christianity and Judaism. Of all the implications of this attachment to the "Holy State in a Holy Land" the geographical dimension is the most perplexing to a humanistic perspective of history.

I propose that it is high time that a new theology of liberation be adopted: liberation of Christian and Jewish ethics and consciousness from the atavistic dictates of the holiness of a special piece of land and the chosenness of a small segment of humanity. With the world becoming a global village, these Old Testament doctrines should be relegated to the basement of religious history. They are as anachronistic as flat-earth doctrines. . . .

Religious Rivalries

Why is it that the three monotheistic traditions—Judaism, Christianity, and Islam—seem to have such a poor track record in promoting moral good in the region of their birth?

All three faiths, it seems to me, harbor a basic problem of identification of divine exclusivity with ethnic-religious exclusivity. Each sees the oneness of God standing in a special relation to a favored people or religious community, whether on an ethnic basis, as in Judaism, or a multiethnic basis in the case of Christianity and Islam. . . .

These rivalries are exacerbated precisely in the territory of the births of these three religions, for this territory is also filled with sacred sites that incarnate these rival claims. The Old City of Jerusalem has, at its center, a rocky outcropping which is both the third holiest site for Islam, the place where Mohammed went on his mystic night journey, and also the Temple Mount for Judaism, where Orthodox Jews and many Western Christians believe that the Jewish temple must be rebuilt in order to usher in the reign of God. Such rival interpretations of the same rocks turn places of holiness into sites of massacre.

Rosemary Radford Ruether, *Sojourners*, June 1991.

The solution to the problem cannot be found in the Bible, which created the problem in the first place and which keeps promoting it among Jews and Christians. Even Muslims have been slightly touched by it, for the Quran recognized the promise to Israel.

This is a human problem and it calls for human solutions. Yahweh and the Bible can only complicate matters here. The religious nature of the problem, the holiness that the three so-called Abrahamic faiths attach to the land, has intensified the conflict beyond any reasonable solution.

Time and effort, and rivers of ink, have been lost on apologetics, on hermeneutics, on putting new wine in old wineskins. The Christian world, as well as the Jews and the Muslims, who in one way or another have inherited this antiquated biblical theory of "gift" and "promise" need a new theology of liberation. It is a theology of liberation from the fossilized doctrine, from

185

the letter that kills.

Dr. Marc Ellis declared that "an essential task of Jewish theology is to deabsolutize the state of Israel." This is a bold statement with which I agree. However, I must admit that it leaves something out and fails to satisfy my maximalist views on the subject. I believe that the deabsolutization of the state of Israel is to be preceded by the deabsolutization of the biblical text which contains the prototype of that state. Christian and Jewish theologians fail in their endeavor to create a liberation theology if their act of liberation does not go all the way to the bottom of the biblical well of particularism and discrimination. In this case the words "liberation" and "theology" seem to me to be contradictory.

The liberal theologians, both Jewish and Christian, preach that the Palestinians have the same right to national self-determination that the Jews have. They recommend negotiation between the two parties. This statement remains hanging in mid-air. It is basically a resolution that political scientists and politicians devise. What should set theologians apart from politicians is the perception of ultimate justice, not just accommodation.

Political accommodations may arrest the strife for a while. But philosophers, theologians, and thinkers deal with what ought to be, not only with what is possible. There is no moral justification for forcing a people to submit, to move out, and to be ruled by occupation and suppression. There is no reason why a Palestinian should be forced to evacuate his home and birthplace to accommodate another, even if that other has been mistreated, just as there was no justification for forcing the Jews out of Germany and Eastern Europe.

God's Children Are Equal

The Holocaust and the territorial theology of Israel should not be allowed to be translated into a license for land robbery. The solution of the two states leaves Holocaust theology and territorial theology almost intact. If we agree that God's children are all equal in His sight, then why sanction the division of the land between two peoples according to race or religion. Politicians do that, but theologians should not.

We have to face this crisis with boldness and new vision: The Old Testament's covenant of people and land has become obsolete—historically, morally and theologically—as obsolete as the rites of animal sacrifice. It is an affliction to our conscience, a burden on our humanity.

"If the Palestinians had the power to do so, they would drive the Israelis out to the sea."

Islamic Beliefs Make Peace Impossible

Richard Rubenstein, interviewed by *The World & I*

Richard Rubenstein is a rabbi and Robert O. Lawton Distinguished Professor of Religion at Florida State University at Tallahassee. In the following viewpoint, taken from an interview in the magazine *The World & I*, he states that the Islamic world will never accept the presence of Israel. He writes that this refusal makes peace between Israel, Palestinians, and the Arab states impossible, and concludes that religious conflict between Islam, Judaism, and Christianity will prevent any effective political or diplomatic settlement in the Middle East.

As you read, consider the following questions:

1. Why have the last two centuries disturbed the Islamic world, according to Rubenstein?
2. Why is oil important to Islam, according to the author?
3. Why does Rubenstein have very little hope for the future of the Middle East?

W& *I:* Could you speak on the Jewish-Islamic issue from the point of view of a Jewish scholar?

RUBENSTEIN: I don't think there is a specific Jewish-Islamic issue. First, I believe that Islam regards itself as the original true religion, whose fundamental meaning was revealed by the Prophet Mohammad, and that Islam regards both Judaism and Christianity as distorted views of the original true religion, so that inevitably Islam has an interpretation of both Judaism and Christianity that neither can accept. Second, I believe that in the history of Christendom there have been three possible and two actual challenges to Christendom. One was Judaism. The second was Islam, and the third was atheistic communism. Judaism was not a real challenge to Christendom for the simple reason that the Jews simply were not that culturally influential or numerous for Judaism to be a challenge after Christianity became the religion of the Roman world.

Islam, on the other hand, was the most powerful of all challenges to Christendom. In 711, Islamic forces occupied almost the entire Iberian peninsula. At one time or another, large parts of Christian Europe were occupied by Islamic forces, including Bulgaria, Romania, the Balkans, southern Italy, and large parts of southern Russia, namely, the Ukraine. Historically, going almost right back to the beginning, there has been this challenge to Christendom which Islam constituted.

Culture Shocks

Now, in the last two centuries, Islam has had a series of cultural shocks. For one thing, Islam was unable to do what the Japanese have done, namely, to meet the challenge of Western modernization. When Islam first entered Europe in the eighth century, it was the superior culture. It had a level of sophistication and culture that was far higher than that of northern Europe. For several centuries, the victories of Islam were such that the victories themselves were taken as signs of the superiority and the truth of the Islamic faith. Therefore, the shock was all the greater when, starting in the eighteenth century, European countries turned out to be quite different. The way the European countries turned out to be quite different was that they had effectively modernized. They had effectively gone through the Renaissance and the Reformation and the Enlightenment, and they had the capacity to develop skills and to advance learning in a way that left the Islamic world behind, at least in the area of power.

What the Islamic world did have, what they have to this day, is the Shari'a, that is, the Islamic way of life as found in the laws that derive from the Koran. To this day, undoubtedly, the Islamic world looks down on the world that came from the

European Enlightenment as a world that lacks real morals and lacks real discipline of the kind that a traditional Muslim would have.

Arab Islam

Arab Islam is the purest form of Islam, uncontaminated or diluted by other influences that have shaped the Islamic religion in, say, Indonesia or Nigeria. Arab Islam, therefore, retains much of the original Islamic passion—to be, as of divine right, the world's supreme religion and to achieve this status by force, if necessary. Religious toleration may or may not be practiced, depending on circumstances, but the idea of religious pluralism is as much anathema to Arab Islam as it was to the Roman Catholic Church of the 11th century. The church has changed. Arab Islam has not. The church has experienced reforms and painful Reformations. Islam has not.

That, indeed, is the problem. All efforts at modernization in the Middle East ultimately are frustrated by a combination of Arab romanticism and Islamic rigidity. The romanticism leads to "heroic" and futile rebellions against the five centuries of Western intellectual, political and military domination.

Irving Kristol, *The Wall Street Journal*, February 22, 1991.

W & I: In the Middle Ages the Islamic world was ahead scientifically and culturally, but then they fell behind. Why?

RUBENSTEIN: The Islamic world fell behind scientifically and culturally because they were so convinced of the superiority of their way that they saw no reason to adapt to modernization, whereas the European Christian nations were able to adapt to modernization in ways that Islam was not.

For two centuries, the Islamic world experienced a kind of inner dislocation because they were supposed to be the true religion and the superior civilization, yet here they saw the infidels as victorious all over. In Asia, the British took over the Islamic domination of the Indian subcontinent. The Dutch took over Indonesia. The British took over Egypt; the French took over Syria. This was not the world that Islam had been used to. Then Islam tried to overcome this world, the new situation in which they found themselves being at least inferior in power to Europe. They tried secularization, modernization, and Westernization. Unlike the Japanese, who also tried modernization and Westernization but were able to do this in a way that allowed them to preserve their cultural integrity, the Islamic world was unable to create this same kind of a synthesis. It is not enough to modernize. If you ruin your culture while modernizing, then

189

modernization has done you no good whatsoever.

I think one of the worst shocks to the Islamic world came in 1967 when the el Kuds, which is what they call Jerusalem, fell to the Israelis. But remember how that '67 war started: The Egyptians made it perfectly clear that they were going to block-ade the Israelis and the UN troops summarily got out of the way. The Israelis pleaded with the Jordanians to stay out of the war, in which case there wouldn't have been any problem with the West Bank. When the Jordanians came into the war, the Israelis, in one fell swoop, in order to defend themselves, took the whole territory of Palestine for the first time in almost two thousand years. Jerusalem, the third most holy city in the Islamic world, fell to the Jews. Of course, Jerusalem is the holy city of the Jews.

Defeated By the Jews

This made matters even worse. Not only had the Islamic world experienced defeats at the hands of the Christian world, whose power was obvious, but this small group of Jews also in-flicted military defeat on them, and for the very same reason, which is that the Jews had learned from the Christians how to adapt to modernization in a way that the Islamic world has not. Basically, had the Islamic world adapted to modernization, then there is no way that the Jews could have won those wars.

W & I: Islamic scholars and religious leaders claim that there is no impediment in Islam to rapprochement between Islam and Judaism, that this is purely a political problem.

RUBENSTEIN: It is not true that, as Islamic leaders and schol-ars claim, there is no religious impediment or no religious ten-sion between Islam and Judaism, that this is purely a political problem. I respect Islam as a culture highly, but there is a real religious difference between both Judaism and Christianity and Islam. That is, Islam claims that it alone is the original true reli-gion of God, and both Judaism and Christianity are distortions. Islam divides the world into the Dar al-Islam and the Dar al-Harb. That is, the Dar al-Islam is that part of the world that is in Islamic hands and is governed by traditional Islamic law. The Dar al-Harb is in the hands of infidels. From the Islamic point of view, since Islam is the true religion, its aim is to make sure that ultimately the whole world falls under the Dar al-Islam. Now, for that which has already become part of the world of the true religion, namely Islam, from their point of view, to fall back into infidel hands is a real defeat. So this conflict is not just political; it is religious as well.

Another very important point: I don't think most Americans realize just how important and how much of a religious signifi-cance the oil boom of 1973 had for the Islamic world. The oil boom of 1973 convinced the Islamic world that a tremendous power reversal was taking place. If you look at where the oil is located, the greatest amount of oil is to be found in those countries that are completely loyal to the most traditional reading of Islam, namely Libya and Saudi Arabia and also some of the emirates. So it was not hard for Islamic thinkers to see this as God's confirmation of the standing and status of Islam. They also saw a direct correlation between faithfulness and fidelity to traditional Islam and the new prosperity.

I think this was very important to them. At the same time, they saw the 1973 war between Israel, Egypt, and Syria as resulting in a victory for the Islamic world, although in reality it was a stalemate.

New Power

They then saw their former colonial masters coming to them and treating them deferentially, as people they were dependent upon for their economic wellbeing. The Saudis, for example, were able to tell the English, you can't show the film *The Death of a Princess* on your television, and the English gave way. The Saudis, the American government, the French—all of them saw this tremendous increase of Islamic wealth and they began to behave towards Islam in a way that they had never behaved before. The oil wealth gave Islam huge amounts of money, which were spent for Islamic causes, for the strengthening of Islam. At the same time, there was a disenchantment with Western ways, not only by Iran but throughout the Islamic world, a turn back to the fundamentals of Islam.

In 1973, after the oil boycott had been instituted and OPEC [Organization of Petroleum Exporting Countries] had quadrupled its prices, one of the Arab ministers said, "This is our revenge for Poitiers." Poitiers (or Tours) was the battle in 732 at which the Christian forces, under Charles Martel, finally stopped the Moslems who had come all the way into Spain and were succeeding in getting into France in the eighth century. These people have very long memories. They now see that, with the oil, they have the possibility of again becoming dominant in a way.

As far as the Jews are concerned, I am absolutely convinced that the Muslims are not going to rest content simply with a Palestinian state. That will be the prelude to the next move, which will be to make the whole area once again part of the Dar al-Islam, that is, an Islamic precinct, which it had been for centuries. That entails either expelling all the Israelis or killing them off. . . .

As far as the Arab-Israeli conflict is concerned, I personally don't think the Israelis owe the Palestinians anything. If the Palestinians had the power to do so, they would drive the Israelis out to the sea. It is that simple. And if you know that people are out to drive you into the sea and—after the Nazi

191

Holocaust—that they are in alliance with people who promised to gas Jews, then you have a situation where the Israelis look at every single Palestinian as an enemy. . . .

When people are that divided, where there is absolutely no trust between them, and where one side perceives the other side as dominating and the other side perceives the other side as, in: "They will stab us to death if they can, in any back alley, et cetera," then you have got a witches' brew.

W & I: When we speak to the two sides, each blames the other wholly for the conflict.

RUBENSTEIN: I don't blame the Arabs. If I were a Palestinian, I would see the Israelis as occupiers. I would see the Israelis as foreigners who have come back to a country that they had left centuries ago. But I am not a Palestinian. I liken this thing to the conflict of Antigone and Creon. Antigone must be loyal to the law of the family, which says she has got to bury her brother. Creon is the king. He has got to be loyal to the law of the polis, which says that the rebel against the polis must not have an honorable burial. So they end up—both of them having some right on their side—in a clash that neither can avoid. That is the way I see the situation.

No Solution

W & I: You used the term *witches' brew* a minute ago and now again you come back to language that suggests hopelessness.

RUBENSTEIN: I don't see any solution to this problem. I have told the Israelis that they will survive as long as they can escalate the cost of killing Jews beyond what the Arabs want to pay.

W & I: So we end there with this hopeless view?

RUBENSTEIN: That's my view. I have said for twenty years that the Israelis will survive as long as they have the weapons that make any attempt to wipe them out unacceptably costly. And basically what this means is that you have got in the Middle East now what used to exist between the United States and the Soviet Union. As long as the Israelis have credible second-strike nuclear capability, they have a chance to survive. The Israelis have got to convince the Arabs that even after they are overwhelmed, the Israelis can unleash so many nuclear bombs that it is not worth the Arabs' trying. And that's, I think, what the situation comes down to. There's simply no way to adjudicate this thing. From this point of view I would therefore not give in an inch. I have no problem coming to a conference like this and having very cordial conversations with Islamic scholars; I enjoy talking to them. The problem is that you have got to find some way that each side cannot see the situation as a zero-sum game, but right now they both see it as a zero-sum game. It may be want of imagination on my part, but I don't see any alternatives, and I have tried to explore all of the alternatives. I

am not saying that this is the way I want things to be, obviously.
I do what I can in the name of world peace. I have done credible work in this field, but I have never found a credible way of
mediating the Israeli-Arab conflict. . . .

The Islamic Threat

The most serious threat to stability in the Middle East and to the
economic future of the industrialized world is the growing influence of fundamentalist Islam—radical, revolutionary fundamentalist Islam—in Middle Eastern politics.

Farid A. Kharari, *Oil and Islam*, 1990.

W & I: You speak like an advocate for the Israeli-Jewish side.
RUBENSTEIN: I haven't closed the door. I don't advocate this
as a way of being. But I don't see any way out. There is a difference between not seeing a way out and wanting things to be the
way they are. I feel these things very strongly, not because I am
an advocate for one side, but because I have spent a good deal
of my life studying Jewish history and the place of Judaism in
the modern world. . . .

Long Memories

Right after the Six Day War, I went to this Arab hotel in
Jerusalem. We had never been to the old city because before the
Six Day War, Jews couldn't go into the old city. So we started to
walk over the old city. A young thin Palestinian, maybe about
twenty, twenty-two, comes up to me and says, "Would you like
a guide?" I thought, well, this would be a prudent thing to do,
let him tell us and show us, et cetera. And for the next two
hours, I heard the most bitter rage and resentment against Israel
I have ever heard in my life. He assumed that we were
Christian. My wife's hair was blonde, she has blue eyes, and
since we came from East Jerusalem he made that assumption.
My feeling in the matter was that it was much more important
for me to hear what he had to say rather than argue with him.
So for two hours I let him talk and it was clear that they were
going to drive them (Jews) out to the sea and they would wipe
them out one of these days—it was just a question of time.

Finally, after two hours, I paid the guide. I said, "There is one
thing I think you ought to know: We're not Christian. We're
Jewish." He said, "Oh, you're Jewish. You Jews have long memories." I said "Yes." He said, "You remember the destruction of
the Temple by the Romans." I said, "Yes, we do. And now we
have Jerusalem back again." He said, "Well, we are your
cousins. What makes you think that we have shorter memories?

We remember the Crusades." I said, "I know you have long memories. That's why there can't be peace between us."

W & I: Maybe you should learn to forget.

RUBENSTEIN: The point is that you are able to forget only if the danger isn't there: If it is a fantasy danger, then you forget. But if the danger is real, and it is, you don't forget. You don't think [Iraqi leader] Saddam Hussein isn't thinking of the Crusades now? You don't think he isn't trying to get the masses to think in terms of the Crusades? Listen to his rhetoric. Read his speeches. I have been following this thing very closely.

Well, that is probably about as bleak an analysis of the situation as you are going to get, isn't it? Remember Elie Wiesel's comment, "Hitler kept his promises to the Jews." These are people who have promised to drive the Israelis out to the sea, and then they still talk like that when they are broadcasting in Arabic. These are promises that I simply take seriously.

W & I: The Islamic religious leaders and scholars tend to say that this is a kind of popular hysteria whipped up for political reasons by unscrupulous politicians and that it is not the real voice of Islam that you are hearing.

Rooted in History

RUBENSTEIN: If you are talking about people like Sheikh Zaki Badawi, who lives in London and is a very cultivated man, I would say, undoubtedly, he is quite sincere about this. But I think you are going to find that there are a lot of Islamic scholars in places like Iraq and Iran who are quite sincere in their particular union of politics and religion, that this is not just manipulation. It is too deeply rooted in history, in their history. They did not conquer as far as they did simply for the sake of material advantage. They conquered on an idea that they have the true faith, that they were giving people the true faith. And very few people whom they conquered and converted ever apostasized from their religion. Their political moves always had a religious foundation, and I believe that is still true today.

"There can be no peace among the nations without peace among the religions."

The Religions of the Middle East Can Work for Peace

Hans Küng

Hans Küng is a well-known theologian who teaches at the University of Tübingen in Germany. In the following viewpoint, he argues that peace will not come to the Middle East until adherents to its three major religions—Judaism, Christianity, and Islam—acknowledge what they have in common and treat each other with mutual respect. He believes that religion, instead of being a cause of conflict, can potentially lead the way to a stable peace in the Middle East.

As you read, consider the following questions:

1. What was the role of religion in the 1991 Persian Gulf War, according to Küng?
2. According to the author, what do Islam, Judaism, and Christianity have in common?
3. How might the status of Jerusalem be resolved, according to Küng?

Excerpted from "Two Flags over Jerusalem" by Hans Küng, *European Affairs*, April/May 1991. Reprinted with permission.

Post-modern humanity needs common values, goals, ideals, visions—a sense of global responsibility based on a global ethos. Only one year ago, no one could have imagined how urgent this demand would become for world politics. Today, we confront once again the aftermath of a war, one which produced ever more devastating military, financial, ecological, social and moral consequences.

A world ethos and world peace also require a special commitment on the part of the world's major religions. As I have asked before: What would it mean for hundreds of millions of people if the representatives of the major religions stopped fanning the flames of war, and instead began advocating reconciliation and peace among the world's peoples? . . .

Religion's Role

One thing must be made clear from the very start: The 1991 Gulf war was not a war between Christians and Muslims, even if it appeared to be one in the minds of both Arab and Christian masses. Nor does there exist an eternal hostility between Jews and Muslims, who until the 20th century often lived together without difficulty. No, the justified outrage against Saddam Hussein may under no circumstances lead to a blanket condemnation of Islam as an aggressive, martial religion without respect for human life. Yet one thing is certain: In any conflict between peoples, the religious dimension also plays a certain role. Religions can have an aggravating, but also a calming, effect; they can provoke and lengthen wars, but they can also shorten and even prevent them.

Peaceful revolutions in Poland, East Germany, Czechoslovakia, South Africa and the Philippines have shown that religion can contribute to achieving peace. Therefore my question—is it an illusion to believe that this war could have been avoided if one had finally taken seriously the Palestine question, an issue which for decades has poisoned relations between the Arab world and the West; if the ecumenical dialogue among Christians, Jews and Muslims concerning world peace, and also the resolution of the Palestine question, had been more earnestly pursued?

I wish to state very clearly: The religious, social and moral dimensions of this crisis must not be ignored in deference to its purely strategic, economic and political aspects. A multitude of misunderstandings between the US and Iraq from the very start paralysed all efforts at diplomacy and made reaching an understanding impossible. Many share the impression that the politicians, diplomats and military leaders stumbled into this crisis because they have no knowledge of the culture, mentality and religion of the peoples in the Middle East. Otherwise they

196

would certainly have recognised that the demand of 'unconditional capitulation' would produce unconditional resistance; that an Arab leader, faced with the alternatives of becoming a traitor or a martyr, would prefer martyrdom; that, for the Islamic masses, the Israel question is everywhere a central (and also a religious) question; that any Western military action for which one makes an appeal to God would reawaken the trauma of the Crusades; and that, ever since the period of Western colonialism and imperialism, the Islamic peoples have felt their dignity profoundly wounded and their religion profoundly despised.

Religions Have Much in Common

All the nations participating in this conflict—above all the United States and Great Britain, then Israel and the Arab states—represent, each in its own way, one of the major world religions: Christianity, Judaism and Islam. But must these religions necessarily stand in opposition and hostility to one another? As prophetic religions, they have much in common. All three of these religions are of Eastern Semitic origin, all three have a prophetic character, and all three trace themselves back to a common progenitor, Abraham. Were they to reflect upon this common origin, these religions could perhaps make a vital contribution to world peace. But at the moment, their first task must be to clarify the misunderstandings, dissolve the stereotyped, dehumanising images which each side holds of the 'enemy', reduce the mutual hatreds, and reflect on all that these three religions have in common.

Obviously, there exist fundamental differences among these three prophetic religions. Judaism concentrates on God's people and land; Christianity on God's son, the Messiah; Islam on God's word and book. These differences cannot and must not be minimised or ignored.

A unity of the major religions is not necessary. A single world religion is an illusion. But what is needed, more than ever after this world crisis, is peace among the religions. For I cannot repeat often enough: There can be no world peace without religious peace. There can be no peace among the nations without peace among the religions. And there will be no peace among the religions without a dialogue being held among them.

The Same God

All prophetic religions believe equally in one and the same God. This common feature must also become politically more effective. In all of them, a prophetic heritage lives on, a heritage which happily has continued to be shared by Judaism, Christianity and Islam:

• Jews, Christians and Muslims believe in the one God who tolerates no other gods, powers, rulers or figures besides Him-

197

self; who is not merely the God of a single people, but of all people; not a national God, but rather the Lord of the entire world, who wishes the well-being of all peoples.

A Point of Unity

Arabs and Jews have a point of unity both can understand: Abraham, the Old Testament patriarch.

All Arabs trace their ancestry to Abraham through Ishmael, whom he fathered through his wife's servant Hagar. All Jews trace their blood roots to Abraham through his son Isaac and grandson Jacob, who, according to the Bible, God later renamed Israel. The name "Abraham" literally means "father of many nations." Having once separated the descendants of Ishmael from the children of Israel, Abraham, 3700 years later, could fulfill the biblical prophecy not only of their unification but of the eventual unification and harmony of all nations and peoples.

Norman G. Kurland, *American-Arab Affairs*, Spring 1991.

• Jews, Christians and Muslims believe in a fundamental prophetic ethos: humane demands for justice, honesty, loyalty, peace and love—justified as the demands of God Himself.

• Judaism, Christianity and Islam are marked by the prophets' criticism of the unjust and inhuman relations under which debased, enslaved, exploited human beings are forced to live—there can be no worship of God without service to other human beings and the vindication of human rights.

It is clear that there is indeed a genuine basis for an ecumenical concordance of the three religions, which together form the ethically oriented monotheistic world movement and which (given their common origin in Abraham) could be called the Abrahamic ecumenical movement. I am convinced that there will be no peace in the Middle East if the Abrahamic ecumenical movement cannot be turned into a worldwide political force. How else can the religious fanatics in all three camps be successfully resisted? In positive terms:

• On the basis of the Hebraic Bible and the New Testament, Jews and Christians should together affirm and support the dignity of the Arab and Islamic peoples, who do not wish to serve as the last colonised peoples on earth.

• On the basis of the Koran and the New Testament, Muslims and Christians should together affirm and support the right to exist of the Jewish people, who have suffered (nearly to the point of extinction) more than any other people during the last 2,000 years.

• On the basis of the Hebraic Bible and the Koran, Jews and Muslims should together affirm and support the liberty of the Christian communities in all the countries of the Middle East.

• Thus, a common commitment of all three religions for peace, justice and freedom, for human dignity and human rights, made (of course) in cooperation with the peoples of the Indian, Chinese and Japanese traditions.

Without a clarification of the religious questions among Jews, Christians and Muslims, no lasting political solution can be found. One need only think of the question of Israel's borders, or the question of the use of force in Islam, or the question of tolerance in Christendom. What can be done concretely, now that the Gulf war is over? The political world, completely fixated on immediate problems, runs the danger of neglecting longer-term perspectives. Allow me to offer a few elements of an overall vision—not for primarily political interests, but rather out of a sense of ecumenical responsibility, an obligation to all three prophetic religions.

Peaceful Cooperation

A new peaceful regional order cannot be imposed, not even by the US. It will demand the cooperation of all participants in the region. Two aspects appear to me essential if there is to be peace in the Middle East. I would like here to briefly address the directly political questions.

A Middle East solution cannot create something entirely new. But it can realign the current constellation of states at several vital points. After the dreadful experiences with the regime of the Shah in Iran and the regime of Saddam Hussein in Iraq, the West simply cannot establish yet another country—whether Turkey, Syria or Israel—to serve as a dominant military power, set up to impose 'order' throughout the region. Regional stability, security and peace will not be attained in the Middle East through an authoritarian 'stabiliser' armed with a dangerous military potential, but rather through more democracy, justice and respect for human rights. A regional balance of powers among the nations, progressive disarmament and economic cooperation are necessary. An inter-Arab 'Marshall Plan' for the just distribution of the oil billions would help the Arabian 'poverty belt' just as much as America's Marshall Plan helped the Europeans after World War Two. And something else must not be forgotten: Many oppressed peoples, such as the Kurds, have a right to at least internal autonomy. These, too, are essentially moral demands to which the three religions can make a positive contribution.

The central problem for any Middle East solution is and shall remain the Palestine question. This question, which has repeatedly jeopardised peace in the entire region, must at long last be resolved, and peace must become possible not simply between Israel and Egypt, but with all of Israel's neighbours. The three religions should reflect on their own programme, in which the word 'peace'—in the Hebraic Bible *shalom*, in the Koran *salam*, and in the New Testament *eirene*—plays such a large role.

A vision of peace must supplant the horrible visions of war and annihilation. And to implement this, there is no way around the creation of a state for the Palestinians. Realistically viewed, this is possible under three conditions: First, secure borders for Israel; second, guarantees by the UN or the major powers, as was the case with Egypt; and third, an economic confederation of Israel with both the new Palestinian state and Jordan (similar to that of the Benelux countries), under terms advantageous for all.

Thus, the state of Israel could be transformed from an army camp bristling with weapons and a highly armed warrior people into a peaceful helping-hand state and a peaceful people. Imagine for a moment: What might it mean for the entire Middle East, for Egypt, Syria, Jordan, Iraq and Saudi Arabia, and all the bordering nations, if a highly developed country such as Israel committed itself to peaceful cooperation?

Jerusalem

Yet the most difficult question is how to find a solution for the city of Jerusalem, which in the course of its 3,000-year history has known so many different rules and which is sacred to Jews, Muslims and Christians alike (and whose status, even for secularised Jews or Muslims, remains anything but a matter of indifference)?

For indeed, it is Jerusalem's unique historical fate to be simultaneously sacred for all three Abrahamic religions, because of Abraham. In addition, each religion has its own specific 'sacred' ties to Jerusalem: for the Jews, it is the city of David; for the Christians, it is the city of Jesus; and for the Muslims, it is the city of the Prophet Muhammad.

Some have demanded the internationalisation of Jerusalem; Tel Aviv could be the capital of Israel, and Ramallah that of the Palestinian state. But perhaps there is another solution. The Palestinians too—with or without Yasser Arafat, who once again appears to have bet on the wrong horse—are seeking a political identity, self-respect, their own flag. One religious symbol need not necessarily exclude another. In a new age of peaceful coexistence, why shouldn't it be possible for two flags to fly over Jerusalem: the Israeli flag with the Star of David and the Palestinian flag with the crescent moon?

This could be the first element of an overall politico-religious solution for Jerusalem. Why shouldn't the highly symbolic Old City—since its renewed division would admittedly be an economic, political, social and religious absurdity—serve as the capital for both the state of Israel and the state of Palestine, a capital which, instead of creating division, unites for the benefit of all? Would that be so unheard of in history? A city with two flags? Don't the flags of both Italy and the Vatican today fly over the once long-disputed city of Rome?

A second element for the future status of Jerusalem could be supplied by making a vital distinction—by no means must a nation's capital and its seat of government be one and the same. There was a long discussion about whether Berlin should become both the capital and the seat of government of a unified Germany. In any event, nothing requires them to coincide. Why couldn't the (purely) symbolic Old City of Jerusalem be a (neutralised) capital for both Israel and Palestine? . . .

One Holy Place

But how should, in the centre of Israel, the questions of the Old Temple Mount, the al-Haram ash-Sharif, be brought to a peace resolution? The three Abrahamic religions need a religious symbol, a common holy place—as a great symbol of the fact that all three revere the one God of Abraham, as a great sign that they have something fundamental in common which could overcome all divisions and all hostility. The fact is that there already exists a holy place for the one God of Abraham. It is precisely this unique holy place on the old Temple Mount in Jerusalem, the 'Dome of the Rock' (in Arabic, 'Qubbat as-Sakhrah'), which is often wrongly described as the Omar Mosque (although it is not, in fact, a mosque). According to both Jewish and Muslim tradition, it is a memorial not only of the commitment of Abraham's son Isaac, but also of both the creation of Adam and the Final Judgement.

Is it therefore so absurd to believe that—after a politico-religious settlement of the relationship between Israelis and Palestinians, Jews and Arabs—Muslims, Christians and Jews could all pray at this holy place to the one God of Abraham? In this way, the Dome of the Rock would become a Cathedral of Reconciliation for the three religions which go back to Abraham.

Is such a vision an illusion? . . . The religions and their representatives, which earlier had remained so passive, must begin to take action and share the burden of the politicians in the search for a lasting peace. Peace should not merely be prayed for but vigorously advocated in every church, synagogue and mosque. To achieve this, we all need a common vision, we need imagination, courage and active, untiring commitment.

Understanding Words in Context

Readers occasionally come across words they do not recognize. And frequently, because they do not know a word or words, they will not fully understand the passage being read. Obviously, the reader can look up an unfamiliar word in a dictionary. By carefully examining the word in the context in which it is used, however, the word's meaning can often be determined. A careful reader may find clues to the meaning of the word in surrounding words, ideas, and attitudes.

Below are excerpts from the viewpoints in this chapter. In each excerpt, one of the words is printed in italics. Try to determine the meaning of each word by reading the excerpt. Under each excerpt you will find four definitions for the italicized word. Choose the one that is closest to your understanding of the word.

Finally, use a dictionary to see how well you have understood the words in context. It will be helpful to discuss with others the clues that helped you decide on each word's meaning.

1. Given Islamic activists' increasing involvement in the democratic movements in many Middle Eastern countries, Americans cannot continue to view Islam as a movement of fanatics *ANTITHETICAL* to democracy.

   ANTITHETICAL means:

   a) directly opposed   c) progressing
   b) favorable resistance d) without

2. There is no widespread enthusiasm for democracy in Islamic countries. Many Muslims *DEPRECATE* democracy because it comes from the West.

   DEPRECATE means:

   a) appreciate   c) worship
   b) disapprove of   d) wonder about

3. Although the United Nations has condemned Israel's treatment of Palestinians, it has been unable to impose economic sanctions and other penalties. Israel has therefore been able to ignore with *IMPUNITY* the decrees of the UN.

IMPUNITY means:

a) severe penalties
b) freedom from punishment
c) a sense of shame
d) extreme caution

4. Religions can have an *AGGRAVATING*, but also a calming, effect. They can provoke or lengthen wars, but can also shorten or even prevent them.

AGGRAVATING means:

a) worsening
b) soothing
c) humorous
d) huge

5. Many Israelis view the West Bank as part of the Jews' promised land. Consequently, they are *INTRANSIGENT* on the issue of relinquishing the West Bank to the Palestinians.

INTRANSIGENT means:

a) flexible
b) unsure
c) careless
d) uncompromising

6. The Old Testament beliefs that proclaim Israel a holy land for only the Jews are as *ANACHRONISTIC* as flat-earth doctrines.

ANACHRONISTIC means:

a) dated
b) timely
c) accurate
d) guilty

7. Some Muslims view Jews and Christians as *INFIDELS* who have intruded in Middle East lands that belong to Islam.

INFIDEL means:

a) soldier
b) unbeliever
c) priest
d) general

8. Unlike the Japanese, who were able to modernize and Westernize yet preserve their culture, the Islamic world was unable to create this same kind of *SYNTHESIS*.

SYNTHESIS means:

a) artistry
b) religion
c) combination
d) division

Periodical Bibliography

The following articles have been selected to supplement the diverse views presented in this chapter.

Shahrzad Azad	"Reaping the Islamic Whirlwind," *Against the Current*, November/December 1990.
Stephen Budiansky	"Bowed Heads and Golden Rules," *U.S. News & World Report*, March 25, 1991.
Christianity Today	"A Crossfire of Loyalties," March 11, 1991.
Edward D. Desmond	"A Revolution Loses Its Zeal," *Time*, May 6, 1991.
Hermann Frederick Eilts	"Islamic Fundamentalism: A Quest for a New Order," *Mediterranean Quarterly*, Fall 1990. Available from Duke University Press, PO Box 6697, College Station, Durham, NC 27708.
John L. Esposito	"The Political Leverage of Islam," *The Christian Century*, April 10, 1991.
John L. Esposito and James P. Piscatori	"Democratization and Islam," *The Middle East Journal*, Summer 1991.
Isaac Hasson	"Blood and Tears in the Holy Land," *American Atheist*, February 1991.
Jon D. Hull	"Farewell to Moderation," *Time*, January 7, 1991.
Timothy K. Jones	"No Shalom in a Land Called Holy," *Christianity Today*, September 16, 1991.
David S. Landes	"Islam Dunk," *The New Republic*, April 8, 1991.
Bernard Lewis	"The Roots of Muslim Rage," *The Atlantic*, September 1990.
Habib C. Malik	"The Future of Christian Arabs," *Mediterranean Quarterly*, Spring 1991.
Daniel Pipes	"The Muslims Are Coming! The Muslims Are Coming!" *National Review*, November 19, 1990.
Rosemary Radford Reuther	"Religion and War in the Middle East," *Sojourners*, June 1991.
Lamin Sanneh	"Reclaiming and Expounding the Islamic Heritage," *The Christian Century*, August 21-28, 1991.
John Alden Williams	"The Revival of Islam in the Modern World," *America*, October 13, 1990.
Robin Wright	"Islam's New Political Face," *Current History*, January 1991.

5 CHAPTER

What Is the Future of the Middle East?

Chapter Preface

Discussions about the future of the Middle East often focus on the prospects of war and peace—the shifting alliances among countries, the resolution of the Arab-Israeli conflict, and the movement and use of military force.

Many Middle East experts, however, believe it is necessary to go beyond these problems when analyzing the future of the Middle East. The prospects for peace between nations, they argue, are directly linked to reforms within the nations themselves. Many experts seem to agree that there is a definite correlation between the autocratic governments of the Middle East nations and the persistence of war in the region. Palestinian economist George T. Abed, focusing on Arab countries, writes:

> To avert future disasters, the Arabs must join the rest of humanity's march toward democracy, tolerance, and freedom. They must be prepared to undergo the social and political transformations needed to establish new values and principles, now almost fully shared in the modern world, but which have not yet fully rooted in the Arab society.

Abed and others believe that because democratic governments are more accountable to the people, they would expend greater effort building their societies and improving the living standards of their citizens.

Some observers, however, reject the prescription that democracy could solve the problems of the Middle East. For example, Prince Faisal of Saudi Arabia has written that democracy in his country would foster divisiveness among its people. Historically, the people in what is now Saudi Arabia consisted of largely nomadic tribes in constant conflict with each other. These violent skirmishes eventually were curtailed after Saudi Arabia was founded and unified under monarchic rule by Ibn Saud, whose descendants rule the small nation today. Prince Faisal and others argue that only continued strong monarchic rule that adheres closely to the precepts of Islam can prevent Saudi Arabia from slipping back into the chaos of tribal warfare. For this and other reasons, analyst N.B. Aragaman writes that "Saudi Arabia and most of the Gulf emirates and sheikhdoms insist that democracy is simply not suited to their countries."

While the Middle East is a troubled region, experts disagree on what reforms would lessen the tension and make peace possible. The viewpoints in this chapter examine these and other issues important to the future of the Middle East.

"The Arab world is more inclined today than ever before toward coexistence with the Israelis."

Middle East Peace Is Possible

Abdul Aziz Said

Abdul Aziz Said is a professor of peace studies and conflict resolution at American University in Washington, D.C. In the following viewpoint, he lays out a peace strategy that he argues could achieve peace in the Middle East and improve the lives of its inhabitants. Steps in his peace strategy include arms control, a redistribution of wealth within the Arab world, and internationally mediated talks between Israelis and Palestinians to determine Palestinian self-determination. Said concludes that his strategy for peace in the Middle East could work with U.S. commitment and involvement.

As you read, consider the following questions:

1. What six issues does Said discuss in his peace strategy?
2. Why does the author believe Islam and democracy are compatible?
3. What should the oil-rich Arab states do to attain Middle East peace, according to Said?

Abdul Aziz Said, "A Middle Eastern Peace Strategy," *Peace Review*, Summer 1991. Reprinted with permission.

This period following the 1991 Persian Gulf War underscores the urgent need to develop a new American-Arab relationship, one that recognizes both parties' interests, affirms the aspirations of the Arab people, and resolves the Arab-Israeli-Palestinian conflict. Although the United States' view—that instability in the Middle East threatens Western economic stability—is valid, viewing the conflict exclusively this way denies the many historically based problems that plague the Arab world, and misses the opportunity to create a better future for everyone.

The Arab Predicament

Let us shift the context of the Gulf tragedy away from Iraq's brutal occupation of Kuwait, from the threat to the ruling families of the Arab states of the Gulf, and from the needs of Western energy consumers, and towards the existential condition of two hundred million Arabs victimized by their leaders, their declining quality of life, and the plight of Palestine in the midst of affluence. This way we can understand the poignancy of the Arab predicament. Since the rise of nineteenth century European colonialism, Arabs have been excluded from history. Saddam Hussein, himself a symptom of this peculiar disease, turned into a messenger who cynically exploited the deep fears and frustration in the collective Arab soul. Arabs are attracted by the pull of his message; the West is caught in the messenger's push.

The tutelage of the superpowers in the Arab world has historically been one of exploitation, acquiescence and victimization. The colonial order in the Middle East, first established by Great Britain, France, and Czarist Russia, and later assumed by the United States and the Soviet Union, is now approaching its end.

The rise of the system of Arab states after World War II brought discontinuity both with the traditional social structures and with the basic precepts and practices of Islam. Traditional Islamic institutions lost much of their effectiveness as organizers and safeguarders of social justice and political participation. The West expected the new Arab states to be imitations of Western nation-states; so did the Arab leaders of the time. But the new Arab states were independent mainly in name.

Given the lack of legitimacy of the newly installed governments, power could only be maintained by corruption and despotism. Granted, some Arab governments are cosmetically better than others, and some are more benevolent; but all remain firmly authoritarian.

The Arab world will never be the same as it was before Operation Desert Storm. Iraq's humiliating defeat represents to millions of Arabs yet another generation lost, another front door to history slammed shut. Arabs may, as in the past, resort to backdoor politics, fundamentalism and terrorism. Still, global and regional forces will have a growing impact in the region. Although the wave of democratization sweeping through Europe and Asia has so far bypassed the Middle East, broader public support will now be demanded of all Middle East governments. There will be no more security in obscurity for Arab princes and military dictators. The Middle East will be in the limelight for many years to come.

The Challenge of Peace

All of the Middle East is facing new challenges. And the choice is sharp: Embrace the modern age or remain an underdeveloped, forlorn, ignorant, hopeless region. The answer is clear. We have to try to build a new Middle East. We have to try to demilitarize, or reduce the military dangers of, the Middle East and introduce a new economic model. Resolving the Palestinian-Israeli conflict and building economic hope for the future is the only solution.

We are facing a great opportunity—all of us, Arabs and Jews, Christians and Muslims. I believe that there is a democratic majority in Israel that wants to take the road of peace, to answer the call of a modern age that has many dangers but also many hopes. That is the prayer of us all: to make the right choice for a historic region so that it will regain what it has lost and remember what it has gained.

Shimon Peres, *World Press Review*, September 1991.

The US could facilitate the Arabs' re-entry into history. Indeed, a US/USSR/European coalition could support the Arabs in developing democratic forms appropriate to their needs, in rediscovering the life-affirming precepts of Islam, and in developing structures that promise a cultural future for the people. Now that the US and the USSR are willing to jointly participate in a new world order, they need to transcend the imperial *policing* mentality. A creative, farsighted policy could combine their expertise and experience to address legitimate Arab grievances and identify viable alternatives.

A workable peace strategy for the Middle East needs superpower support of these six issues: the transfer and control of arms; an Arab-Israeli-Palestinian peace plan; social and economic justice; appropriate political participation; an Arab role in the emerging world order; and regional security under American leadership. I will discuss each of these items in detail.

The introduction and proliferation of ballistic missiles and nuclear and chemical weapons have altered the Arab-Israeli power balance. The US will have little success in reducing proliferation unless it holds Israel to the same standards it applies to Arab states. So far, the US has sought to frustrate the transfer of new, more lethal weapons technology to the Middle East, hoping that the military balance would still favor Israel and other US friends; local disputes would be resolved through peaceful negotiations; and the high cost of advanced weapons technology would prohibit states from achieving a security advantage. These hopes have been dashed as Middle Eastern governments continue to purchase conventional weapons while exploring opportunities to gain a qualitative advantage by acquiring chemical weapons and new ballistic missile systems.

In the context of the proliferation of nuclear weapons, new policy approaches are needed in the US government. The US needs to recognize that exclusive possession of weapons-related science and technology is a thing of the past. The US should recognize that the Arabs have access to both technological knowledge of weapons and suppliers of military technology.

The United States has a particularly significant role to play in seeking to moderate the pace of missile and chemical weapons proliferation. For starters, the US should make clear to Israel that continued transfers of missile technology to China, South Africa and other nations cannot be tolerated. Past US acquiescence in such transfers makes a mockery of US participation in any missile-control agreement, and weakens Washington's credibility in seeking to secure European control over technology transfers to the Arab states and to Iran.

The United States should invite the Soviet Union into a peace partnership in the Middle East—the Soviets certainly have a stake in peace and stability in the region. Washington and Moscow can jointly offer incentives to Israelis, Palestinians, Syrians and Lebanese grounded in an international legal framework. UN Security Council Resolution 242 of November 22, 1967, could be amended to include a call for Palestinian self-determination, peace negotiations under the auspices of the two superpowers (with the blessing of the permanent members of the Security Council), a recognition of legitimacy of the claims of all parties to the conflict, a moratorium on violence, and finally, an American/Soviet sanctioned arms-free zone in the Middle East for the duration of peace negotiations.

United Nations' Role

The peace process could be conducted either under the auspices of a special authority created by the United Nations or a private nongovernmental organization such as the Harvard Mediation Team or Search for Common Grounds. In any case, Israelis, Palestinians, and other concerned parties should consult in selecting a mechanism for conducting the talks.

No party should demand any concession of any other party as a condition for participating in negotiations. A condition could preclude options that might later prove fruitful. Initially, several possible maps would have to be drawn, and several formulas for limiting Palestinian and Israeli sovereignty within a confederation would have to be devised. The right of Jews to settle in some parts of their holy land would have to be recognized, as would the right of the Palestinians to settle in some parts of their ancestral land. These are rights of peoples, not of states.

The tension between the population-poor but resource-rich Gulf states and the surrounding resource-poor but population-rich countries can only be resolved by the Arabs themselves. Otherwise, the relation between people without resources and resources without people will trigger more violent confrontations. A developmental approach is needed, sponsored by the oil rich Arab states, using oil revenues to support economic and social development in the Arab world. The rich Arab states should become the keepers of their less fortunate brothers and sisters, and participate fully in the creation of an Arab economic community.

Economic Development

Both a public development authority and private assistance are needed. The former would include organizations such as an intra-Arab development bank; the latter would include an Arab trust fund to work closely with international economic agencies such as the World Bank. This private structure could fund and support approaches for helping the poor that have proven successful in other Third World nations. Small loans, for example, have been very successful for starting small businesses and making agricultural improvements. This development strategy has the added advantage of minimizing opportunities for graft and corruption, and keeping the bureaucracy of implementation small.

Development is the process through which human beings choose and create their future, within the context of their environment. The goals of development are to realize the potential of human beings and human societies. Development in the Arab world cannot easily fit any prevailing Western model. Arab development can be reconciled with Islam once the concept of development is freed from the linear, rational idea of progress that has been canonized by the Western mind.

Development includes both modernization and humanization. Modernization is the process of adapting technology for the uses of the society, and attempting to make that society more rational, efficient and predictable, especially through the use of comprehensive planning, rational administration and scientific evaluation. Modernization also carries the connotation of a more

211

productive society, at least in economic terms. Humanization is the process of enlarging and making more equal the dignity, freedom, opportunity for creativity and community, and welfare of individual persons in society, as well as the restructuring of the society's institutions and culture to support these goals.

Reconciling Islam and Democracy

The reconciliation of Islam and democracy is a crucial first step toward a new regional Arab order. Democracy—Western or Islamic—is not practiced anywhere in today's Arab world. Does this mean that Islam and democracy are not compatible? No.

The substance of democracy is a human society that has a sense of common goals, a sense of community, wide participation in making decisions, and protective safeguards for dissenters. The form a democracy takes is cast in the mold of the culture of a people. There is nothing in Islam that precludes common goals, community participation and protective safeguards. It is true that western liberal forms of democracy—with their provisions for political parties, interest groups and an electoral system—are alien to Islamic tradition. But democracy is not built upon institutions; it is built upon participation. The absence of democracy in the Arab world is more the result of lack of preparation for it and less because of a lack of religious and cultural foundations. There are democratic precepts in Islam as there are in other religions. There are also Islamic traditions, as there have been in other religions, which in practice result in transgressions against those ideals. In Islam, democratic traditions have been more commonly abused than used.

Arabs are forced by today's conditions to make the connections between democracy, modernization and Islam. There is no model available now for *modern, democratic and Muslim*. At the close of the nineteenth century, when Egyptian liberal thinkers began to explore these concepts, they accepted the Western norm as the only reality. In so doing, they began to hang an Islamic garb on these concepts. It did not work then, and it is doubtful that it will work now.

Neither the Muslim fundamentalists nor the Arab secularists represent a genuine revival of Arab civilization, but rather negativism and identification with the enemy. What is required is an Arab alternative that is neither a superficial compromise nor a schizophrenic reaction: a response based on Islamic values which reflects the historical development of Islam and responds to the challenges of contemporary life. Mainstream Islam should regain the moral high ground and emotional momentum from fundamentalism. This can be done when Arabs gain self respect as full-fledged citizens of the modern world. In the long run, it is better for the Middle East to develop through its own Islamic tradition. Otherwise, the people of the region will con-

212

tinue to suffer from the contradictions between traditionalism and secularism, fundamentalism and Westernism.

The oil rich Arab states can contribute to a new world order. Saudi Arabia, for example, can take the lead in planning for and promoting a long-term global transition from fossil fuels to non-greenhouse energy sources. The new Saudi oil discoveries could ease the transition with less risk of conflict over increasingly scarce oil. Without strong and enlightened leadership in the West, however, Western politicians will probably use the additional oil as an excuse to put off dealing with the energy problem. If that occurs, oil rich Arabs will be increasingly at risk of armed conflict over control of dwindling oil supplies. It is very much in everyone's interests to promote a smooth transition.

Middle East Hope

Hope stems from the growing understanding among all Middle Easterners that war is a dead-end street. Increasingly, Middle Easterners have come to see that no one group can have all it asks for.

Helena Cobban, *The Christian Science Monitor*, May 19, 1991.

The oil rich Arabs can undertake [these] initiatives. First, Saudi Arabia can promote the development and use of environmentally responsible energy sources and energy using technologies. A special emphasis should be placed on meeting the needs of developing nations, particularly, in the Arab world. The goal would be to enable these nations to achieve economic development without risking the unacceptable environmental damage that the industrialized world is experiencing. This calls for new, more advanced and environmentally benign technologies.

The Arab world can stabilize the oil market, and hence the world energy market, by negotiating a long-term agreement between OPEC and the oil consuming world. This would transform the relationship between OPEC and oil consuming nations from one of conflict and competition to one of cooperation. This goal is compatible with a smooth eventual transition from fossil to non-fossil energy sources. Those realists who would scoff at the possibility of productive cooperation between the producers and consumers of oil should consider the dramatic changes in international relationships away from competition and towards cooperation that have occurred in only the last two years. A key initial agreement would be a willingness to supply oil to the US and other industrial nations, for their Strategic Petroleum Reserves, at a low and fixed price. This would begin to build mutual confidence which might facilitate a producers/consumers agreement. . . .

There is a tremendous amount of thinking to be done by the United States about the Middle East. The great and glaring fact of international relations today is that an era has ended; a handful of states can no longer control what goes on in the world. Great Power strategy has become a historical curiosity. Today the only workable instrument for the ratification of interstate decisions is a broad consensus of governments and peoples.

Consensus—the distinctive political tool in relations among equals—has already gone far to replace armed force as the preferred instrument of national policy. Those international relations specialists who call themselves Realists may object to the naiveté, the instability, or the shortsightedness of some manifestations of consensus, but it would be a sheer folly to challenge either its existence or its power. As a method of reaching binding international decisions, consensus is so new that mistakes and contradictions in its application are inevitable. But we have little in the way of alternatives: the emerging global order will either learn to live with mass opinion or it will not survive. . . .

What are some characteristics of cooperation that would enhance security in the Middle East? One is the identification and acceptance by Arab people and governments, Israelis and Palestinians, Americans and the great powers, of shared objectives that can only be reached through cooperative efforts. Each party has to have an expectation of personal benefit from the cooperative effort. Parties are not obligated to contribute to an enterprise from which they expect to get nothing back. And there must be a fair distribution of the benefits and costs of cooperation. Heretofore, the people of the Arab world have carried most of the cost. . . .

U.S. Role

The prevailing order of uncertainty in the Middle East could degenerate rapidly into chaos unless Arabs, Israelis and Americans take the road to peace in the very near future. The current situation offers little predictability, even less stability, and carries with it the risk of devolution into wholesale violence. Yet, the Arab world is more inclined today than ever before toward coexistence with the Israelis. Washington's crisis and security managers, and the country's neo-isolationists, can benefit from active diplomacy toward the Middle East. Only the United States can make peace possible.

"*The Middle East will continue to be marked by glaring disparities between the rich few and poor many.*"

Middle East Peace Is Unlikely

James E. Akins

James E. Akins, a former U.S. Foreign Service Officer and Ambassador to Saudi Arabia, is a consultant on international affairs. In the following viewpoint, he argues that the Middle East has fundamental conflicts not only between Israel and the Arab nations, but within the Arab world itself. Because of these conflicts, he is pessimistic that the Middle East can ever attain lasting peace.

As you read, consider the following questions:

1. What false hopes were raised by the 1991 Persian Gulf War, according to Akins?
2. What role do the Palestinians play in the Middle East, according to the author?
3. What examples of Arab division does Akins describe?

Excerpted from "The New Arabia" by James E. Akins, *Foreign Affairs*, Summer 1991.

The 1990 Iraqi invasion of Kuwait was an immediate disaster for Kuwait and the Palestinians and an ultimate calamity for Iraq. Nonetheless, many Americans, including President Bush, thought good would come from this evil.

A New World Order?

There would be a "new world order" in which aggression would not be tolerated. Furthermore, the entire Middle East would be transformed. The disparity between rich and poor Arabs was clearly an unstable configuration and would be changed. After the final victory, the rich would move smartly to improve the lot of the poorer 90 percent of the Arab world. Future investments of the oil-rich Arab states would be in North Africa, Syria, Jordan and Yemen, not in Europe, Japan and America. Some American academics proposed that rich Arabs could put a substantial portion of their oil income into a special account for development of the entire Muslim world. Secretary of State James A. Baker thought the rich Arabs should form a new bank to finance projects in the poorer countries.

It all seemed reasonable and just. Unfortunately, to one who has spent most of his professional life dealing with the Arab world, it is all only a utopian fantasy. Secretary Baker, for instance, might well have discussed his bank idea with the Arab leaders before he announced it. While Egypt and Syria were enthusiastic, those countries with the financial resources were not. The idea of an Arab bank died before it was born; so did the dreams of a new Arabia—or a new Islam—with its wealth more equitably shared.

I can agree with confidence—not necessarily satisfaction—that the future Middle East will indeed be different from what we have known, but it will bear no relationship to the idealized picture of generous gulf Arabs using their riches to transform the Arab world. Instead, the signs of the Middle East will continue to be marked by glaring disparities between the rich few and poor many, and among diverse national and ideological forces in competition for the soul of Arabism.

Feelings of Betrayal

Every gulf Arab knows or remembers the grim poverty of decades past. All remember the contempt in which they were held by Syrians, Egyptians, Jordanians and Lebanese. No gulf Arab feels any moral obligation to those states now that their relative positions are reversed. While there is some gratitude for the stance taken by the Egyptian and the Syrian leaders during the Gulf War, there are strong feelings of betrayal by the incipient democracies—Jordan, Yemen, Algeria—and by the Palestine Liberation Organization (PLO).

216

The bitterness against the Palestinians in the gulf countries—especially in Kuwait—is intense. Some were expelled immediately after the Iraqi invasion. It was made clear to those remaining that as their contracts expired they would not automatically be extended. Only the most needed and trusted Palestinians would be allowed to stay in the gulf. There is little appreciation of the fact that most Palestinians who stayed in Kuwait during the occupation had no place to go and were forced to cooperate with the occupier. Many were active in the resistance. The common Kuwaiti line now is to condemn all Palestinians: "We took them in; we gave them good jobs; and now they stab us in the back. Never again will we do anything for them."

Dick Wright. Reprinted by permission of UFS, Inc.

The attitude of rich gulf Arabs toward Jordan and Yemen is only slightly less hostile; it springs from the same admiration for their own past generosity and shock at the lack of present gratitude from the recipients. . . .

The second of August 1990 will be as important in Arab history as the second of November 1917, the date of the proclamation of the Balfour Declaration providing for a Jewish homeland in Palestine. A large Arab country attacked, occupied and absorbed a smaller Arab country with which it had diplomatic relations. No Arab state endorsed the Iraqi invasion of Kuwait. All Arab governments and the PLO demanded Iraqi withdrawal. Jordan, Yemen, Libya, Algeria, the Sudan and the PLO insisted that the problem could and must be settled by the Arabs themselves.

Others, led by Saudi Arabia and Egypt, thought outside help was required, and Riyadh invited American troops to Saudi Arabia to defend the kingdom, to liberate Kuwait and ultimately to destroy the army and the economic infrastructure of Iraq. This presented a problem; the United States had good relations with the GCC [Gulf Cooperation Council], but it was still the main supporter of Israel as well. American outrage at the Iraqi invasion of Kuwait was widely contrasted with its tranquil acceptance of Israel's defiance of a series of U.N. Security Council resolutions on Jerusalem, the West Bank, the Golan Heights and Lebanon. But all this was dismissed in the panic that followed Secretary of Defense Dick Cheney's convincing report to the Saudis of an imminent Iraqi invasion of Saudi Arabia and the rest of the Arabian peninsula.

Costly Principles

Nonetheless, the Saudi invitation to the United States was extraordinary. Countries that had long opposed "imperialism" and "Zionism" turned to the primary Western military power for protection against another Arab country. Jordan, Yemen and the PLO found this "solution" offensive and dangerous, and they condemned the subsequent American destruction of Iraq. Their principles have cost them dearly. Jordan's markets in Iraq disappeared in the early days of the crisis. All subsidies from the gulf Arabs to Jordan, Yemen and the PLO stopped; Saudi Arabia ceased delivery of oil to Jordan and stopped buying its agricultural produce. Altogether Jordan lost half of its gross domestic product.

The damage to Yemen has been almost as severe. Some 800,000 Yemenis who had been long-term residents of Saudi Arabia were dispossessed and expelled. They had been peaceful, even docile, residents of the kingdom; they had taken no action against their Saudi hosts; there were no demonstrations, no sabotage. Yet they were forced to leave their homes on short notice, sell their businesses for small fractions of their value and drive to the Yemeni border where their vehicles and remaining possessions were confiscated. Their expulsion was ordered presumably because the Saudis disapproved of the position held by the government in Yemen—that Iraq could be persuaded or forced to leave Kuwait without war—and possibly because the Saudis believed that the Yemeni government was part of the infamous "plot."

The secretary general of the GCC has said that the gulf Arabs would "never forgive and never forget the betrayal" by the poor Arabs. It will also be a long time before the wounds inflicted on Jordanians, Yemenis and Palestinians are healed. The Koranic injunctions to forgive and show compassion have been temporarily suspended by all. Those who opposed the invitation to the Americans accused the GCC and its allies of treason to Arabism and to Islam, but in the GCC itself there was little opposition. In short, the invasion of Kuwait and the Arab reaction to it marked the end of the period when Arabs maintained the pretense that they were part of one great nation.

The change was long in coming. It started even before Egyptian President Anwar Sadat's "betrayal" of the Palestinians in order to get a bilateral agreement with Israel and to secure Israeli evacuation of the Sinai Peninsula beginning in 1979.

With the "Arab awakening" in the period between the two great wars, educated young Arabs deplored the artificial boundaries in their new world. Only one border, that between Saudi Arabia and Yemen, had been drawn by Arabs. All others were products of imperial ambition: Turk, French and British. Yet all have assumed an astounding sanctity. The immediate explanation was the one used by Italian and German nationalists in the middle of the nineteenth century: the kings were attached to their thrones and their privileges; they dismissed the wishes of their peoples.

Possible Arab Groupings

There were several "natural" Arab groupings. A Greater Syria including all the countries of the Fertile Crescent had many adherents in the period immediately after the Second World War; it seemed reasonable and some, most notably Syrian President Hafez al-Assad, still advocate it. The unity of the Nile Valley has been pressed by Egypt for more than a century, but the Sudan is not even united itself. A united Arabian peninsula had much to offer; so did a united Maghreb: Libya, Tunisia, Algeria, Morocco and Mauritania. None was achieved. They were opposed by the various heads of state and local politicians. They were also opposed by Arab nationalists who thought such regional conglomerations were deliberate attempts to postpone the greater good of a complete Arab union.

Many Arabs aspired to lead the Arab nation but only one, Gamal Abd al-Nasser of Egypt, captured the imagination of Arabs from Morocco to Oman with his vision of a united Arab nation restored to its early glories. His admirers thought he was the new Bismarck, but Nasser lacked the subtlety, the cleverness and the power of the Prussian leader. Egypt was not Prussia; it did not have the finances to buy leaders of rival states or the military strength to force its will on those who would not be bought. Muammar al-Qaddafi of Libya aspired to fill the role of Arab leader after Nasser's death. He failed. He had money but he lacked everything else. His followers were limited to those whom he paid and their loyalty did not outlast their subsidies.

Arabs and Jews

At least until the mid-1970s young Arabs were usually "nationalist," but as they matured they almost always became "realist." They might cherish the concept of an eventual unity, but they abandoned the dream of seeing it in their lifetimes. The Palestinians were an exception. They retained a pure nationalism. They had been deprived of their homes, and their only hope of regaining their homelands rested with the Arab states. All Arabs agreed that the creation of Israel and the displacement of Palestinians by European Jews was unjust. Many Arabs had sympathy for the Jews but thought that those who had persecuted them should cede land for the Jewish state, not Arabs whose record of tolerance toward minorities was better than that of the most enlightened European state. All Arab states supported the Palestinians; all voted properly in U.N. deliberations on Palestine; some gave Palestinian leaders and institutions financial support. The rich states of the Arabian peninsula employed Palestinians and gave them new homes. Kuwait allowed the PLO to collect taxes from Palestinians employed there.

No Solutions in Sight

The one long-standing conflict in the Middle East—the protracted Israeli-Palestinian struggle—offers no immediate solution, nor even signs that one is in the offing any time soon. . . .

The Palestinian problem has always been an Arab problem, before it became Israel's. No Arabs on their own have ever resolved any Middle East conflict without help, and the Gulf war is only the latest example of this. The only way the Israeli-Palestinian conflict will be resolved is through an Arab initiative—that is, when an Arab regime is ready to deal with Israel.

Amos Perlmutter, *The Washington Times*, February 26, 1991.

The Arab-Israeli wars before 1973 were fought largely because of the Palestinian problem. The 1973 Yom Kippur War was different. Egypt and Syria fought to regain territory seized by Israel in 1967. The peace treaty ultimately signed by Egypt and Israel provided for the return of the Sinai to Egypt. Sadat called the agreement the first step toward a more comprehensive treaty assuring the rights of the Palestinians; so did President Jimmy

Carter. Israeli Prime Minister Menachem Begin made it clear that as far as he was concerned the treaty was only with Egypt; it held neither promise nor implication of more. The Camp David agreement marked a victory for Israel. It isolated Egypt, the largest Arab country, and forced Israel to relinquish only the Sinai, which Zionists had never considered part of Eretz Israel. Israel could now devote greater attention to the absorption of Judea and Samaria.

On the basis of all available evidence most other Arabs reached the same conclusions as Begin, for they did not share the optimism of Sadat or Carter. They assumed that the Israeli leader had hoodwinked the Egyptian and the American, and President Carter himself now wonders if he was deceived. The Arab states broke relations with Egypt, but they would do nothing for the Palestinians.

With Egypt isolated and neutralized, Begin was free to move into Lebanon and destroy the Palestinian forces there. Without even the pretense of a provocation from the PLO or the Lebanese, Israel invaded in 1982. It occupied all of southern Lebanon, destroyed much of Beirut and killed at least 15,000 Palestinians and Lebanese. The international community condemned Israel but did nothing more. In Tel Aviv there was a massive demonstration against the invasion. There was none in any Arab capital; most Arab leaders feared that anti-Israel demonstrations might be turned against themselves. In fact, there was little popular indignation in any Arab country. Arab television screens at the time were dominated by the World Cup soccer matches, not by scenes of carnage in Beirut.

A Loss of Honor

No Arab forgets the humiliation of the loss of most of Palestine in 1948 and the rest in 1967. Arab honor was at stake and Arabs know they will have no peace as long as Palestinians are clamoring for justice. . . .

None of this should imply that there is much love or affection for the Palestinians. By 1982 most gulf Arabs were bored by the Palestinians. They worked too hard; they were too intelligent, too educated, too aggressive, too ambitious, too intent on talking about the injustices committed against them. It was sometimes said they had become the "Jews" of the Arab world; their Arab "brothers" reacted against them with some of the same discomfort that polite Christian antisemites show toward Jews. It would delight most Arab leaders—and many others—if both Israel and the Palestinians would simply disappear. But Aladdin's lamp is long lost and no one can remember when a genie last appeared to grant unseemly wishes. All sides will be stuck with a difficult peace process.

221

"The Middle East is on the verge of profound change."

The Economic Future of the Middle East Is Promising

James Flanigan

James Flanigan is a reporter and columnist for the *Los Angeles Times*. In the following viewpoint, he argues that the Middle East could be on the verge of an economic boom. He states that Islamic beliefs can promote economic development, and that an increasing number of Middle Eastern business and government officials are encouraging a shift to free-market policies.

As you read, consider the following questions:

1. What is unusual about the economic output of the Middle East, according to Flanigan?
2. What two trends does Flanigan predict will sweep the Middle East?
3. How does the author support his statement that Islam does not prevent free markets in the Middle East?

Americans looking at news reports might think that little has changed in the Middle East as a result of the 1991 Gulf War.

Saddam Hussein, although reduced in power, remains on top in Iraq. The Kuwaitis are back in their homeland, but like the Bourbon kings after the French Revolution, they seem in some ways to have "learned nothing and forgotten nothing." Israeli Prime Minister Yitzhak Shamir has stated publicly that the war has left the region "unchanged."

Profound Change

But listen to officials and business people from the Gulf to North Africa and look at what's happening and you see that the Middle East is on the verge of profound change.

Change is badly needed. The economic output of this region is curiously low.

"The gross national product of all the nations of the Middle East does not equal that of Italy," says Mohammad Imady, economics minister of Syria. Indeed 200 million people in 15 or so Middle Eastern countries, including Iran, produce fewer goods and services annually than California's 30 million people, to say nothing of the 60 million people of Italy.

And more output will be needed because this region is undergoing a tremendous baby boom. With birthrates of 3.5% to 4% in every country, population will double within 20 years—meaning that the Middle East will have a larger population than the European Community.

Meanwhile, easy money is drying up.

"One effect of the war is that the financing system based on oil wealth has been destroyed," says Mirwan Ghandour, deputy director of the central bank of Lebanon. He means that grants from Saudi Arabia and the Gulf states, which for two decades helped finance governments and economies in Jordan, Lebanon, Egypt and other countries, won't continue in the 1990s.

What does all that mean? Two powerful trends you'll be hearing about: The spread of Islamic fundamentalism and, less noisy but ultimately more important, a shift everywhere to competitive, free-enterprise industry that could bring about the gradual spread of democracy.

Islamic fundamentalism, seen demonstrating recently in Algeria and in power for over a decade in Iran, is the region's fastest growing political movement. Islamists hold more seats than any other party in Jordan's Parliament.

Islamic Economics

Islamic economics is not incompatible with free markets, although the present fundamentalism may be incompatible with democracy.

"The economics of Islam demand that capital be fully employed, and they are concerned with justice," explains Prof. Hatem Karanshawy of American University Cairo.

The Economic Benefits of Peace

Breaking the stalemate between Israelis and Palestinians calls for epic compromises. . . . Both sides seem intractable and stiff-necked. What they too often ignore are the immense *economic* benefits of peace—and the staggering costs of prolonging the struggle. A settlement would help bring Israel the investment capital needed to absorb Soviet immigrants. It would unleash the Palestinians' formidable business talents, planting a budding Hong Kong in the Middle East. The result could be a new generation of Arabs and Jews with a stake in prosperity, not war. If ever two people could *benefit* from each other by working together, it is the Arabs and the Jews.

Any settlement above all must be built on free trade. Peace dividends would flow in abundance from combining a patchwork of economically isolated states and territories into a common market. Says Milton Friedman, the Nobel Prize-winning economist: "Peace would produce a textbook example of the benefits of free trade."

Shawn Tally, *Fortune*, May 20, 1991.

"To have land idle is sinful; even land that can be drained and used must be. Also, idle capital should not earn, so there is no predetermined interest on bank deposits. Instead, both depositor and bank are said to share the return when a loan is made for investment in machinery, or to create housing," says Karanshawy, who has a doctorate in developmental economics from Oxford University and is a consultant on project financing.

"The emphasis is on abundant production," he says, "so Islam forbids monopoly in any form, including monopoly by the state."

Islamic economics, based on religious principles, is an ideal, similar to the "just price" theories of St. Thomas Aquinas in the Middle Ages or the many commentaries on markets and fairness of Talmudic scholars through the centuries.

They call for fair wages and profit sharing for employees. And although the Third World is notorious for exploiting cheap labor, some notable merchants and industrialists run businesses on Islamic principles.

In Syria, Riad Seif, a carpenter's son who worked as a street vendor to pay for his education, shares profits of his shirts and ladies wear factory with his workers. It is very successful. "And within five years every employee can buy an apartment," he says.

But Islamic economics does not approve of today's extremists in the streets, says Karanshawy. "Economic growth [does] not result from instability."

And politically, Islamists tend to be undemocratic and counterproductive. Islamists headed five ministries in Jordan's recent government. But they proposed rulings that outraged Jordanians, such as a rule that fathers could not attend field days at their daughters' schools because girls would be in gym clothes. So King Hussein sacked the government and appointed a new one this month—pointedly excluding Islamists.

Because of the fundamentalists' intolerance of modern life, most Middle Easterners see fundamentalism as lacking answers to today's problems.

One problem is that the Middle East remains a series of uneconomic, one-country markets. There is no car production in the Middle East, but imported Mercedes are prominent on every street in Amman and Cairo, Damascus and Riyadh.

To get car production, with its spur to development of jobs and skills and wealth, the region's countries must cooperate to take advantage of their combined home market of hundreds of millions of people.

But doing so will force a change in today's state-dominated economies, in which business depends on the favors of a king or a national socialist government. In such patronage economies, monopolies and corruption are inevitable. Business is limited to what it can take from the local pie and so lacks the regional vision necessary for building larger markets, and a more productive Middle East economy.

The antidote is independent, competitive enterprise. And, indeed, that's the trend. As governments in the region find money tight, there is a general call for the private sector to become the engine of economic growth. State corporations are being privatized; local merchant and engineering companies that had existed on government contracts are being encouraged to invest their own capital and grow.

A Region of Promise

Ultimately, if enterprise becomes truly private, this historic but underdeveloped region will finally get competitive democratic politics too.

"With U.S. encouragement, within five years this region could open and develop," says Husain al-Jasem, the thoughtful deputy chairman of Kuwait Petrochemical Industries Co.

What's in it for Americans? A lot more than recent exaggerated expectations of billion-dollar state contracts to rebuild Kuwait. The trend could produce a Middle East advancing toward the economic output not of Italy alone but all of Europe. The promise is awesome.

225

"It is evident that the Middle East as a whole
will be much poorer in the 1990s than in the
1980s."

The Economic Future of
the Middle East Is Bleak

Yahya Sadowski

The Middle East has been marked by widespread poverty and
uneven economic development. In the following viewpoint,
Yahya Sadowski states that this dismal economic performance
will continue in the future. The expenses of the 1991 Persian
Gulf War, he argues, will burden even the oil-rich nations of the
Middle East and greatly worsen the condition of nations without
oil. He concludes that the economic problems and disparities in
the Middle East will inevitably lead to continued political conflict. Sadowski is an editor of *Middle East Report* and an analyst
at the Brookings Institution in Washington, D.C.

As you read, consider the following questions:

1. How was Saudi Arabia affected by the Persian Gulf War,
   according to Sadowski?
2. What is the importance of labor migration in the Middle East,
   according to the author?
3. What do you think Sadowski means by the "Arab cold war?"

Excerpted from "Power, Poverty, and Petrodollars" by Yahya Sadowski in *Middle East Report*
#170, May/June 1991, pages 4-10. Reprinted by permission of MERIP/Middle East Report,
1500 Massachusetts Ave. NW, #119, Washington, DC 20005.

For anyone who "follows the money," it is evident that the Middle East as a whole will be much poorer in the 1990s than in the 1980s.

Those in Washington and elsewhere who hope that the 1991 Gulf war will midwife a "new economic order" in the Middle East pin much of their hopes on contributions from Saudi Arabia—historically the largest oil exporter with the largest petroleum reserves, highest cash income earnings and most pivotal political position of any Gulf state.

Costs of the Persian Gulf War

Saudi Arabia emerged from the fighting relatively unscathed. A handful of Scud missiles hit Riyadh; Iraqi artillery set fire to the refinery at Khafji; and oil spills threatened desalinization plants. Yet the Saudis are finding their economic assets drained by the Gulf war. The day Iraq invaded Kuwait, business confidence in Gulf investments plummeted. The crisis dashed Saudi hopes that foreign concerns would invest $5-6 billion in new petrochemical works at Jubayl. The government had to cancel a dozen major projects as $10 billion of anticipated investment dried up. The Saudi stock market crashed. Saudi citizens began converting their savings accounts into dollars in preparation for fleeing the region, triggering a run on most banks. Eleven percent of all bank deposits were withdrawn, and the government had to pump $4.4 billion into the financial system to keep it from crashing. . . .

Using even the most conservative estimates, the cash cost of coping with the Gulf crisis drained $27.9 billion from the Saudi treasury by the end of 1990. By August 1991, Saudi Arabia will have spent some $64 billion on the war and associated costs, and some well-placed Saudis estimate the sum may actually reach as high as $80 billion. . . .

Most petroleum industry analysts agree that the actual Saudi receipts from oil sales in 1990 totalled $40-41 billion. This represents $14-16 billion more than the kingdom had expected to earn from oil sales before the Gulf crisis erupted. The expenses Riyadh incurred as a result of the crisis exceeded the value of this windfall by at least $10 billion. . . .

Saudi Arabia is not about to become a "poor" country, but the costs of the Gulf war will exceed all of its petrodollar windfall and most of its liquid assets, compelling Riyadh to borrow abroad. In early February 1991, when Iraq dumped oil from Kuwaiti terminals into the Gulf to imperil Saudi Arabia's desalinization plants, Riyadh reacted cautiously: the kingdom lacked the money to contemplate any massive effort to clean up the spill. On February 13, 1991, the *Washington Post* noted that the Saudis were preparing to make major sales of their holdings in U.S. government securities, and later that month Riyadh borrowed $3.5 billion as a loan syndicated by J.P. Morgan Co.

The war's economic burden will weigh less heavily on Saudi Arabia than on most of the other oil-rich Gulf states. The emir of Kuwait, like King Fahd, has been making handsome contributions to allied war coffers. He also has had to pay $500 million a month to sustain the Kuwaiti refugee population. Estimates of the cost of rebuilding Kuwait now generally start at $60 billion. Kuwait has earned no oil export revenues since August 2, and Iraqi troops dynamited 60-85 percent of its wells before they withdrew. It may take 5-10 years to restore the emirate's oil production to pre-war levels. The costs of rebuilding the country will have to be paid largely by liquidating part of Kuwait's $90 billion portfolio of foreign assets and taking out sizable loans secured against the rest.

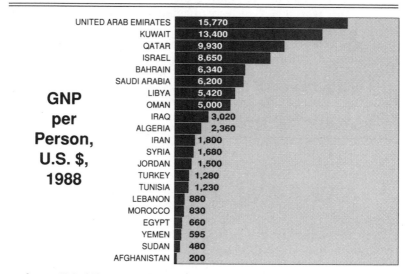

GNP per Person, U.S. $, 1988

UNITED ARAB EMIRATES	15,770
KUWAIT	13,400
QATAR	9,930
ISRAEL	8,650
BAHRAIN	6,340
SAUDI ARABIA	6,200
LIBYA	5,420
OMAN	5,000
IRAQ	3,020
ALGERIA	2,360
IRAN	1,800
SYRIA	1,680
JORDAN	1,500
TURKEY	1,280
TUNISIA	1,230
LEBANON	880
MOROCCO	830
EGYPT	660
YEMEN	595
SUDAN	480
AFGHANISTAN	200

Source: United Nations Development Programme, Human Development Report, 1991.

Iraq has been economically demolished by the war. On August 2, 1990 Baghdad was already shouldering a $23 billion fiscal deficit and $80 billion in foreign debts. Once the UN embargo was imposed, it began to lose $1.25 billion a month in oil revenues. Allied air strikes rapidly erased much of its economic infrastructure: bridges, power plants, factories and refineries. Now that the war is over, Baghdad may find commercial bankers unwilling to roll over old credits, much less extend new ones. Foreign firms, which built many of Iraq's industries, may be reluctant to resume work in a country where their employees have been held as "guests by force." As for Iraq's foreign assets, confiscated shortly after the invasion of Kuwait, the allies plan to hold them as part of the reparations owed to the victims of Saddam's invasion.

Some of the smaller states of the southern Gulf—Qatar and the United Arab Emirates—have been hit less hard by the war. But even before the conflict, their oil revenues were not large enough to make a major contribution to the economic development of the region. The US proposal to orchestrate the economic reconstruction of the region through a Middle East Development Bank, then, suffers from a major flaw: no state in the region really has the assets necessary to fund such an institution.

The diversion of oil profits into the Gulf war and reconstruction (and away from development projects) is going to have a major impact on the economies of the Middle East for years to come. It is too soon to make hard predictions, but certain broad effects are already apparent.

Shaky Banks

Within the Gulf states themselves, the war has dealt a body blow to the one economic sector—apart from oil—which had shown potential: finance. In March 1990 Offshore Banking Units (OBUs) in Bahrain held $73.3 billion in deposits and seemed to be on the verge of recovering from the problems which had afflicted them in the 1980s. When Iraq invaded Kuwait, thousands of their depositors withdrew $13.7 billion in assets (21 percent) and sent them abroad. Local commercial banks lost 15 percent of their deposits. A similar run consumed 11 percent of Saudi bank deposits and in the UAE [United Arab Emirates] withdrawals rose to 25 percent of liabilities. Kuwaiti banks ceased operations entirely. Iraq looted KD $365 million in securities and $800 million in gold which had been deposited with the central bank of Kuwait. . . .

The Gulf banks had been one of the major channels through which petrodollars had percolated from the Gulf into the rest of the Arab world. Aid from the oil-rich countries to their poorer neighbors had been declining throughout the 1980s. As the Gulf states divert their revenues to meeting war and reconstruction costs, aid will probably become even less available. Aid to states which appeared sympathetic to Iraq was suspended almost immediately. Saudi Arabia and Kuwait completely halted their contributions to the Palestine Liberation Organization, which had been running over $100 million per year. Jordan, too, quickly lost the $300 million in aid it had been receiving annually from Iraq and Kuwait, and now Riyadh also has cut its support, suspending concessionary oil shipments to Amman (worth

$1 million per day and representing half of Jordan's consumption). It also suspended economic aid to Amman, which had totalled $200 million annually and supplied 15 percent of the state budget.

Restricting aid to the Palestinians and Jordan freed up monies which the Saudis could then reallocate to countries which supported the kingdom in the Gulf conflict—chiefly Egypt, Syria, and Morocco. A similar change, benefitting Saudi allies while punishing "unfriendly" states, was evident in the most important single mechanism for redistributing petrodollars: labor migration. Before the crisis, all of the oil-rich Gulf states had employed large numbers of expatriate—largely Arab—workers who provided professional services (teachers, doctors, lawyers, engineers) or performed manual labor (construction, agriculture) which local citizens either could not or would not. Remittances formed a major source of hard currency for their home countries. The invasion of Kuwait massively disrupted this system. . . .

The substitution of Egyptian workers for Jordanians, Palestinians and Yemenis in Saudi Arabia and Kuwait will reinforce the same pattern evident in the reallocation of aid from those two states. Egypt and Syria may enjoy some relief from the economic constraints which had plagued them in the 1980s. Jordan, Yemen and Sudan, which the Saudis felt had shown too much sympathy for Baghdad, will find their economic problems enormously aggravated.

A Poor Outlook

Overall, the economic outlook for the Arab world is bleak. Remittances, tourist receipts, and financial aid will decline. Military spending and capital flight will increase. To the extent that the region's already heavy debt burden does not grow, it will largely be because credit is not available. The United States and its allies will not be able to ignore the Arab countries' economic troubles, but neither will they be able to address them successfully.

Joe Stork, *World Policy Journal*, Spring 1991.

This does not bode well for any "new economic order" in the Middle East. The Gulf war has made the region as a whole much poorer than it was in 1989, and the inequalities between the "have and have-not" states are likely to become even more pronounced. The growth of poverty and income disparities will translate into popular resentment and sooner or later will fuel political conflict. Instead of a "new order," the future probably holds a return to "the Arab cold war."

"There were significant stirrings of democratization across the Arab world well before the Gulf crisis."

Democracy Will Spread in the Middle East

Michael C. Hudson

Michael C. Hudson is a professor of international relations and government and Seif Ghobash Professor of Arab Studies in the School of Foreign Service, Georgetown University, in Washington, DC. In the following viewpoint, he argues that many Middle East nations have held elections and enacted other democratic reforms. He believes this demonstrates that democracy can become common in the Middle East, and that people who believe otherwise are stereotyping Arabs.

As you read, consider the following questions:

1. Why have there been few studies of the prospects for democracy in the Middle East, according to Hudson?
2. What examples does Hudson give of democratic reforms in the Middle East?
3. What predictions does the author make concerning the Middle East?

Excerpted from "After the Gulf War: Prospects for Democratization in the Arab World," by Michael C. Hudson, *The Middle East Journal*, vol. 45, no. 3, Summer 1991. Copyright © 1991 by the Middle East Institute. Reprinted with permission.

The military victory of the US-led coalition against Iraq has fueled speculation in the press and the think tanks of Washington about the possibility—perhaps the inevitability—of liberalization and democratization in Arab politics. This speculation in itself is surprising given the conventional wisdom in academic circles and educated public opinion that "Arab democracy" is virtually an oxymoron. In looking into this topic further, however, it is important to note that there were significant stirrings of democratization across the Arab world well before the Gulf crisis. We also should consider the possibility that the impact of the Gulf crisis could impede rather than accelerate this trend, at least in the short run.

Arab Stereotypes

The editors of a recent four-volume survey on democracy in developing countries ignored the Arab world entirely. To be sure, authoritarianism has been the dominant feature of modern Arab politics. In 1990, for example, *The Economist* observed that only five of seventeen major Arab states could be considered to exhibit an element of pluralism or, by generous standards, be called emerging democracies. Still, those five countries—Algeria, Egypt, Jordan, Morocco, and Tunisia—have a combined population of around 115 million people, or roughly 57 percent of the total Arab population. One might have thought that this might be sufficient evidence at least to pique the curiosity of specialists. Has the Orientalist stereotyping of the Arabs, so evident in parts of American academia and the news media, blinded mainstream analysts to the possibilities of more participatory politics in this region?

Prejudice and ignorance may have played a part in this curious neglect, but in fairness we should also look to our own paradigms and research agendas as well. Given the predominance of authoritarianism, political scientists working on the Middle East understandably have concentrated on explaining the *absence* of liberalism and democracy, to the neglect of studying less prominent countervailing tendencies. We have focused on society and political culture, portraying them as lacking in "civic" qualities, infused with patriarchal values, divided vertically by "traditional" or "primordial" loyalties and horizontally by social inequalities and immobility. What kind of political structure does this unruly social conglomeration sustain? We have identified it as the *mukhabarat* (national security) state, an authoritarian-bureaucratic Leviathan whose stability derives more from fear than legitimacy. We have also been able to chart its dramatic growth from the 1960s up through the mid-1980s, in terms of budgets, number of employees, internal security capabilities, and the like. Supporting that state, in the view of many

232

analysts, is the international political and economic order, which is shaped by the major industrialized countries whose governments—official positions notwithstanding—prefer to deal with dependent dictators.

Yet, notwithstanding all these apparent requisites of authoritarianism, there have been some remarkable rumblings of political liberalism and even democratization in the past several years, and recently a small number of Middle East specialists have begun to analyze them. Egypt under President Husni Mubarak is perhaps the "trailblazing" case, and, lately Algeria, Jordan, and newly unified Yemen have experienced significant openings. The Palestinians, despite (or perhaps because of) their lack of a territorial state, have developed a relatively open and participatory political process. There have also been less successful efforts, as in Morocco and Tunisia and in Kuwait before the Iraqi invasion. Sultan Qabus of Oman announced in November 1990 his intention to widen the representation in his country's consultative assembly within a year, and henceforth to exclude government membership in it. Also in November 1990, even Saudi Arabian King Fahd reaffirmed his intention to establish a long-promised advisory council, its members to be appointed, not elected. We have even seen gestures, albeit more cosmetic than substantive, in the highly authoritarian systems of Syria and of Iraq before its invasion of Kuwait. Finally, and clearly on the debit side of the ledger, a democratization experiment in the Sudan collapsed in a military coup in June 1989.

Moving Toward Democracy

While free multiparty elections have been rare in the Arab world, the region has not been the desert of dictatorships and absolute monarchies which critics often allege. Some countries such as Sudan have long histories of party politics, though they currently languish under military rule. Several, most notably Jordan and Algeria, are moving, in fits and starts, toward genuinely competitive pluralist systems. Others (Tunisia and Egypt, for example) are cautiously feeling their way toward genuine competition. In other states—Mauritania and possibly Kuwait in the near future—internal opposition pressures have pushed the government toward opening up the system.

Michael Collins Dunn, *The Washington Report on Middle East Affairs*, August/September 1991.

Multiparty electoral competition, a rarity 20 years ago, is making modest advances. Egypt has held regular legislative elections since 1976, the most recent in 1990. Morocco, too, holds regular elections and has a limited multiparty system. In 1989, Jordan held its first full legislative elections since 1967; party participation was illegal but tolerated. The now-defunct Yemen Arab Republic (YAR) held free legislative elections in 1988, and, while parties were banned, surrogate political groups were active. Tunisia, in the post-Bourguiba era, held parliamentary elections in 1989 in which some opposition parties were allowed. Even Iraq—the quintessential mukhabarat state—held parliamentary elections in 1989 which were swept by the ruling Baath Party and its tame allies, an event of little intrinsic importance: yet, officials in Baghdad, interviewed before the Gulf crisis, saw these elections as the opening step in the government's plan for constitutional reform and limited political relaxation in the post-Iran-Iraq War period. Following Iraq's defeat by the US-led coalition in February 1991, President Saddam Hussein publicly announced his government's decision to move toward a democratic society, the rule of law, and a multiparty system.

In June 1990, there was a flurry of electoral activity around the Arab world. Syria held elections to its People's Assembly; only tame parties were allowed, but independent candidates increased their share of seats. Tunisia and Algeria held municipal and provincial elections, the former's swept by the ruling party, but the latter's by all accounts a wide-open genuinely free election—a rare event, indeed, in the contemporary Arab world. With the declaration of unity between the two Yemens a new transitional parliament was created, joining the legislatures of the former People's Democratic Republic of Yemen (PDRY) and the YAR, with the addition of 31 appointees to represent previously excluded parties and tendencies. The case of Kuwait was to prove especially interesting. In June 1990, Kuwait held carefully controlled elections to a new "national council," to prepare the way for reconvening the parliament, the National Assembly, dissolved in 1986 by [the Emir's] decree. Following the liberation of Kuwait from Iraqi occupation in February 1991, greatly intensified pressure to democratize was brought to bear on the ruling Sabah family both by the traditional opposition and by the Kuwaiti resistance movement that developed during the Iraqi occupation. . . .

War's Negative Impact

What, then, of the impact of the 1991 Gulf War? Although the reverberations within the region are still far from clear, this author is inclined to think that they will set back the process of democratization—if such it be—in the short run. This is mainly because political insecurity, tension, and even instability emanating from the conflict are likely to have put mukhabarats throughout the area on a heightened state of alert. Regimes will be increasingly uneasy about allowing free public expression or political organization. The "state of emergency" mentality that inhibited political openings in the past will now be more pervasive and less tolerant. The increased tension will arise both from the substantial new economic damage that has been done throughout the region as a result of the crisis and also from the new political animosities it has spawned. Regimes will have some reason to fear the consequences of mass protests, whether they arise from economic or political grievances. They will fear even more the possibility of terrorism, armed attacks, assassination, and other forms of subversion. They will wonder whether the Pandora's Box of ethnic and sectarian hostilities opened wide by the postwar rebellions in Iraq will spread, or at a minimum, whether such hostilities will not polarize fragile experiments in political participation. They will worry that Islamic movements—perhaps the major beneficiaries from the feelings of humiliation so widely generated by the war—will become too popular and uncontrollable. . . .

The Rise of Public Opinion

The stereotype of Arab leaders as autocrats free to ignore the popular will is fading as the phenomenon of public opinion emerges in the Arab world. The development of more vocal popular sentiment reflects advances in literacy, access to media, and increasing awareness of events outside the region; it is leading to a growing sense of empowerment that partially constrains the policy choices available to presidents and monarchs.

Muhammad Muslih and Augustus Richard Norton, *Foreign Policy*, Summer 1991.

Long-run predictions are even more hazardous. While the immediate aftershocks of the Gulf War may generate a climate inimical to democratization, the deeper trends that were evident before the war may continue to have their liberalizing effect. The growing popular disgust with authoritarian rule, that is not only often cruel but also incompetent, is not likely to be diminished by the behavior of Iraqi president Saddam Hussein and some other Middle Eastern leaders. At the same time the process of developing a more effective civil society, while probably set back by the particularist feelings unleashed by the war, is driven inexorably by the socioeconomic changes, even the painful ones, that are ubiquitous throughout the Arab world. Direct US government efforts to promote "democracy" will probably be counterproductive, and it is debatable just how much Washington really wants it. Yet, as Arabs contemplate their place in the "new world order" it is likely that they will demand—and finally achieve—more representative government than they have had in the past.

=====

"The traditional Arab weakness for despots does not seem to have diminished over the decades."

=====

Democracy Will Not Spread in the Middle East

Danielle Pletka

Most Middle Eastern countries are run by monarchies or military dictatorships. The sweeping political changes in Eastern Europe and elsewhere have caused much speculation as to whether Western-style democracy could be established in the Middle East. In the following viewpoint, Danielle Pletka argues that cultural and religious factors, such as the role of Islam and a legacy of tribalism and ethnic conflict, prevent Middle Easterners from accepting democracy in the region. Pletka is a reporter for *Insight*, a weekly newsmagazine.

As you read, consider the following questions:

1. Into what three basic groups does Pletka divide the Arab countries and their governments?
2. Why are there no underground pro-democracy movements in Arab countries, in the author's opinion?
3. How might Iraq's 1990 invasion of Kuwait change Arab resistance to democracy, according to Pletka?

There are 19 Arab states, 20 if you count Palestine, and 21 with Iran, which is not Arab but casts its Islamic shadow over the Arab world. Not one qualifies as a democracy.

Algeria comes closest. An economic quagmire and ebbing government popularity sent the nation's single party in an unusual direction: The National Liberation Front, which has ruled Algeria since independence in 1962, abdicated its monopoly, wrote a new constitution, allowed some 20 new political parties and held free local elections in June 1990.

Less happily for the secular-minded, the legalized fundamentalist party swept the vote. So far, that means fundamentalists control only the towns and regional councils. But the exultant winners were quick to demand national elections. They were as quickly refused by the powers that be. Still, it seems certain that in any national poll, the fundamentalists could repeat their stunning performance. And that, some suspect, will be the end of democratic experiments.

Rigged Elections

Tunisia and Egypt, the Arab world's other two daring democrats, have avoided a similar problem with fundamentalists by simply banning the peskiest religious parties. That leaves other opposition groups in play, but it is only play. Elections are rigged and real power is never up for grabs.

Unlike their North African counterparts—forced into elections because they cannot afford to buy legitimacy from their subjects—the wealthy sheikhs of the Persian Gulf shun the free-for-all of representative politics. Their populations are much smaller and their people have lots of money, pay no taxes and get most everything they need free from the government. People with good jobs and warm homes worry less about legitimacy. Then too, they know that a word amiss can mean jail, torture and death.

Several Gulf sheikhdoms have toyed with national assemblies or consultative councils. But these are merely forums in which citizens air their gripes of the moment, rather than political bodies. Indeed, in 1986, when Kuwait's National Assembly began to take itself more seriously than the emir expected (it criticized the regime and was accused of "democratic tendencies"), he quickly closed it down.

Military dictatorships such as those in Iraq, Syria and Libya are less free with cash than their palace counterparts. For one thing, most cannot afford to dole out the perks that the oil royalty can. And they would rather spend their money on arms.

The curious will search in vain for a pro-democracy underground in any of these states. "There are no mass movements out there; there isn't even a samizdat literature, no Vaclav

Havels," says Samir al-Khalil, the pseudonymous Iraqi author of "Republic of Fear." "The Arab world is in a different historical period than Eastern Europe. It's 20 years behind, at least."

One reason is that almost all popular discontent manifests itself as Islamic fervor. Islam has become the religion of rejection, whether of the shah and American clientism, as in Iran, or of the existing regime, as in Algeria, or simply of the excesses of the oil-rich 1970s. The very nature of Islam, say some, precludes the possibility of democracy. "For a majority of Islamicists, there is no room for democracy, freedom of belief, freedom of expression," says Abdulaziz Fahad, a Saudi lawyer.

Three Traditions That Hinder Democracy

New York Times reporter Thomas Friedman . . . argues that regimes in the Middle East are the product of three different but intertwined traditions: tribalism, authoritarianism, and the culture of the modernizing bureaucracies. Tribalism is characterized by the belief that resources are scarce; that you need power to secure enough for yourself, your kin, and your tribe; and that to survive you must punish and make an example of those who would trespass on your tribe's, clan's, or family's space. In the authoritarian tradition, itself the product of societies divided along tribal, ethnic, confessional, and other lines, power is concentrated in one man who can maintain order and whom all are expected to obey. The modernizing bureaucracies are determined to use centralized power to create modern nation-states in countries where state traditions are weak or nonexistent. This, too, is a formula for considerable concentration of power in the hands of a ruling group.

Shaul Bakhash, *Dissent*, Summer 1991.

Among other inbuilt problems, Islam dictates the unity of church and state. Law is Islamic law, and legitimacy is in the hands of Koran-toting imams. Though Islamic parties have found their way into democratic politics in Egypt, Jordan and North Africa and have vowed to operate within the confines of that system, this flexibility may condemn them to overthrow by more dogmatic Islamists.

More inimical to democracy than the religious mania is enduring tribalism. Take Lebanon, divided among a dozen sects and as many militias. Beirut's weak central government had no hope of combating the armed tribes that rose to conquer the nation for themselves. And after 15 years of civil war, Lebanon was finally taken over by someone strong enough to cow any militia: Syria's Hafez al-Assad.

Some argue this was inevitable, that the Arab world *needs* strongmen: They are the only glue that can bind the tribes cobbled into states half a century ago. Assad, indeed, has had remarkable success in quelling his local rivals. Lacking oil to grease the wheels of national unity, he has terrorized his population into peace. Thus Syria has been ruled by a member of its most hated minority, the Alawis, for 21 years.

Adib al-Jader, the Geneva-based president of the Arab Organization for Human Rights, dismisses the strongman theory out of hand. "That's stupid," he says. "You need a strong government, but you don't need one man. Strength comes from the participation of all people in government."

Weakness for Despots

Yet if [Iraqi leader] Saddam Hussein is any example, the Arab masses do not subscribe to Jader's ideas about democracy. The traditional Arab weakness for despots does not seem to have diminished over the decades. Like Gamal Abdel Nasser before him, Saddam has mesmerized the masses with rhetoric about Arab unity and self-respect. And like, Nasser, he has led the Arab world to war.

"It is the human propensity for shortcuts," explains Fahad of Saddam's appeal. "People who are frustrated tend to want shortcuts to overcome all their difficulties. One way is with a Stalin-like character who makes the trains run on time, and the other alternative is meticulous institution building. Unfortunately, we have a sufficient number of people who want to do it the short way."

Each new despot tantalizes the Arab world with a return to the glory days of yore. Like Saddam, who overthrew his predecessor, and the Ayatollah Ruhollah Khomeini, who took over from the shah, each holds out the hope of restoring Islamic pre-eminence. And on their way to power each finds it useful to talk about democracy and giving voice to the aspirations of the Arab masses.

"The people who objected to the shah spoke the language of free speech and human rights, and the ayatollah was quick enough to say he would implement those things," says David Pryce-Jones, author of "The Closed Circle," an interpretation of the Arabs. "What he actually meant was that he was going to take power for himself and cut off the heads of all who opposed him."

The Middle East's organized opposition groups today seem hardly better than those they seek to depose. Anti-Saddamites are largely Iranian-backed fundamentalists who would replicate the Iranian-style theocracy in Baghdad. Other opponents are rival Arab socialists backed by Syria's Assad, indistinguishable from the Iraqi ruling party but for their sponsor.

Outside the religious fanatics and roving gangs of terrorists, the opposition to the autocrats of the Arab world is powerless and largely in exile. Intellectuals run newsletters out of London and Paris in their spare time, holding only a local audience of Arab expatriates in their thrall, with little or no influence in their home countries. Most despair of change. "We have a war generation everywhere," says Khalil. "The best minds of Arab intellectuals are professional cynics of the first order. They lack any hope."

Democracy and Israel

Even in Israel, where only three out of four residents enjoy democracy (Arabs in the occupied territories are fully excluded, those behind the Green Line partially so), the topic will not disappear. Quite understandably Israelis and Arabs are obsessed with the question of freedom. The cacophony ranges from calls for a Palestinian state to a dispute within the Israeli right about whether Israel can simultaneously be a Jewish state and a democratic one. Yet despite the vigorous commitment of the Israeli government to democracy for Jews, it is no less committed to withholding this freedom from Arabs. Can a polity in which only three-quarters of the residents enjoy democracy be called a democracy? What of the other 25 percent?

Jerrold Green, *American-Arab Affairs*, Spring 1991.

That leaves the forces of change in the hands of the leaders—the kings, emirs and presidents for life—who may find that their survival depends on greater attention to questions of legitimacy.

The Arab world continues to grow at an astonishing rate—on par with the most prolific of Third World nations. In the wealthy and underpopulated petrocracies, pressure for political liberalization is more a reflection of middle-class ennui than seething discontent. Next door, however, in those states where the population is expanding and poverty and ethnic cleavages make democracy a nonstarter, the favored response to dissent at home is adventurism abroad, as Saddam ably demonstrated when he found support from the Arab masses for his Kuwait grab.

Ironically, it may be Saddam who frightens the Arab world out of the 13th century. The 1990 Kuwait invasion laid bare the mirages of the Middle East: unity, brotherhood, stability—the myths that once saved the rich and powerless states from the poor and powerful. "People found that all these regimes are not stable," says Jader. "And all these establishments—the Gulf Cooperation Council, where is it? Just on paper. Where is the Kuwaiti army?

There is no such thing. Iraq went through in six hours.

"People started thinking something's wrong," he adds. "In the States now, we watch hearings and Republicans and Democrats debate the secretary of defense, the chief of staff. You don't find that in the Arab world, so people compare: Why is this happening? What is wrong? Why don't we do the same thing?"

Suddenly, the most lethargic of societies has come alive. A former Saudi minister of information published an unheard-of question in the once moribund Saudi press: "Are not the Arabs responsible for their own failures? Are not their own fingers worse than the world Zionism with which we frighten our children?"

New Promises

Such heresies have been noticed in the Gulf's palaces. Saudi Arabia's King Fahd ibn Abdul Aziz has said he will set up consultative councils around the country, a promise he and his predecessors have reneged on before. The exiled Kuwaiti government has vowed to reconstitute the National Assembly dissolved in 1986. Oman's leader has ordered the creation of a consultative council, to be made up of representatives from all 42 Omani provinces.

Will they keep this year's promises? Saudis privately admit that if the government can get away with it, the status quo will prevail. And, says Khalil, it will continue to prevail because the outside world will always jump in and rescue the Arabs. "Arab must fight Arab," he says. "By fighting over a question like the invasion of Kuwait, one is fighting for a new order. A war over the restitution of sovereignty is a war over principle, and that principle is a fundamental one to democracy."

As yet, however, the Arabs are relying on 400,000 Americans to do the fighting. And when the Americans leave, they may well take their principles with them.

a critical thinking activity

Recognizing Statements
That Are Provable

We are constantly confronted with statements and generalizations about social and moral problems. In order to think clearly about these problems, it is useful if one can make a basic distinction between statements for which evidence can be found and other statements which cannot be verified or proved because evidence is not available, or the issue is so controversial that it cannot be definitely proved.

Readers should be aware that magazines, newspapers, and other sources often contain statements of a controversial nature. The following activity is designed to allow experimentation with statements that are provable and those that are not.

The following statements are taken from the viewpoints in this chapter. Consider each statement carefully. *Mark P for any statement you believe is provable. Mark U for any statement you feel is unprovable because of the lack of evidence. Mark C for any statements you think are too controversial to be proved to everyone's satisfaction.*

If you are doing this activity as a member of a class or group, compare your answers with those of other class or group members. Be able to defend your answers. You may discover that others will come to different conclusions than you do. Listening to the reasons others present for their answers may give you valuable insights in recognizing statements that are provable.

P = provable
U = unprovable
C = too controversial

1. The Saudi Arabian stock market crashed the day Iraq invaded Kuwait.

2. The Arab world will never be the same as it was before the 1991 Persian Gulf War.

3. No Arab state endorsed the Iraqi invasion of Kuwait.

4. The tension between the rich and poor Arab states can only be resolved by the Arabs themselves.

5. The wave of democratization that has swept Europe and Latin America has so far bypassed the Middle East.

6. Israel invaded Lebanon in 1982.

7. It would delight most Arab leaders if both Israel and the Palestinians would simply disappear.

8. The gross national product of all the nations of the Middle East does not equal that of Italy.

9. According to population growth figures, the population of the Middle East is expected to double within twenty years.

10. The Middle East is on the verge of an economic boom.

11. The economic outlook for the Middle East is bleak.

12. The Palestinians must be granted their own state in order to achieve peace between the Arabs and the Israelis.

13. The Arab world needs strong dictators.

14. Tunisia and Egypt are two Arab countries that hold elections.

15. Bias against Arabs has blinded the U.S. media to the possibilities for democracy in the Middle East.

16. Arab democracy is an oxymoron.

17. Following their liberation from Iraq, many Kuwaitis called for democratic reforms in their government.

Periodical Bibliography

The following articles have been selected to supplement the diverse views presented in this chapter.

Fouad Ajami	"The End of Arab Nationalism," *The New Republic*, August 12, 1991.
Naseer Aruri	"Trouble in the Wake of War," *Dollars & Sense*, June 1991.
Hossein Askari	"Restoring the Gulf's Health," *U.S. News & World Report*, March 18, 1991.
Shlomo Avineri	"The Impact of Changes of the Soviet Union and Eastern Europe on the Arab-Israeli Conflict," *Mediterranean Quarterly*, Winter 1991. Available from Duke University Press, PO Box 6697, College Station, Durham, NC 27708.
Shaul Bakhash	"Democracy in the Arab World?" *Dissent*, Summer 1991.
Lisa Beyer	"Let the Game Begin," *Time*, October 28, 1991.
Stephen Budiansky et al.	"Saying Hello to a New Era?" *U.S. News & World Report*, August 19, 1991.
Helena Cobban	"Meeting Mideast Fears," *World Monitor*, June 1991.
Christopher Dickey	"What If the Talks Aren't All Talk?" *Newsweek*, November 4, 1991.
Global Affairs	"The Middle East in Transition," Fall 1991. Available from the International Security Council, 1155 15th St. NW, Suite 502, Washington, DC 20005.
Fred Halliday	"The Post-Crisis Crisis: Balancing the Mideast," *In These Times*, April 10-16, 1991.
Samir Al-Khalil	"In the Mideast, Does Democracy Have a Chance?" *The New York Times Magazine*, October 14, 1990.
Daniel Pipes	"Is Damascus Ready for Peace?" *Foreign Affairs*, Fall 1991.
Richard L. Rothstein	"The Middle East After the War: Change and Continuity," *The Washington Quarterly*, Summer 1991.
Alvin Z. Rubinstein	"New World Order or Hollow Victory?" *Foreign Affairs*, Fall 1991.
Lamin Sanneh	"Winning the War and Struggling with Peace," *The Christian Century*, April 10, 1991.
Shawn Tully	"The Best Case for Mideast Peace," *Fortune*, May 20, 1991.

Chronology of Events

1897	Theodor Herzl convenes First Zionist Congress, which designates Palestine as an appropriate Jewish homeland. Less than 10 percent of Palestine's population is Jewish.
1914-1918	World War I. Arab nationalists cooperate with Britain against Turkey. Turkey's Ottoman Empire collapses.
1917	British foreign secretary A. J. Balfour declares Britain's support for a national homeland for the Jewish people in Palestine, a declaration that conflicts with promises to the Arabs.
1920	Lebanon established as French Mandate.
1920-1948	Britain rules Palestine under agreement with the League of Nations. The British Mandate approves limited immigration for Jews.
1921	Military officer Reza Khan rules Iran after a coup and begins a secularization campaign that abolishes many Islamic customs.
	Faisal I, with the support of the British, is made king of Iraq, which is comprised of three former Ottoman Empire provinces.
1922	At the Uqair Conference, the modern borders of Iraq, Saudi Arabia, and Kuwait are drawn by representatives of the British government.
1928	The Muslim Brotherhood is established in Egypt as a movement of fundamentalist reform among Sunni Muslims.
1929-1939	Arabs rebel against British rule; Arabs fight Jews for the right to live in Palestine.
1932	British rule over Iraq ends. Iraq is admitted to the League of Nations as an independent state.
1939-1945	World War II. Six million Jews are killed by Nazi Germany. Jewish population in Palestine swells to 608,000 by 1946.
1941	British and Soviet forces, concerned that Reza Khan is allied with Hitler, invade Iran and depose the monarch, replacing him with his son, Muhammed Reza Khan Pahlavi.
November 1943	Lebanon achieves independence with government posts given to members of each of the main religious groups. Because Christians outnumber members of the other groups at this time, the president is a Christian.
March 1945	Egypt, Iraq, Jordan, and Lebanon found the Arab League.

November 29, 1947	UN General Assembly votes to partition Palestine into Jewish and Arab states with Jerusalem being an international city. Arabs refuse.
May 14, 1948	State of Israel is proclaimed. Five Arab League states attack Israel. At the war's end, Israel takes more land than originally assigned. More than one-half million Palestinians flee Israel.
September 17, 1948	Jewish terrorists assassinate UN mediator Count Folke Bernadotte.
1952	Officers of the Egyptian army overthrow King Farouk and replace him with their leader, Gamal Abdel Nasser.
July 1956	U.S. and Britain refuse to support a loan to Egypt to build the Aswan Dam; in retaliation, Nasser nationalizes the Suez Canal. After Britain freezes Egyptian assets held in England, Egypt closes the canal.
October 1956	The Israelis, with military aid from Britain and France, invade Egypt. They take the Gaza Strip and the Sinai Peninsula, which they later return in a peace settlement.
1956-1958	First Lebanese civil war. Pre-war conditions are restored by U.S. after a stalemate between warring religious groups.
1958	Faisal II, who had succeeded Faisal I as king of Iraq, is assassinated. Gen. Abdul Karim Kassem installs himself as military dictator of Iraq.
August 1959	Jordan offers citizenship to all Palestinian refugees.
January 1961	Iran, Iraq, Kuwait, and Saudi Arabia found the Organization of Petroleum Exporting Countries (OPEC).
May 1964	Palestine Liberation Organization (PLO) is established.
May 1967	Nasser orders UN emergency forces to withdraw from the Sinai, declares a state of emergency in the Gaza Strip, and closes the Strait of Tiran to shipping to and from Israel. Israel and the U.S. warn Egypt to remove blockade.
June 5-10, 1967	Six Day War. Israel attacks Egypt, Jordan, and Syria and captures the Sinai, Gaza Strip, West Bank, and Golan Heights.
November 22, 1967	UN Security Council Resolution 242 calling for peace in the Middle East is adopted. The resolution asks that Israel return land acquired in the Six Day War and that Arabs respect Israel's boundaries.

1969	Yasir Arafat and Fatah (the largest Palestinian group) take over the PLO and give it a more aggressive role.
	Muammar Qaddafi overthrows King Idris I of Libya.
1970	Nasser dies at age fifty-two. Vice President Anwar Sadat takes over leadership of Egypt.
	Libyan leader Qaddafi removes British and U.S. military bases from Libya.
1970-1971	Jordanian civil war. King Hussein crushes Palestinian guerrillas and invading troops. Palestinians move offices from Jordan to Beirut, Lebanon.
October 6, 1973	Yom Kippur War. Egypt and Syria surprise Israel in a two-front attack. The U.S. and USSR, who are both involved, urge a cease-fire.
October 18, 1973	First day of five-month Arab oil embargo cutting off or sharply curtailing oil exports to countries that support Israel.
November 11, 1973	Egypt and Israel sign a cease-fire.
February 28, 1974	U.S. and Egypt renew full diplomatic relations.
October 1974	The UN grants the PLO observer status and allows it to participate in debates on the Palestinian question.
April 1975	In Lebanon, Christian Phalangists attack Palestinians, touching off large-scale confrontations between Christians and Muslims. Syria participates on the side of the Muslims.
November 9-21, 1977	Sadat makes the first visit of an Arab leader to Israel to promote renewed peace talks.
September 5-17, 1978	Camp David summit meeting between U.S. president Carter, Sadat, and Israeli prime minister Menachem Begin leads to an Egyptian-Israeli peace agreement and accords on the Palestinian question. Most of the Arab states, the Soviets, and the PLO denounce the agreements.
January-February 1979	After months of unrest, the government of Iran is overthrown. The shah is replaced by Muslim fundamentalists led by Ayatollah Khomeini.
July 1979	Saddam Hussein seizes power in Iraq.
November 4, 1979	Militants storm the U.S. embassy in Tehran, Iran, and hold fifty-two Americans hostage for the next fourteen months.
September 1980	Iran makes air attacks on Iraqi towns. A few weeks later, Iraq invades Iran, beginning what will become an eight-year war.

June 7-10, 1981	Israel bombs a nuclear reactor in Iraq "to prevent another holocaust." The U.S. refuses to deliver promised military equipment to Israel.
October 1981	Sadat is assassinated by members of the Egyptian army. Vice President Hosni Mubarak takes over the government.
February 1982	Syrian leader Hafez Assad's troops crush a Muslim Brotherhood uprising in the city of Hama, killing more than ten thousand people.
June-September 1982	Israel invades Lebanon; it occupies Beirut and demands that the PLO leave the city. U.S. Marines help oversee the PLO evacuation. The PLO establishes its headquarters in Tunisia.
August-September 1982	Bashir Gemayel, a Maronite Christian, is elected president of Lebanon. He is killed one month later. His brother, Amin, is elected. Christian militia massacre hundreds of Palestinians in Sabra and Shatila refugee camps.
April 18, 1983	Sixty-three people are killed in the bombing of the U.S. embassy in Beirut.
May 17, 1983	Lebanon and Israel sign an agreement to withdraw Israeli forces from Lebanon. Israel refuses to withdraw completely until Syria also withdraws.
October 23, 1983	A pro-Iranian suicide bomber drives an explosive-laden truck into U.S. Marine headquarters in Beirut, killing 241 people. U.S. troops later redeploy offshore.
January 1984	Reagan administration officially lists Iran as a supporter of international terrorism and cuts arms sales to Iran.
March 16, 1984	William Buckley, CIA station chief in Beirut, is kidnapped by pro-Iranian Muslim group. He is later tortured and killed.
May 16, 1985	Journalist Terry A. Anderson is kidnapped and held hostage in Lebanon. He becomes the longest-held American hostage of the eighteen kidnapped by various Islamic groups in Lebanon between 1982 and 1991. The hostages are taken to extract various political and financial concessions from the U.S. and other nations, including the release of Islamic prisoners in Israel and Kuwait. Of the eighteen American hostages, three died or were killed in captivity, one escaped, six were released before 1987, two were released in 1990, and the remaining six were released in 1991.

June 1985	Shiite gunmen hijack TWA flight 847 and hold its 153 passengers hostage. They kill a U.S. Navy passenger. Most passengers are released except for 39 Americans, who are taken to Beirut. Iranian officials help negotiate freedom for the Americans.
October 7, 1985	Four Palestinians hijack the Italian ship *Achille Lauro* and hold four hundred hostages. They kill Leon Klinghoffer, an elderly American Jew.
April 14, 1986	Reagan, arguing that Libyan leader Qaddafi supports anti-American terrorism, orders the bombing of the Libyan cities of Tripoli and Benghazi. Dozens of Libyans die as many homes are hit, including Qaddafi's.
November 1986	The U.S. government reveals that it covertly sold arms to Iran and diverted profits to the Nicaraguan contra resistance in Central America. The scandal becomes known as the Iran-contra affair.
January 20, 1987	Hostage negotiator Terry Waite is himself taken hostage while seeking the release of two Americans.
May 17, 1987	An Iraqi fighter plane attacks and disables patrolling U.S. warship *Stark*, killing thirty-seven members of its crew.
June 1, 1987	A bomb explodes on board a plane carrying Lebanese prime minister Rashid Karami, killing him instantly.
December 1987	Four Palestinians are killed when an Israeli army truck rams their car after they attempt to run a military roadblock in Gaza. During their funeral, Israeli troops clash with mourners. The event marks the beginning of widespread Palestinian protests and rioting that come to be called the *intifada*.
July 3, 1988	U.S. Navy ship patrolling Persian Gulf accidentally shoots down Iranian commercial airliner, killing 290.
August 1988	Iran and Iraq accept UN peace terms and announce cease-fire. The eight-year war leaves more than one million casualties. An estimated 100,000 Kurds flee to Turkey amidst reports that Iraq is attacking them with poison gas.
September 22, 1988	President Amin Gemayel of Lebanon, minutes before his term expires, names Christian general Michel Aoun leader of a provisional military government.

November 1988	Palestine National Council (PNC) meets in Algiers, votes to accept UN Security Council resolutions 242 and 338, which call for Arab Recognition of Israel and Israeli withdrawal from territories occupied since 1967. PLO leader Yasir Arafat declares Palestine an independent state.
December 1988	The U.S. establishes a "diplomatic dialogue" with the PLO after Arafat renounces terrorism and states that he accepts the right of "Palestine, Israel and other neighbors" to exist in peace.
February 1989	Iranian leader Khomeini calls for Muslims to execute Indian-born British author Salman Rushdie, whose novel *The Satanic Verses* Khomeini calls blasphemous.
May 23, 1989	Egypt attends an Arab League meeting for the first time in ten years.
June 3, 1989	Iranian leader Khomeini dies in Tehran.
November 8, 1989	Parliamentary elections are held in Jordan; Islamic fundamentalists win thirty-two of the sixty-two contested seats in the eighty-seat parliament.
November 22, 1989	Days after his election, Lebanese president Rene Moawad is assassinated; Elias Hrawi is elected president by Lebanese parliament; military leader Aoun denounces election.
April 2, 1990	Iraqi president Saddam Hussein claims Iraq possesses advanced chemical weapons; threatens to destroy half of Israel if it launches any preemptive strike against Iraq.
May 22, 1990	North Yemen (Yemen Arab Republic) and South Yemen (People's Democratic Republic of Yemen) unite to become the Republic of Yemen.
May 30, 1990	Palestinian terrorists in two speedboats try to land on Israeli beaches in an attempted terrorist attack but are captured or killed by Israeli security forces. The Palestine Liberation Front, a faction of the PLO, claims responsibility; PLO chairman Arafat denies official link between the incident and the PLO. U.S. later suspends its dialogue with the PLO, citing Arafat's failure to condemn the incident.
June 21, 1990	Earthquake in Iran kills 35,000, leaves 400,000 homeless. U.S. offers humanitarian assistance; Iran accepts.
August 2, 1990	Iraq invades Kuwait. The emir of Kuwait flees to Saudi Arabia. The UN Security Council passes Resolution 660 condemning the invasion and demanding Iraq's immediate and unconditional withdrawal from Kuwait.

August 6, 1990	The UN Security Council passes Resolution 661, which imposes a trade embargo and economic sanctions on Iraq.
August 7, 1990	U.S. president George Bush, after consulting with the leaders of Great Britain, the Soviet Union, Japan, Egypt, and Saudi Arabia, sends U.S. forces to Saudi Arabia to protect it from a potential Iraqi invasion.
November 8, 1990	Bush orders a near doubling of U.S. forces in the Persian Gulf.
November 29, 1991	The UN Security Council passes Resolution 678 authorizing the use of "all necessary means" to force Iraq from Kuwait if Iraq does not withdraw before January 15, 1991.
January 9, 1991	Talks between U.S. secretary of state James Baker and Iraqi foreign minister Tariq Aziz take place in Geneva, Switzerland, but fail to resolve the crisis.
January 16, 1991	Coalition forces launch massive air attacks on Iraq. Israel declares a state of emergency and imposes a curfew in the occupied territories.
January 18, 1991	Iraq attacks Israel with Scud missiles, causing light casualties. The U.S. responds by sending troops to operate Patriot anti-missile systems in Israel.
February 23, 1991	The U.S.-led multinational coalition launches a massive ground offensive against Iraqi troops.
February 27, 1991	Bush declares victory over Iraq and announces the liberation of Kuwait. He orders Allied combat suspended at midnight. A permanent cease-fire is later negotiated.
March 1991	Iraq releases prisoners of war. Civil unrest spreads throughout Iraq as a Kurdish rebellion begins in the north and Shiite Muslims rebel in the south. The rebellions are brutally crushed by forces loyal to Saddam Hussein.
April 1991	The UN Security Council passes resolutions establishing a formal cease-fire between Iraq and the UN coalition, requiring Iraq to destroy its chemical and nuclear weapons, and condemning Iraq's treatment of the Kurds. U.S. troops enter northern Iraq to protect returning Kurdish refugees and to assist humanitarian efforts. U.S. secretary of state James Baker makes numerous trips to the Middle East to promote an international peace conference.
May 22, 1991	Lebanese president Hrawi and Syrian president Assad sign a cooperation treaty that many believe reflects Syria's control over Lebanon.

June 2, 1991	The emir of Kuwait announces that parliamentary elections will be held in October 1992.
June 4, 1991	Algeria's first multiparty legislative elections are postponed indefinitely as a state of emergency is declared in response to a twelve-day nationwide strike.
June 28, 1991	Iraqi troops fire warning shots over the heads of UN inspectors who are trying to photograph heavily laden trucks leaving a base near Falluja, thirty miles west of Baghdad. The trucks are believed to be carrying equipment used to make fissionable material for nuclear weapons.
July 4, 1991	After four days of clashes around Sidon, Lebanon, the PLO agrees to withdraw from its only military base near Israel.
July 7, 1991	King Hussein of Jordan cancels martial law conditions imposed following the 1967 Arab-Israeli war.
July 15, 1991	The last of three thousand Allied troops, who had been protecting and assisting the Kurdish refugees, withdraw from Iraq into Turkey.
September 17, 1991	After months of negotiations, the U.S. announces it will host an international peace conference to be held in Madrid, Spain.
October 30, 1991	International Middle East peace conference is convened in Madrid, Spain. The event marks the first open and direct negotiations between Israel, Syria, Jordan, Lebanon, and the Palestinians. No treaties or agreements are signed. The participants agree to meet for further talks.
December 4, 1991	Terry A. Anderson, the last U.S. hostage held in Lebanon, is released after more than six years of captivity.
December 10, 1991	Delegations from Israel, Syria, Lebanon, Jordan, and the Palestinians meet in Washington, D.C. for a second round of peace talks.

Organizations to Contact

The editors have compiled the following list of organizations that are concerned with the issues debated in this book. All of them have publications or information available for interested readers. For best results, allow as much time as possible for the organizations to respond. The descriptions are derived from materials provided by the organizations. This list was compiled upon the date of publication. Names and phone numbers of organizations are subject to change.

Americans for a Safe Israel
147 E. 76th St.
New York, NY 10021
(212) 628-9400

The organization disseminates information on conflict in the Middle East. It believes that a strong Israel is important for American security interests. Its publications include books, pamphlets, news updates, articles, videos, and the monthly magazine *Outpost*.

Americans for Middle East Understanding (AMEU)
475 Riverside Dr., Rm. 241
New York, NY 10115
(212) 870-2053

AMEU's purpose is to foster a better understanding in America of the history, goals, and values of Middle Eastern cultures and peoples, the rights of Palestinians, and the forces shaping American policy in the Middle East. AMEU publishes *The Link*, a bimonthly newsletter, and books and pamphlets on the Middle East.

Anti-Defamation League of the B'nai B'rith (ADL)
823 United Nations Plaza
New York, NY 10017
(212) 490-2525

The ADL works to stop the defamation of the Jewish people and to promote understanding among people of different races, creeds, and ethnic backgrounds. The ADL publishes a wide range of books, films, pamphlets, and other educational materials on Israel and the Middle East. Materials include the *ADL Handbook on Israel, Talking Points on Israel and the Middle East Conflict: A Guide for Discussion, Jews of Syria: A Chronicle*, and *A Search for Solid Ground: The Intifada Through Israeli Eyes*, which includes a video and accompanying study guide. Call or write the Middle Eastern Affairs Department for a catalogue of available materials.

Center for Middle Eastern Studies
The University of Texas
Austin, TX 78712
(512) 471-3881

The center was established by the U.S. Department of Education to promote a better understanding of the Middle East. It provides research and instructional materials. The center publishes three series of books on the Middle East in addition to monographs, essays, and translations.

253

**Duncan Black Macdonald Center for the Study of Islam and Christian/
Muslim Relations**
Hartford Seminary
77 Sherman St.
Hartford, CT 06015
(203) 232-4451

The center is an educational organization that seeks an increased understanding
of Islam and improved relations between Christians and Muslims. It sponsors
studies of political and social developments in the Islamic world, including the
Middle East. The center publishes *The Muslim World*, a quarterly journal.

Foundation for Middle East Peace
555 13th St. NW
Washington, DC 20004
(202) 637-6558

The foundation assists the peaceful resolution of the Israeli-Palestinian conflict
by making financial grants available within the Arab and Jewish communities to
promote peace. It publishes the bimonthly *Report on Israeli Settlements in the
Occupied Territories* and additional books and papers.

The Institute for Palestine Studies (IPS)
3501 M St. NW
Washington, DC 20007
(202) 342-3990

IPS is a pro-Arab research, documentation, and publication center specializing
in the Arab-Israeli conflict and Palestinian affairs. It publishes books, papers,
and the quarterly *Journal of Palestine Studies.*

Israeli Embassy
Department of Information
3514 International Dr. NW
Washington, DC 20008
(202) 364-5500

The embassy officially represents the government of Israel in the United States
This diplomatic presence seeks to maintain understanding and good relations
between the citizens of the United States and Israel. The embassy's Department
of Information provides pamphlets, studies, reports, and maps published by the
government of Israel. It distributes information packets designed for both students and teachers interested in Israel.

Jordan Information Bureau
2319 Wyoming Ave. NW
Washington, DC 20008
(202) 265-1606

The bureau provides political, cultural, and economic information on Jordan. It
publishes factsheets, speeches by Jordanian officials, government documents,
and the bimonthly *Jordan Issues and Perspectives.*

Jordan IS Palestine Committee
PO Box 7557
New Hyde Park, NY 11040

The committee believes the Arab-Israeli conflict can be solved if Palestinian Arabs would recognize that Jordan is the Palestinian homeland. The committee distributes article reprints and provides film and slide presentations.

Middle East Institute (MEI)
1761 N St. NW
Washington, DC 20036
(202) 785-1141

MEI seeks to promote interest in Middle Eastern history, culture, economics, and politics through lectures, publications, and programs. It publishes books, the quarterly *Middle East Journal*, and *Middle East Organizations in Washington, D.C.*, an annual guide.

Middle East Outreach Council, Inc. (MEOC)
c/o Middle East Studies Association
1232 N. Cherry Ave.
University of Arizona
Tucson, AZ 85721
(602) 621-5850

MEOC was established in 1981 as a nonpolitical organization that provides factual information about the lands, cultures, and peoples of the Middle East. The council publishes a resource guide on other organizations and embassies, text evaluations, classroom materials, and other materials for teachers and nonspecialists.

Middle East Policy Council
1730 M St. NW, Suite 512
Washington, DC 20036
Tel: (202) 296-6767   Fax: (202) 296-5791

The organization, formerly known as the American-Arab Affairs Council, publishes books and reports examining current issues in U.S.-Arab relations. Among its publications are the quarterly journal *American-Arab Affairs*.

Middle East Research and Information Project (MERIP)
1500 Massachusetts Ave. NW
Washington, DC 20005
(202) 223-3677

The project provides information, research, and analysis of Middle East social, economic, and political issues, including U.S. policy in the region. It publishes the bimonthly magazine *Middle East Report*.

The Washington Institute for Near East Policy
1828 L St. NW, Suite 1050
Washington, DC 20036
Tel: (202) 452-0650   Fax: (202) 223-5364

The institute is an independent organization that produces research and analysis on the Middle East and U.S. policy in the region. It publishes numerous position papers and reports on Arab and Israeli politics and social developments, military affairs, and U.S. policy in the region, including *The Future of Iraq* and *Building for Peace: An American Strategy for the Middle East*.

Bibliography of Books

Laila Abou-Saif	*Middle East Journal: A Woman's Journey into the Heart of the Arab World.* New York: Charles Scribner's Sons, 1990.
Ewan W. Anderson and Khali H. Rashidian	*Iraq and the Continuing Middle East Crisis.* London: Pinter Publishers, 1991.
Geoffrey Aronson	*Israel, Palestinians, and the Intifada.* New York: Kegan Paul International, 1990.
Nazih Ayubi	*Political Islam: Religion and Politics in the Arab World.* New York: Routledge, 1990.
Greg Bates, ed.	*Mobilizing Democracy: Changing the U.S. Role in the Middle East.* Monroe, ME: Common Courage Press, 1991.
Leonard Binder	*Islamic Liberalism: A Critique of Development Ideologies.* Chicago: University of Chicago Press, 1990.
Elias Chacour with Mary E. Jensen	*We Belong to the Land.* New York: HarperCollins Publishers, 1990.
Congressional Quarterly	*The Middle East.* 7th ed. Washington, DC: Congressional Quarterly, Inc., 1990.
Charles F. Doran and Stephen W. Buck, eds.	*The Gulf, Energy, and Global Security.* Boulder, CO: Lynne Rienner, 1991.
Kevin Dwyer	*Arab Voices: The Human Rights Debate in the Middle East.* Berkeley: University of California Press, 1991.
Gloria Emerson	*Gaza: A Year in the Intifada.* New York: Atlantic Monthly Press, 1991.
John L. Esposito	*Islam and Politics.* 3d ed. Syracuse, NY: Syracuse University Press, 1991.
Robert Fisk	*Pity the Nation: The Abduction of Lebanon.* New York: Atheneum, 1990.
Robert O. Freedman, ed.	*The Intifada.* Miami: Florida International University Press, 1991.
Robert O. Freedman, ed.	*The Middle East from the Iran-Contra Affair to the Intifada.* Syracuse, NY: Syracuse University Press, 1991.
Thomas Friedman	*From Beirut to Jerusalem.* New York: Farrar Straus Giroux, 1989.
David Fromkin	*A Peace to End All Peace.* New York: Henry Holt, 1989.
Charles Glass	*Tribes with Flags.* New York: The Atlantic Monthly Press, 1990.
Andrew Gowers and Tony Walker	*Behind the Myth: Yasser Arafat and the Palestinian Revolution.* London: W.H. Allen, 1990.
Colbert C. Held	*Middle East Patterns.* Boulder, CO: Westview Press, 1991.
Mark A. Heller and Sari Nusseibeh	*No Trumpets, No Drums.* New York: Hill and Wang, 1991.
Simon Henderson	*Instant Empire: Saddam Hussein's Ambition for Iraq.* San Francisco: Mercury House, 1991.
Amin Hewedy	*Militarization and Security in the Middle East.* New York: St. Martin's Press, 1989.

Dilip Hiro	*Holy Wars: The Rise of Islamic Fundamentalism.* New York: Routledge, 1989.
Albert Hourani	*A History of the Arab Peoples.* Cambridge, MA: Harvard University Press, 1991.
Samir al-Khalil	*Republic of Fear: The Inside Story of Saddam's Iraq.* New York: Pantheon Books, 1990.
Farid A. Khavari	*Oil and Islam.* Malibu, CA: Roundtable Publishing, 1990.
Charles A. Kimball	*Religion, Politics, and Oil.* Nashville, TN: Abingdon Press, 1991.
Marcia Kunstel and Joseph Albright	*Their Promised Land.* New York: Crown Publishers, 1990.
Peter Mansfield	*A History of the Middle East.* New York: Viking, 1991.
Jamal R. Nassar and Roger Heacock, eds.	*Intifada: Palestine at the Crossroads.* New York: Praeger Publishers, 1990.
A.F.K. Organski	*The $36 Billion Bargain: Strategy and Politics in U.S. Assistance to Israel.* New York: Columbia University Press, 1990.
Daniel Pipes	*The Long Shadow: Culture and Politics in the Middle East.* New Brunswick, NJ: Transaction Publishers, 1989.
David Pryce-Jones	*The Closed Circle: An Interpretation of the Arabs.* New York: Harper Perennial, 1991.
John Quigley	*Palestine and Israel: A Challenge to Justice.* Durham, NC: Duke University Press, 1990.
Ze'ev Schiff and Ehud Ya'ari	*Intifadah.* New York: Simon & Schuster, 1990.
Jerome M. Segal	*Creating the Palestinian State: A Strategy for Peace.* Chicago: Lawrence Hill Books, 1989.
Micah L. Sifry and Christopher Cerf, eds.	*The Gulf War Reader.* New York: Times Books, 1991.
Emmanuel Sivan	*Radical Islam: Medieval Theology and Modern Politics.* New Haven, CT: Yale University Press, 1990.
Emmanuel Sivan and Menachem Friedman, eds.	*Religious Radicalism and Politics in the Middle East.* Albany: State University of New York Press, 1990.
Alan R. Taylor	*The Superpowers and the Middle East.* Syracuse, NY: Syracuse University Press, 1991.
Kitty Warnock	*Land Without Honor: Palestinian Women in the Occupied Territories.* New York: Monthly Review Press, 1990.
Robin Wright	*In the Name of God: The Khomeini Decade.* New York: Simon & Schuster, 1989.
Daniel Yergin	*The Prize: The Epic Quest for Oil, Money, and Power.* New York: Simon & Schuster, 1991.
Rosemarie Said Zahlan	*The Making of the Modern Gulf States.* Boston, MA: Unwin Hyman, 1989.
Sami Zubaida	*Islam, the People and the State.* New York: Routledge, 1989.

257

Index

262